THE

DECEPTION

OF THE

THRUSH

The Deception of the Thrush

©2014 by Bruce P. Spang

Published by Piscataqua Press
an imprint of RiverRun Bookstore, Inc.
www.riverrunbookstore.com
www.piscataquapress.com

ISBN: 978-1-939739-42-1

Printed in the United States of America

Cover photo: *Swimmers, 2003*
©David Hilliard

Section headings are from "The Four Quartets"
by T.S. Eliot, *Collected Poems.*

brucepspang.wordpress.com

"*The Deception of the Thrush* by Bruce Spang is a story of personal transition that is at once comic, authentic, irreverent, and at times, shocking. From brutal fraternity hazing to the assassination of Martin Luther King and the times leading up to the 1968 Chicago Democratic convention, Jason Follett's coming of age tale is marked by both the complexity of his emerging sexuality and bearing witness to historical events. What Jason calls his voyage is unique in its own evolution, and yet a journey so representative of those taken by the many who struggled to find moral balance during the turbulent Sixties. This first novel is a fine read."

Dan Guenther, author of *Glossy Black Cockatoos*,
the 2010 Colorado Authors' League
Award selection for Genre Fiction.

THE

DECEPTION

OF THE

THRUSH

BRUCE PARKINSON SPANG

For Dr. Russell Compton, Dr. John Eigenbrodt, who taught me to question and to believe in the life of the mind and, my mom, Ann Elizabeth Spang who taught me to believe in my heart. And to Ralph Wagner Spang, my brother, who has taught me courage in the face of adversity.

This book would never have found the light of day without the immense help and expert guidance of Ellen Lesser and Richard Foerster who made suggestions both about its shape, its organization, and its language. I'm indebted to Baron Wormser and Dan Guenther for their insights about how to best frame the story. I couldn't have shaped the book in its present form without the suggestions of Kara Whitney, Ann Pike, Dick Schmidt, and Skip Spang for their careful editing and reading of the book. And particular thanks to my sister-in-heart, Nancy McDaniel, who combed over the manuscript and teased out the typos and grammatical errors. As always, I'm indebted to my partner Myles Rightmire for his love and support.

Shall we follow?
Quick, said the bird, find them, find them,
Round the corner. Through the first gate,
Into our first world, shall we follow
The deception of the thrush?
> — T.S. Eliot, *Four Quartets*, "Burnt Norton"

"The impossible gives birth to the possible."
> —Karl Mannheim, *Ideology and Utopia*

Permit Me Voyage

Take these who will as may be: I
Am careless now of what they fail:
My heart and mind discharted lie
And surely as the nerved nail

Appoints all quarters on the north
So now it designates him forth
My sovereign God my princely soul
Whereon my flesh is priestly stole:

Whence forth shall my heart and mind
To God through soul entirely bow,
Therein such strong increase to find
In truth as is my fate to know:

Small though that be great God I know
I know in this gigantic day
What God is ruined and I know
How labors with Godhead this day:

How from the porches of our sky
The crested glory is declined:
And hear with what translated cry
The stridden soul is overshined:

And how this world of wildness through
True poets shall walk who herald you:
Of whom God grant me of your grace
To be, that shall preserve this race.

Permit me voyage, Love, into your hands.

James Agee, *The Collected Poems of James Agee*

Table of Contents

Part I: The Testing

The Harvard of the Midwest   1
The Outcast   5
The Leaving   11
Pledging   16
The Brothers   24
The Beast   32
Frogs   38
The Bonfire   42
The Waking   45
Alone   49
Resigned   57
The Arm   62
Confession   67
Pressure   71
Hanging Out   76
The Party   82
The Necklace   86
The Closet   91
Rebellion   94
Bad Egg   97
The Relay   99
Axis Mundi   104
The Samaritans   108
Even Steven   112
The Flag   116
Capture the Flag   120
The Accused   124
Change of the Guard   128
Street Smarts   130
The Show   132
Mugged   134
The Incursion   139
Girlfriend   143

Play by Play	146
The Poet	149
The Visit	151
The Primitive Terror	153
The Guide	156
A City Divided	162
Home Away From Home	164
Home At Last	166
Leadership	170
The Image	173
The Princess	177
The Shrimp Boats	182
Aborted	185
Hunger For Glory	188
Sacrifice	191
A Different Light	197
A Nazi	201
The Proof	208
The Blow	210
The Trial	218
The Sentence	223
The Long Walk	227
The Break	230

Part II: The Wakening

The Lectures	237
The High Life	243
Private Club	248
The Apartment	254
New Roommate	259
The Artists	266
The Date	270
Adult Books	273
War Hero	278
Club Championship	282

Nineteenth Hole 287

Close Call 288

The Professor 290

The Visitor 293

Basic Belief 298

The Seamstress 304

Confrontation 309

Final Adjustment 316

New Tenants 318

Manhood 324

Terra Haute 327

Taming the Lion 333

Closing Out the Year 344

The Real World 347

The Veteran 351

Upside Down World 362

The Bottom Line 367

The Wedding 372

Pledge Brother 375

The Dream Deferred 389

1-A 401

A Special Night 409

Dead End 412

The Interview 415

Goodbyes 421

Assassination 431

The Line Drawn 436

The Salesman 438

The Lake 447

Part I

The Testing

I: *...This is the use of memory: For liberation—not less of love but expanding of love...*

The Harvard of the Midwest

My mother eyed it first—a billboard on a hillside with gold and black letters "Ashbury University, the Harvard of the Midwest, 25 miles," scrolled across the top and, below it, an image of students like religious pilgrims headed toward East College, a century-old brick building with a bell tower. Pointing to the sign, she turned to look at me, "It's a good school, honey. Don't worry. I'm sure you'll be happy there." But she wasn't really sure any more than I was. Her face broke into an easy smile. She wanted to boost my confidence since my acceptance at Ashbury, or any college, had been doubtful. Pep talks, that's what my parents thought I needed to assuage my own self-doubt before cutting me loose.

My dad added, "Just buckle down, son. You'll do fine."

He believed ambition trumped ability, and anyone could rise to the top. Even if you had dyslexia and struggled to read, as I did, it did not matter. If you played your cards right, if you worked hard—as he had, late at night and on weekends—you could become, just as he had, Vice President of Motorola and have people who parked your car, opened the door and let you into your personal elevator to your office with its private bathroom, conference room, and bar hidden behind a bookcase.

Whenever I'd gone to his office with him, Dad's secretary would stand to greet me, "Good morning, Jason," and ask if I wanted an orange juice, a muffin, something else to eat. I felt like royalty, and, as such, was expected to comport myself well in public and be successful—or at least act successful—in whatever I did. My dad often told me, "I don't care what you do—be a lawyer, a businessman or bum—but be the *best* at whatever you do, the very best, even if it's the best bum in the world."

My mother was more concerned that I be happy. She worried that I did not have many friends and tended to be a loner. As we drove by the hundredth cornfield, she asked, "Did you see Jeff before he left for college?" My mother liked Jeff, my best friend, and knew I would miss him. He often stayed at our house so much he practically lived with us. His dad was a football coach and pressured him to be number one at everything,

1

paying him a dollar for every point scored in a basketball game, for every hit in a baseball game, and ten dollars for first place in a track meet. Jeff earned a lot of money—sometimes $40 a week—but it was earned pushing himself to be better than he wanted to be. He wanted to be an average guy, not the best. Though my dad wanted me to excel, for some reason I never understood he never pressured me to be tops in sports, or, for that matter, in my school work. He expected me to earn whatever wages I earned by making an honest effort, to act right and have good manners and to *look* like a success. As long as I worked hard, he was happy.

Before packing for college, I'd seen Jeff at his house. We sat on his front stoop, looking at the late summer light that filtered through one of the domelike elms left on his street that hadn't yet succumbed to the Dutch elm disease. For several years, a large, red X was sprayed on diseased elms, so that, by graduation, the town had been denuded, the once shaded avenues exposed like open sores to the sun.

"You going to visit me in Urbana?" he asked. "You promised you would."

"Sure, I'll hitchhike," I told him, although I'd never hitchhiked and had no idea how far it was from Greenview, Indiana, to Urbana, Illinois.

If I'd had my way, I would have gone to the University of Illinois with Jeff and with six other classmates, but my poor grades ruled that out, as well as my dad's insistence that I not go to his old hometown where his father, a restaurant owner, went bankrupt during the Great Depression. Because our next-door neighbor knew the dean at Ashbury and because my dad could pay full tuition, I managed to get in. I'd convinced myself, however, that I did qualify on my own merit as a three-sport letterman. My C average was nothing to boast about, but at least, when the dean told me that I had to have a B average my last semester, I studied and did what he asked.

The cornfields flickered by and, in the distance, by an immense oak, horses grazed in a pasture as they did in back of my home. I remembered one night with Jeff, how he and I had gotten drunk, stripped and, lifting the barbed-wire fence, crouched down, careful not to castrate ourselves, and trotted into the field where Morgans—huge jumpers—grazed on the tall grasses under moonlight. We crept up to them, bent down, interlopers, getting as close as we could. They stared at us, their moon-glow eyes wide and yellow, their breath visible and white in the cool evening air. They snorted like primitive gods.

Jeff turned to me and said, "Let's race 'em!"

"No way! They'll trample us," I whispered, pulling on his shoulder, trying to back up.

"Come on," he yelled and stood up, flailing his arms and leaping about screaming, "hey-ya, hey-ya," like a warrior.

The horses' heads jerked up. They whinnied, their eyes enormous, then reared, fierce and immense. I turned to flee, but they simply trotted away. Jeff took after them with the graceful stride of a runner, his white buttocks diminishing in the dark. Soon he was beside them, and I sprinted to catch up, the two of us racing alongside the beasts that trotted, three astride, with one in front like a general charging into the misted dusk. Over a dried-up creek, up hillock and into a swale, the clods of earth and tufts of grass smacking against our feet, we heard the deep breath of the horses heaving, felt our straining to keep up with them in our lungs. But we laughed too, when we realized we were one of the herd, our naked bodies in tandem with theirs. They slowed to an amble and stopped to graze again. We patted and leaned against their sweaty flanks, and thick muscular legs, feeling emboldened with beings more powerful than either of us. At the house, later that night, sleeping together, I felt Jeff's body nuzzle next to mine and let his arm stay, draping over my shoulder. We woke, together like that, somewhat startled, but mostly pleased with our bodies pressed against each other, and dressed, coyly, sensing something magnetic in our bond yet uncertain what to name it, that first of many nights we slept together, discovering the magic of our bodies.

"Look, honey," my mother called out, "a Greenview sign. We're almost there."

The town unrolled before me: the railroad depot, the Monon Grill, a line of run-down three-story residential homes, plain, some with porches, some without, set back a few feet from the road. I felt a jolt of excitement with the realization that in a few hours I'd be on my own, far from my parents, and could do whatever I wanted to do. Up ahead, a town square had a monument of a WWI soldier, his rifle like an assassin's aimed right at us; and, surrounding the square, brick storefronts squished together in a indistinguishable line; and, interspersed on several corners, wooden storefronts, some three stories, some two, had paint peeling like picked scabs. Up a hill on the far side of the square, a road sign to the right pointed to "Ashbury University." We turned on Washington Street, and then took a right on South Locust Street. We passed by large brick sorority and fraternity houses, a quad with three dormitories and, across from them, the Memorial Student Union. My mother, I noticed, reached over to my father and took his hand.

"We're here, honey," she said with breathlessness in her voice that belied a fear, perhaps, remembering that, not a year ago, she had left my older brother Jack at Ohio State University. The closer we came to the university, the more nervous I became, thinking of how many things could go wrong, and had already—at least for my brother.

The Outcast

For years, we'd had been a pair, the Follett boys, which is what my father called us with a sense of pride because we were to him, and to our mother, two handsome, well-mannered boys who knew to stand when someone came to the dinner table, to hold the door for a lady, to assist with her chair, to use correct table manners and dress impeccably in Brooks Brothers' suits. That had been our trademark: the look of success. Or least until last year. My brother, a year older than I, had left for college and, after a bumpy second year, came home, before school ended, with hepatitis B. Having nearly flunked out, he wallowed in a hospital bed, gaunt, weak, his skin sallow. Although my father rarely said anything about Jack's bungling of his second year, I knew that he harbored a fear that I, too, might end up like my brother. I'd struggled in elementary school with dyslexia. In third grade, the teacher discovered I read like an Asian: backwards, from right to left. A college student worked with me to train my eyes to move along the page and sound out each word. My dyslexia plagued me throughout high school. I had to work twice as hard as other students to comprehend books. But I'd done it. I'd gotten by. I now had to prove I could do it in college and be a success.

Isolated at St Luke's Hospital in Chicago, for several weeks, Jack became a nightly subject of dinner conversation as if he were some foreigner, no longer a member of the family, an outcast who had violated the implicit family code: be a success.

"Have you heard from him?" my father asked mother.

"Jack?"

"Yes, him."

"The doctor says he's improving," Mother said. She cleared the plates. She had the long quick gait of a golfer—she'd won several Chicago district tournaments—and quickly piled the dishes in the sink, then came back to the table.

"Hum," my father responded. "Good." He leaned back in his chair and brushed his hair with his hand, something he did when he was agitated. He combed his hair straight back from his forehead like Richard Nixon, the former presidential candidate, and had the same loose jowls as Nixon, with the same slight stoop to his shoulders from working at a desk.

"I did talk with him," Mother said. "He feels better and Jason will visit him tomorrow."

"Good."

"Have you time to drop by from work this week?"

"Not sure. Very busy. New product line coming out."

"Oh."

Although Father never said it, I knew what happened when Jack fell off the success train. He became invisible. That would never happen to me.

When I finally went to see Jack, I had to pull on a mask and a white gown before entering his room. Mother had warned that he didn't look good and was feeling down. She asked me to pick up his spirits.

"Joke with him. Tell him what's going on at the country club. Be positive," she said.

"Sure, Mom, I can do that," I said.

The nurse told me not to stay long: He's weak. Jack was propped up in bed, watching TV. His thin arms hung out of a paisley hospital gown like sticks. Not having seen him since his hospitalization, I was dumbstruck by his appearance; I gawked at him.

"What's wrong?" he asked.

"Nothing," I said. But something was wrong: His skin had the milky transparency of a lampshade. It was drawn tight against the bones of his eye sockets and cheekbones so that his face seemed skeletal like that of a war prisoner.

I rubbed my eyes—damn tears— and looked out his window.

"Nice view," I said.

"You *must* be kidding. Who wants to look at the interstate?"

"Well, it's better than an alley."

I pulled up a chair and scooted it near the bed, inspecting him, his skin that, on closer inspection, was the same lemony tint as his eyes.

"You all right?" he asked.

"Yeah, just allergies. How are you, Jack?" I asked, not sure what to say.

"What do you think?" he said. "Sitting here with a god-damn TV and some lame books and nothing else to do is not exactly my idea of fun."

"Sorry I asked," I said. Like Jack, Dad had a lighter fluid temper that ignited with the least provocation.

I gazed at a print on the wall—an evening skyline view of Chicago, from the lake, looking at Lake Shore Drive and the Gold Coast, their lights glimmering against a rib of night. I decided to change the topic. "How long before you can come home?"

"A few more weeks. My immune system needs to be back to normal," he said, pushing on his night shirt, smoothing it out. "But let's not talk about me. I'm sick of me."

"What will we talk about?"

"Anything but this stupid illness."

So we talked about baseball, the dismal heat, the bland hospital food. Not having seen him except for brief stints during holidays for a year, it felt as if I was talking to a stranger, someone who'd lived an entirely different life from mine. To pick up his spirits, I told him about Ashbury because he wanted to transfer there from Ohio State. He admitted that he wasted the year, spending most evenings in the dorm, playing poker, getting smashed, and writing maudlin poems to girls he met. Now he planned to reform.

Before I left, I hugged him. His shoulder blades and spine felt like the carapace of a horseshoe crab, hard and fleshless. I didn't want to let him go and pressed him close to me.

"I love you, Jack," I blurted out.

"Okay, okay," he said and pulled back from me. "I know you love me, but this is not the end of the world. I'm just sick."

I stepped back and took several steps toward the doorway. He smiled and said, "it's okay. I'm all right. You need to go. Say 'hi' to Dad and Mom. And thanks for coming. I'll be out in no time." The stick in his hospital gown waved. I slipped out the door, tore off my mask, and fled to the car as if death were stalking me. I turned the radio on high, let it blast the Beatles' "I Want to Hold Your Hand" and followed the East-West Highway home.

Our father at first did not outright disapprove of Jack's behavior—he

7

often said to us that "sowing one's seeds" was part of college—but he was peeved over his poor grades, his hepatitis, and his needing to drop out. He told him that he would not have one of his sons wasting his life nor his father's money. If he wanted to be a bum, he could damn well do that. What irked him even more, however, was the gossip among our parents' social circle. It buzzed and stung my mother who heard every derogatory rumor. People heard that Jack had "some difficulties" at college and made sure Mother knew how concerned they were when, in fact, they licked their tongues and prattled about what a drunk and wastrel Jack was. Soon, the story became so contorted that Mrs. Benson reported back to Mother at their weekly bridge game about how awful, dreadfully sad it was that Jack had an DWI and had been arrested—all unfounded and untrue.

Before being diagnosed with hepatitis B, Jack got a dose of Father's wrath —and I did too. Jack had called during dinner one night to inform Dad that he intended to buy a motorcycle. As if someone had flipped a switch, my father lashed out, screaming into the phone, lambasting Jack in front of Mother and me.

"Listen Jack. Do you hear me? You will not," he snarled into the phone, "buy a motorcycle or anything else. Get this straight: I'll have none of your foolishness. None of it. Drop that harebrained idea. Grow up. No. No, I said NO. This conversation is over," and slammed the receiver down, his ears as red as the heating unit on an electric stove turned up high.

He leaned with his fist pressed against one of the kitchen cabinets and stared at the wall. "I expect better," he said, seemingly not referring to anyone in particular.

Mother said, "He'll be fine."

I pushed the peas on my plate into the mashed potatoes. My mother reached over to me and patted my hand, whispering, "He's not talking about you."

My father sat down, cut into the steak into little pieces, and took a bite of one, chewing it as if he'd ripped a morsel of raw meat me off the cow with his bare teeth. He picked up his wine glass, took a sip, and looked at me. "I *am* talking about you. I *do* have expectations," he said. "You know what they are as well as he does."

"Sure, Dad," I said. That's when the knot in my stomach, the fear of disappointing him and not living up to my name, first began to tighten like a bolt that held me in check as I realized how quickly my brother had fallen from grace and how I might be next in line.

My father named me Jason, an unusual name in 1945, after his grandfather who was one of the first Folletts to arrive in the new country—an explorer, a voyager, and one of the most successful members of his family. He started a small restaurant in Urbana that was left to my dad's father as a thriving enterprise until the Great Depression plunged him out of business, forcing the family, for a while, to live on the government dole, to go from a large house in a prosperous neighborhood to a two-bedroom home out in the Appalachian hills in southern Ohio. It was 1932, the year of Dad's mother's suicide.

A sophomore in high school, Dad had come home to find the front door locked. The windows were sealed shut, too. He broke the side door, prying it open with a crowbar from the shed. The house was quiet. The kitchen door was closed. He had to jimmy it open because dish towels were stuffed under it. He pulled them away. The air felt heavy as if stuffed with cotton. He stepped back and took a deep breath. His mother, bent like a woman in prayer, slumped face down on the oven door. There was a fifing sound like a tire leaking. The gas was turned on high. He turned it off. He knelt down. His mother was limp. He shook her. Her knew she was dead, but he called to her anyway, "Mother, Mother," and held her tight against him, rocking back and forth. He felt dizzy. He set her back on the floor and he shoved open the windows. And made the calls, one after another standing in the living room where he could see her shoes sticking up like miniature tombstones.

Success distanced that awful day from him, made it seem possible for him never to be on his knees begging, "Mother, Mother." He never wanted, as the eldest son, to have to call his father and to tell him to come home, something terrible had happened and to call his younger brother and tell him that their mom was dead. He wanted to carry on as if his family was as it had been, a normal family going through hard times. He would expunge the irreparable taint of suicide with hard work. Success erased the past because it led to a bright future. We, his sons, would follow in his footsteps and be as successful as he had become, and, by doing so, his mother, although her name was never mentioned, would not haunt us.

That is, until my brother and I discovered a photograph of his parents in a desk drawer and asked him about the woman who we'd never seen with wire-rimmed spectacles next to Grandpa. He grabbed the photograph.

"Where did you get this?" he asked.

"In the upstairs desk."

"Put it back. It's none of your business," he said. His jaw tightened, and the skin on his cheeks flared as if he'd been slapped hard. He said something to Mother and then abruptly went for a walk. Our mother was left to tell us of the suicide and of the little she knew about his mother.

"Your grandmother was a writer, a poet of sorts, who, it seems, was very sensitive. The loss of the family restaurant and move from a university town, from her arts community, to rural Ohio with its dire poverty and all just proved to be too much for her," she said. "Now you must put that photograph back and promise never to inquire about his mother again." We stuck the photograph in the drawer, as she asked.

That way the woman in spectacles would never cast a shadow, never be a reminder that, like a curse, death can darken any door, even a door that had long ago been closed off to any whiff of death. Success assured Dad that he'd never have to face her again. The past remained past. And he— and we—were supposed to carry on as if it never happened.

The Leaving

After Dad parked the car, we went to the Student Union where a woman whose smile looked a little too perfect like ones in a Colgate toothpaste commercial, gave me a schedule for the day and instructions about what preliminary tests I needed to take to see if I qualified for advanced placement. I was assigned temporary housing—a private residence in town, five blocks from campus—since I intended to pledge a fraternity. We dropped my suitcases off at my temporary housing—a small house with so many antiques that I had to walk sideways to get to my room, avoiding some chair or pedestal with an ornate vase. We met Mrs. Hughes, a silver haired woman with an Old World manner, who assured my mother that she would take good care of me. In her gravelly voice, she told my mother that she would make sure I had a good breakfast every morning and was in bed at a reasonable hour. My parents thanked her and gave her their telephone number.

They took me to lunch at the Student Union, a brick building with an expansive portico with white columns. It sat kitty-corner from the dorms on Hanna and Locust Street. Students lounged in chairs under the portico and on the steps, the union seeming to be a hive at the center of campus. My parents said how pleased they were to have me staying with Mrs. Hughes. She reminded them of my grandmother, a firm and disciplined woman who ran a strict household, and they felt assured I'd be safe.

"Now, do you have everything?" my mother asked once we found a table for lunch, looking at the checklist that she had made earlier in the week. "Your toothbrush, your schedule, your..."

"Mom, it's fine," I told her. "I'm fine."

She smiled weakly, looked up at me, her brow furrowed, and said, "Excuse me, I need to use the ladies room," and hurried off, her long athletic stride carrying her quickly by several tables and into a lobby where the restrooms were.

"This is hard on your mother," my dad explained, and, using a phrase I'd heard often when he was launching into pronouncements, "Now, son,

11

let me say this: your mother and I know you'll do well. We expect no less. You will not let us down. This is your chance. Make the best of it. I've assured your mother that *you* will not disappoint us. *That* is what we expect. Is that clear?"

"Yes, sir," I said, sensing that he was not really speaking to me as his son, but an employee who worked for him, and, as an employee, I knew the job that had to be done, what the marching order was, and I would do it as if I'd been drawn into a tread of expectations that like a spider's web was intricately woven to hold me in place as the dutiful son. I pressed my fingers into my burger, gripping it tighter. The red juice leaked down the bun onto the plate. It drained toward several French fries, which I picked up and ate, the salt titillating my tongue.

He smiled his professional smile, the one he used to show approval, and tapped his fork on the table and whispered, "And, along the way, have a good time too, but," he hesitated, trying to make sure he used the right words, "work before pleasure, if you know what I mean.' He winked.

"I got it," I said.

"And, son," he lowered his voice, leaning forward. "Please do me a favor. Hold it together. No crying when we go. You understand? This is very hard on your mother as you know."

"Got it, Dad," I said, noticing my mother coming back to the table. She wiped her eyes several times with a handkerchief. Dad stood up, and I followed, as she approached the table. I pulled her chair out so she could sit down and noticed my father winking at me in approval. He looked elegant. Even on a drive to my college, he wore a sports jacket, tie and sports pants—impeccably dressed and handsome, his thick dark hair combed back, every strand in place, patted down to perfection.

Since my father was Vice President of Motorola Corporation, I'd grown up with men who were important, men who knew they were important, men of great power, presidents of corporations, entertainers with big careers, men who'd won major tournaments, who lived off their reputations, men who comported themselves in such a way that I easily believed that they were men of significance and men who lived up to and had high expectations. Was it any wonder that I had come to believe that how I looked, how I behaved, and what I did was the essence of who I was?

I had learned to spend hours looking in the mirror, making sure I appeared as I should—my hair combed carefully, my clothes matching, and my face shaven and clean. My body was never quite what I wanted it to be. Acne set up a permanent encampment at the edges of my nostrils. My thighs were too big and felt as if they were going to burst out of my pants. My hair, even when combed, flared out in an insuppressible revolt. None of that mattered, however. As long as I looked good in the eyes of the world, things would be good.

As his sons, whenever we went out in public, my brother and I were always dressed in tailored suits and expensive ties from the finest stores, even as children, so that we looked the part of being the proper sons of the Follett family.

"Now Nixon is still the man, believe me, who knows what America needs," my dad had changed the topic when my mother returned from the restroom. He tapped his finger on the table. "Look at his stand against Khrushchev; he told him off and argued that we made a better product than they did. He knows what makes America strong and that is a strong economy. Look how he's come back from that defeat in California and supports *our* candidate for president. Isn't that inspiring?"

I nodded. My father always assumed that *his* candidate for president would be *my* candidate, and I did not question it.

I sat in the student union that day with my hand around the last sliver of my hamburger and nodded my head, not sure what to say because we rarely talked about politics in our family. As a high school freshman, I'd listened to the Nixon-Kennedy debates and knew for the first time that I was a Republican because, well, I didn't really know what a Democrat was and had never met one, so I was not about to differ with my father and had learned to go along with him when he brought up politics.

"Sure, Dad, he's great," I said.

"You bet he is. Mark my words: he'll be one of our greatest presidents someday."

"I bet he will," I said and took a bite of the hamburger, medium rare, just as my dad and I liked it.

When my father took a bite of his hamburger, my mother quickly engaged me in conversation and asked if I had any preferences for fraternities. I told her that I had none, although I did, having decided, after a visit to the DEA house in the spring, that I preferred them. Opening her purse, she pulled out a small packet.

"This is for you," she said.

I opened it up. A packet of stationery, stamps already on the envelopes. I smiled and kissed her.

"I'll write. You know I will."

"I do." She kissed me on the cheek.

My father put his napkin on his plate, thereby announcing that lunch was over.

We walked to the car. Several vehicles pulled up and doors swung open. Students lugged trunks up the stairs to their dorms. Parents trailed after them with lamps, rugs, and radios. A soft wind worried the leaves in the maple along the walkway. When we came to the car, my father opened the car door, and rolled down the window. He came back to the sidewalk.

"Well, this is it," he said, smiling.

He hugged me with our chest touching, and, as was a custom in our family, he kissed me lightly on the lips and offered half a smile, grabbed me by the shoulders and peered down—at 6'3", he was four inches taller than me— and then, patting my head, let go of me.

"Be good, son."

I felt a knot in my stomach, the one that had been growing over the years when I thought how I had to be a success. My father looked at me sternly. I took a deep breath.

"Say goodbye to your mother."

My mother hugged me. "Be happy, and, honey, I love you," she said, holding me close to her.

I told her that I loved her too. I hadn't expected to be sad. But I did not cry. I was not going to let him down. She patted me on the cheek as if to make certain I was still there.

"Oh, honey, I hope you'll be all right," she said.

"I'm fine," I said. "Don't worry."

As she turned to the car where Dad had already was, the knot in my throat tightened. I stood for a moment, watching my mother close the car door and their white Chrysler New Yorker with its wide fins pull away, head down the street, turn and blend into the traffic going out of town. On the corner of Locust and East Hanna Street, right in the middle of Ashbury University, they left me and I waved at them, but they were already gone.

Pledging

Not sure what to do with myself on campus with no parent to help me decide, I figured I should find someplace to wait until the formal orientation of all new students started.

It seemed strange to be entirely on my own. I never knew how much I relied on my mother—the whole routine of waking to the smell of bacon and going to sleep, having eaten a good meal. Now I had to fare for my own self, to find a good place to eat and to do my own laundry. Although I had just eaten, I felt hungry again.

At Jiminotts, a cafe across from the DAE house, I ordered a hamburger and a butterscotch milkshake. I liked observing the couples coming in, sitting across from one another, in the booths; I wondered what they might be thinking about each other. One couple looked as if they had just met. The guy had a very large mouth and was leaning forward, his elbows on the table and talking animatedly to the girl who slouched back, staring at his mouth, which looked as if it would never stop, probably wondering if she could stick something in it to shut him up.

The front door opened. A large-framed girl with bangs covering her forehead came in and stood, looking for a place to sit down. She spied me, alone in my booth and came over.

"Do you mind if I sit with you?" she asked.

"Not at all," I said, pointing to the seat opposite me.

She smiled, her face lighting up. She shoved her hand under her green and white knee-length skirt, and scooted into the booth. She put her plump hands on the table and wrinkled her nose, squinting somewhat to appraise how I looked.

"Hi, I'm Sue. So who are you?" she asked.

I told her who I was, where I lived and, surprisingly, she told me about her life—how she planned, after her sophomore year, to quit college and marry her boyfriend who would finish his degree that next year.

"You're going to get married now?"

"Yes," she said. "Why do you ask?"

16

"It seems so soon. I mean you are so young and all."

She laughed. "It is not as if I'm a teenager. I'm twenty and know what I want."

"That's amazing," I told her.

"Now you can't tell any of my sorority sisters," she said. "If they found out, the rest of the year would be utter misery. They'd want to persuade me not to do it or I'd have them fawning over me, wanting to do a wedding shower. Gad, that would drive me crazy. You know what I mean? People nagging you, wanting to know why you're ruining your life, not finishing your education. I have heard enough of that from my parents. I told them that I'm not ruining my life. Bob, my fiancée, he wants me to finish school. He wants me to work. We're just in love, so we figure better sooner than later, you know what I mean?"

"Yeah, it makes sense to me."

"You have a girlfriend?" she asked.

"No."

"Great, then you and I can be friends and, if you don't mind—I pretty much say what I think, as you'll find out—you can be my date for those occasions I need a date. That way I don't have to be with some guy who, well, is interested in me and who I have no interest in. Is that okay with you?"

"Sure, why not? Saves me having to get to know some girl who I may not like."

We hit it off. That week, we often met to have milkshakes at Jiminotts. She liked strawberry, I preferred butterscotch. She liked being with me: I wasn't pushy and, in addition, was a good listener since she loved to talk.

My classes started up later that week. For my first class, eight am on Monday, I sleeked in late after searching for the room in the wrong building. It was a Freshman English class with a gaunt, frail professor, who didn't even notice my late arrival. He looked as if at any moment he'd keel over. Shriveled up like a desiccated apple and hunched over like a bent question mark, he spoke so quietly that we had to lean forward to hear him. His voice chirped like a parakeet. He was a Professor Emeritus, and we were his class, his "cherubs of words" as he called us. My other classes were Cultures of Man, a demanding course surveying cultures from Egyptian to modern times, Elementary Spanish with an instructor from Ecuador who spoke stilted English and American Government with a bespectacled professor who wandered back and forth across the room, pacing and reciting monotonously from the text book he wrote and clearly had memorized. After drooling several times on my notes, large pools that obscured much of what I had written and dribbled in a miniature waterfall on my leg, I had to take two NoDoz at lunch to keep my eyes bulging like bulldogs and wide awake in his class.

In the afternoon, I hurried to football practice which seemed a replica of high school practice—drills, drills, drills, and, the coach screaming at us to "be men and move your asses."

Then, hot and sweaty, we stripped off our uniforms, stepped into showers, gulping cool water from the shower heads, letting the water titillate our bodies until we were numb, and then, allowing the hot soothing water splash over us and relax every fiber in us. Afterwards, I grabbed a burger with Suzie at Jiminotts, while we did homework. I wrote on an essay for English or read about the Egyptian sun king Osiris. Poor fellow, his brother Set killed him, sliced him into forty-two pieces, and strew his body in the swamps along the Nile River. But at least Osiris's sister, Isis, retrieved the parts and put him together, which was a pretty nifty when I thought about it, and he came back to life and ruled Egypt. After several days of football practice, my body felt like Osiris's—bruised and torn from the pounding on the field. Suzie was Isis. She kept telling me to hold it together and to get through Rush Week.

At night, participating in Rush Week, I was busy, literally rushed, going from one fraternity to another, trying to keep an open mind as my dad had instructed me to do. The whole week I never had a moment to myself except late at night. I came back after ten. Mrs. Hughes, sitting in a rocker, greeted me.

"So tell me about your day, Jason." I told her about my classes, the different fraternities. She offered me an oatmeal and raisin cookie. I ate it. I told her what I had for homework. She smiled and wished me good night. I twisted and turned through the antiques to my bedroom, careful not to knock over several table lamps that look as old as Mrs. Hughes and plopped on the bed. Without changing into pajamas, I'd lie there. From my one window, the moonlight cast a soft light over the bed. I thought how I'd entered a totally different life where the pressure to succeed or fail rested on my shoulders. Then, before I knew it, I'd fall asleep until my alarm woke me, announcing another day rushing from one thing to another.

Every night, those first couple of weeks, I would make the rounds, visiting different fraternity houses. Members of each house would greet us, a gaggle of freshmen, at the door, shake hands, pat us on the back, give a tour of their facilities the dining areas, lounge, and student rooms and propound their philosophy of brotherhood—what they believed was important for creating a good fraternal experience. Then, in separate rooms, we would meet with a few upperclassmen who asked us questions about ourselves—what were our interests, our ambitions, our future plans. On most of these questions, I learned to tell them I wanted to be a lawyer, had planned to major in history (the one subject I consistently passed in high school) and wanted a fraternity that both supported sports and liked to have a good time. We, in turn, could ask them questions. Mostly, I was at a loss knowing what to ask, so I often smiled, shrugged, and let the session quietly end. The more houses I visited, the more convinced I became that the Delta Alpha Epsilon house was the best fit for me.

I'd spent a number of weekends at Ashbury earlier in the spring semester, getting familiar with the different fraternities. On the first night on campus, after going out with several DAE upperclassmen to a movie in town, I'd returned to the house where Bill Harris, a junior, and I had a long talk. He pulled out a beer and asked if I minded him having a drink.

"Go ahead," I said. "Can I have one, too?"

"You drink?"

"Yep," I smiled, proud of my already knowing how to drink.

We talked and other guys came in the room. Soon, I had polished off four beers and was feeling pretty good and they asked me to pledge. I told them I would; they patted me on the back and cheered and I felt like I had won an election. I felt special. They liked me. They wanted me. I wanted to be one of them. It was something I never felt before: I belonged.

When my parents came to pick me up that weekend, I did not let on that I had pledged. They introduced themselves to Bill and several other fraternity members and made small talk. As a way to show how savvy he was, my dad motioned for Bill and the other fraternity members to come to the rear of his Chrysler, opened the trunk and showed them a metal thermos.

"What do you think this is, boys?" he asked, holding it up. A green metal thermos with a silver top, it seemed unimpressive.

Bill ventured a guess, "Coffee for the road?"

"No," my dad said, opening it up and holding it out for Bill to smell. "Martinis. You must always be prepared in case you stay overnight in a dry county!"

He winked at Bill and put it back in the trunk, shook hands with each of the guys gathered around the car. I shook their hands too and said I would be in touch.

On the car ride back home, when I announced that I had pledged, my father jerked the car to the side of the road and turned to face me, his ears bright red, pointing his finger, saying, "in no under certain terms" (that was his favorite phrase) that I could not pledge a fraternity after being there only one weekend. He informed me that I had shut out other, much better houses and should immediately withdraw my pledge.

"When we get home, you need call and inform them that you will not—you hear me?—you will not pledge until the fall. Is that clear?" he said, staring at me with his mouth drawn in a straight line like a knife blade until I nodded my head.

As I lugged my overnight bag upstairs, time seemed to reverse itself, each moment like a guillotine cutting off what preceded it, until I heard Dad call, "Come down here, son. I need you to take care of business." So not five minutes after we came home, he handed me the phone, and, standing over me, told me to dial the number and withdraw my pledge. Once my father told me what to do, I learned that I had to do it—no questions asked. Embarrassed at having to retract my commitment, sweating at the thought of having to say no, I bungled into a polite conversation with Bill, telling him how great it was to meet him and to get to know the other guys and then told him that I was sorry but that, after consulting with my dad, I had to go through Rush Week and, then, make a decision. Bill seemed to understand, but I felt humiliated and wondered if

I had ruined my chances of pledging the DAE house. But it turned out that they still seemed as interested in me as I was in them, but I still wanted to keep an open mind, honoring what my father had said.

After several days of making the rounds, we identified our top four choices and found out if those houses we liked had liked us. One fellow in my group, a Southern guy from Birmingham named Dwight, whose father was a Sigma Nu, broke down in tears when he found out that he wasn't asked back. He dreaded telling his father.

My father called me mid-week, asking what house I planned to pledge.

"You're not set on that DAE house, are you?" he asked.

"No, Dad. I'm keeping an open mind."

"That's good. I've talked to Bud Benson. You know Bud wrote you a strong recommendation. He said Delta Tau Delta is a strong house, a top notch house. Look it over carefully. Bud tells me they're very interested in you. I think it might be the right choice," he said.

"They're on my list," I said, knowing that he liked their house, a new building, recently refurbished with a large endowment from alumni such as Mr. Benson.

"Keep an open mind," he said. "You understand?"

"Got it."

"That's my boy."

I knew that the Deltas were his choice. But I was not sure they were mine. By the end of the week, I had a few interviews left, DAE as one, Delta Tau Delta as another. In my first interview, pressed by the DTDs to make a commitment, I deferred and refused to commit so they upped the ante.

One fellow, a center on the football team who had seen me at practice, came over to me, pulling up a chair—I was sitting on a couch—and sat on the back of a desk chair, his feet on the chair seat, looming over me and gave me a piece of his mind as if doing an imitation of my dad.

"Listen, Jason, you're a good athlete, starting material. We have more players on the varsity teams in DTD than any other fraternity. This is the place for you. Don't give it a second thought. Come on, what do you say? You know you want to pledge us, come on," he said, staring down at me.

I felt sweat bead on my forehead. How did he know that I wanted to pledge DTD?

Here was this big lug pressuring me. He reminded me of the football coach, leaning over me, shouting, "Keep your legs moving. Come on. Do it." I squirmed in the couch. "I'll give it some thought," I said.

"Thought?" the beefy center intoned.

"Yeah, thought."

"Give it more than that," he said and told the other brothers in the room to leave me alone for a while for me to "give it some thought."

Initially, I had seemed interested in DTD—they had an enormous house, twice the size of DAE with bigger rooms and I had one friend from high school there, a teammate, Bob Dusing, a tackle, who I knew pretty well and liked. When Bob was in the room, we talked about high school, and I felt relaxed.

Why they believed pressure might sway me I was not sure, but it had the opposite effect. Alone in the room for ten minutes, I stared at the posters of Y. A. Tittle, the New York Giants quarterback who almost singlehandedly beat the Bears in the 1963 playoff game. Looking at the books, mostly history, and mulling my decision, finding myself getting more irritated by the minute, I felt my arms tense. I felt more abandoned than confronted, more outraged than intimidated. When the center came back in, sitting, as he had before on the back of his desk chair, he scooted closer to me than he had been, his head five inches from mine.

"Well, you know I'm right," he said, smiling, reaching out to shake my hand. He seemed like a salesman convinced he'd sold me the best car in the lot.

I shook my head, pulling back in the seat, "I need to give it more thought."

He hopped off the chair and said, "Well, I think you are making a big mistake."

"I may be."

"May I ask what house you have left?"

"DAE."

He laughed. "DAE?! Those fucking bums. You must be kidding me! Are you out of your mind?"

"No," I said, wiping the sweat off my forehead, "I'm not."

"I think you are. They're on the bottom of the rung. Losers."

"Are we finished?" I asked.

"Yes, we are."

I started to walk by him, but I stopped. His black leather shoes were scuffed and unpolished.

"What are you looking at?" he asked.

"Your shoes need polishing," I said and walked out the door, off into the night.

The next night, I met with Bill and other DAE members. No pressure. No put-downs of other houses. They chatted with me, asked what I thought and I told them that they were my choice. It was simple. They accepted me, and the week was over and I was officially a freshman pledge, learning to find my way in the university and to make my own decisions. I had, however, to make one phone call to make.

When my dad answered the phone, I chatted about school, trying to maneuver to tell him what I knew he did not want to hear.

"We pledged tonight. It was the last night," I said.

"And?"

"I pledged DAE," I said.

I could hear breathing on the other end. And a sigh.

"Really?"

"Yes."

"May I ask why?" he said, his voice hard yet querulous.

"I like the guys."

"That's your reason?"

"Yes."

"That's disappointing,' he said. " But it's your decision. I hope you, ah." He hesitated. "You don't regret it."

"So do I," I said.

"Well, appreciate your letting me know. Have a good evening."

I hung up. My palms were sweaty. I wiped the sweat off the receiver and hung it up. Out the window, the leaves in a maple were shuddering nervously. I took a deep breath. I'd made a decision. It was mine.

The Brothers

Although small compared to most fraternities—some four-story mansions looked like plantations in *Gone With the Wind*—the DAE house had ample space for its forty-five members. It had dorms with bunk beds on the third floor and, on the second, study rooms—two to a room—with desks and couches. On the main floor a large foyer spilled on the right into a long, narrow sun-room with couches, chairs, and a TV. To the left, it opened into a formal living room. At the far end of the living room, a separate space, set aside for the housemother, included a bedroom, small sitting room, and bathroom. From the foyer, if you walked straight ahead, it led into a small library with several tables for studying and a floor to ceiling bookshelf on the right side wall. But beyond the library were four sets of glass doors that, when opened, provided access to the dining room and the kitchen. The exterior was a three-story Tudor style with large oaks looming in the front and back of the house like huge hands blessing it.

After moving in, I met my roommate, Paul Pierce, who, I soon learned, studied night and day, bent on getting a 4.0 as he had in high school. From Hannibal, Missouri, he loved literature and, when we first met, asked if I'd read *The Adventures of Huckleberry Finn*—he lived up the street from Twain's childhood home—which I had only partially read, but never understood since I could never make sense of the dialects, and because of my befuddlement, thought too difficult to comprehend, although I didn't tell Paul.

Tall and skinny, Paul majored in theater and seemed pleasant enough. He wore a smart smelling cologne, almost a lime scent and was dressed impeccably—in an Oxford button-down shirt, pressed slacks and penny loafers with no socks. Initially, he intimidated me: he passed all his entrance exams and, already, was taking advanced math, English, and science classes. Claiming to be an existentialist, he said he didn't believe in God and immediately leapt into a discussion about His existence.

"Do you believe in God?" he asked.

"Well, I haven't given it much thought."

"As far as I'm concerned, I pretty much agree with Nietzsche. He says that we've murdered God and that, without Him, we're like madmen. And, hey, God's just a fiction; some guy we made up to justify what we do," he said.

"Who's this Nietzsche?"

"He's dead!" Paul laughed. "But he's interesting, a German philosopher. I have a few of his books here." He picked one off the shelf, *The Birth of Tragedy.* "Borrow it anytime."

I emptied my suitcase, putting the shirts in one drawer, socks and underwear in another, hanging up my pants in a closet, thinking, if Paul was a typical Ashbury student, I'd be like a little league player in the big leagues and have some difficulty competing.

"Hurry up," Paul said. "Before dinner and orientation, you'll have time to meet your new brothers."

We gathered in the formal living room to meet our fellow pledges. Paul knew most of them because he'd pledged in the spring and had been involved in Rush. He took me around, introducing me. I found I became so engrossed in what they said or how they looked that their name would not stick in my brain. It was as if the name like a moth at a screen door flitted against my brain and fell off, disintegrating on the floor. I tried to see if, as my father had suggested, I associated a name with something about the person—their appearance, their interests, their likes or dislikes—I could remember their name.

Paul introduced me to Luis Underhill, a slight, skinny guy, from Cincinnati. He dressed as if, like a model, he'd stepped out of a New Yorker magazine advertisement, his shirt, pants and shoes the latest style. He liked to party and informed me that Tom Wilson liked to party, too. I thought to myself, *Luis and party, Good Time Luis.* I turned to look at Tom. Standing out from the rest, Tom was a handsome guy from Long Island—Port Washington—and was the tallest of the group—six foot three. *Tall Tom: that would be easy to remember.* He smiled at us. His eyes were a brilliant blue like the water off Boca Raton— water where I'd snorkeled amid sand sharks and tropical fish. Coming right up to Paul and me, he introduced us to his friend Jerry Evans—they had pledged in the spring—who looked the opposite of Tom, squat and homely, and a local boy, hailing from

Indianapolis. The skin on his face, pock-marked from acne, had angry pimples on it, two quite swollen with white pus visible. I kept my attention on his eyes so that I didn't embarrass him by focusing on them, although I had a strong urge to pop one of them.

"Where'r you from?" he asked.

"Chicago."

"The Windy City!"

"Not really, a suburb west of the city, Glen Brook," I said.

"Never been to Chicago. Never been out of state," he said, his right cheek flinching as he spoke, a quick tic that came on and, after a few seconds, left.

"Maybe you could visit sometime and I'll show you the city," I offered.

"Nice. Yeah, that'a be nice," he said.

Jerry the...I could think of nothing to associate with him except the pimples, and that was gross, so I decided to wait to associate him with something positive. His appearance did give me pause, even revulsion.

As I spoke with Jerry, I checked to see where Tom had gone. He was chatting with one of the upperclassmen, tapping him on the chest as if trying to make a sales pitch. I wanted to head over to talk with him and get to know him better.

But, while I was conversing with Jerry, another pledge came around, barging in, presenting himself as if he were running for political office, going from one person to another, explaining that he believed we had the best pledge class ever. I had a vague recollection that I'd seen him somewhere else. He shoved his hand at me and squeezed so hard that my pinky buckled under and popped.

"Trevor's my name, what's yours?"

He explained that he was a football player, a defensive end. I remembered him from practice, always on the go, a sparkplug, short but stocky, who exuded raw physical power that never seemed to need recharging. He squinted his eyes.

"Do I know you?" he asked.

"I'm on the football team."

"Right, right," he exclaimed and patted me on the back. "One of the team! A back, right?"

I nodded. When he shook my hand, I felt as if he might shake it loose from my arm. Since he had not met everyone, he moved away from me as soon as he knew my name.

By this time, I'd met five guys whose names were rapidly blending together like credits at the end of a film, so I sat down in one of the lounge chairs, going over their names. *Party Luis. Then Tom*, I thought, *Tall Tom. That would do. Jerry, Pus Face. No, not good. Jerry... Crater Face. No. Maybe, Local Jerry. Okay. And Trevor, the Force. That would do.* I stood up and peered around the room. *Where was Tom?*

From behind, someone slung their arm around my shoulder, nestling close, and whispered, "Hey, buddy, what you think? Odd mix, isn't it."

I turned to face him. His cologne was a brisk lemony fragrance, the smell of Florida, of the beach and sand, of tanned bodies in the sun. His eyes squinted as he smiled. I smiled back.

"Guess so," I said. "I've only met a few."

"Oh, you've need to meet them all," he said, swiveling me around the room. "Who haven't you met?"

His hand pressed into my shoulder, squeezing it affectionately. I pointed to two guys by a wall.

"Who are they?" I asked.

"Oh, they're something else. Might as well meet them," he said, an indifference in his voice. "I'll catch you later." He scrunched my shoulder again gently and patted me on the back. He reminded me of my friend Jeff— the same easy rapport and affection.

The guys by the wall seemed as shy and reserved as I was, so I went over to them. Jacob, a short kid with a crew cut and medium build, looked like a poster boy for the military, his formal manner and stiff ramrod posture made him appear to be at attention all the time. When he told me he wanted to be in the Air Force like his dad, it was not a surprise. Larry, who hung around Jacob as if he were his puppy dog and smiled a lot, only answered questions with a polite yes or no, so I initially had no idea who he was and wondered if he knew who he was. It stuck me that some people did not want to be remembered. They wanted to evaporate. *How to remember them?* Before I could think, another pledge came over to greet us.

Joseph Stein, who lived in Wake Forest, Illinois, proudly informed us that he was the first Jewish pledge in the fraternity's history. Some national advisors opposed his being a pledge, but local leadership ignored the advice and admitted him. With the dubious reputation of being a party fraternity, a place where sawdust was strewn on the floor and wading pools had semi-naked couples paddling around, DAE had difficulty getting pledges who wanted to work hard and be good students. Everyone knew, if you wanted to drink, go to DAE house: the booze was always flowing, night or day any day of the week and the parties last long into the night and sometimes well into the next day. But this year, it had managed to collect Paul and Joseph who seemed to be bright and capable students. Joseph Stein made it a point of shaking each of our hands and learning our names. He claimed he could remember everyone's name and, nodding at the different pledges sitting and standing around the room, recited them all. That's something I could never do. He also had the densest 5 o'clock shadow, almost as dark as Nixon's, that I'd ever seen. I would soon learn he needed to shave two, sometimes, three times a day. *Bearded Stein,* I thought and realized I completely lost the names of the previous two guys, even the one who looked like a cadet.

I searched for Tom, but he was nowhere in sight. Where had he gone? He entered and exited the room like an actor who knew his cues and would slip off stage unnoticed and reappear when his scene demanded his being center stage. But I couldn't figure out what part he was playing. It was a mystery. I only knew I felt drawn to him as if he had some mysterious quality in his presence that had captured my imagination and I needed to investigate what it was.

To one side of the room, a large fellow, named Steve, probably weighing close to two hundred ninety pounds was dressed to the nines in a pin-striped blue suit with a red and blue tie, almost as if he had leapt out of a Brooks Brothers' catalogue. *Steve, the Stout. Easy to remember.* He waddled over to me. He came from southern Illinois, near Springfield and had, faintly, a Southern drawl. His head seemed much too large for his body— wide and round like a pumpkin with large eyes. He seemed pleasant enough, although anxious. His eyes darted around like a frog anxious to find a fly.

"I'm so nervous," he said. "I don't know anyone."

"Neither do I," I said.

"Right, right. But you're cool. I can tell. You look like someone who's done this before."

"Well, I guess I have. My parents threw lots of parties and I..."

"See, I told you," he whined. "But for me, Jees, I never much went out and I'm..."

"You'll be fine," I interrupted him, searching for Tom since I felt that, if I stayed with Steve, I'd soon be counseling him and have to determine my hourly rate.

"Just give it time," I said, squeezing his shoulder as Tom had done to mine.

One pledge, John Hayward, was actually famous by association: his dad was Art Hayward, the actor in the TV show, "The Newlyweds." A stick of a guy, with long blond—almost white—hair that fell over part of his face like Andy Warhol, he made a point of acting as if he were just a regular guy—not haughty but soft-spoken and sincere, someone who wanted to know more about you than he wanted you to know about him. I liked talking to him. He told me that he kept to himself, and liked to strum a guitar. Laid-back to the point of being nearly somnolent, he opened up to me about growing up in his dad's limelight and how, no matter what he did, he could never quite shake his dad's fame and being Hayward's son. At his private school, he said he sang in a band. *John, guitar.* I liked how he had no pretense, no air of being special.

Another pledge, Brian Ibbitson, nicknamed "Ibby" played in a band and aspired to be a professional musician. With long hair like the Beatles, combed over his forehead, he had a passion for the Beach Boys music and carried around a skateboard and—I soon discovered—would slide up and down the sidewalk, his arms outstretched, zipping in and out of pedestrians as if he was riding an enormous wave, a California boy stranded in Indiana. Despite his artistic bent, he remained a true patriot, wanting like Jeff to enlist in the Air Force and serve his country. *Beach Boy Ibby,* easy to remember.

The leader of the group, it seemed, was Eric Ritmas who had pledged early and knew everyone in our pledge class by name and by town. Broad shouldered like a swimmer, he had striking features: a well-chiseled face with high cheek bones, almost Native American in appearance, and long black hair, parted neatly in the middle, and combed back, no hair out of place. It turned out he actually was a swimmer, aspiring to be in the Olympics. After fifteen minutes of milling around, he rounded us up and told us that he had great hopes for us to transform the DAE house into one of the best houses on campus, not just a party house.

Tom caught up with me after I made the rounds. "Well, what you think?" he asked.

"You're right. We're a motley crew."

"Told you so. But we're going to make waves. Wait and see," he said, winking at me. "They'll never forget us." He seemed mischievous. I liked that about him. I sensed that we'd be making trouble before the year was over.

After getting to meet our pledge brothers, each of us was assigned a pledge father, an upperclassman, who would show us the ropes as well as someone we could talk to if we had problems. Sam, the president of the fraternity, an avuncular guy, stocky, who did not take himself too seriously, was mine. Taller than I was, he slung his arm over my shoulder and said, "Tell me about yourself."

Over dinner, I told him about my family, my dog Sam who had died after being hit by a car, my sports career, and my fears about doing well in college.

"Listen," he said. "No matter how good you are, no matter how academically successful you were—and I can tell you that I was not a stellar student in high school—college is a whole new game. You'll do fine. Trust me. Just buckle down and do the work."

Funny he used the same phrase as my father had used. *Buckle down.* He invited me to his room after dinner to go over the routines: we had to study a certain number of hours each day in the house or school library, we needed to have a passing grade point average, we could not use alcohol, we had to do our chores every day, which would rotate among us, and we needed to be on time for every meal. Not being able to drink seemed pretty strict, so I asked him about how strict it was.

"It's a new rule here. Since I became president, I wanted to change the norms here. I know some of you actually drank when you visited in the spring and I heard from Bill that you had some difficulty with your dad and

I was not happy about it," he explained. "So I met with the other members of the house and said, 'Let's make a change and put performance before party' and mostly everyone agreed. Do you have a problem with that?"

"No, I don't think so."

"Think so?"

"No, I don't.

He smiled. "That's better. Get your grades first and you'll have plenty of time to party."

Sam sounded like my father. For that, I admired him. For a semester, I thought that I could refrain. I liked his attitude and his approach to reshaping the image of the fraternity. His dark hair fell partially over his forehead so he had to flip it back to keep it out of his eyes. His eyes at one minute effused with humor when he cracked a joke and the next intent and serious as he spoke about his hopes for the fraternity. Not only could I respect him but I also felt I had someone I could talk to about my struggles, if any came up in the future.

The Beast

A week after I pledged, Sue called the house and asked me to do her a favor: could I go to a cookout with her on Saturday night, which meant we could stay out as late as we wanted. The girls in her sorority were having a party with some of the guys who waited at the house. Her best friend was going, and she wanted to go and needed a date, so I complied, figuring that it would give me a chance to meet other students. My fellow pledge, Luis Underhill who waited at the sorority and dated a girl there, had been invited too, so I would have a new friend with me.

Luis was very excited about going since there would be no DAE upperclassmen there.

"We can forget the pledge rules and get wasted, drink as much as we want. No worry. Let's have a blast!" he said.

"Sure," I said, not wanting to be a prude. Luis, a scrawny guy, had already regaled me with his sexual exploits as quite a lady's man and had a reputation for being a big drinker too. Though I felt uncomfortable with Luis's idea about drinking, I felt that I'd manage to figure out what to do once we got to the party.

"What's your broad like?" Luis asked while we waited on the front steps of the fraternity.

"She's nice. Met her having a milkshake first day of school."

"Man, you're fast," Luis said. He looked me over. "Some stud."

"What's your date like?" I asked.

"Haven't met mine. Hope she's hot. It's be a good night to get laid," Luis said and grabbed at his crotch.

"Good luck."

"You too, man."

After Sue picked us up from the front steps of the fraternity, we drove our small caravan of cars out of town, out past the cornfields, into another country, down past a small stream where the water undermined the limestone ground, leaving enormous sinkholes. We followed a dirt road that lead to a sinkhole that spilled down a slope to a sandy basin and a quiet stream. On the far side of the clearing, a newly constructed road led up a hill into a glade of trees, and, beyond it, a dense forest with tall hardwood and pine. At the bottom of the hill rested an excavator, with it long crane like neck bent over as if it were sleeping. We emptied the cars and set out our eight blankets for the sixteen of us—all couples—and arranged the coolers of beer and food alongside the blankets. The guys took command of the charcoal and grill, stoking the fire in a matter of minutes. The girls got out the snacks and plates. I didn't know anyone except Luis and Sue, but everyone acted friendly. An older guy with long hair was standing by the open cooler. I asked if he had some soda and he grimaced, "Soda? You kidding me?"

Sue came up behind me, handing me a beer. "It's all right, Jason. You don't have to worry. I know you are not supposed to drink, but, hey, enjoy yourself. I'll take care of you."

My last three years in high school, I had the reputation for being a big drinker, so I felt quite at home with a beer in my hand, and decided to enjoy myself. Several guys brought guitars and strummed some Bob Dylan tunes. We sang along to the favorites "The Times are A Changin'", singing out the one line we knew, "The times are a'changing," while the long haired guy sung the lyrics that seemed to be speaking directly to me.

I didn't know if the song were speaking the truth about the sons and daughters being beyond the mother's and father's command. But I did feel free.

Several girls gathered, stacked up wood and constructed a small bonfire. I tossed a rock into the fire and watched it drown in the flames, sinking into the pink swirl of flames. Sue stroked the coals on the grill for the hamburgers and hotdogs. We drank another beer. Luis who sat with his head in his date's lap—a girl with long brown hair and thick eyebrows, at least for a girl—decided that we needed wood for a bonfire, so we trailed off into the woods, scaring up dried branches and toppled tree trunks.

"What do you think of my date?" he asked.

"She seems nice," I said.

"I think she's ugly. You notice her eyebrows?"

"They're big."

"Ugly!" he said. "I'm going to get royally drunk tonight."

33

After a few more beers, we sprawled on the blankets, chatting quietly. Sue let me lie in her lap and stoked my hair.

"You know you have lovely hair. I mean most girls probably envy you. It is naturally wavy, but not too much, just enough to give it body," she informed me.

"Thanks," I said.

"Your eyes, I just noticed, are not blue. They're hazel. And..." She laughed. "You've got the tiniest eyebrows. Where'd you get the scar by your eye?"

"I fell out of a tree."

I told her about my dad, how he was Vice President of Motorola, and how we lived forty minutes from Chicago in a fancy house he designed. She kept giving me beers, telling me how cute I got as I drank. Normally, I felt uncomfortable being affectionate with a girl, afraid I might come on too strong, but, with a few beers, I lay in her lap and massaged her hand and she seemed quite pleased with my attention.

Luis asked if I needed to take a leak since he was going, and since the light was failing somewhat, he wanted to fetch more wood for what he claimed would be the biggest bonfire in human history.

"We could roast three Joan of Arcs on it," he exclaimed.

"Clearly," Sue said, "he must be an Englishman."

"I think he's French," I said.

"Oh, then he's in big trouble with the Pope," she said. "Joan's a saint."

I raced after Luis. We stumbled down the hillside to the creek and, walking along its embankment, found a spot in a swale far from the girls. As we took a leak, I noticed, not a hundred yards from us, what appeared to be a large boar wallowing on its side in the creek. The beast, I thought, had chosen a perfect spot to bathe.

"Look," I pointed to it.

"What?" Luis asked, somewhat stupefied, having drunk nearly a six pack.

"Look, by that log where the creek bends," I explained. "A hog, I think."

"Jeez," he exclaimed after a quick survey of the beast, "Let's see if we can stampede it back to the girls."

"I don't think we should mess around with it. I've seen whole ones roasted on a spit," I told him.

"Really?"

"Yeah, at the country club, they'd hang it over a fire all day, turning it, head and all. It's amazing. The fat from it sparks in the fire and the smell of pork carries everywhere," I said, adding, "but this one is alive and I don't think he'd like it if we disturbed him."

"Shish," he cautioned me. "We'll just pretend we are like Indians and make no sound."

We crouched down, tiptoeing along the creek, stepping over a downed tree to within twenty feet of the animal. From its backside, the bristly hairs stood upright, and its body, round and fat, made us hesitate: it was humongous, nearly half a ton, and definitely a boar. Its head was nearly as large as a bull's with its ears flopped over. The stench of its body wafted over us, putrid as if it has wallowed in its feces. His head bent down, seeming to slop up water, he acted oblivious to our intrusion. I wondered if it might attack as wild boars do, their tusks flaring out of their jaw.

Flies swarmed around him in looping circles, each in its own flight pattern, searching for a place to land.

"Be quiet," Luis said, putting his hand on my chest, cautioning me to move closer more slowly.

Ten feet from him, we sensed something was wrong. He didn't stir. Maybe he knew we were stalking him. He was merely biding his time until we came closer and then, with his head down, would charge us. I crouched, stepping back toward to the fallen tree. I didn't want to take any chances. Luis leaned to the right side, stepping into the creek, his foot soaked—*he'll ruin his loafers,* I thought— and took several more steps toward the beast, his eyes transfixed on him, indifferent to his shoes filling with water.

"What are you doing? Get away from him!" I told him, expecting the beast to stomp down a hoof and turn on us.

"Oh, my God, look at it. Just look at it," Luis exclaimed, holding his hand to his mouth.

"What?" I asked, still holding back.

"Come here and look. You can really see it from this side," he explained, motioning me with his hand to come where he stood.

Hopscotching on flat stones and tiptoeing through the water, not wanting to get my shoes drenched, I balanced on several steppingstones and gingerly moved downstream to his vantage point. He pulled me close to him, his arm around my shoulder. I squinted and noticed a phalanx of flies, a massive, dense black cloud of them, swarming at its open jaw and into its eyes, and, in each socket of its eyes, a thick pulsing black mass seemed to undulate in and out of the holes, cascading in a ghastly fluidity. Beetles the size of a thumb darted in and out of holes in the rotted flesh.

Neither of us said, "It's dead," because death announced itself with such a ferocity in the decay, the bloated skin, drawn taut against the bone, and the gruesome smell, almost overpowering, that we understood death presided a mere five feet from us, and yet we also understood in a strangely contradictory manner that the beast, festered with myriad insects, seemed more alive in death than it might have been in life.

"Amazing," Luis said, whispering the word as if, somehow, by speaking in a normal tone of voice, we'd be desecrating the magnificent gift of this once powerful creature now manifested in its humble garb of death. Luis inched closer. I held his hand and followed him, tiptoeing as if we still believed we might awaken him. The humming, distinct and intense as the vibrating of a violin, enveloped the air. We could see that the massive layers of insects, all types—beetles, flies, and maggots—had invaded the carcass, taking it over fully so that, in death, the body seemed in the process of resurrection, exuding new life. It was a phenomenally active invasion, consuming it with a fierce intensity. The chest heaved back and forth as if he were breathing, yet, the closer we got, the more we ascertained that the movement came from the swarms of insects that trafficked in and out of him like infinitesimal motorists zigzagging into the heart of a city, driving around and over one another to garner the latest succulent goods. We huddled there, not speaking, for several minutes and then, in gradations, slipped back as if we had trespassed into a sanctuary.

I felt Luis's arm on my shoulder, our faces nearly cheek to cheek, and our breath slow and quiet as we watched the consumption of the beast by the sprawl of ravenous insects.

"Makes you think," Luis whispered.

"What?"

"What killed it?"

"Maybe old age?"

"Not likely. Seems too big and fat and healthy."

"Maybe what it drank or something it ate?'

"Fuck, I don't know. Might have been suicide: he knew his fate—another pork loin and slab of bacon—and hightailed it out of there," Luis said, laughing.

"Sad," is all I managed to say. I could not help but think that someday I too would make a good feast for them, their eating out my innards until I was bone.

We heard a cry from the camp. "Come and get it! Burgers and dogs are ready!"

The hotdogs and burgers were ready.

As we turned and sloshed through the creek, trudged up its bank, I looked back to make sure what we had seen was not an apparition. It felt as if someone had played a terrible trick on us, putting it there. I felt vaguely sick in the stomach. I pushed aside saplings, took a deep breath, and saw in the clearing where the girls had set out plates of the grilled meat along with coleslaw, baked beans, and potato chips. Sue greeted me with a kiss on my cheek.

"Where have you been?"

"You would not believe it," I said.

"Try me," she said, taking a sip of her beer.

"We saw a dead pig, a big one, right in the creek."

"Gross."

"That's what I think. Maggots and beetles and flies. "

"You all right?" she asked, stroking my face. "You look sick."

"Yeah, you're right. I don't feel so good."

"Let's go for a walk," she offered.

Frogs

We wandered up the road into a field, wide and long, with the russet grass trailing along the road for miles. We walked, talking about how my first week had been, how I felt good about pledging DAE and how I enjoyed being with her.

"Too bad you're hooked up already," I said, taking her arm.

"I'm taken," she said, sighing, "but that does not mean I'm gone. I'm still here and I like being with you"—she put her hand in mine—"so let's just enjoy each moment."

After strolling down the road a way, I told her that I felt better and we returned to the party.

We sat down and I ate heartily, having two hotdogs, and drank several beers. Sue held me in her arms and I leaned back against her. She stroked my hair and I felt as if she might love me. I cocked my head to look up at her and she smiled and kissed me on the forehead. "Silly boy. You're a sweetheart."

My head felt dizzy. I sat up and looked at the other couples, some sitting up and chatting, some curled in an embrace, off in worlds of their own.

Occasionally, Luis would glance over at me and, I suspected, he was thinking the same as I was: how we were eating the flesh of a cow and pigs and how, just five hundred yards from us, the insects were eating the flesh of a pig and how we shared in the fate of every living thing: the living eating the dead.

Since the girls had started the bonfire, after we had eaten, they told us to get more wood. For half an hour, the guys fetched wood, doing the girls' bidding. Luis decided to explore the forest up the hill, while I remained near the campsite where already plenty of limbs lying about for the harvesting. On one of the outings, I heard an engine roaring and raced back to the clearing to see who had decided to leave, but the cars were where they had been parked. Instead, Luis had found the keys to the excavator and, in halting jumps and starts, he hiccupped the excavator up the trail, its long cupped arm swinging back and forth like an elephant's trunk.

"Look at me!" Luis cried out. "I'm fucking driving it."

I ran over to the machine and called out," Luis stop it, stop it. You'll get hurt or ruin the thing."

Before I finished speaking, the bucket of the excavator rammed into a slight ash, and, rippling back, the driver's cabin reared up and plopped down with smoke billowing out of the engine. Luis, shaken loose from the driver's seat, fell sideways and slid off the frame, toppling over and over down the hill. I hurried to his side. He lay on his back, his arms stretched out to his sides, legs splayed, unconscious, looking like someone who had fallen from the sky. I knelt down and called his name, "Luis?" and, afraid not to harm him, sat beside him, stroking his cheek. With a smile on his face, he looked none the less for wear and opened his eyes.

"Man, tha-as-som-ride!" he slurred.

Drunk, no doubt about it.

I picked him up and, holding him by the shoulder, dragged him back to the bonfire where we joined the others and had another round of food while we sang some more songs. Sue had gotten pretty drunk, too, and had me hold her in my arms.

"You know," she said, "I sometimes wonder if I made the right decision."

"About marriage?" I whispered.

"Yeah. It seems so final like that door is closed and it will never be opened again."

"Well," I said, brushing the hair from her forehead "Put it off."

"I can't."

"Why not?"

"I just..."

"Oh, sure you can, why not put it..."

"Stop asking me!" she blurted out with fire in her voice and sat up, pushing my hand away from her. "I can't. That's all." She stomped off into the woods. I stood, dumbfounded by the outburst, staring at her silhouette in the woods, and raced after her.

"I'm sorry," I called.

She stopped, turned around, rubbing her hands across her forehead. She did not glance up at me.

39

"I'm a little drunk. It's not you. It's not you. Just let me be for a while. Okay?" she said, finally letting her eyes meet mine. Putting her hand on my cheek, she held it there for a moment—I could see tears in her eyes— and then, she turned and walked away, her long legs carrying her into the dark.

I put my hand on my cheek and felt how cold my own fingers felt compared to the warmth of hers.

I went back to the campfire and Luis gave me another beer. After several more beers, I had to pee again and, on Luis's suggestion, decided to visit our friend the boar. We headed toward the creek again but missed it and ended up in a bog where we heard bullfrogs, big ones with stentorian voices, and, as we stood there, our ankles in water, we began to mimic their croaking. I'm not sure what happened because I'd never caught a live frog in my life. But I think that we were no longer thinking as human beings think, nor sounding as human beings sound because the frogs recognized us as kin and leapt to us as we sang "Ahhruubhaa" over and over again, making a gurgling sound in the back of our throats, and first one, then another kept coming up to us, sitting right in front of us, their skin glistening in the moonlight so that we were able to hold them in our hand, our fellow frogs, croaking along with them deep into the night. They felt like gelatin, soft and pliable and, with the slightest pressure, lay still in our hands. Luis looked over to me and I looked at him, astonished that these creatures had put their trust in us and let us pick them up and hold them. I'm not sure how long we were in the bog but we saw fifteen frogs leaping right up to us.

"Do you believe it," Luis said, showing me one in each hand.

"They must think that we're frogs," I exclaimed. "Wait till the girls see them."

I felt the cool water ooze in my shoes and did not care. I was one with the water, one with the frogs, one with everything. They kept singing to us as we held them close to our faces.

We put a few frogs in our pockets to show the girls. They'd be impressed.

When we got back to the fire, several girls shrieked and told us to let them go to take them back to the bog. I noticed Sue was not among them. I asked where she was and the other girls said that they had not seen her.

40

Worried, I trekked into the woods to find her. I called her name. I stumbled across a log and banged my head into a small tree, cutting my forehead. I staggered back to the clearing and noticed that she was standing by the bonfire, drinking. I went over to her.

"You all right?" I asked.

"I saw it."

"What?" She didn't answered but her eyes seemed to dink in the fire.

"The pig?" I asked.

"Yeah," she said. "How awful. By itself, there. Dead."

"Pretty gruesome."

"I wonder how it got there?" she asked.

"That's what Luis and I wondered. What do you think?"

"I don't know, but I know it made me feel sick and, when I saw how decayed it was, I just cried," she said, handing her beer to me. I took a sip and handed it back.

"It's pretty sad."

"Oh, I was not crying for it. It's dead."

"What then?"

She drank the rest of her beer and laughed an oddly bitter laugh. "For me. I cried for me."

I put my hand out to pull her close, but she put her hand out. "Don't. Get yourself something else to drink." She smiled weakly and stepped back from the fire. "Enjoy yourself, really, don't mind me, have a good time, be happy" she said and she walked briskly away, stopping, as she did, to fetch another beer from the cooler.

The Bonfire

Luis and I drank several more beers, more than I had drunk in a long time, and I found that I could not walk straight anymore, so when I decided to take my biggest frog back to the bog, I smacked into another tree, scraping my cheek, and gave up trying to return him. I nestled him softly in my pants pockets, just slipping him in there since he didn't seem to mind being there, close to me. Luis suggested that we head back to the bonfire. I wanted to find Sue and ask if maybe we could date, maybe she needed to give herself a second chance, but she was nowhere in sight. *Why had she pushed me away? I only wanted to help. Women, I wish I understood them. One minute it seems like she cares for me, even likes me, maybe loves me and the next I'm disposable.*

I asked the other girls if they have seen her. They hadn't.

Luis called me over to his blanket, patting it, "Sit here, Jason. Sit right here and have another beer."

Luis folded his arm around me, pulling me next to him. "It's nice to have a good buddy," he said. I scooted down, nestled close to him, resting my head on his lap. I gazed at the fire. Glowing deep red and pink with pulsing waves of heat flowing upward into the pitch of night, it seemed like a lake of fire that I could almost dive into.

"Hey, what's up?" Luis asked.

"I'm cold," I said and sat up, leaning close to the fire.

"Really?"

"Yeah, but that fire feels fine" — I held up my hands to radiant heat— "It's warm and lovely," I said. "It looks inviting."

"I suppose," he said. "But it *is* fire. Here, have another beer."

He passed me another beer and I felt wonderful. I'd been drunk before, but not this drunk. The trees and bog and fire swam around me in a lovely symphony. Particularly beautiful were the colors emanating from the fire. The girls had stoked it, tossing in anything that would burn—logs, branches, vines—so that the coals glowed in a bright pinkish orange even brighter than they had been earlier in the night. I stood, stumbled, but righted myself so I stood properly like an admirer right beside it. Flames flicked up from the coals. It seemed so appealing I felt like leaping into it, just to step right into the warmth of it, become one with it, letting myself lean out and swim in its ecstasy. The tongues of flames licked upward deliciously, inviting me to join them. One of my feet rose up. It stepped forward to test what it was like. Like the pig on the spit, the flame and the flesh.

I heard shouts. Someone grabbed my arms. The fire kept calling me—lovely and warm, better than I expected. I could feel it on my face. I broke loose and stepped into it again. It felt warm. Voices cried, "No, No, No," and I felt my feet dragging backwards. Someone yelled, "Get him the hell out'a here." I shoved someone away. The flames were around me, but they were kind and didn't hurt. I felt an arm around my neck. Someone held my arm against my back. It hurt. We were moving quickly. A door opened. Someone called, "Sue, Sue, for god's sake get over here." The door closed. I was on my back. Someone was holding me down. The door opened. Then someone kissed my cheek and said, "There, there, you'll be fine sweetheart." Someone else had me by the arms. He was pressing on me. I felt his legs on mine. There was a grinding. A lurch. We were in a car. "Go, go, get him out'a here." The door slammed again; we were moving. I liked the feeling of swaying side to side, and the feel of someone's long hair on my face and a hand patting my cheek. There was a body on my body. He pressed against me. His arms on my arms. It was nice. The curves in the road, the acceleration and deceleration, the rocking in her arms, the pressure of his arms. Time swerved. The sway and counter sway. The stillness and the starting. Her hand on my face. "I'm sorry, I'm so sorry." She was crying. We stopped, the car, the engine died. There were more voices. A door opened. Cool air on my face. "Sit up, honey." Her letting me go. His getting off of me. Someone pulling on my arm. It was Luis. "Hi, Luis." "Hi, Jason. You're drunk." "Yes I am. I'm very drunk." Someone told me to walk. I'm on my knees. The ground is cool. I want to stay here. I'm upright. Someone kissed me on the cheek and held me close to her and said, "It's my fault. Oh, God, what have I done?" "He'll be fine. We'll take care of him." "Look, he's burned his pants and shoes." "Should we take him to emergency?" "Jees, look at his face." Another said, "Shish. He'll be fine. He's a freshman. We need to get him in the house. Let him sleep it off. Come with me, the back way." The girl brushed my cheek.

The soft caress of her hand. Nice. It felt nice. Cool. "Wash him off, he's a mess," she said. I felt my legs going forward although I could hardly see anymore. Smoke must'a gotten in my eyes. We were going up stairs, 1, 2, 3, 4... I lost count. Someone was taking off my shoes and socks. I was sitting up. Arms around my waist. My shirt was off and my pants—hey, where are my pants?—and underwear, what is going on? There was water on my face. Someone said, "Get that off his face and arms. Is it burned?" Another door opened and it was cold then warm. It was like rain, warm rain. Someone was rubbing my skin, his body next to mine. It was nice. Someone held me up. The water stopped. Then something soft. Someone was drying me off. Someone put one leg and, there, the other in something cool. Pajamas. I was on something soft. Voices, quiet, talking in whispers and a "Thank-you" and "Goodnight" and "Will he be all right?" and "Sure, he's fine; he'll be all right." A laugh. Someone gasped. "There is a frog; look, it's dead, a dead frog in his pocket." I wondered where it came from—the frog. Then I remembered. I wanted to see if it was alive. It was mine. What went wrong? I tried to stand up. "No, no, go to bed." I was not in bed. Where was I? "Calm down. You're in a room. Go to sleep. Everything is fine." A face was smiling at my face. It had blue eyes. A hand patted me on the chest. "Go to sleep." I sat up. The hand pressed me down. "Go to sleep." I knew the voice and I liked it and did as it told me. The fire kept leaping at me, its fingers grabbing at me like her hand on my cheek. I wondered how it was, how it would be to give myself over to it, how I wanted to leap into it still. My face felt hot, burning, and thoughts flickered and died out and the night, the embers of it faded, and the dark of it, drew near, and it was over.

The Waking

I woke on a couch in my room, covered with a blanket, and, by the angle of the sun in the sky, figured that I'd slept most of the morning. Pressing my hand to my head, I tried to recollect what had happened, but it seemed like trying to piece together strands of an unraveled tapestry, only little fragments coming into focus and others largely clouded in smoke. In high school, I'd found that getting drunk was one sure way to shed my doubts and inhibitions, but in the haze of the last night, my doubts redoubled and my inhibitions had gone wild. I didn't like waking. I wanted to go back to sleep and pretend it never happened. My head hurt. Standing up, holding onto the couch to steady myself, I staggered to the bathroom. Promptly I threw up. Once, and then a pause, a breath, spasms, and again. My face against the toilet stall, I lingered there, letting the cool metal soothe my cheek before going to the sink to wash my mouth. My face, flushed with some smudges on my cheeks, did not look pretty, but I washed up, took a cool shower and prepared for the day: do some studying, get back to classes, call Sue and apologize for how I'd made a fool of myself.

If I was going to get breakfast, I needed to get to the kitchen to fetch some grub. I was hungry, but the kitchen, which only served breakfast until 8, was most likely closed. After cleaning up in the bathroom, I noticed my face was not only puffy, but reddened, probably from the fire, and it felt sore. I touched it: warm as if still heated by the fire. Back in my room, the clothes I'd worn were smoky and my pants had both cuffs blackened and burned. I tossed them in the closet and got out new shorts and shirt and gathered my books so I could get to my first morning class.

Trevor greeted me in the hallway. "Heard you were fire dancing last night."

"Shit," I said, "the word is out."

"Afraid so." He looked at my quizzically. "Don't you remember us carrying you into the house?"

"That was you?"

"Yeah. Me and Tom and Jerry. You were out of it." He laughed. "Never seen someone so drunk."

Tom came up the stairs and pointed at me. "Hey, there he is, the drunk of the century, he's standing on his own."

"All right, all right," I said, holding up my hands. "You have me. I'm guilty."

Tom stepped by Trevor and put his arm around me. "You all right? You looked like someone punched you in the face."

"I'm fine and I'm late to class."

"Let me get my books," Tom said. "I'll go with you."

Before I escaped from the house, four other guys poked fun at me. I told Tom, "Let's hurry. This is getting embarrassing."

The day was unusually hot, nearly 88 degrees, and a sleepy drugged quality pervaded the campus. The only evidence that people were alive was the blare of radios, the speakers facing out from windows in the fraternities, blasting the Beach Boys' "Surfin' Safari", followed by similar summer tunes. The sound of competing radios blasted into my head as if someone had struck it with a hammer and would not stop. Ibby bolted past us on his skateboard.

"Hey, guys, the surf's up," he cried.

"Go for it," Tom called.

Beneath the incessant cacophony, motionless bodies, stripped of nonessential clothing, and slathered with coconut-smelling Coppertone, would twist and stir like reptiles on their small blankets and towels, spread out on lawns, roofs, porches, any place safe from traffic yet exposed to the sun, catching the remains of summer.

While I staggered to classes in a golf shirt, shorts, and penny loafers, I ogled at the bodies, mostly bleached white from being indoors. Sunlight streaked on the white facades of the fraternity and sorority houses, leaving a pained glare set off by the heavy shadows of trees and adjacent buildings, creating an illusion of a harsher light, much like the illumination of a street lamp in the pitch of night. For a second, I could not tell if it was night or day. My vision blurred. But the confusion lasted a second and passed quickly before my eyes, the afterimage of what I'd seen spilling away. I stopped and walked back a step to see if I could see it again. But the white glare bothered my eyes even more than it had, forcing me to squint, so that I could not recreate the strange dissociation of time that the light caused. Momentarily, I lost my balance, staggering sideways on the sidewalk.

"You all right?" Tom asked. He grabbed me to hold me upright.

"Fine. I'm fine," I said. But I wasn't fine.

Flushed, I put my hand to my face. It still felt puffy and irritated and hot. When I pressed my fingers on my cheek, the skin felt as if it had been overinflated, but I ignored the feeling and kept walking, heading to my classes and taking in the clamor of campus life.

I heard from a sorority's porch the next latest hit—a Roy Orbison number, "Oh, Pretty Woman,"— confound the air. Languid bodies, absorbed in the sounds, never noticed me walking beside them. The noise numbed them. They retreated behind their eyelids, into a world of sound where the rhythms became the reality. There were girls on their bellies, their tops unknotted, strewn loosely on the sides like a promise, and guys, their penises evident in their skintight Speedos. I stared at them. Like young gods, they cupped their hands under their heads, proud of their ample anatomy as if advertising that, yes, they were proud, the proof of their masculinity there for the looking. Gazing at them, the allure of their being passive, a few paces from me, caused me to shudder and feel dizzy again.

They stared blankly back at me looking at them, those boys and girls, as if already giving up their bodies to anyone who was interested, having shed their clothing to the sun's admiration, forgetting any loyalty to style, to fashion, to slacks or dresses, to Oxford shirts and Christian Dior blouses. Baby Leon and the Presidents, the local rock band, their Negro jive, strident and strained, stung the air. Legs wobbled back and forth. A finger snapped. White bodies converted to darker rhythms. It didn't matter who thinks one race is better than another because they were all interfused in a universal rhapsody of sun and sound.

"You sure you're all right?" Tom asked. "You're just standing there like a zombie. What's with you?"

"I don't know. I feel weird."

He laughed. "Man, you *are* weird."

He peeled off to his English Literature class. I strode to my class, knowing only a few of us would show up for Russian History in such weather because the professor, a man with a flattop haircut and the disposition of a military sergeant, lectured the whole period, rummaging through the lives of one czar after another, giving out dates and times, times and dates, recounting the bloody history of the dynasties and drumming out one fact after another so that, if I dared lift my pencil, I missed a half century.

Alone

At lunch, Paul mentioned that I looked funny, my eyes seemed red and my skin—it looked redder too. My throat was sore, making it nearly impossible to swallow. I didn't feel right. The dizziness I'd felt on the quad came back intermittently. Excusing myself, I went to the bathroom mirror and looked at my face, which was normally long and angular but had puffed up, my forehead, cheeks, and chin protruding like a pumpkin. It itched too. Paul came in to check on me.

"You better see the clinic, man," he told me. "You're blowing up like a balloon."

At the clinic, the doctor pressed my skin, looked down my throat and asked a few questions—if I'd been in the woods. (I had.) Was I allergic to poison ivy? (I was.) Had I been exposed to it? (Not sure.) But then it hit me, I had leaned over the fire. Could I get it from smoke? He nodded his head. Yes. My throat was inflamed and my face was bloated from poison ivy smoke. He told not to scratch my face and to apply a saline solution to it every few hours and to keep cool. Sweating could cause it to spread. He gave me a shot and told me to take antihistamines. They would calm the rash in my throat and reduce my reaction.

On the way back to my room, I noticed others staring at me. I tried to cover my face with my hand, but it only made it worse. My face burned. I wanted to scratch it so badly that I felt like screaming. At the house, I flushed my face with the solution and went to the dorm where a cool breeze wafted through the window. When I went to dinner, hoping to swallow something soothing, but there was one thing I could eat: mashed potatoes. Sean, one of the upperclassmen, laughed at me and called me, "tomato face," which lead to a chorus of laughter. My face, already burning, enflamed with embarrassment, I wanted to punch Sean in the mouth. Paul, who was sitting next to me, said, "Forget it."

I glared at Sean and, as soon as dinner was over, retreated to my room where Paul helped me dab the saline solution on my skin and suggested that I get some rest. I told him that I would and consigned myself to the dorm where I spent the next four days, pressing my hands into the sheets to keep them from touching my face. I fell in and out of a coma like sleep from taking antihistamines. I thought how, much of my life, people had called me "fat" and "tubbo"' when I was overweight in elementary school and mocked my "buck teeth" before I had braces and "scar face" after I got a staph infection from a football strap and how I wanted to disappear in those years and how, even as a young adult, I still dreaded being seen as ugly, dreaded thinking that someone would see me as disfigured, as anything less than handsome. I did not like to admit it, but I still carried within me the fat, bucked-toothed little boy whom everyone saw as ugly, and so I often wanted to hide, to disappear, to pretend I did not exist, did not have the mixed-up feelings about being who I was. I could not take people not seeing me as good-looking, which I counted on for my passport to acceptance. Without it, I felt stripped and naked and ashamed. Invisibility seemed the right choice. I would disappear from view until I looked right, a strategy I'd used often in my life, retreat to a room where I could mull over what happened to me.

At mealtimes, Paul, who had taken pity on me, would come to our room with some food and we'd chat, going over notes from the Cultures of Man class.

"Aren't you going crazy lying around in bed?" he asked.

"No. It gives me time to think."

"About what?"

"I never told you, but at the party last weekend Luis and I came upon this enormous pig—I mean huge—that was dead and bloated and infested with insects. There were beetles the size of a quarter coming in and out of its eyes. Gross. But I couldn't take my eyes off of it. It fascinated me. Its skin looked like a balloon, all stretched out, the way it gets before it bursts. And I was thinking how it seemed so foreign and unreal. But now with my face swollen and my skin feeling as if it might pop, I've been thinking how I'm like that pig, feeling like my body is just skin and innards, and I too will rot and decay," I told him.

"Shit, that's gross!"

"You think?" I touched my face, still sore and taut. "I think it's just how it is."

50

"You say crazy things sometimes. Hurry up and eat. I need to get back to the library. I've got a research paper already in Psychology."

I gobbled the meatloaf and mixed vegetables—flaccid overcooked beans and carrots like melted plastic.

"Thanks for doing this," I said. "I just don't want to be in public. I look pretty bad don't I?"

"Like a bloated pig!"

"Shut up!"

"You asked."

"I just don't want to be seen like this."

"Makes sense," he said, taking my plate as he was leaving. "With it so hot out, your face would just bake if you weren't in the shade."

Eventually my hiding away in the dorm became a daily pattern. I enjoyed being left alone. Well after the last guy in the dorm moaned, yawned, and dragged himself out of his bunk and the creek of the floorboard groaned, signaling he had stepped into the hallway, the door clicking shut, and I'd lie on my side peering out the windows at first one, then two students hurrying along the sidewalk to class. Then more. They'd carry their books under their arms or like a papoose held in front of them as they rushed to 8 o'clock classes. Sorority girls, their faces made up—lipstick bright as cherries—clustered together, moving seamlessly as a unit, talking animatedly, swept forward by the momentum of their own voices. The boys hustled after them or skirted in front of them, with their long masculine strides. Hour after hour, they went and returned like a herd heading up to pasture before returning later to their stalls. Soon I would join them, coming and going based on a schedule and never give it a thought, never consider how I too was regimented, programmed, and consigned to follow the herd, one more body headed toward some destiny, toward a diploma which, when I held it in my hand, would open a gate to another life where, as my father, I would get up each morning, gather my papers and march off to work, returning at night for a meal and rest so I could start up again, a never ending pattern of doing what one was told and of being what one was supposed to be. For a few days I had stopped and observed how I'd been trained to follow—not that it was bad, nor that I would not continue to do it, but that I'd never seen it, not when I was caught in its flow. It seemed absurd. Comic.

Inevitable. Something one did, something that was as much our fate as eating and loving and breathing.

With my faced turned to the window, I could see how the screen had torn; the fine filaments of wire were ripped apart. The tiny hole provided some entertainment. One morning a bumble bee, stout and persistent, wiggled through it, and, when it tried to get out, bumped into the screen, tirelessly, flying at it, being deflected off it and then popping into it. I took pity on it and pried the screen loose, pulled it out and the bee fled, heading toward the oak tree in the front yard. The tree provided amusement, too. Two squirrels romped from branch to branch, hanging on one, dropping to another, chasing after each other, swinging from the higher limbs to lower ones by free-falling and catching the lower branch and, without missing a step, scampering along it. I watched them for hours, how they loved the acrobatics, grabbing ahold of something sturdy and letting go, knowing—I am not sure how they knew—that there was a branch below them, something to catch onto so they could carry on.

In the early morning and evening, birds—some finches, sparrows, and chickadees—serenaded me, flitting from branch to branch, opening their throats and, just for the pleasure of it, singing. Over the days I could identify their voices, how they chirped, and the notes, in little rhythmic patterns, signaled it was the one with the ruddy chest or the black striped one that never seemed still. They seemed perpetually happy. They loved to make music as I did, too. I'd had sung in a church choir when I was in elementary school. How lovely it was to feel the sound in one's throat, the song coming out—it was magical that a voice could make music. Enchanted, I'd listen to the birds call in the day and sing goodbye at night.

While sequestered on the top bunk in the back by the window, where whatever small breezes that blew could soothe my burning face, being as invisible as I wanted to be, I became unwittingly an interloper for some pledges and upperclassmen who snuck into the dorm and, closing the door, would pull down their trousers and jack off. When a senior, a pre-med student came in, I had been asleep and only half-consciously was aware of his being in the dorm. I heard a rattling sound and, not sure what it was, cautiously turned over and saw two legs sticking out of the bottom of a bunk bed that was shaking back and forth. Not wanting to embarrass him, I froze and let him finish, turning my back on him in case as he got up and noticed that I was there. He did not, nor did others. The blanket heaped over me and my head facing the window to catch any hint of cool air must have given the impression of a jumbled bed.

It was practically an assembly line on some days, one after another. I'd avert my eyes and turn on my side in case they spied me. Most of the time, they came in, got down to business and were done with remarkable efficiency. Two brought in magazines that they gazed at while they fantasized their dream lover. What surprised me was Jacob, my pledge brother, who seemed so asexual in his conventional dress with his crew cut and Air Force cadet demeanor. He was a frequent flyer at the dorm: on most days, coming up in the morning and afternoon and sometimes even at evening with no end of supply, he'd prime his pump. The way he did it reminded me of someone pulling a cord on a lawn mower, and it worked as well as a starter cord, since he was off and running in no time.

As I sat around, not feeling clearheaded enough to read my text books, I read the papers that Paul brought up to the room, the *Indianapolis Star* and the *New York Times*, the one he bought at the bookstore.

With the presidential campaign heated up between Goldwater and Johnson, and with news that Robert Kennedy had resigned as Attorney General and was running for the New York senatorial seat, separating himself from the president, the daily newspaper proved to be more interesting than my history text. *The Indianapolis Star*, normally a conservative paper, remained neutral, not supporting Barry Goldwater whose conservative ideas—his support of business, his threats to use tactical nuclear weapons in Vietnam, his fervid anti-communist stance—made him seem more radical than rational. My dad liked him although he did not agree with his convention statement "extremism in the defense of liberty is no vice," but, as a family, we rarely talked about politics, never mentioned a speech made, nor a campaign ad viewed, almost as if such talk was impolite, an egregious violation of etiquette, like talking about masturbation.

When I had lunch with Paul, he noticed that I had read the paper and asked what I thought about the campaign.

"I don't know," I said, shoving the paper aside, avoiding the need to state my own thoughts as almost a habit.

"Come on," he insisted. "You're reading the paper. Right there, Goldwater is being accused of being unstable. Look at the number of psychologists who claim he is. What do you think?"

"I think they may be right. What person in their right mind would use nuclear weapons when we've seen what they do—obliterate whole cities," I said.

Paul stood up, took a few steps back, tilted his head, squinted as if appraising some fancy piece of jewelry in a store window.

"Damn, I do not believe it! You actually said what you think. I bet your pap wouldn't agree with you," he said, smiling broadly.

"Shit, no. He loves Goldwater. Well, maybe not him, but anything Republican."

"You bet he does, as do most businessmen. I bet he loves Nixon too," he said.

"How'd you know?"

"That's how they are."

I laughed. "My dad even looks like Nixon and talks like him too."

"You poor sap."

"Do you think all businessmen talk like Nixon?" I asked. "You ever notice how he acts, how he uses certain phrases over and over?"

"Damn if I know. I don't obsess about politicians," he said and, pushing the BLT sandwich in front of me, added, "I wish we could continue, but hurry up. I got to get to class."

I scarfed the sandwich, one of my favorites, and handed Paul the empty plate.

After Paul left, I thought about what he said—"obsess"—that's the word he used. I did obsess about Nixon. By growing up with corporate CEOs, I became fascinated with men in power and with one in particular—Richard Nixon. My fascination stemmed from his reminding me of my father—the way he talked and how he knew how to put on the right smile for the right people.

When I was fifteen, a freshman in high school, Nixon was campaigning and he came to Hook County where we lived because it was known to be a Republican booster shot. Whenever a Republican candidate needed an emotional lift all he had to do was come to Hook County where everyone was a Republican. My mother drove us to Wheaton, some six miles from our house in Glen Brook, and we stood on some side street, forty or fifty of us. It was hot, late August during his 1960 campaign against Kennedy—and I was sweaty and impatient, wanting to get to the Glen Brook Country Club to caddy, when a caravan came by us with Nixon, wearing a blue suit, and sweating too, sitting next to his wife on the back of an open convertible, waving and pointing occasionally into the crowd until he came right by us and pointed at me, winked and gave me a thumbs up sign. I returned the sign and he smiled. I remember how I smiled back at him, thinking that he had acknowledged me, picking me out from the crowd as if I had been chosen by him for something important.

That was how it started—my interest in him and his career. I was stuck by how handsome he was in person, how his dark, five o'clock shadow was clear evidence that, had he chosen to, he could have grown a thick beard like Lincoln in no time, made him seem more handsome than he did on TV, where he seemed sallow, almost sickly. What also struck me was how even with all the adulation (we waved and shouted at him), he looked mildly ill at ease, just as my father, who with all his success, his being a corporate leader of a major Fortune 500 company, his being on the board of major corporations, was always very self-conscious of how he had to act right, to be dressed properly, attired in the best suits and to look the part of a corporate executive, and, if anything was out of place—his tie not perfectly knotted—he would become upset. Even after he came home, he remained in his suit while my mother and he drank their martinis and while we, as a family, sat at the dinner table with him, the chief executive of our corporate family. He used the same emphatic statements as Nixon and as I'd heard other businessmen use, "Let me make this perfectly clear," which is what he said when he wanted to cut off discussion and conclude the conversation. If anyone did disagree, he would settle the argument with the statement that he had made his point "in no uncertain terms," which meant that in his mind, the discussion was over and compliance was the only option.

That afternoon, before dinner, Tom Wilson came to visit me in the dorm, something he did every day, sitting on the bed across from me, asking how I was doing. He'd rub my back and noticed how tense I was. "For an invalid, you're back is strung tight as guitar strings."

"I carry a little tension."

"You bet you do. I'd hate to see it when they snap," he said, laughing.

I showed him my face and he said, "Ugly."

"Yeah," I groaned. "Was afraid you'd say that."

"Hey, don't get me wrong. It looks better. I mean a few days ago you looked like a Porky Pig and now you look more like Elmer Fudd. That's improvement!"

I swatted him with my pillow and he took his pillow and swatted me and we laughed.

"Seriously," he said. "I think by tomorrow you should be fine. You need to get out of your cocoon, Jason. Really. The swelling's gone. And the color is more normal. Get off the pity pot. Have you looked in the mirror?"

I had. The swelling had diminished, leaving the skin, although still flushed, looking more normal than it had been. In my self-isolation on the third floor, with no one to tell me what to do or what to think, I realized I'd become more assured of myself. Although I was still the type of guy who would just as soon go along with what my dad—or others—said, I had read the newspapers and thought long and hard about the three boys murdered in July and whose bodies were discovered last August in Mississippi. The FBI arrested eighteen of the murders, but the state refused to bring them to trial because a lack of evidence. It seemed so unfair. What must it have been like, cornered as they were by the Ku Klux Klan on some dark road, to face death? What must it have taken for them to risk their lives for a cause? I had to put those thoughts aside. I knew Tom was right. I said goodbye to the birds, the bumble bee, and the squirrels. I folded up the newspapers. I noted that there was talk now in Washington about The Voting Rights Act. The world seemed to turn upside down while I was in my bed. Now it was back to a normal—and busy—life of being a student.

"All right," I said, hopping off the bed. "Time for reentry into the real world."

Resigned

During the first weeks with the DAE, I used to toss the football in the front yard, playing catch with Eric, who was quick, and with Norm, a sophomore, who could cut on a dime. In my senior year at high school, I worked out in the basement of the school gym where we had an indoor track with a low ceiling, twenty feet high at most. When we tossed the ball, we had to rifle it on a straight line or it would hit the ceiling, and so I learned to zip a football twenty yards on a straight trajectory. Bill Harris who noticed that I had a good arm told me that the house had never competed in the school intramural program because they never had a quarterback and asked me if I wanted to do it. I told him that I would think about it. But that would force me to make a big decision. I had to quit the football team, which had been my passport to acceptance at Ashbury, not something easily forsaken. After missing practice most of the week, I'd had time to think about my interest in being on the Ashbury team. I felt an obligation to give it my best since my athletic ability had been a major factor in my acceptance at Ashbury.

Every afternoon I went to the gym, pulled my uniform from the locker—the shoes with the cleats, the shoulder pads, the jock, the jersey, the helmet and the pants— and took off my clothes. The other players, the upperclassmen, dressed quickly, shucking off their clothes and yanking on the elastic pants, anxious to get on the field. The practice field, adjacent to the stadium, had blocking sleds and dummies strewed at one end, set at odd angles like abandoned farm equipment. After calisthenics, we jogged to the sleds. The coach stood on the sled, pointed at me and yelled, "Eighty-four, come on candy ass, move it, move," and I drove with the legs, pushed him down the field, yard by yard, until he barked out someone else's number, "Sixty eight" who shoved him back up the field. We repeated one drill after another: running backwards as the coach moved the football to one side after another, sprinting up and down the field, and repeating a play over and over. The whole time the coach barked out commands. "Get over here." "Hit 'erm harder." "Move your lazy ass." Sweat poured over my face, drenched my jersey and soaked my pants. In lulls, Trevor told me he wanted to earn a starting position and became a favorite of the coaches. He hustled to the blocking sleds and practiced before and after practice. I told him that I just wanted to survive.

I had expected college football to be different from high school. Since I knew how to block and how to rush passers, I didn't want a coach yelling at me and telling me to hurry up and do a job I knew how to do. The whole practice routine became as monotonous as it was in high school. Day after day we slammed into a blocking sled, into the dummy, into each other, body on body, my legs driving, my head jamming into leather, into shoulder pads, stumbling, getting up, calves sore, forearms bruised, neck taut, day in, day out, sweat dripping down the forehead into my eyes, sweat drenching my jersey, chafing the inner groin of my pants, the inside of my helmet, day in, day out, the coaches' taunts, "Move your ass" "Hit harder," "Hurry up, faster," "Come on, pansy" and, on a break, the cool salve of water in a towel, some relief from thirst, and yet the pushing on, run a play, hit the hole, once, twice, "Come on, damnit, cut on the block," and the waiting to run it again, do it right, do it again, do it so often my legs knew better than I did where to cut, how to evade outstretched arms until I stood by, letting another runner go, a breeze cool on my wet jersey, the light tilting down in the pines at the edge of the field, the exhaustion at the end of practice, the wind sprints, twenty-five yards, up the field, down the field, fifty yards, up the field and down, the pep talk, "We need better improvement," the long walk back to the locker room, no one talking, the shedding of my jersey, my pads, my shoes, and the showers, cool water from the shower head in the mouth, the taking it in, the thirst like a hunger, like a yearning, unquenchable, the other bodies naked, scrubbing off of dirt, blood and grass, soap cleansing the body of the hard labor, the drudgery, the hours of doing what one was told, and then like soldiers back from the war, slipping into civilian clothing, the soft press of cotton shirt, loose cling of undershorts and shorts, with pockets that the scarred hands slide into like forgetfulness, into the safe confines where they do not have to fend off or grab anything, where they can just press like lovers against the thigh, and the feet step down the stairs down to the sidewalk, to the evening light, and to the quiet, inviting, undemanding air.

"Have you ever played on a team?" I asked Paul.

"Yeah, centuries ago in elementary school. Baseball, I think. Why you ask?"

"I'm wondering about football. The fun's gone out of it. It's just drudgery, and some guys want me to play intramurals, to be the quarterback," I said.

"Do you have some obligation to play?"

"I don't know. The dean told me that my athletic ability was an important factor in my being considered as a student. Before I got accepted, I interviewed the coach. He thought I could play in the conference, be a starting back."

"But that was then. What about now?"

"Not sure. All I know is that I'm fed up. My heart isn't in it. I don't just want to be another running back. I would prefer to play quarterback. Besides, these coaches treat you just like the ones in high school did. They yell. They scream at us as if we were dumb. They run us through drills. Endless drills. Nothing is ever good enough. Besides, I don't know anyone on the team except Trevor who is, well, you know, a bit over the top like someone whose engine is always on overdrive."

Paul put down his pen. His eyebrows raised and his lips pulled in tight. He shook his head.

"I think you've answered your own question," he said.

"What?" I asked.

"Your heart isn't in it."

After my classes the next day, I went to my football locker, collected the pads, jersey, pants, helmet and shoes, piled them up so I could carry them. I felt strange. I'd never quit a sport, no matter how bad the coach, how much he yelled, I had stuck it out, finish the season.

At the coach's office door, I knocked.

"Come in," the coach said.

The coach sat at his desk, his thin brown hair combed back on his head like my dad. Standing by him, Assistant Coach Kansa, a dark, powerful man, was pointing to something on a sheet of paper.

He greeted me, "What's up, Jason?" As the back and receiver coach, he knew me better than the head coach who worked mostly with defense and linemen.

I piled my uniform on the coach's desk. He looked puzzled.

I said, "I don't want to be on the team." My heart felt as if it were about to burst through my chest. Sweat broke out on my forehead.

"You don't?" the head coach said.

"No."

Coach Kansa came around and put his hand on my arm, "Is there something wrong, Jason? You still sick from the fire?"

"I'm fine coach," I said and smiled at him.

"What's the reason? Can you tell us why?" he asked.

The head coach stood, placed his hands on his hips, and tilted his head to the left. The paper on the desk had names listed by positions. I saw my name. It was circled. I stuffed my hands in my pockets.

"Well?" Coach Kansa asked. His eyebrows narrowed to a point that almost met.

"The uniform didn't fit," I said and shrugged.

Coach Kansa laughed. "Didn't fit!?"

"Well, you wanted a reason," I said. "And that's all I have."

I wiped the sweat from my forehead.

Coach Kansa stepped back and nodded his head in disbelief.

"Is that it?" he said.

"Pretty much."

"You're a piece of work, Follett," he said and sighed deeply. "I'm sorry to hear that. We figured you might start with us someday soon." He tapped his finger on the sheet of paper with my name on it.

"I'm sorry, coach," I said.

"It's your decision," he said. "Are you sure?"

"Yep."

"Is there anything we can do?"

"No."

"All right."

I shook his hand and the hand of the head coach who did not look me in the eyes. He kept looking at the paper. I turned, walked out the door, took a deep breath and felt as if I'd cut out my heart. But, too, I felt relieved as if, once again, I turned another corner, made another decision, and was coming into my own.

The Arm

To prove myself as an athlete had been, since junior high, the one sure way of impressing others and being noticed. I enjoyed how other people, if they saw me play well, assumed that I had some special qualities, some gifts that set me apart, gifts that made me important, so I was excited about being the quarterback of our DAE team.

In our first game against Sigma Nu, we managed to score four touchdowns by means of several long passes to Norm who knew how to make a quick spinout where he sprinted straight ahead, stopped—the point, at which I threw the pass—turned, caught the ball and then dashed up-field without losing a step in speed. But even with our four touchdowns, we lost 32-24. We needed better defense and so recruited Jacob, who was quick on his feet, and several other guys who could do better coverage of the receivers. Under Bill Harris's tutelage, we recruited several blockers for me so I would have more time to read the defense and make passes. We also rounded up big men, including Tom, who could rush the opponent's quarterback. By the second week, when we played the Beta Beta Chi, the previous year's championship team, we had more depth. From being a nobody at the house, I had suddenly become a somebody.

At dinner, the president made an announcement. "For four years, DAE has never competed in intramural football, but this year, we have the makings of a winner. My pledge son, Jason"—he pointed at me, motioning me to stand up—"has made us contenders against the Betas. We have a big game against the traditionally best intramural team and, if I were a betting man, I'd say, although we're an underdog, we can be the top dog. I want to see every member of the house at the game. We're going to change history for DAE." Everyone stood and cheered. Tom patted me on the back. I smiled and acknowledged the support.

"Speech, speech," Luis chanted.

I shook my head, but everyone was chanting speech. "Hey, what can I say? We're a team and we plan to win."

A cheer reverberated in the room. Everyone stood up and clapped, even

62

Mrs. Mayford, our housemother. After dinner, as I walked back to my room, guys would shout out, "You can do it!" and I smiled at them and gave them a thumbs up. But secretly I had my doubts. I'd scouted the Beta team and it had not only a good quarterback but quick wide receivers. With the game coming up, I turned my attention to perfecting my throws, going out in a side lot with Norm and Eric, making sure that I could anticipate the second that they turned or cut either right or left on a route that I could deliver the ball to them.

When I arrived for the game, every DAE was there, lining the field. They cheered as we practiced, tossing short routes to warm up my arm. We did not do any running plays in practice, wanting Betas to anticipate our using the pass as our primary weapon.

Sue came too. Before the game started, she walked over to me.

"Big game, huh?" she said, putting her hand on my arm.

"Yeah."

"Nervous?"

"Suppose I am."

"You'll do great. I know it."

"Thanks for coming."

"I wouldn't miss it for the world," she said, smiling.

"Even for your boyfriend."

"Even for him," she said. "And, hey, you're my boyfriend too."

I laughed. I suppose I was and I liked it.

When I walked back to the team, Tom asked, "Your girlfriend?"

"Yes, I guess she is."

"Guess?"

"She is."

The first quarter, we surprised Betas by running the ball with Jeffery, a junior who once had been a running back, but had never played because our teams had been so bad. He could cut and accelerate amazingly, so, as long as we could block, he made five yards, eight yards, fifteen yards—all steady pickups—and we moved down the field. From scouting reports, they expected me to pass, and we did not until we were twenty yards from the goal line at which point we faked a run with Jeffery and I hid the ball for a second, stopped, and zipped a pass to Eric who had sped to get by the defense. Norm continued to be a reliable weapon, getting clear whenever I needed a quick out. In the last quarter, we were tied. The Betas quarterback could not only throw but run. Several times when I was rushing him, thinking I could tag him, he put one foot out and I lunged in that direction and he darted by me, leaving me grasping at air. Tied 28-28, with our having the ball deep in our territory, we huddled and Eric told me that we had not run an in-seam pass, which would be quite risky because it meant I had to pass right up the middle of the Betas defense. He would have to line up to the right side, spring ten yards straight ahead, cut to inside, heading across the field and, right at the midpoint, cut up field, splitting the two defensive backs. The difficulty with the play was that I could not pass it straight into his body because linebackers and running backs would be in back and either side of him and they could snatch it for an easy interception. I had to pass it over his shoulder so that, as he was sprinting downfield, the ball would fall over his head and into his arms. If he caught it, he would have no one who could stop him since he could accelerate from first gear to fifth gear in a matter of seconds and run by all the defenders. It was like tossing a ball at someone doing a hundred yard dash. The downside, if I miscalculated the throw and tossed it to his right or left side, not directly over his shoulder, was that he could not adjust to an errant throw. The throw had to be pinpoint like tossing a dart and needing it to be in the exact middle of the board.

With five minutes left in the game, if we could score, we might be able to hold them off and have an upset. But an in-seam pass was risky and Eric and I had not practiced it much.

"Come on, I know they'll expect the down and out as we have done the whole game. They don't expect us to do one down the middle," Eric said.

"I need good blocks," I said.

Bill growled, "You always have good blocks. Don't worry, man. We have you covered."

Steve, the stout, who had joined the team and who surprisingly had done well with competition after losing ten pounds by working out more, proved to be a big barrier to rushing defensive lineman. "We'll get them," he said. "You just worry about the throw."

I agreed to try it. The snap was clean. I looked at Eric and when he made his first cut, I faked a throw, which froze the defensive back. Eric cut to the left, coming down the line right in front of me, not ten yards away. I shuffled to the right, holding the ball up as if I was going to flip it to him and then, he cut, ripping downfield and I set and threw the ball more at an angle knowing it had to come down softly over his shoulder. He raced by the defensive backs, turned to look in the air for the ball and adjusted slightly because I threw a little to his right, but I'd thrown it the correct distance and he snared it, tucked it under his arm and, head back, darted to the end zone. The Beta players turned around and watched him, their hands on their hips.

Undefeated in the previous two years, they could not believe what happened. When they got the kickoff, their quarterback decided to prove his mettle and made several quick moves, raced up the sideline, trying to outfox us, by pulling off a nifty touchdown. He held the ball up to show off his having outdone us and replicated what we had done. But he had not looked to his left side and failed to see Jeffery who came up and slapped the ball out of his hand. The ball bounced several times and Eric scooped it up, then darting the other direction. The kickoff team had slowed to a trot confident that their quarterback had pulled them out of the fire and definitely did not expecting the see Eric racing down the sidelines in the opposite direction, so with a few blocks by Bill and several others, he was standing on the end zone, the nail in their coffin.

After the game, Sue raced over to me and gave me a hug and kiss on the cheek.

"You were fabulous. It was so exciting. That toss you made was something," she said, holding onto my arms and jumping up and down.

"Thanks." I looked at her face, gleaming, full of excitement.

"Let's meet later," she said. "But you need to go with your team and celebrate."

I kissed her on the cheek. She ran off, waving. I joined the team and headed back to the house.

Our victory caused quite a stir in the intramural circles. My photograph was plastered on the campus newspaper with "DAE Upset Betas" as headline. We won several more games as I got more comfortable passing, learning more plays, and getting used to the different receivers. Although our team did not make the finals—we lost to the Delta Chi team in the semi-finals, we made a name for ourselves and knew that, if we could get one or two more good players, we might stand a chance the next fall to go all the way.

Having proved myself as an athlete and being in a key position of quarterback, I gained the respect of many of the upperclassmen and realized for the first time that college, if I could keep up my grades, was going to be fun. I felt I had it made, that I had acquired a certain power that made me stand out from other guys. I cultivated that glorified image of me that came from my ability to face the pressure of oncoming linemen. I liked the feeling that others thought there was something special about me that set me apart, that guys looked at me differently and envied me. I'd learned a violent game, to avoid tacklers, to give and take hits. Early in my football career, I'd come to trust in the importance of being tough, of being a man, of being special.

Confession

After the Beta upset, I met up with Sue at Jiminotts. She asked me about football since she had never paid much attention to it and it was a side of myself that surprised her.

"It seems like a really rough sport. I don't mean this to be negative. But you are such a sweet guy, I can't imagine you playing it. It's so violent," she said. "Do you really like it?"

"Yes, I do. Someone else told me that, too. A guy in high school said I was such a calm, easygoing guy, but on the field, I turned into a monster," I told her. Then I explained to her why football had been such an important part of my life, but how I too had doubts about what it might do to me if I lost perspective and only thought about winning at all costs.

"When I played high school football, after becoming first string, I wanted to prove myself to my coach. On defense on a kickoff, I raced down the field and saw, right ahead, a running back coming in my direction. It was him and me. Trying to fake me, he darted to the right but I had him in my sights and slammed right into him, head first, driving him back and landing right on top of him. Once we were down on the ground, I realized that he was a slight kid, weighting probably 25 pounds less than I did. I jumped to my feet and jogged off the field. My coach rushed up to me, slapped my helmet and called out, 'Great tackle, Follett. Great tackle.'"

"When I stood beside the coach who patted me on the pads, I saw that the runner had not gotten up. Several referees rushed over to him, then the opposing trainer and coach. They kneeled over him, lifted his head, but he was out. Finally, they had to get a stretcher and carry him off the field. He sat in the sidelines and never played again that day.

"Later that night my father asked at dinner, 'Weren't you upset that the boy you tackled was carried off the field?'

"I didn't miss a beat because I was so proud of myself. I told him, 'No, in fact, I was praying he would not get up.'

"'Not get up?' my mother asked.

"'Yep.'

"She looked at my dad, her eyes tight, and he looked at me, quizzical. Finally, my mom said, 'I'd hope you wouldn't think that.'

"'Why?' I said.

"'You might have paralyzed him,' she said. She reached out across the table and touched my hand. 'Jason, listen. He's a boy just like you and, think about it, you might have hurt him. Permanently hurt him. That isn't right.'

"'But...' I started to say, wanting to let her know how the coach told us at halftime what a terrific tackle I'd made.

"'But nothing," she said, a firmness in her voice that almost scared me.

"I thought about what she said and, most of all, the distress in her eyes— or, maybe it was more than distress—it was fear. I pulled my hand back from her in disgust. I cut another piece of meat.

"'Sorry mom, I just never thought about him,' I said. It was then that I realized that my wanting to prove myself may have its limits. I have to keep it in perspective, knowing it's just a game that I happen to be good at."

Sue nodded her head. "I'm glad you realize that. Your mom was right. But how could you become so cold and indifferent to what you had done?"

"I supposed it was because I'd become convinced that hitting was the ultimate goal, since when we blocked, when we tackled, we cried out 'Hit, hit, hit.' I believed if I made a good hit I had done my job and I deserved all the accolades. Face it, I liked the attention. I loved how the coach told other players to do it like Follett," I said.

Sue listened attentively and took a sip of her soda, "I suppose we all get duped."

"Duped?"

"It means tricked. You know how sometimes we get a strange notion in our head and then, weeks, months, even years later we realized we'd been fooled? Well, it seems you got fooled into believing that hurting someone else was okay. You don't think that now."

"I don't. I just like to compete," I said.

She reached over and patted my hand like my mother had.

I pulled my hand back.

"Hey, I'm not your mom," she said and paused to make sure I realized what I had done. "That's okay to like competition. It's the violence that worries me."

"Me, too."

"Be careful, it's not like you," she said.

"I will," I said and told her about my classes, how I was doing. She told me that she'd not heard from her fiancée, not for several weeks.

"Is everything all right?" I asked.

"I think so. He gets busy. I do, too. That happens," she said, brushing several crumbs off the table.

"Are you worried?"

"Well, since we're being honest with each other, I am. There's this problem."

"What was the problem?" I interrupted, noticing how her eyes tearing up.

"He wants me to convert."

"Convert?"

"He's Catholic and I'm a Congregationalist."

"Same as me!"

"Well, you know that pretty much means I'm nothing. As long as you are doing well economically, God is happy with you. But Catholics are strict. They want you to toe the line. Follow the script. And religion," she sighed, "religion is not important to me."

"Did you tell him that?"

"Yeah, and that did not set too well with him. He's big on religion."

"So?"

"I don't know," she said, tilting her head back and taking a deep breath. "Can we not talk about it?

"Sure," I said. "Was I too forward in asking about..."

"No. No. Not in the least," she said. "But I do have to be going. So nice to talk. You're a good friend." She slid out of the booth and kissed me on the forehead. I sat finishing my butterscotch milkshake. I had to stir it with the straw to loosen up its thickness. I thought about what we discussed.

Having to prove myself as a man seemed a curse, something that a man had to do, something I strove to do yet never seemed to succeed at. And yet I was content to bask in my success for the time being. I thought too about Sue, how her dreams of happiness and marriage were crumbling around her, how little I could do for her, and how our fates drew us in directions that we know little of and yet rule our lives.

Pressure

When upperclassmen came to my room just to chat with me or to strategize about the next game, I was no longer a pledge with no authority, but a luminary. I felt my confidence grow each week. I put Sue out of my mind. I enjoyed those moments of glory when I knew I was good and others did, too. It became easy to convince myself that I was better than they were.

Whatever insecurities I felt about dating or just going out with girls which, in turn, led to my lingering doubts I had about my own sexuality— my attraction to some guys and my fear of girls—vanished during the intramural season. It seemed strange how everyone assumed if you were a successful jock you must, almost inevitably, be a stud, a ladies' man, a first-class heterosexual. It was not true, I knew that, but everyone seemed to believe it as if athletic prowess meant sexual confidence.

"You could have any chick you want," Luis told me one evening on the way back to our rooms from dinner. "I mean the girls go for a jock and, man, you are good-looking, too. All you do is hang around with that girl— what's her name?"

"Sue."

"Yeah, her, but she's already committed. You need to get out, man, and date some chicks that really want a man."

"Sure, sure, that's easy to say when you are a ladies' man," I joked, poking him in the ribs.

He grinned, pushing me on the shoulder. "Yeah, I'm pretty good, I admit. But you, man, you could have girls eating out of your hand. I mean it; they'd jump if you gave them a call."

"Trouble is, I barely have time as it is to do my studies. I'm not the best student in the world and I..."

"Excuses, excuses. Don't give me that. Don't you like girls?" he asked.

"Sure, I do."

"Well, then prove it. Get with the program. I mean we have a reputation here at DAE. This is an A-number-one stud farm here. Look at Joe: he dates two girls a week. And Tom—he's already got a reputation," he pressed me, grabbing me by the arm. "Let's make some phone calls. I know some girls who have already asked about you."

"Really?"

"Yes, really. They're hot for you, man. Big football star. Let's call them right now!"

Pulling my arm back, I said, "Come on, give me a break. I'll take you up on it. I will. I promise I will. But now I *really* need to study."

Luis leaned against the wall, tilting his head back, and said, "Okay. But by this weekend, you'll call?"

"I'll call."

In my room, I opened the American Government text, reading about the Constitution and the balance of power, the legal challenges between the executive and judicial branches, the same topics that I'd studied in junior high school. I found it hard to focus. I doodled on a page, drawing a river with willows hanging over the edge and thought about Huckleberry Finn, how he drifted down the river with Jim, and remembered my school friend Doug.

When we were teenagers, he'd been the first boy who'd I'd had a crush. It was mutual. When he'd slept over at my house—or I at his—we had difficulty keeping our hands off each other, although both of us had resisted, except for beating off together, for fear that the other one might think we were queer. We were like two magnets that were doing our best to keep from being pulled together. When we were fifteen, he invited me to ride down the Illinois River in his boat—a Chris-Craft—with a small cabin and upper pilot deck with a windshield.

We packed food and sleeping bags and meandered like upscale Huck and Jim down the river, stopping on an uninhabited island. Covered by sand dunes and scrub pines along its ridge, which also rimmed around the shoreline, the island had a pristine pond in the middle with water so clear we could see fish on the bottom. We set up camp in a sand dune carved out of the ridge, just our sleeping bags, a kerosene stove, and a lantern. In the evening, we discovered that the island was a lovers' lane: couples would steal over to the island—young men and girls—and lay down a blanket, and, depending on the couple, disrobe and go to it. We secreted ourselves in eye-shot of them and watched them make love, or, in some cases, try but ending with the girl tossing the boy off of her and trotting away in tears. Most left by ten o'clock. Left to ourselves, at night, lying out on our sleeping bags, after skinny-dipping, we discovered each other and, as boys do, played with one another, touching each other, getting aroused, pretending that it was nothing——just play—but kept on until we had let go. We acted as if it had nothing to do about being attracted to one another. No pressure to be other than we were, enamored with our bodies and their pleasures. But, over the next few years, whenever we were together, the subject of sex came up and I would find myself wanting to touch him and he, more diffident than I, would shy away until, the last year in high school, after he had transferred to a private school, he came over to see me.

He wanted to talk. He seemed distressed. I invited him to our rec room in the basement, a paneled space with a pool table, TV, and bar. We sat next to each other on a couch. I looked into his blue eyes, a liquid blue that when I was young I feared I might drown in, and noticed how intently he focused on me. He was blunt.

"I've been at a private school," he said. "While I've been there, I was thinking a lot about us, you know, especially that trip down the river."

"Yeah, that was cool."

"And at private school, it's all boys, you know."

"I suspect it is."

"It is and, well, there is a lot of, well, you know...homosexuality." He glanced up at me.

I noticed that he was groping himself, rubbing his penis. "And there is not much else to do, so I got involved, if you know what I mean."

I nodded, squirming in my chair, feeling the old attraction to him heating up in my body.

"What do you think?" he asked.

"I guess it's all right," I said, staring out the window at a ginkgo tree, its leaves fluttering in the wind. I could feel myself getting aroused and shifted in my chair.

"All right?"

"Yes, you know, we all do it some."

"And?"

"And what?" I asked, getting up and going over to the bar, "You want something to drink?"

"Sure, a Coke."

I fixed up Cokes, pouring them in glasses with ice. Mortified by the topic, I tried to change the subject, although, secretly, I wanted him to go on, to tell me more, to ask me if I wanted to start up where we left off. With his hands in his pocket, he kept rubbing his penis—the outline of it against his pants visible like a wand with its special magic to draw me toward it, as it had in junior high when we had hard-ons all the time. I tried not to look and somehow, out of my own frustration and confusion and urges, made an excuse that I had to go out to meet someone. I was determined to put my attraction aside, to relegate it to the past as if it belonged to someone else and had nothing to do with me. He stood up. He rubbed his hand around the lip of the glass, making slow circles.

"You all right?" I asked.

He finished his Coke, one last sip.

"Can we get together sometime?" he asked. "I mean, it might be nice just to hang out."

"Sure," I said, but I did not mean it.

He thrust his arms around my neck and pulled me close to him. I could feel his whole body. The house was empty. No one would be home for hours. But I pulled away.

"Good to see you," I said.

"You, too."

That was the last time I'd seen him. I'd heard he went to college in the East.

Luis knocked on my door. "Hey," he said. "I have a girl, Janet, who really likes you. She's seen you play football. Shall I tell her you're interested?" he asked.

"Sure, that's fine."

"Cool," he hit me in the arm. "You'll like her."

Just when I thought that sports might save me from having to date, to give me a reprieve from proving myself, always having to show I was a real man, I found that it was having the opposite effect: making it more incumbent on me to be a true jock and show that I could have any woman I wanted. I put a Johnny Mathis album on the record player, singing along with "Chances Are":

Guess you feel you'll always be
The one and only one for me
And, if you think you could,
Well, chances are your chances are awfully good
The chances are, your chances are awfully good.

It made me feel better, like one of those birds I'd heard in the tree, just feeling my voice in the room joined with his and I felt awfully good, yet awfully alone.

Hanging Out

One weekend at the end of October, after studying late, I decided to go to Jiminotts, across the street from our house and have a soda and fries and see if Sue was hanging out at a booth. I had not seen her for several weeks. But she was there. She told me that her plan to get married continued to spiral out of control. Another weekend with her boyfriend had not gone well.

She inquired about my classes, the new Psychology class and I told her the experiments we had done on perception, how an afterimage was held in the eye after you stared at an object. She sipped her milkshake. I asked more about her fiancé to show I was listening to her concerns. She flipped her hand in the air.

"Not something I want to talk about, if you don't mind," she said.

I swirled my milkshake between my hands, seeing how fast I could spin it. She stared at it. We smiled at each other.

"I better be going," she said. "Exam tomorrow. You know how it is." I stood. She held my hand and squeezed it and did not let go as if, when she did, she'd fall off a cliff. She signed, "Oh well," and we parted.

When I came to the street, I noticed Jerry holding Tom upright, literally propping him up, pushing against him as if he were the straw man that Dorothy had snipped from his perch, wobbly-legged, tilting left and right. I thought maybe Tom was sick, so I trotted over to them.

"Can I help?" I asked.

"Damn right you can," Jerry said. "Get a hold of his other arm and keep him steady."

"What's wrong?"

"He's drunk."

"Drunk?" I gasped, startled that he'd put himself at risk as a pledge. If any upperclassmen saw him, they could report him and he could be put on notices, given a black ball demerit and possibly be expelled from the fraternity.

"You heard me."

76

"We need to get him out of here," I cautioned. "He could be put on probation."

"Shit, I know, I know," Jerry groaned trying to right Tom who listed terribly toward the pavement.

Tom was singing a song, quite oblivious to his surroundings and his precarious position, "The cows wouldn't milk and the corn wouldn't grow if it isn't okay with Eddie OJ and it isn't okay with me...." I didn't recognize the song, but I did recognize the way he was slurring his words and changing his pitch, fluctuating from one octave to another like someone was changing the speed on a record player. He was more than a little drunk: he was totally out of it, as bad as I had been the night of the bonfire.

Before we could move Tom out of the intersection to an obscure place, he took several steps forward with his arms extended like a man on a high wire, balancing them promptly, took a wide stance and proceeded to unzip his pants. I stepped up behind him and pulled him back a few steps.

"That's not too wise, not here," I cautioned him.

"It's all right. I gotta go bad."

Before I could stop him, he started to urinate in the street, nearly in the middle of the intersection, the street light illuminating him as if he were center stage. He insisted that I hold him up so he could aim better.

"Feels so good," he exclaimed, his face tilted upward, staring at the stars.

A couple came by, heading to Jiminotts. They stopped in their tracks, were aghast, and I smiled at them and, trying to be nonchalant, said, "Hi. Nice evening, huh?"

Several girls who came out of Jiminotts, saw him in midstream, put their hands over their mouths, tittered, and raced down the street toward another set of girls, calling out, "Look, look at the guy in the intersection."

I thought that, well, he was certainly getting good exposure. Every girl in town will know he's well-endowed.

By the time he finished, quite a crowd had gathered around us. Jerry and I, initially dumbfounded, quickly gathered our senses and grabbed Tom by his arms, one of us on either side, and escorted him down Elm Street toward the Biester Gym, moving rapidly, hoping to get him out of sight and, equally, hoping none of the DAE brothers had seen him. He veered to the left and right as we aimed him down the side of the street as far from the overhanging street lights as we could.

After depositing him in back of the gym in a grove of trees, leaning against the back of an oak, Jerry told me to get coffee, lots of it. I bought four large cups. We plied him with one, trying to sober him up. Jerry drank from another, seeing if it could sober him up, too.

After fifteen minutes, Tom was more coherent. When we told him about peeing in the intersection, he denied it—or, at least, did not remember it.

We decided to take him for a walk to sober him up some more.

"We need to get him out of here," Jerry said, making an assessment of the situation. "We better head in that direction to get off of the main campus. It's not safe here. Too many students."

The coffee emitted tiny puffs of steam from the holes in the lids and seemed to burn their mouths, but Tom and Jerry kept on drinking as we staggered along the sidewalk down one street and another. I was not sure where we were headed.

When we were out of sight of the restaurant, Jerry halted and unzipped his jacket.

"Here," he said, handing me a bottle of whiskey. The label was torn off so I had no idea what sort of liquor it was, and I don't know why, but I took a swig, and gasped for air. Powerful stuff. Each of them took swigs, too, as if it was soda pop and passed it back to me. We stood there, under an elm along a side street, passing the bottle back and forth for ten minutes. By the time the bottle was empty, my head had lit up and I felt as if it were floating away from me, brains and all, soaring over the elm into the blackened sky. Tom began to sing his song again, "The milk wouldn't grow if it isn't okay with Eddie OJ and the cows would crow if the milk wouldn't grow if Eddie OJ don't care... ," the words making less and less sense as he sang. Jerry and I were singing along, all of us arm in arm, walking down the street when a police siren blared like a scream.

Tom and Jerry literally dove to the ground and sidled down a hillside, rolling a few feet out of sight and hid by a large oak. I stood momentarily and then quickly followed their example. A police car whizzed by. We clung to the ground as if we were teetering on a fault line of an earthquake.

"They after us?" I inquired, sensing something wrong.

"Could be," Jerry said.

"Why?"

"We put a motorcycle on some guy's car, you know one of those little foreign cars. We sat it right on the top," Jerry giggled.

"How'd you do that?"

Tom smiled, "I did it. Didn't think I could when I started but I lifted that sucker right up. Nothing to it. Set it right on the roof."

There was a silence. Tom and Jerry looked at each other, then laughed.

Finally, Jerry admitted, "We could be in big trouble. That squad car was headed to the place we did it."

Tom nodded. "We need to keep under cover, right?"

Jerry patted him on the back. "Right."

My heart was throbbing. I never expected to be in trouble. And this looked like it could be big-time trouble.

"Shit," I said.

"It will be fine," Jerry said. "I know a way back to the house that's out of the lights. Help me carry him."

We managed to get Tom back to the house, going down back streets and, finally, carrying him up the back stairs. We sequestered him in his room, leaving him on the floor to sleep it off, a blanket to cover him. I stayed up talking with Jerry, who told me about his family, how he hated his dad who was a drunk and how he and Tom, when they met on a visit to campus, had hit it off and gotten drunk with Bill Harris. I told him that I had too.

After that night's escapade, Jerry, Tom, and I became good friends. When Tom realized how out of control he was and how he could have easily been caught and been thrown out of the house, he promised us that he put his energy to school work. We studied together, walked to classes, and pored over our books. I'd learned how to allot time to reading, to writing and working on assignments, preparing for class, developing a routine: early morning, breakfast, read at library, attend classes; lunch at fraternity, hang out for an hour, head back to library, attend afternoon classes; evening, have dinner and hang out with Tom, Jerry and Paul, back to library, preparing for next day's assignments.

As autumn progressed, the cool autumnal air riffled the leaves. The greens tarnished into a coppery orange and fell almost as if unsure they should let go. In time, the maples shed whole basketfuls of them like a lady carrying groceries and dropping them as if startled in a terrible fright. The spines of trunks stood out, charcoaled against the gray skies like dark gods of a forgotten time, distant and unbidden, that spoke in another language that none of us had as yet learned to understand.

The closer the end of the semester came, the more my friends and I talked about getting initiated and about Hell Week which, we'd been warned, was coming up soon. It was a rite of passage, a test we had to go through before we were initiated as full active members of the fraternity. My pledge father told me, "No big deal. It's a series of challenges to test your strength and endurance, like boot camp in the army, challenges meant to bond you together as a class."

This year, as officers in the house, Sean, a guy from Alabama, and Randy, a guy from New York, planned it. They told us that we had some surprises in store for us, some challenges that had never been done before.

"Don't worry tomato face," Sean said. "You can handle it." I glowered at him. "Oh, Jason, don't be such a sour puss," he laughed. I walked away, not as worried about what might happened to us as other pledge brothers, but more concerned with Sean in charge. I had endured the raging hot August football practices that ran morning and afternoon, sweating, being told to run wind sprints back and forth until I wanted to die—so I figured Hell Week would probably be a piece of cake, even with Sean in charge.

One evening, while lounging in Tom's room, he asked me to tell him about my dad.

"Not much to say. He's been good to us. He's a success, a vice president of a big corporation. We belong to a country club and I get to play golf there," I said.

"No, not that. What is he like," he asked.

"Well, he's a hard man to be with. If you don't do exactly what he wants you to do, he flies into rages."

"Really?"

"Yeah, once he told me to put the salt in the water softener. I said sure,

I would and went about finishing something I was doing—can't remember what—and he came downstairs ten minutes later and asked if I had done it. I said no. He screamed, "When I ask you to do something, I expect it to be done," and stormed off, getting the salt and doing it himself. He didn't talk to me the rest of the day."

"Jesus, that sucks."

"It's just how it is," I said. Wanting to shift the focus off of me, I asked him about his father.

"Nothing like yours. He's gone a lot, over in the Middle East. He works for Gulf Oil and meets—it's really neat—with shahs, going to their palaces, eating with them on rugs, you know, working out oil leases. When he's home—and that's not often—we go to Yankee games and shows downtown. He's low key, a good listener," he said.

"Can we trade?" I asked.

"Not on your life!"

Tom suggested that I should come out to visit him on Long Island, maybe on Christmas break, but when I asked my father over the phone, he said, "Absolutely not, not this year but, perhaps, another year," and asked if Tom wanted to visit with us. Tom said no. He had a girl friend to see, and she was hot.

The Party

Back home Christmas break, the rooms with the paintings of the Seine in Paris, the misty figures idling on its banks, the long dining room table with its lion's paw feet, and the circular stairs up to my room on the second floor, seemed more set pieces for a movie and less like my own house. Of course, I belonged here, but I felt like a stranger too.

After a few days, however, I fell back into the family routine. At dinner one night, mother said, "I thought I'd have a little Christmas party."

My father looked up, glanced at me and my brother, smiling. "And when would it be?"

"On the 28th. I called the caterer. Does that work for you, dear?

"Of course. How many were you planning to invite?"

"Just a few couples."

I glanced at my brother who, in turn, looked at my father, who raised his eyes and took a breath.

"Mary, how many is that?"

"Ten or so," she said, cutting her steak without looking up.

I laughed. "Mom!"

"Yes, honey," she said, tilting her head toward me.

"Just ten?"

"There may be a few more. I haven't decided."

My father nodded, taking a sip of his wine. "So it will probably be a big party."

My mother sighed and took a sip of wine. "If you don't mind."

"Sounds good to me," my father said, "The more the merrier." He winked at my brother and me.

My mother would often get an idea to have a few friends over for dinner, but, after she invited one, another friend would get word of it, and mother would invite them and so, by the end of the invitations, we'd have a hundred people coming over for cocktails and food, sometimes in two shifts. Before such parties, mother would have my brother and me polish the silver trays and coffee pot, polishing them so finely that, when it was set on the table, our faces would shine in it like a mirror. We'd gingerly removed the Waterford crystal glasses and placed them on the sideboard. Everything had its place—and she knew where it was. On these occasions, I carried trays of hors d'oeuvres to the guests, making small talk and asking them if they wanted refills of their drinks.

My brother said, "You know these parties are like a graduate course in how to succeed."

"You kidding?" I asked.

"No, really," he said. "Look at all the people who will be here. Mr. Warren—he's President of Sears; and Mr. Hayward—he's with NBC. You get to meet the bigwigs. You learn what they think, what they're interested in and, before you know it, you have the inside scoop on what makes corporate American tick."

"I don't know about you, but I get so nervous at these parties, I feel like throwing up. I never know what to say."

"Hey, don't think too much. Just enjoy yourself. I nip a few as the party heats up and feel no pain," he said.

"Isn't that bad for your liver?"

"Screw my liver. I'm mostly fine. Nothing serious," he said. "Let's get dressed. Mom wants us to look our best."

"I know."

We hurried upstairs and changed into dress shirts and our best slacks and went to the front door to greet the guests, take their jackets, and, as the party progressed, brought around trays of shrimp wrapped in bacon and stuffed mushrooms.

We were expected to chat with guests about topics that were of no interest to me, so I made the rounds with the trays, asking guests if they wanted crackers with cheese, to avoid being entangled in some conversations about how I like college, if I were dating and what I planned to do professionally after college. I had no idea what I wanted to do. Hell, all I hoped to do was pass my classes and finish out the first year. I recognized one Mrs. Benson, a short woman with startling green eyes, who had a son still in high school, a tall thin boy who acted in plays and whom I'd seen at the country club by the pool. She pulled me aside and asked about college, if I'd met a girl, how my classes were going, whether I played sports and then abruptly changed the topic.

"Do you remember Scott, my son?" she asked, holding me by the arm and drawing me to the side of the room by a window. Snow covered the two pines with pointed white hats. We looked at the yard for a moment. A wind dusted the snow up in a swirl.

"Do you remember him?"

"Yes, I saw him in *Our Town*. He's a good actor. He dances and sings, too," I said.

"He certainly is," she said, her face softening in a momentary recollection of him.

"But that's not the point." She put her face close to mine and whispered, "I'm afraid he's a homosexual."

"Really?" I tried to act surprised.

"Yes. He's not like you. He's not like other boys."

"What do you mean?"

"Well, he's involved with arts and never dates. I mean *never.*"

"I didn't date much either in high school," I said, trying to assuage her fears.

"But you did date, right?" I nodded my head. "And you're such a good looking boy; the girls must fawn over you."

I laughed. "Not really. I mean..."

"Don't be modest. I bet they do."

I pasted a grin on my face and held it. She pinched my cheek. I dropped my eyes, noticing her open-toed black high heels. She continued to talk about her son.

"He hangs around with other boys who are, well, odd."

"What do you mean?"

"They are not like you—big strapping football players—" She pulled me close and squeezed me as if to confirm her appraisal of me. I could now smell the liquor on her breath. "His friends are strange. Theater types. Nice boys, don't get me wrong. But, well, kind of feminine."

"That doesn't mean they are..."

"I know. I do. I really do. But there are things that a mother knows. I'm afraid he's one. He's a... you know."

I nodded.

"What should I do?"

"Don't worry if his friends are different. That's okay."

"You're so cute."

"Do you want another drink?" I asked.

"Oh, yes, that would be good. Martini, dry, an olive."

I took her glass and she called after me. "Thanks, you're a dear for listening." I refilled her drink, brought it back to her and she said, "You're such a lovely boy. I wish Scott was more like you." A sadness settled about her eyes. She patted my cheek. "Oh, well," she said and wandered off into the crowd with her secret.

After the party, I helped clean up, drying dishes, stacking them, gathering glasses from different corners of the house and tossing on the napkins in the clothes hamper.

"Thanks, honey," my mom said. "I'll finish up. You can relax."

My brother went downstairs to play pool with my dad. I went to my room and sat at the window. The snow clung to the branches of a maple like a white glove. I thought about Mrs. Benson, how she inquired about her son and how she trusted me, some college kid to assuage her fears. It took some courage for her to tell me. Maybe she sensed something in me that could identify with him. An attractive kid with startling red hair, he swam at the club pool. He had a nice body, lean, sinewy. I wondered what it was like for him. Did he know that his mother suspected that he was a homosexual? Probably not. It was a topic that remained as taboo as talking about infidelities. She would stew about it. Was he a homo? How could she tell? He looked like other guys. Heck, he looked like me. There was no way of telling.

By the end of the holiday, I was eager to get back to school and be with my friends. Immersed in the college routine, the first weeks went smoothly. A cold gripped Indiana. Snow whipped across campus for several days, blanketing the campus and turning the sidewalks into a labyrinth of chest-high paths spilling out into the various academic halls. Tom, Jerry and I built a huge snowman in the front lawn, eight feet tall with a hat and a cigar and two black eyes. I kept focused on my school work, wanting to prove that I could make it, getting back to my routine of going to the library to prepare for classes.

The Necklace

Without warning, near the end of January, one night at eleven o'clock, we were rousted from bed. Upperclassmen screamed, "Get up, come on, move your ass," shook our beds, and prodded us down two flights of stairs to the basement with paddle boards—boards pledge fathers gave pledge sons that harkened back to the days when initiation included hazing. Some of us slept in running shorts and a T-shirt, some in pajamas, some in underwear. It did not matter. We lined up on a far wall and Sean, decked out in a safari hat with a wide brim, paced back and forth in front of us.

"Look at these sorry wimps," he shouted, pointing at us. The upperclassmen stood behind him, legs spread, with paddles in their hands like military police.

"Stand at attention when I talk to you," he blared and poked Paul in the belly with his paddle, "Pull in your chin," and turned to me, "Wipe that shit-eating grin off your face."

Half-asleep, still in the grip of a dream of a river and of being stranded on an island in the rapids, I'd thought Sean looked like a preppy Mussolini, strutting back and forth, head back, chin up, slapping the stick in his hand, and the whole spectacle seemed more a joke than a serious matter. I snapped to attention and saluted him.

"Follett, step out, tomato face. You will not mock me, you hear?" He motioned to Jerome, a red haired, pre-med major, whom I'd seen in the library and at meals, but who never lounged around in the TV room with other guys--a loner, an academic type.

"Let Mr. Follett be the first to wear a special Hell Week DAE necklace." With his eyes on the floor as if he were balancing on a beam, Jerome came up to me.

He looked distressed, his face tightened, his eyes with a faraway sad expression. He did not like doing what he'd been instructed to do. He had twelve strings looped over his arm, each with a large onion and what looked like four smaller onions. He took one of the strings off and, not looking at me, hung it around my neck.

"Now, Mr. Follett, since you find this so amusing, you can be the first the taste a special delicacy we have prepared for each of your classmates." He tapped the necklace with his stick, "Presto," he chirped in a high falsetto voice, and then snapped a piece of the small bulbs and ordered, "Take it and eat it."

I grimaced, "What is it?"

"Eat it, Follett," he growled, narrowing his eyes, "Eat it." A chorus joined in, the flank of upperclassmen, chanting, "Eat it, Follett. Eat it."

I grabbed it from his hand shoved it in my mouth. The initial taste shot like a firecracker in my mouth. I bit into it and then spit it out.

"Shit," I gagged. A few people tittered.

Sean tapped another bulb and barked, "You don't like it? It's special. When I said eat it, I mean eat it!"

I snapped off another clove and chewed on it, the bitter taste spreading across my tongue, causing me to gag. After chewing it, I swallowed, my face grimacing from the taste. I'd heard my mother warn us not to eat garlic since it smelled terrible. She never cooked with it, never. But I'd seen my father crushed cloves of it when he made Caesar salad.

Laughter erupted again. A stick poked me in the ribs, "What you just ate, my friend, is a delicacy: garlic. Get back in line Follett." Sean motioned to Jeff to drape the strings on everyone's neck.

"If any of you smile," Sean said sternly, "if any of you smile, you will have to eat the garlic. You need to have this on your neck at all times and I mean all times: at night, in bed, in the head, in the shower, at breakfast, in your classes and the library, on campus—everywhere. You are to have them with you always. Do you understand?" He turned to us. "When I ask a question, you are to say, 'Yes, sir.' Let us try that." He repeated, "Do you understand?"

We shouted, "Yes, sir!" He repeated the question five times until we shouted in unison, louder each time.

When he was finished, Randy stepped forward, wearing an army cap. He tipped it at us as a gentleman might tip his hat to a lady. "Gentlemen," he nodded at each of us, looking us in the eye. "For this week, each of you will have a special name, a name you need to know because when an upperclassman asks what your name is, you need to snap to attention and repeat your name to whoever calls you out." He waited a moment, and then asked, "Any questions?"

With that, he called each of us to step out of line and gave us our name, which we repeated several times.

He started with Paul whose name was, "May I please blow you, sir?" Paul laughed when he heard his name—and hesitated to say it aloud— and had to take a bite of his garlic. Then he had to repeat his name four times, each time louder, the last time on his knees in front of Randy. With his dramatic flair, Paul decided to ham up his part and acted as if he were Romeo wooing some Juliet—but in this case, some Julius. He brought the house down with laughter. Randy patted him on the head and said, "Nice job."

Then, Ibby was named, "Let me eat shit, sir," and Steve, "May I kiss your ass, sir," and Rick was "Kick me, sir," and Tom was "May I give you a flying fuck, sir." Larry was "I'm an ass," Jacob had "I have a tiny weenie, sir"—each of us with some name meant to humiliate us and each name ending with "sir." By the time I stepped forward, I expected the worst and got it: "FUBAR—fucked up beyond all repair."

"What is your name?" Sean asked.

"FUBAR, sir."

He didn't like how I said it. When he had me repeat my name, I spit the words at him to which he grinned, knowing he'd gotten me riled.

"Funny, Follett, I don't remember—you know how much trouble I have with memory. What does your name means? Could you tell me what it means?"

I stared at him, expressionless.

"Come now, Mr. Follett, certainly you can do better than that."

I stood immobile. I glared at him. If hate could ignite my eyes, I'd focus them on him and roast him to a crisp.

"Your friend, Mr. Wilson, gave us a unique opportunity to see how, with his enormous size, he could fuck and fly, much to our edification, right guys? So, yes, I am sure you can show us what FUBAR means, can't you, Mr. Follett?"

"FUBAR" is all I said.

He backed up, "No sense of humor, Follett? That's not good."

I glared at him as he sat down, leaning back in his chair, his feet stretched out on the mahogany table, a cigar dangling from his mouth. He clenched the cigar between his thumb and middle finger, peering at me under his round safari hat. We were frozen in a tableau for a minute, each of us peering at one another. The noise in the room dampened to an occasional shuffle of a foot. An uneasy tittering subsided, followed by a few coughs and the rustling of jeans in wooden chairs. I felt like a gunfighter in a duel waiting for the other gunslinger to reach for his gun.

But by the quizzical expression on his face, I sensed that he knew shouldn't push me, that I might have punched him—I'm not sure—but I would not take any more of his harassment.

He pointed his cigar at me and waved it. "That's enough Follett," taking his eyes off me. "I think you just *did* show us what FUBAR means, boy. Stand back."

By then, my fists were clenched and my body felt as if it were coiled like an iron spring. Not meant to challenge us, or bring us together as a class, this evening was intended to humiliate us.

After I stepped back, I continued to glare at him, so, even while he spoke, I could see his eyes darting at me. He called on Jerry Evans, whose appellation was, "May I please jerk off, sir." As Sean joked with him, he suddenly flipped his chair down, slammed his hands on the armrests and, straightening himself up, addressed me, "Quit it, Follett. Get your fucking eyes off me. If you want to make trouble for yourself and your brothers, just keep it up. Otherwise, quit it. Understand?"

I responded without shifting my gaze off him, "Yes, sir."

Tom nudged me, "Cool it."

With the silence in the room, Sean turned back to Jerry and in a high-pitched voiced asked, "Mr. Evans, what is your name?" to which Jerry replied, "May I please jerk off, sir?" and Sean, mimicking someone opening his zipper, cried out, "You may jerk me off!" The room broke out in laughter, and I, much to my dismay, could not help cracking a smile. Sean looked at me and grinned.

Guffaws rung out with each new name, the upperclassmen enjoyed our shouting them out and some of them were funny—"May I sing you a song, sir"—which was John's name, an appropriate name since he loved to sing.

After John called out his name, Randy turned to him and said "Why, yes. Sing me a song. " John pushed back his blond hair and sang a refrain of Sinatra's "Pennies from Heaven," and then a refrain of some Dean Martin's song "Everybody Loves Somebody."

Randy liked to mock us. He chided us, sometimes asking, "What do you want to do?" We would then repeat our name again and again, and everyone would laugh. Even when I found it funny—because some played along with Randy and acted outrageously, as Paul had—I refused to show that I was amused. I'd tightened my lips and grimaced, refusing to give them another laugh. I felt that it was not funny: it was cruel. I'd defy them. Rage boiled inside me as it had, when I was younger, when my father yelled at me, when his face flared and I cowed in corners, waiting for the blow. I'd stare at my father with no expression, though I never dared question him. But now I felt a righteous anger burn in my chest, the heat of it rising.

Sean kept eyeing me during the naming ceremony. After Randy was finished, Sean came and stood in front of me, smiling. I imagined that he was an apparition whose body I could see through and that with one hard breath I could send him fluttering across the room. He posted in front of me for several minutes, trying to get me to crack, then he turned around, pointed to the stairwell, and instructed Randy to dismiss us. We walked single-file out of the room and up the stairs, some upperclassmen taking a moment to ask our name, which added one final ripple of laughter before we slunk back to our beds at nearly 2 a.m.

The Closet

Each night, at some unpredictable hour—12, 1, 3—we'd be awakened, marched to the basement to endure another "challenge." The fourth night, we were startled out of bed with a fog horn blasting through the dorm about 1 a.m. We were ushered in silence to the front foyer and instructed to pack into a coat closet, which meant some of us had to crouch down, while others, the shorter ones, went to the back under the hat rack. Once we were snugly inside, Sean asked if we felt close because the brotherhood meant intimacy and sharing everything with each other. Then we were each given a large lighted cigar. If anyone moved, his cigar would scorch someone next to him. Once we were all crammed inside, Sean announced the challenge: We were to stay in the closet until every cigar—every last one—was smoked to the nub. He told us that what we were to share was smoke. The door was closed. Cigar embers shone like demonic eyes.

"I don't smoke," Jerry moaned. "I'm allergic to smoke. Shit, I'm going to be sick."

Tom said, "Give me your cigar and kneel down here, be as close to the floor as possible and breathe the air coming under the door sill."

I felt Jerry scrunching down, slipping between our legs, spreading out as best as he could, his face by the door sill, his breathing heavy and quick.

"Can you breathe?" Tom asked.

"Better," Jerry affirmed.

"Let's do this as quickly as possible or we will be asphyxiated," Paul suggested. "You don't need to inhale, just suck on it and blow it out. Blow the smoke up, away from you. Go."

I puffed on mine, quick puffs, noticing the end glow and darken with each puff, trying desperately not to notice the density of smoke which burned my eyes and throat. I felt dizzy. Someone next to me moaned, "I can't breathe," and began long raspy coughs, gagging as he did. It was Ibby; he carried an aspirator and had a history of asthma.

Eric said, "Quick, Jerry move over; let Ibby down."

We moved our feet as best as we could as Ibby who was in the back, since he was one of shorter pledges, swiveled his body, turning one way and another like a corkscrew, in and out of us in an effort to reach the front. His body heaved violently as he coughed.

"Bend down now, get your face on the floor," Paul told him.

Before he could bend down, however, his body went slack and he crumbled against me, his cigar nose diving with him. I grabbed at it and caught it, the burnt end searing my palm, until, by using my other hand, I held it up over my head with my own cigar.

"This is madness," Trevor shouted, banging on the door. "Someone is going to die. Let us out, you motherfuckers."

A chorus of laughter rose from the other side of the door.

"Come on wimps, show us you've got balls," Sean chided. "A little smoke never hurt no one. It's a good Southern tradition to enjoy a cigar with friends."

"Where there's smoke," someone else shouted, "there's fire. Fire up, boys!"

It was getting even harder to breathe. Eric whispered, "Listen, listen, I've got a knife. I'm here"—he waved his cigar back and forth. "Pass me your cigar and I'll cut it down and keep the stubs in my pocket. One at a time, come on, hand 'em over."

We passed him our cigars, and systematically, he cut them and returned them, until we had less than a quarter inch to smoke. Eric said, "Be quiet. Don't say a word. They'll begin to worry if we don't complain. They might even think we've died." We finished smoking them and then, taking turns to duck down and catch the little air coming from under the sill, we waited, not saying a word, and listening to low-level machinations coming from outside the door.

Someone outside complained, "This is not funny anymore. We need to check. We don't want them sick."

"Fuck off," Sean said. "I've got this under control. They can't die from smoke."

"You fuck off," the other voice said. "This is a fraternity and we don't treat our brothers like this."

"We are testing them," Sean retorted. "We want them to prove themselves worthy."

"Bullshit," someone else shouted and the door flung open, the smoke blasting out into the faces of the twelve men outside the door. They covered their faces and coughed, darting out the front door into the fresh air. Tom and I lifted up Jerry who had passed out and dragged him out into the front yard, while Eric and Paul attended to Ibby.

"Where the hell do you think you're going?" Sean yelled.

"To a picnic," Eric snarled, "and get the fuck out of our way, you sadist!"

"What did you call me?" Sean snapped.

"A sadist," Eric said evenly. "Look at Jerry, look at Ibby—they're sick, you bastard! They could have died, the little that you care. They should have never been there with their lungs as bad as they are. Do you give one god damn about them? If this is your perverted idea of fraternity initiation, I don't want any part of it."

Putting his hands on his hips, Sean bellowed, "No part of it?"

"Damn right, you sadist."

"I will not have a pledge call me a name," Sean snorted, grabbing Eric by his shirt.

Charging out from the living room, Sam, the president, took Sean by the arm, "Get over it and let them go. They have had enough for one evening. They need air and they need sleep." Sean tried to pull away from Sam, and clearly was prepared to stand on principle of his authority over us, but Sam tightened his grip and pulled Sean's feet off the floor—he was a good eighty pounds larger and a half-foot taller than Sean—and Sean, seeing that he'd been usurped, gave in and said, "It's over boys. Our esteemed president has spoken." He pushed Sam away and called to his minions, "Come on, we're outta here."

Rebellion

On our way upstairs, Eric asked if he could speak with me, privately.

I went to his room where he began pacing back and forth. He didn't ask me to sit down, but blurted out, "I'm resigning. I can't take this shit!"

It didn't take me a second to respond because I was boiling with rage, too.

"Let's do it!" I said.

We marched down to Sam's room, knocked. "What?" he called out.

"Can we talk?" I asked.

"Door's open," he said.

In his bathrobe he was sitting in his easy chair, and John, the bespectacled vice-president was sitting across from him in his PJs and white socks. John never put on airs. He engaged with us pledges as he did with his classmates. Some evenings, he'd come into my room, flop in the chair and announce, "I need a break; let's talk," and we'd chat about his girlfriend in Long Island and his wanting to get into med school and become a psychiatrist. Since I had taken an Introduction to Psychology course, I'd ask him questions and he always had the answers. He'd read about Freud, Jung and Skinner. He'd enjoyed explained their different views.

Sam motioned for us to sit on the couch, and John said, "Hey, you guys look like you've had a bad day."

"What's up?" Sam asked.

Eric laid it out: how we were fed up being treated like dogs, how Sean had crossed over a line not only endangering our lives but belittling us, how we couldn't do our friggin' homework we were in such a daze and how we'd become the laughingstock of the campus, smelling as we did like a garlic factory. We could not take any more and wanted out. At that moment, I thought, perhaps, my father had been right: I'd made the wrong choice. I should have gone with the Deltas.

John put up his hand because Eric kept up his rant, citing what Sean had done to us in private—the demeaning comments, the slurs, calling us "faggots" and "pussies" and swatting us with his paddle. "Okay, okay, we

94

hear you," John said. "We were just talking about it. Some upperclassmen believe we need to rein it in."

I directed a question at Sam, "Did you go through this?"

He looked at his hands for a second, rubbing them together, "Well, we had a Hell Week."

"That's not what I asked," I shouted.

"Calm down, Jason."

"Calm down?"

"Yes, calm down," he leaned over to me and patted my knee. "We did have a Hell Week, but not like this." He gazed over to John who nodded his head.

Sam continued, "As John said, we have been talking. And listen, Eric, Jason, we want you here. We need guys like you. You are right. We hear you. You have important things to say and do. So don't cut and run. Give us time. We will take care of it."

Eric leaned back and rubbed his hands through his hair. He tapped his foot, the taut skin on his cheeks still enflamed. He shook his head. "You don't get it. I don't treat anybody like this, not even an animal. This is like Nazi Germany. You know what happened there when everyone clammed up. Millions exterminated. Gas chambers went right on cooking. People shrugged their shoulders and said, ' Let's just wait and see. It's not so bad.' I'm not willing to do that. You hear me, not willing to do that!"

John stood up and walked to the door, his back to us, his hands in his pajama pockets. He pressed his fist against the door and pounded it several times. We looked at him. He did not move for a minute, just standing with his back to us.

He turned around and pursed his lips. "Listen up. Sam and I are going to have a talk with Sean. You hear me? We will make sure he hears our concerns."

"Hear your concerns?" Eric shouted mockingly. "I'm sure that will help."

"I know you have a right to be cynical. But I do mean we will make sure he toes the line. Trust us." He rubbed his chin and stared at us intensely. "Listen, we can't just end Hell Week because, well, there have been some indiscretions. You will have challenges—one I guarantee will piss you both off, but one I guarantee we all have had to go through—so, please, do me a favor, lighten up, have fun with it and we'll tamp down Sean. Trust us. We will take care of it."

"Trust us?" Eric retorted.

"Yes," John said firmly. "Trust us."

Eric looked at me. I nodded. We agreed to do the best we could. They shook our hands, assured us that our conversation would be confidential, and told us to come back if Sean got out of line again. We felt justified in our complaints, and they heard us loud and clear.

Bad Egg

The next morning we were given tokens to carry with us for the day: one fresh egg and one calf's liver, wrapped in a paper towel. Both were placed in our jockey shorts and needed to be with us all the time. With our cloves of garlic hung like a primitive necklace around our necks, no matter how much cologne we splattered on ourselves, it made no difference.

Our history professor, smelling us when we came in the room, shook his head, "No, no, this is not going to happen," and he pointed to the back of the room where he opened the window, letting the cold air waft in the room to disperse the noxious odor. Cold, embarrassed, ostracized, we sat there trying to be invisible. Again, I felt the slow boil of rage roiling in my belly. Looking out the window at the limbs of a maple swaying in the wind, I took several slow breaths, trying to calm down and to do, as I had promised Sam and John, my best and not overreact.

On the way back to the fraternity, Eric, Ibby, Tom, Jerry, and I were moaning about Hell Week to several Kappa Kappa Gamma girls, the sorority next to our house, since, for the last several nights they had heard screaming coming from our house at weird hours of the night.

"What is going on at your house?" one of the girls, Suzie, asked.

Ibby, recounting how he had fainted in the closet, suddenly stopped midstride. We stared at him, his face flushed and eyes bulging, as he cried out, "No, no, no," and leaned forward, cupping his hands over his groin. The girls put their hands to their mouths. I reached out to help him. He appeared to be hemorrhaging.

"Are you all right?" I asked, putting my arm under his arm.

"Oh shit," he moaned. "The damn egg."

We looked as a splotch spread across his pants, a yellowish stain.

If he had not burst into laughter, we might have tried to keep our composure but soon we were all laughing and he, not to be the brunt of a joke, slapped at my groin and I felt my egg yolk ooze across my penis, and Tom, starting to bolt, was brought down by Ibby, and, SPLAT, he too was eggnog, and Jerry holding up his arms in surrender, called out, "All right, all right," and, closing his eyes and wincing, slapped at his own groin. Eric stood by himself, watching it all. He crouched like a wrestler and motioned with the tips of his fingers, daring anyone to come after him.

"I'm going to protect my egg," he said, smiling. "I'm a virgin and I plan to stay one!"

We surrounded him, Tom and I behind him, Jerry and Ibby in front. The girls, giggling, stepped aside. We charged him, and, like a weasel, he slipped out of Tom's grip, sidestepped me and was wheeling around to make a break for it when Jerry, who, small as he was, hid behind several girls, and by extending his leg, tripped him. That was all it took: hands outstretched, he toppled forward and SPLAT hit the ground, crying out, "Jesus Christ." By this time, the girls were laughing hysterically and a crowd had gathered around us, to watch the viscous stains spread across our crotches while making comments about leaky diapers and broken condoms. I noticed Sue standing to one side, smirking.

"What nonsense is this?" she said, gazing down at the stain on my pants.

"Another challenge for Hell Week," I said.

"Men," she said.

"What do you mean?"

"Do you always have to prove yourselves?"

"I suppose," I said, shrugging.

"It seems such a waste of time."

I stopped in front of the DAE house and she smiled at me.

"I have to get changed," I said, feeling the slick yoke on my penis.

"Oh, you poor boy!" she explained. "You must call when it's over." She patted me on the shoulder. I trotted upstairs to my room, gathered a new set of underpants and pants and headed to the showers where Ibby, Eric, Jerry, and Tom were finishing up.

Before lunch, the word got out about our eggs and we were applauded by the upperclassmen. John winked at us, knowing that we had decided to take the initiation less seriously. We were awarded with fresh eggs.

The Relay

Not until 2 a.m. that night were we awakened. Half-drugged from lack of sleep, we were told that we had a relay. Sam and John intercepted Eric and me as we stumbled downstairs and pulled us into Sam's room.

"Listen, you're going to hate this one. But it's one that we do every year. Sam did it; I did it. It may seem impossible but go with it, see if you can make it fun," John said. "It's not the end of the world, although it may feel like it." John gave us each a hug and patted us on the back.

We agreed and hurried to the basement where the pledge class was lined up. Strutting around with his paddle in hand, Sean explained what we would do: it was a relay race and the winning team would get a special prize. We surrendered our livers to Randy, who brought them into the kitchen, and, unbeknownst to us, replaced them with cooked livers that were dropped into a large bucket that gave off a dreadful smell. Our task was to take the liver from the bucket in the basement to one of the two buckets on the third floor, but to do it on our hands and knees. Once we got to the third floor, we had to eat the liver. The basement smelled like puke: the buckets contained limburger cheese mixed with beer, and the livers were bobbing in it like turds. We had to fish the livers out of the mix with our mouths and carry them like dogs, no use of our hands, up three flights of stairs.

I said, "I'm not doing this. It's gross."

Eric pulled me aside. "Hey, we promised to go along."

"But this is sick."

"You're right. But play along, okay?" I nodded.

Eric and I were separated as the pledges were put into two teams. The team that filled their bucket first won if, in turn, they'd eaten all their livers.

The whole fraternity gathered along the stairs to cheer us on. The first two guys, Jerry and Ibby, as they dunked into the bucket, vomited into it. A cheer went up as if they had scored a touchdown. They each fished out a liver and, on their knees, climbed up the stairs out of sight. Two more pledges, Eric and Paul, ducked into the slop; they managed not to vomit there, but, before they got to the stairs, they both heaved, large convulsive pukes that splattered on the shoes of several upper class men. The upperclassmen shouted, "Gross," and leapt back. But the puke kept coming, splashing on their pants and shirts.

I smiled and made eye contact with Eric who winked at me, and I realized he had planned to get sick, to toss his cookies on the upperclassmen. I chuckled to myself. What a brilliant idea. I looked at Tom with whom I was paired in the competition and whispered, "Did you see that? Eric planned it. What you say we give it a try?"

He smiled. "I've got an idea," and whispered in my ear. We watched poor Jacob, who was always dressed impeccably, even for bed, and Larry who looked like a Bassett hound on his hands and knees, as each crawled over to the pot. Looking pitifully at Sean, Jacob asked, "Do I have to?"

"Damn right." He raised his paddle to swat him but, looking up at Sam, caught himself and patted Jacob on the head. "Good doggie, you can do it. I have faith in you."

"Can I change my shirt?" Jacob asked, pointing to his newly pressed pajama top.

Sean laughed and gently plunged Jacob's face down. I stepped forward, wanting to grab Sean and shove his face in the bucket, but Tom grabbed me by the arm.

"Wait. We'll get him."

I took a breath. I'd forgotten our plan.

Poor Jacob retched several times, which provoked Larry to do the same. It took some time for them to recover and, while they were being attended to, Tom grabbed my arm and told me what strategy he thought would work best, since we were last to go:

"Take a deep breath and see if we could hold it until we get to the top floor," he said.

Sean ran up the stairs to announce the winners.

I bent over and crawled to the bucket. I looked at Tom. He winced. Although I had nearly retched twice from the smell that seemed to clog the back of my throat, I took a deep breath as we bent over the slop. The remaining two livers bobbed among green and yellowish bile. I ducked my head and nipped one in my teeth, trying not to let my lips feel it. The stench nearly knocked me out, but I could see Tom, his liver in his mouth, eye me

100

and knew what he meant: we had to do it. We had to make it. My stomach convulsed and I jerked my head back and took air in the sides of my mouth, cool air, and the nausea passed. Tom was waddling toward the stairs and I caught up with him. We wanted to make it look as if we were competing, so we jostled each other as we made our way up the stairs, first one flight, then the next, the liver wagging back and forth in our mouths like golden retrievers with dead game.

The upperclassmen, loved our jostling and cheered us on. When we got to the top floor, we could see the pale wraiths of our pledge class standing in back of Sean and Randy who were whooping it up, raising their fists, cheering us on as Tom darted ahead of me and I shoved him with my shoulder, then shuffled ahead of him. By the end, we were neck and neck. Just as we got to our respective buckets, we shook our heads, as dogs would with their teeth on a toy, and let our livers fling against the wall.

"Pick it up!" Sean yelled.

"Put it in the bucket," Randy yelled. "The winning team is the first in the bucket."

I bent over and picked mine up and, to my left, Tom did the same, and as I leaned over the bucket, smelling the limburger cheese and beer and puke, the rancid puke—several green beans floating among brown and orange globs— I felt my stomach riot and, afraid I might lose my control right in the bucket, stood up, opened my mouth, and all I remember is seeing Sean's hands coming up to cover his face because, when I let loose, it seemed the whole inside of my body upchucked, propelling the puke outward. The force of it, after it was released, drove me back on my heels and onto my butt. I hadn't seen what Tom had done. But when I looked up, he was on his knees, holding onto his stomach, groaning, but his head was facing in Randy's direction.

There was a cheer and clapping and laughter. Our pledge brothers were picking us up and raising our arms up as if we'd just slain Goliath. Sean was leaning against the wall wiping puke off his face and shirt while shouting, "You bastards, you bastards!" and Randy, gagging, was shoving guys aside to make a dash for the bathroom. The other upperclassmen were laughing along with us as Randy sank to his knees in the doorway and threw up all over himself.

"That was a photo finish if I have ever seen one," Bill Harris cried out.

With everyone laughing, Sean and Randy had no choice if they wanted to save face but to laugh too, so they did, and, after taking off their shirts. Sean graciously told us the night was over: that was it, clean up and go to bed, acting as if he had no other plans for us.

Several hours later, however, we were quietly roused by seven upperclassmen who told us to go to the formal living room. Sitting in a large emperor chair, Sean said, "I'm afraid, boys, there is more in store for you."

We were blindfolded and taken to different parts of the room and put in odd positions. I was placed on the floor on my hands and knees and had to lift my left leg like a dog at a hydrant. Once we were positioned, Sean told us that we had to keep that pose until he told us to stop. Fifteen minutes dragged into twenty and twenty into forty. My leg shook. Eric called out, "That's enough."

There was no reply.

"Take off your blindfolds, guys," Eric said. "We've been had."

As I pulled mine off, I saw Jacob bending over at the waist with one leg off the ground, Joe with his leg up the wall like a dog—and others in strange positions. Eric muttered, "The bastard left us here and went to fuckin' bed." Snatching the onion and garlic strand from his neck, he held it up and swung it violently at the wall where it splattered and then, picking the remnants up again, flung it at another wall, cursing the whole time.

Jacob, always the good cadet, the one to do the right thing, to follow instructions to the T, called out, "You shouldn't do that. They told us to keep our onion. You should be careful." Jacob cupped his hand over his necklace protectively.

"Oh, fuck you!" Eric cried out. "Careful? I have an exam tomorrow in psychology. Does he care? No. I quit. I cannot take this anymore," he fell to his knees and sobbed. Tom went over and patted him on the back, putting his arm around him, holding him next to him.

"One more day," he reminded him, "That's it. One more day and Hell Week is over. Hold on. One more fuckin' day and then we'll be in charge."

We sat in a loosely configured circle and watched Eric cry, his body heaving up and down, while he moaned, "He doesn't care. He doesn't care," until his moan subsided and trailed off to a whimper. Tom's patted Eric's back and Eric pressed against him, his body slack, compliant, soothed. It seemed so natural. I looked at Tom who smiled and nodded at me. Maybe it was envy, but I suspected that many of us wanted to join Eric and feel the comfort of Tom's embrace. Together, two by two, we left the whimpering and headed up the stairs, back to the dorm to get what little sleep we could before breakfast. Morning was less than two hours away, an unwanted glimmer of light and classes to attend. Exhausted as we were, as much as we could, we managed to go to classes in a daze, trying to make notes and remember what it is that the professor had said, and hoping that we'd seen the end of Hell Week.

Axis Mundi

The next day at dinner, no one mentioned a word about Hell Week. Sean, who had been angry the night before, was ebullient at dinner. He held up some newspaper, pointing to a photograph of a black man. He tapped his fork on his glass to announce that Malcolm X had been taken care of by his own kind—fellow Muslims shot him down.

"You don't have to worry no more about that nigger threatening our way of life. I think we need a round of applause!" he said.

A few men clapped, but I didn't even know what he was talking about. Later, I asked Paul what it was all about. He told me that Malcolm X was a Black Muslim that he'd broken away from the leader of his sect and been assassinated while giving a speech in Harlem, gunned down while his kids were there watching him. Paul handed me a *Ramparts Magazine* with an article on how Black Muslims were fighting for their right to define who they were. Yet, even in their own movement, they were divided. It seemed a shame. Yet here we were in a supposed fraternity with brother violating brother.

"How can Sean get up and make racist remarks?" I asked. "Isn't this supposed to be a fraternity—brotherly love and all that?"

Paul told me, "Let it go. When it is time to act, you'll know. Trust me. Sean will get his comeuppance."

On Friday evening, after dinner, Sam had us gather in the formal living room. He explained that the last challenge was one that every prior class had done. His class had done it in a blinding snow storm. Sean sat beside him but did not say a word. The message was clear: he had overstepped his authority and the senior officers were not pleased.

"This last challenge will require all of you to step forward. It will not be easy, but you need to work as a group and, as we did four years ago, you will succeed if—and only if —you pull together," he admonished us. He stared at me and Eric and gave a slight nod. Clearly, he expected us to live up to our promise to him.

He turned to Sean and said, "Now Sean will explain what you need to do."

Not looking at Sam, Sean weakly smiled at us and, began: "We'll take you to a destination out of town. It is cold out. And the snow and slush will make it hard. Sam wanted to make sure I told you that you will need to keep warm so wear your warmest clothes. Your job will be to bring a log back to the house. Some of you will need to find out where you are and all of you will need to take turns carrying the log. You need to have it back here in the fraternity before breakfast at seven. Hear that? Here in the fraternity. Get ready and be back here in ten minutes."

We hurried to our rooms, grabbing jackets, boots, gloves, scarves and hats. When we arrived back in the living room, we were blindfolded and separately escorted to cars, driven for what felt like a half hour to a location and dropped off. Our blindfolds were removed. Sean stood by his yellow Mustang and pointed to a log, recently cut, fourteen feet long, a foot or more in diameter, on the side of the road. Its bark hung loosely, some pieces broken off, some intact.

"Here it is. Good luck," he said and hopped back in his car. The air was raw and cold with flecks of an icy wind whipping at us. With no clear leadership, Trevor stepped forward, "Listen guys, I have a football practice at eight tomorrow. So we just need to tackle this," his announced, grabbing the end of the log. "Suck it up. Someone take the rear. We'll take turns."

No one stepped forward. I walked off, looking out in the field, an anger boiling in me. Another wasted night. Another foolish task. Another power play by Sean. I wondered why I'd ever pledged in the first place. Maybe my dad was right.

Larry said, "Look, if we don't show up, they'll come out here and find us. I'm not busting my balls for some stupid log. Not for that asshole. I'm staying put."

"Not me," countered Tom. "The idea of sitting here on a freezing night is not my idea of a good time. Let's do what Trevor said: let's get on with it."

Angry as I was, I joined Tom, picked up the back of the log. It was very heavy and dense with moisture, way beyond my strength alone. In short order, we figured out that it would take six of us to carry it.

In one mighty effort, we lifted it straight up, so that it stood for a moment like a telephone pole. Three of us held it there. Ibby started to dance around it, chanting and waving his arms as if in some ancient tribal dance. Soon others joined him, whooping it up, acting as if it were the center of our world. We laughed and, for a moment, as I looked up at it pointing up into the misted sky, it did look like some sacred center, a stark pole in the middle of nowhere, aimed up at the interminable dark.

"All right, all right," Trevor called out, "enough of the voodoo. We need to get this sucker into town."

Tom and I took one end, Brian and Eric at the other, and Trevor and Steve the middle. Step by step like mourners carrying a casket, we marched off. While we were carrying the log, the other pledges checked out the roads and calculated the directions back to the house. We had no idea where we were: no road signs, no familiar landmarks, only an occasional farmhouse. Sleet spit across the sky in the distance and, further off, a dense line of trees snaked along the landscape parallel to the road, which wound slightly to the right. We trudged. No one spoke.

As careful as we were to keep a steady pace, if someone up front moved too quickly, the people in the middle and end staggered and lost their grip and dropped the log. Eric suggested that someone, as in a drill team, yell out "step, step, step" to keep everyone in cadence. That worked, for a while, but the log was so heavy that no one could lug it for long.

My cloth gloves soon soaked through and my hands became numb. Pressing the log against my hip, I managed to keep one hand and arm around it. Yet it slipped and Tom was left holding it, until I could latch onto it again. After fifteen minutes, I asked for a substitute, who might last ten minutes before he needed someone to take over. The littler guys—John, with his wiry frame and Joseph with his flaccid body— barely lasted a few minutes. And Steve, with his enormous weight, who we thought would be a workhorse because his girth, could not hold the log close to him, and so proved useless.

Instead, we decided to let him walk and shout the cadence despite his asthma acting up.

When we tried to stop and rest, the wind bit into our hands and the perspiration under our coats quickly went from hot to icy in a few short minutes.

During one transition to exchange the log, Ibby dropped it and smashed his left foot. Another time, Brian cut his hand when the log slipped and cut a long gouge in his palm. Jerry, who looked like a midget next to the log, tripped and bruised his knee. We trudged like wounded soldiers retreating from a battle. It seemed to me such a stupid waste of time. I did my part, but I wanted to cut and run, to get as far away from the log and my pledge brothers and the night as I could.

After an hour, we found a road sign and figured out which way to go. We were South of Greenville, and we had six miles ahead of us. As the hours plodded by, Ibby had us sing "Ol' Man River" which befit us as we "sweated and strained, bodies all achin' and wracked with pain." He was our cheerleader, whooping it up when we reached another intersection, "Come on guys, we can do this. Chin up. We're the best!" Using his singing voice, he bellowed out "to your left, your right, your left." He'd have us sing our fraternity songs: "Come sing to Delta Alpha Epsilon, and to brothers who have come along..." and show tunes like "Climb Every Mountain," until we were hoarse from singing. But we kept on singing. The music lifted our spirits and in way, our log, too.

The Samaritans

Along one stretch of road, a beat-up blue Chevy Corvair pulled alongside us. The driver, a bearded man in a blue uniform, asked us what we were doing. We told him.

"Now, guys, I never saw much in going to college. Never had the smarts. But I'll tell you that's downright dumb, if you ask me," he said. We agreed. He told us that he had just gotten off work; he was a night guard at a company down the road. Reaching under the seat of his car, he held up a bottle of whiskey.

"Boys," he said. "You need some antifreeze to keep you going. Want some?" He held the bottle out of the car. Tom went over to him and said, "Much obliged," and took a swig. Trevor followed, then, to my surprise, Eric and, by the time Joseph took the last swig, we had all drunk from the bottle. It felt like something holy, a communion.

We asked him how far it was to town; he guessed four, maybe five miles. He took the last swig and said, "You boys be careful, now. There are a lot of weirdos out this hour of the night." He honked his horn and dove off.

An hour later, two trucks, big Ford trucks, roared by and, about 500 yards down the road, turned around and drove slowly by us. A big pudgy man with a baseball cap pulled down over his head leaned out the window.

"My, my, if it isn't Paul Bunyan's little elves."

He stopped his truck and spit on the pavement. Chewing tobacco. He turned to his friend in the cab and offered a commentary on us, "Lookie here, fatso can barely walk, the sap looks as if he's dressed for his own funeral. And, over there, Josh, there's an albino. Wonder if he is one of them faggots. I wonder if they're all fags? And that log, so nice of them to bring it to town for us. We could use it. Mighty cold out. You got several more miles, boys, and I'll tell you where to put it."

Trevor strode over to the truck, "Listen wise-ass, leave us the well-enough alone or I'll show *you* where to put it."

The driver cut his engine and called out to his friend, "Well, listen here, Josh, someone is itching for a fight." He waved his hand toward the truck in back, motioning for his buddies in the other truck to join him.

Though wiry and half the size of Trevor, Luis stepped in front of him and held up his hand, nudging him back. He sensed the danger. Two men from the second truck had positioned themselves in front of the headlights, illuminating their silhouettes.

Intent to make a stand, Trevor pushed at Luis, trying to get to the driver of the first truck. Luis, who never lost his temper, turned around and grabbed Trevor by the collar and told him, "This is no fuckin' time for heroics." And then he whispered, "Take a look to your right. These lugs mean business. Back off," and shoved Trevor into my arms. I held him and whispered in his ear, "Let Luis handle it."

Trevor attempted to get loose, but, saw that Luis had walked up to the driver and shook his hand. Trevor figured it was no use to stop Luis since he was already talking to the driver. Luis pointed at the log and I could make out some of what he said—we were tired, had some cash, would he mind helping out. He asked where the driver was from, noted that he came from Cincinnati and his dad owned a trucking firm. The driver said his dad was a trucker. They made more small talk. Luis patted the driver on the shoulder and told him how it was mighty cold and we could use a helping hand. The driver called to his other friends, who, once I got a better view of them, were large men with necks as thick as their heads. They came over and joined the huddle with Luis and the driver. After a few moments, Luis shook each of their hands and said, "Hey, guys, no need for those bats, unless you want to play some baseball," which led to awkward laughter. He then turned to Joseph. I was not sure why. But maybe he had a sense that Joseph as the son of a wealthy banker, might have a better sense of how to negotiate money. Luis gave Joseph instructions as he continued to chat with the men, showing them the log, sizing it up to see if it would fit in the back of the truck.

Joseph came to each of us, telling us to contribute to the cause: we needed fifty dollars. Once Trevor understood Luis's plan, he charged forward, his fist raised.

"We're not doing this!" Trevor shouted.

"What do you mean?" Tom asked.

"We *are* going to carry it ourselves. It is our challenge."

"Are you nuts? We'll never get it back," Tom said, kicking at the log that had already iced over in the short time it sat on the side of the road. He moved toward Trevor to calm him down, trying to reach around and pat his back.

"Get your fuckin' hand off me! I'm not going to compromise. It's our challenge and we *are* going to do it as a class."

"Come here," Tom said, moving away from the road. "No need to yell. Let's talk."

Eric joined Tom, and Jerry and I followed along too, sensing we might need to use force.

Trevor followed Tom out into a field about ten yards from the rest of us. Their faces were intent, nose to nose. Trevor pointed at the log. Tom pointed in our direction. Trevor shook his head. The sleet stung my cheeks and felt as if someone had slapped them. I turned to Jerry.

"What the fuck does Trevor think he is doing? He acts as if he is speaking for all of us. *We* will carry the damn log. *We* already carried it for hours! I'd like to bust his teeth..." I said.

Eric grabbed my arm. "Hold on."

Jerry shook his head. "Just calm down. Let Tom handle it. He knows Trevor. Come on, let's take a walk." With his arm around my waist, Jerry walked me down the road. "We can't be fighting among ourselves. It never comes to any good."

"I'm at the end of my rope. Trevor is acting like an ass. Can't he fuckin' see that we are exhausted? Ibby's hurt. John's hurt. Steve can't breathe," I exclaimed.

Jerry put his hand on my chest. "Calm down. Tom will take care of it."

I gazed up at the mist. The skin on my face felt as if someone had pulled it tight against the bones. The muscles in the back of my jaw tightened. I wanted to walk over to Trevor and grab him by the collar and tell him to cut the bullshit. But Jerry kept telling me to calm down, take a deep breath, and I did.

We turned around, looked back at headlights illuminating the sleet. I took long breaths as Jerry suggested and we headed back to the trucks.

Luis continued to talk to the guys while Joseph came around to collect money. I gave him five, as did Jerry, and I saw more bills coming out of wallets.

Steve stepped forward and put several bills in Joseph's hand. Startled, Joseph said, "That's too much," but Steve insisted, "Hey, I've not been much use. Let this be my contribution."

Joseph counted it out.

"Thanks, that should do it," he said and returned to Luis.

Tom and Trevor were still out in the field pacing around each other in a circle like two gamecocks. We could see Trevor's hands flailing up and down, hear him pleading. "No, no, no." punctuated the air. Tom pointed at the sky and then in our direction. Trevor stopped and stared at us. He took several steps back. His hand out, as if exasperated, he ranted for a minute, his gestures like those of a broker I'd seen on the New York Stock Exchange. Tom shook his head and turned abruptly and pointed again at us and then, toward the sky. Trevor stood like a soldier at attention. Then he looked down and said something. Tom put his arm around Trevor's shoulder and they hugged. When they came back to the group, Trevor stood by himself, his hands in his pockets, and wouldn't look at any of us. Tom went over the Luis who, in turn, passed some cash to the driver, telling him that the rest would be paid once we were delivered to campus.

The driver, who introduced himself as Earl, instructed his three friends to get the log, which, without much effort, they lifted up to their shoulders and flung in the back of the truck. Earl then told some of us to hop in the back his truck and the rest in the other truck.

During the drive to town, I wondered what Tom had said to Trevor to convince him to abandon his principles. Had he threatened him? Had he paid him off? Offered him a bribe? I looked up at the misted sky, the cold rain spitting in my face, the street lights like little moons zipped by as we passed under them.

When we came into campus, past the quad and past the tall brick spire of East College, I still had the knot in my stomach. I wanted to hit someone—Sean for his insolence, Trevor for his self-righteous assurance. Then I realized my anger was of no use. It was over. I thought about how the log, standing upright by the road, seemed, as Ibby had sensed, like some powerful emblem of our weeklong struggle and how, despite the bickering, we had proved ourselves. We had prevailed.

Even Steven

Pulling up on Elm Street, just in front of the house, we prepared to make a grand entrance. It was 5:21 a.m. While we staggered the last five hundred feet to the front door, the early light began to streak though the tops of the oaks like ornaments. Larry, who normally said very little, suggested we carry the log upstairs and, just as a final touch, jam the dorm door with it. When Trevor protested it was not right, Larry straightened himself up.

"Listen, guys. We have over an hour. I remember what Sean said. He said we had to be *in* the house by seven." He smiled, "Now that to me meant we, including the log, need to be inside!"

We laughed. Several slapped him on the back and, despite Trevor's misgivings, thought it was a grand idea.

"We'll stick it to them," Steven said.

"No, we'll log it to them," Larry said.

We entered the front door, careful not to make a noise. No one was up. It would be a perfect revenge: when the upperclassmen tried to get out, they would have to go down the fire escape to the front door in their pj's or skivvies. Quietly, we maneuvered the log up the stairwell, twisting and turning as we went until eventually we were able to set it against the dorm door. There was no way to dislodge it from inside the dorm.

With the log in place, we headed to the shower, eager to strip out of our clothes and wait in line, naked, with only a towel around our waist, as each of us took his turn under the hot spray. We went to our separate rooms, and, on the floor, in chairs or on couches, fell into a restless sleep.

About an hour later, we could hear banging and, swearing followed by the sound of feet on the metal fire escape, the front door flying open and the approaching thunder of footsteps on the stairway like kenneled dogs released from their pen. Several upperclassmen barged into Eric's room, demanding an explanation. Sean and Randy were among those in his room. We had agreed if there was a confrontation that we would stand by one another— as a pledge class. We filed into the hallway, congregating outside Eric's room. But Eric knew exactly what to say when they asked what the hell was going on.

"Sean, you told us to bring it back to the house."

"That's what you were supposed to do," Sean shouted, "but, instead, you bastards pulled a prank and that was not part of the deal."

In a matter-of-fact tone, Eric said, "You never told us where to put it, so we decided to put it where we did."

Sean stomped his foot and yelled, "Fuckin' bastards, get your asses to the basement. I'm not done with you. I'm not going to let this pass, you bastards. You will pay...."

Sam, who was standing at the end of the hall, interrupted, "Hold on, Sean. Eric is right. You told them to get it here *in* the house before dawn and, well, Sean, they did." Sean looked at Sam. Like two gunfighters, they stood facing one another. Neither spoke. Another door opened.

The hallway in back of them filled. John came out, brushing sleep from his eyes.

"What's the problem?" he asked.

Sean pointed at us. "They pulled a prank!"

"What they do?"

"They jammed the door in the dorm and locked us in!"

John laughed. "That's a good one. First time any class has done that."

"They need to pay."

"No," said John. "They need to get to classes. Hell Week is over."

Sam nodded and laughed. "Well done, guys. You're the first class to have made it all the way back and be on time. Go get yourselves some breakfast. And, Sean, let's have a talk."

We never found out what was said, but a month later, Sean and Randy moved out of the house to claim a room in the annex, a two story building that the DAE house owned, known for being the place for juniors and seniors to party. And they did.

At the morning breakfast, Sam told us to resume our normal activities and to remember that we needed to keep our grades up, and not cause any trouble. The upperclassmen, he said, still had to vote on each of us. If any one of the members did not support a pledge, he could black ball him.

After dinner one night, I asked Tom what he had said to Trevor.

He laughed. "It wasn't easy. He was as adamant as a bulldog. He saw

113

that log as our last challenge. He thought it was like football practice with pads before the big game. He kept saying, 'If we can't show what we are made of now, how can we ever play the big game when we are the first team?' He had a point."

"What did you say?"

"For a while I did not know what to say."

"So what did you do?"

"I pointed to you guys and said, 'Is that a football team?' He stared for a moment at you, then asked, 'What's your point?' I told him that someone—Steve I knew for sure, but probably others—would get hurt more than we already had. Someone would get really sick if we continued. That maybe valor isn't all it's hyped up to be. That we needed to settle for what we could do. I pointed to you guys and said, 'Look at them. Do they look like they're going to make it?'"

"He agreed?"

"Not right away. He had suggestions about how we could carry the log more effectively and said that he would take the load. He would do it himself if he had to. But I said that he had practice and might end up being worthless to his team. That got to him. He was supposed to start. He knew that he was compromising his place on the starting team."

"And that was it?"

"Yep. He actually laughed when he looked over at you, and said, 'They look like more like prisoners of war than a team.' He suggested that we get it over with as quickly as we could. He said that he supposed that he didn't need us to be a football team. We were just pledge brothers."

Although Hell Week was over, I still felt a sense of violation that I could not shake entirely. It was as if I'd witnessed something dark and evil, something primitive and dangerous, too real to deny. I talked with Paul and he said that our time would come.

"When we are no longer pledges, we can stand up to them and make sure this never happens to anyone else." He stood at his dresser, staring at himself in the mirror. I could see anger in his eyes, a hard metallic look. But he could see me, too. Then his face softened it and he smiled at me. "We will make them see, just you wait."

And so winter yielded to spring. In March, the talk on campus and in the news was our increasing involvement in Vietnam. President Johnson approved an operation called "Rolling Thunder," which led to ongoing air strikes on something called the Ho Chi Minh Trail and to our first combat troops arriving in Vietnam, some 3500 Marines landing at China Beach. The President claimed we needed to defend the American air base at Da Nang—places foreign to me. Yet Paul told me that, if our involvement escalated as it had for the French, I shouldn't be surprised to find myself drafted, something that I'd never thought about and startled me like the blind blast of a horn from an oncoming truck. What would I do?

I didn't consider myself a pacifist. But I could not imagine killing someone. No one in my family had served in the military. I had no interest in war, particularly one that was in a part of the world I had never been and scarcely heard of. For the time being I was content to put away such thoughts and have the center of my world here in Indiana.

The Flag

In early March, the same day Dr. King started his first march for voting rights from Selma to Montgomery, Paul and I were coming back from our World Civilization class. Paul was concerned about what might happen.

"Dr. King is taking a big risk. Governor Wallace, a racist, will do anything to stop that march. He'll tear them to pieces, just wait, you'll see," he said.

"How do you know?"

"I read the papers. Johnson has tried to get Wallace to back down, but he thinks that if he takes a strong stand, he'll keep what he wants most: the white votes."

Paul told me that King had to cross the Edmund Pettus Bridge in order to start the fifty-four mile march down Highway 80. When the march crossed the bridge, it faced the onslaught of club-wielding Alabama state troopers. Before class, we'd heard reports of the attack on the radio. Paul said, "Someone is going to be killed."

As we turned down Locust Street toward the house, we saw, the Confederate flag flying over our house.

On the porch, sitting with his legs on the railing, shouting "Dixie forever," was Sean and two of his friends. We checked our steps, and Paul glared at Sean and then turned to me, "Don't say a word." Since we were still pledges, we knew that if we questioned an upperclassman, we would be put on double duty for cleaning toilets and forbidden to talk, maybe even blackballed.

Sean called out, "Hey, you see that flag? We're making a statement: Freedom of speech. First Amendment. Pretty neat, huh?"

Paul smiled at him and whispered to me, "Keep walking." We walked by them and up to the second floor.

Once inside our room, Paul slapped his hand on the desk, "Bastard. He thinks he can do what he wants. He doesn't represent us. He's a racist pig and all we can do is smile and act as if we didn't care." He paused for a moment, both his hands on the desk, the side of his jaw tightening. "But I do care. Damn it. Why didn't someone else tell him to take the fuckin' flag down? Where the fuck are the upperclassmen?"

"Maybe they think it's his right to disagree? He said it's a First Amendment right," I replied.

"What? You side with him?"

"No. I don't agree with him."

"Good. There must be others who feel the same way. But no one is saying anything."

"Maybe they're afraid of him."

"No. That's not it."

"Well, what is it?"

"They don't give a shit," he said.

I flopped in the armchair, lifting my arms behind my head, and looked out the window at the flag. "It's a fuckin' disgrace, but he has a point. It's freedom of speech. We're still pledges. We can't risk it. He still holds all the cards. Eric and I told Sam and John we'd not make waves."

"Jesus, what are you saying?

"I mean he..."

"Mean nothing. Don't you see he's making a statement about what all of us feel and, to boot, what we believe. He's saying DAE is racist. Is that what you want?"

"Well, no, but..."

"But nothing. We need to do something," he said, thumping me in the chest with his forefinger.

"Maybe we can talk to some upperclassmen?" I offered.

"Sure, that might work, but I don't think so."

"Why?"

"Because, if someone wanted to do something, the flag would not be there. Sam or John would have said something. Maybe they will. If they do, fine. If not, we need to do something."

"That's a bit risky," I said, trying to think what we might do that would not get us into trouble.

"But what is worse," Paul moaned, "is that no one, it seems, cares."

We stared at one another. He was furious and I felt a quiet fury burn in my chest too, but one that did not come so much as from righteous anger as from being put on the spot. I hated having to take a stand, but it seemed I had no choice.

Paul stared at me. "Do you want to do something?"

"Yeah. I supposed we have to."

"Suppose?" He frowned at me.

"We need to do something."

"Good. We're in agreement. But now the question is: what to do?"

We agreed to think about it. In the meantime, we turned to our World Civilization books to the chapter on the Roman Empire since we had a test coming up, to distract ourselves, but the raspy singing of Sean, half-drunk from sipping his sour-mash whiskey, rose through the window as if it were chasing us: "Oh, I wish I was in the land of cotton/ Old times there are not forgotten. Look away! Look away! Look away! Dixie Land..." I remembered reading how President Lincoln loved the song. But that was when he hoped for reconciliation, before the country was ripped apart. The anthem seemed now an undisguised affront, a lyrical boast to racism.

After no one said anything at dinner about the flag, after we checked with other pledges to see if anyone else was concerned, and after we found no one who did have concerns, it seemed too risky to speak up and, anyway, as pledges, we carried no clout. Many agreed with Sean: it was freedom of speech. Frustrated by the lack of support, Paul nodded to me, "Let's go the library to study, whatta you say?"

I hated the library, being sequestered in those sterile carrels, staring at the empty walkways and bland academic halls, whitewashed, like bleached minds.

"No thanks. I'm going to our room."

He rolled his eyes and shook his head, "No, you're not. You need to go to the library to do some research, right?"

I knew something was up so I gave in and said in a voice that Sean and his buddies could hear, "Yep, I gotta do some intense research for World History."

"Right," Paul smiled, "World History it is." He told Sean that we'd be putting in several hours at the library. Sean flipped his hand indifferently, "Hey, good for you. Someone should be learning something from history. Check out Hitler. He did a job in his day," and then caught himself, noticing that others were listening to him. He added, "Good for you, boys. Make us proud with straight A's."

On the way to the library, we took the long route around by the gym and halfway to the football stadium, plotting to get rid of the flag. After we shook on it, we separated for the rest of the evening so that no one would suspect that we were in cahoots. We agreed that, even if we got caught, even if we were reprimanded, we would stick together and if need be, resign from the fraternity. Still, I had my misgivings because I somewhat agreed with the idea of the flag being free speech, and I did want to be a full fraternity member, but I also I did not want to let Paul down.

We also decided that if we succeeded in getting rid of the flag, we would never tell anyone. It would be our secret.

Capture the Flag

After coming back from the library separately, talking with friends, getting undressed, we headed up to the dorm along with the other pledges. We went to our bunks and acted as if we had fallen asleep.

The moon, still visible through the bent arms of the trees, cast a fractured light though the dorm. After we were certain everyone was asleep, Paul and I crept out of the dorm a half-hour apart. After getting dressed, we met at midnight in the upstairs hallway. The stairs creaked as we tiptoed down them, trying to keep from making any noise. We made our way to the window over the front entryway of the house and pried it open to where the flagpole held the limp Confederate flag. We pulled the clamps off it and gently hauled it in, checking, as we did, to see if anyone was on the street. The flag felt thinner than a blanket yet heavier than a sheet— its own distinct weight— a soft fine fabric made with care. It showed the signs of wear—a frayed edge, a thinning of color in the two blue bands where the thirteen stars ran crisscross across the red. Sean had boasted at dinner that his dad had given it to him with some pride, a family heirloom, full of tradition. Paul and I had no such feelings, but we folded it carefully, neatly, hand over hand, as we had learned to do in Boy Scouts. We pulled down the window and latched it as it had been. Paul stuffed the flag inside his shirt and hurried down the stairs. I waited several minutes, went to the bathroom, stopped in our room to pick up a pair of scissors, checked the hallway, then, taking the back stairs, followed him outside to the designated rendezvous: down the street, across from the playground, near the baseball diamond. As I often did when I was anxious, I had begun to sweat. My forehead beaded up and trickles of sweat ran down my nose. I took a deep breath and I sprinted to the woods.

He was crouching behind a large maple. We surveyed the streets — empty —and, keeping low, crept along the line of trees by the baseball field for a hundred yards into the woods. Several large rocks rested by an oak. We lugged them to a clearing and stacked them in a neat pile , then, after brushing aside the damp leaves, dug in the ground with the scissors, using our fingers to scoop and draw the dirt and stones into another pile until we had a hole about two feet deep. It took about fifteen minutes. We laid the folded flag there, then pulled the dirt back tamping it down, first with our palms, then with our feet so that it would be perfectly level and leave no clue that something was buried there. Then we scattered leaves over it, matching as best we could the other leaves around it, and finally rolled large rocks haphazardly around the spot.

We left the woods through the far side, backtracked around the block and came down to Elm Street from the campus end, opposite of where we had been.

We saw the glimmer of lights on the second story of the fraternity and heard some guys yelping near the front door of the annex, each in backlight. They were peeing in the bushes and singing some incoherent lines from Dixie. We waited until they staggered back into the annex, then retraced our steps, and crept up the side steps of the main house and ascended the back stairwell. Midway up the first flight, we heard a door open and several voices. I was paralyzed, certain we were caught. I had no idea who it was, but when they spoke, I knew immediately: it was Randy and Ralph, Sean's two buddies.

Randy, who normally spoke in a distinct clipped northern tone, slurred his words. "Let's go back to the annex. Sean got's a keg in his room and some broad from Kappa Gamma is comin' over," Ralph belched. They were coming our way.

I turned to back away, but Paul had come up behind me and draped his arm around my shoulder. His face went slack. I stared at him, trying to pull away, thinking we could skedaddle before they identified who we were.

"What the..." I said, seeing by the slack expression on his face, that he had decided to do an improvisation.

He whispered, "I'm drunk, okay? Play along."

I put my arm around his waist and he uttered in a slurred voice, loud enough to be heard by Randy, "Come on, no one will see us. Just get me to my room before I puke."

Randy stopped at the head of the stairwell and blurted out, smiling broadly, "Well, what do we have here?"

I grabbed Paul and tried to turn around, pretending to be startled, and wanting to get away.

"Hey, pledges, stop right there," Randy ordered, stepping down to where I stood, propping up Paul who had gone slack like the scarecrow in *The Wizard of Oz*.

"What's his problem?" Randy put his hand under Paul's chin and tilted it up.

"Nothing, no problem," I offered, swaying slightly and grabbing the banister for balance.

"You bastards are drunk!" Randy roared. "Where'd you get the stuff?"

I muttered, "I'd rather not say."

He leaned close to me. "What do you mean that you would rather not say?"

I pursed my lips and stared right at him, "If I tell you, it might compromise my source and since we are not supposed to drink and this person, well, he knew Paul here was feeling down — problem with his girl, see. Well, he, you know, might be compromised and all."

Randy laughed, "Jason, you're such a fuckin' diplomat. You should work for the goddamn State Department."

Paul's knees buckled and he started to tilt forward. His act was getting out of hand.

"Damn it, Paul," I snarled, "Fucking stand up; you're killing me!"

I turned to Randy and Ralph and pleaded, "Can't you see I need some help here?"

Delighted to see us in the same state that they were in, they swung their arms around Paul as if he was a long-lost comrade and gestured to me to let go. As they hoisted Paul up the stairs, his feet slapped against the risers. They dragged him down the hallway carpet to our room and deposited him in the chair where he slumped like a rag doll.

I played up to Randy, "I know we could get in big trouble here — we're not supposed to drink as pledges — but Paul here just found out his girlfriend back home is..." I hesitated and leaned back on the desk as if I had lost my balance because I had no idea what excuse to make up and Randy, shorter than me, grabbed me and held me up, and saved me from saying something absurd.

"Don't you worry about a thing," he consoled me. "We all have girl problems. The bitches are fucking us up all the time. And I am glad to see you ain't no pussies and like a good time every once in a while. And to think I thought you both were straight arrows!" He patted me on the back, "Go ahead, take care of your friend and we'll just let this one go. Just between you and me."

He laughed again, shaking his head in amusement. "When I was a pledge, I got smashed every weekend and no one knew the better. This will be our little secret and when you are initiated, we'll get blasted every week. You owe me one."

He swung his arm around Ralph and they headed off to the annex, laughing.

When they had gone, Paul piped up, "How was I?"

"You asshole, too damn good. You nearly broke my back, but I'm sure glad you can act."

"You did a great job yourself," he said, looking out the window where we could see the tops of trees in the wooded area where the flag was buried.

The Accused

The next morning, Sean, Randy and Ralph came into the dining area late, loaded up their plates and sat at a table together, talking quietly among themselves. Their faces were puffy, clearly hung-over. Paul and I watched as several other brothers leaned over and whispered something to them. Sean asked a question and slammed his fist on the table.

"You got to be shitting me!" he shouted and beelined it to the front door, where another loud, "Fuckin-A!" and "Shit!" could be heard.

He stomped back into the dining room and stood, his legs apart, hands on his hips, "Whatever asshole did it — took the flag — you better fess up or I will find out and when I find out, it'll be hell to pay!" He glared over at our table and announced, "I want to talk with each and every one of you bastards, one at a time, in the living room." He picked up his tray, nodded for Randy and Ralph to follow him, and went to the couch in the living room.

By the time Paul and I went in we had heard about the routine: Where were you last night? Did you hear anything? Give us the facts, just the facts. Sean was acting as if he were Sergeant Joe Friday on the *Dragnet* TV series, grilling people, checking to see if they had an alibi, having Randy and Ralph keep notes so they could go over them and see if there were any loopholes. Paul went in first and came out five minutes later and winked at me, "Next, " and then crouched down and softly muttered, "You seem quite hung-over."

I sat in the chair across from them and held my head, hoping that Randy would remember that I had also been drinking and that he promised not to tell.

Sean asked, "Something wrong with you, Jason?"

"No, just a bad headache, migraine," I said.

Randy nodded at me and smiled, "Late night cooking the books?"

"Yep, World History exam. I studied late and went to the dorm right afterward and slept through the night."

Sean inquired if I had seen anyone leave the dorm. I said no. He ground his teeth and lowered his voice, "You better not be lying to me."

"No, why would I?" I said.

He tilted his head and grinned, "Because you are a Northern Liberal, that's why."

I rubbed my temples. The things I wanted to say to him flashed through my mind, but I held my tongue and kept rubbing my temple.

"Well, aren't you one of those I-am-so-much-better-than-you liberals?" I glared at him.

Randy interceded and changed the topic, "You feeling sick?"

I smiled slightly and looked up at him, "Not well; I'm not well."

Sean shot back, "Well or not, tomato face, you're a Yankee liberal and that makes you a prime suspect."

I took a slow breath, "You may think, Sean, you know who I am but you are mistaken. Just for the facts: My parents are Republicans. They voted Goldwater. I don't think that makes me liberal."

Randy laughed, "No. That would make you a conservative."

"All right, all right," Sean waved his hand at the door, "get out'a here."

After Sean had grilled each of the pledges, Randy came out and bent over the table where I was eating a second helping of scrambled eggs. "You done well, kid. It's our little secret," he whispered.

"Thanks," I said. "I owe you one."

He tapped my shoulder, "Later."

By lunchtime, a rumor circulated that another fraternity had swiped the flag and was hiding it. Randy heard it from a friend in his psychology class. I know Randy wasn't a racist, but he would go along with the search for the culprit as a way to cement his friendship with Sean and also to defy his Northern liberal, overbearing, father. He knew that if he could get the flag back, he would win big points with Sean. He'd do anything for Sean. He idolized him.

Randy heard that "some Jew from New York," the president of the Sigma Nu house had threatened to tear the flag down and he was probably the one who took it. Besides, the Sigma Nu house had been an archrival of our house for many years. They had lost to us in football and the story was that they wanted to get even.

Randy was never one to waste time thinking something over when he could act, so he took action. He made a threatening call to the Sigma Nu house, using a Southern dialect. He told them that they'd find a burning cross in their front yard. That same night, he flung a brick through their fraternity's bay window, smashing it.

The police arrived two hours later at the annex and asked who had made calls on the annex phone. A pledge who had picked up a pizza and had just come from Sean and Randy's room told the officers that they were the only two in the annex, since the other residents had gone to a dance. The police interrogated Randy intensely. His high-pitched voice matched that of the person who made threats on the telephone. Sean defended his friend and attested how he would never threaten to burn a cross. That statement, as it turned out, sealed Randy's fate, since the police had never mentioned a cross. Randy, in tears, finally confessed, told them how the Sigma Nu president had stolen Sean's flag, how that violated—didn't it?— freedom of speech and how he didn't mean any harm.

From our window in the fraternity house, we saw police lead Randy, handcuffed, to a cruiser and later heard that he'd been booked at headquarters. When Sean stepped out of the annex after him, he looked shaken, his head bowed. Sean took his car and followed the officers to the station. The next day, Randy's parents told the police he could "rot" in jail, and so Sean's parents posted bail.

To celebrate Randy's release, he and Sean went that evening to Fast Track, a local bar, and got drunk, recounting their story to anyone who would listen. They staggered home, singing a Ray Charles tune, "Born to Lose," at two in the morning. When they awoke the next morning, no one was in the mood to listen to their story any longer. The adviser of the local chapter of the fraternity, a distinguished lawyer in his fifties, called from his office in Indianapolis, and later that day, drove down, had a meeting with the upperclassmen and said that he did not want to hear about any Confederate — or, for that matter, any "goddamn flag"— nor any trouble with the police or heads would roll. In side conversations that we overhead at meals, Sean still bragged how his father had called the police station and made the cops squirm. However, Randy's parents picked him up the following day and he did not come back for several weeks, at which point he moved back into a room in the main house. His parents had given him an ultimatum: cease his relationship with Sean or they would cut off financial aid.

Paul and I hated what happened to Randy, given he had kept his end of the bargain that night: he'd never snitched on us and, because of him, we were never real suspects. We felt obligated to help him out and discussed how to get him off the hook, but every option implicated us. Randy was beyond our help, and so we kept quiet and let the wheels of justice grind away.

The missing flag quickly became legendary with theories of who actually did it changing from month to month. Some claimed that the girls in the Delta Gamma house, known to be a liberal bastion, had done it. Others said some radical group in the dorm that promoted free love had used a ladder to grab it and someone now had it in their room. Still others claimed that Randy had done it just to stir up trouble with Sigma Nu house since they were our football rivals. Of course, as the investigation into Sean's claims about Sigma Nu continued, the president of Sigma Nu denied that he had anything to do with the flag. Eventually, Randy got off by paying for the damage to the window and no one discovered what actually had happened.

The flag, folded neatly, remained buried in the woods.

Change of Guard

Following Hell Week, two major changes in leadership swept through the house. My pledge father stepped down and John Hatch, a junior and the vice president, became president. He was a level-headed guy who had listened to Eric and me during Hell Week. Instead of Sean getting the vice president's job, Randy did. Since his return to school, he'd broken off his friendship with Sean and put more focus on his academic work. People were impressed with his resolve to reinvent himself. That left Sean in the secretary position, something he resented but took. He claimed it did not matter and informed everyone all he wanted to do was party. And he did.

With Hell Week over, we were officially done being pledges. We could choose where and when we studied. The official initiation ceremony confirmed us as members in full standing. And yet with all the build-up, the actual induction when it finally came seemed like a farce.

In jackets and ties, we were sequestered in the library and told to wait while the rest of the membership filed past us into the dining room. At an appointed hour, Randy, outfitted in purple robes like a grape and a pointed cap like a sorcerer's, came to get us. We were ushered single-file into the dining room where all the tables but one had been removed and the curtains drawn so that the only light came from candles on the table. Behind it, John, Randy, and Sean stood with their hands folded across their chests. Their robes had gold insignias blazoned on them and, on the cuffs, gold embroidery. Their faces looked like those of ministers at funerals: kindly but serious. We lined up in front of the table, which was covered with a gold and purple cloth. Atop it, golden bowls with something in them sat by a large rolled-up parchment scroll that was tied by a purple ribbon. Upperclassmen crowded in back of us, dressed in coats and ties. After welcoming us and reading something in Latin, John said that it was his honor to initiate us as new members of DAE. He felt that we would all be true gentlemen during our college years as well as in our lives, and represent the best of DAE's traditions. He asked everyone to read our creed, which, during our time as pledges, we had to memorize:

128

The True Gentleman is the man whose conduct proceeds from good will and an acute sense of propriety, and whose self-control is equal to all emergencies; who does not make the poor man conscious of his poverty; the obscure man of his obscurity, or anyone of his inferiority and deformity; who is himself humbled if necessity compels him to humble another; who does not flatter wealth, cringe before power, or boast of his own possessions or achievement; who speaks with frankness and always with sincerity and sympathy; whose deed follows his word; who thinks of rights and feelings of others more than his own; and who appears in any company a man with whom honor is scared and virtue safe.

John Walter Wayland wrote that in 1899, the year before the old century ended. I wondered if when such ideas seemed reasonable, even then. Certainly, in 1965 they were more an idealized relic of manhood than anything worth paying attention to. And yet in the ceremonies everyone seemed to take such prattle seriously. When I looked at Sean, his serious demeanor, I almost burst out laughing. His actions contradicted nearly every sentiment in the creed, but he, not any of his more level-headed classmates, was still an officer and, as such, supposed to represent the True Gentleman. How was it, I wondered, that such buffoons ended up in leadership positions? The True Gentleman had been embalmed long ago but left exposed like Lenin in his tomb for everyone to look at and admire as if still living.

After the ceremony, Sean tapped a keg and everyone got thoroughly drunk except those who did not drink—John, the president and several of his friends.

Street Smarts

After the induction, we planned a weekend trip to Chicago to celebrate and to visit the National Headquarters of DAE in Evanston, Illinois. We rented a bus and booked a motel on the Northside near Lincoln Park. Our first day in the city, being good pledges, we hopped on a bus to Evanston and made the rounds of the National Headquarters, but once we dispensed with the formalities of being new members, we reverted to the luxuries of being foot-loose and fancy-free in Chicago. We toured the bars in the Old Town area of Chicago to scope out the women and entertainment. One particular bar had a racially mixed group, and though some of us felt uncomfortable there, we stayed. After a while I noticed Ibby buying drinks for two Negro women. One had blond hair, the other had red hair. With their high heels, they towered over us. I quickly discovered they loved to tell off-color jokes. Soon they were running their hands over us as if testing whether we were man enough for them. Ibby whispered that they were hookers and that he had invited them to come back to the motel and perform for us. I was impressed since I had never seen a prostitute before. I took a mental inventory of their heavy makeup with silver eyeliner and bright red lipstick, their skirts that left little to the imagination: skin-tight as swim suits. They told us we would not be disappointed if we hired them. They gave us a group rate and as soon as we forked over twenty dollars apiece, they took us by the waist and marched out the door. Tom and Ibby, both of whom were terribly drunk, led the way, but after turning down one street and up another, we were lost. The women were not sure which motel we were staying because none of us remembered its name.

Ever vigilant, Trevor acted like a scout on reconnaissance. He looked down a dark street and noticed, at the other end, lights of a bigger boulevard, which, to him, looked familiar.

"That's our street. Let's go this way," he ordered.

Tom told him that it was not wise to go down dark streets and the two women agreed, and pointed several blocks ahead to a well-lit avenue. We were all pretty drunk. Suddenly, Trevor and Larry suggested we have a race

130

back to the motel. I was surprised that Larry wanted to race, but, when he drank, another side of him emerged as if, hidden inside him, was a whole other personality that was suppressed under a mask of passivity. Trevor said that the first team to get there would get first chance with the girls. Trevor and Larry would go down the side street and the rest of us would go to the other way, and he bet an additional ten dollars apiece that he would win. We gave Tom the money, and he agreed to distribute it among the winners. I volunteered to go with Trevor and Larry because supposedly I knew the city better, having grown up in the Chicago suburbs. Yet, truth be told, my only experience in Chicago had been to go on the L to Chicago Bears games. Before I could step over to join them, Jerry grabbed me by the arm and pulled me aside.

"Hey, if they want to be fools, fine. But you know as well as I, it's not safe. Come with us."

I knew he was right and backed off. Instead, I announced that I would signal the start of the race. "On your mark, get set"—-there we were, crouched like runners in set positions and I yelled "Go." We raced down the street, nine guys in slacks and dress shirts and two women in tight, thigh-high shirts and high heels hustling along the sidewalk, laughing, while Trevor and Larry, sprinted at full speed, disappeared down the dark side street. I was sure they were going to win easily. But, to my surprise, even in high heels, the women were quicker than we were. One whose name was apparently Sugar called out to us, "Move your ass, boys, we're gonna make some quick cash."

The Show

We arrived at the motel before Trevor and Larry who seemed to have lost their way, since, even after twenty minutes, they failed to show up. The women grew impatient; they wanted to get down to business and began flirting with us, running their hands down our necks, twirling our hair in their fingers. I felt a wave a panic rush over me. Here I was in front of all the other guys and these women were showing us their bodies, and I felt nothing but discomfort. They stripped and began to kiss, fondle and caress each guy in turn until he was nearly rapt with seeming ecstasy. Then, they'd laugh and wander over to another one of us. I looked at Sugar, her enormous bosoms, and failed to feel aroused, yet discovered that by watching guys get erections I'd gotten an erection too. The tall blond eventually landed in my lap and swiveled her legs around my waist and flung her arms around my neck.

"Lookie here, Katie, we've got a shy one," Sugar called out to her friend. She cocked her head to the side.

"Why, you're cute. Look at that smile. You're some hunk," she said, putting her lips on mine and kissing me like she meant it. Her tongue darted in my mouth. Her hand slipped down my pant leg and soon she discovered my erection and called out, "We have a live one here," and began to stroke me through the fabric. Katie helped out, rubbing my thighs and encouraging me, "You go for it, honey child, you go for it." Sugar pressed her breasts against my face. But they enveloped my face as if in padded vice. I squirmed left then right, trying to catch a breath.

"Oh, honey, that feels so good," she exclaimed and pulled my head against her. Sugar's heavy sweet perfume, made me dizzy. I gulped a quick breath as she pulled back to throw a kiss at Tom. *This would be a really embarrassing way to suffocate,* I thought. She swung her breasts back and forth which felt like being smacked by two punching bags. They were powerful, and she knew how to use them. I put my hands up to push her away. The guys were howling with laughter. The only things I could locate were her breasts. I latched on and shoved back gently, tilting my head up to gasp for some air.

"Well, you are some man. Look at you just taking hold of me," she sung out as I held onto her breasts, my fingers around them as if were palming a basketball in each hand.

She moved back. "That feels real nice. You keep that up, honey."

Sugar's bright teeth glistened. I bared my teeth. Sugar had a round face that radiated kindness and delight. I liked her. I liked how she enjoyed my body, rubbing her hands over my chest and abdomen, how she laughed with her whole body, how she unzipped me, made me feel oddly at ease. She knew how to make what might have been an awkward scene with callow college boys into a playful encounter, a nibbling into sexuality. Katie had this whole time been flicking her hand on my erection. Just when I felt as if I was going to explode, my lap lady stood up and smiled at me, "Save your virginity for some special girl, honey cakes. You are much too sweet to be wasting it on us."

Then they turned their attention to Tom, who was already at full mast. Katie announced that he a good-sized one, one she wanted to try out before they left. Tom smiled at me, looking down at his erection which Katie was fingering furiously. I looked on too. It was large, that was for sure. Any sense of privacy among the guys had been dismissed. I could see the other guys looking at Tom who was smiling, pleased with all the attention. But Sugar and Katie left him on the brink, just as they had me and went, one by one, to the other guys, exposing their erections, fondling them, then letting them go. We yelped and drank and ogled at the spectacle. Any racial barrier, if there was one, became irrelevant when it came to sex. And any modesty we might have laid claim to back at the fraternity house for the moment at least had evaporated.

Mugged

After two hours, the women collected their money and were about to leave when we heard a knock on the door. Jerry opened it. Trevor, his face bruised and his shirt torn, and Larry, his mouth bloody and his head bandaged, staggered in the room. We poured them a glass of beer and they told us what had happened.

About halfway down the alley, three white guys accosted them, demanding their wallets and watches. Trevor told them to bug off and tried to run, but one of the men had a knife and brandished it at Trevor's face. Larry, who'd trained in ROTC at his prep school, attempted to kick the knife out of the guy's hand, but the guy flipped Larry on his back and kicked him several times in the head, while another guy put his foot on Larry's chest to hold him down. Trevor did not fare well either: the third guy slugged him several times—quick jabs— in the face, and knocked him down. They stole their wallets and watches, but before fleeing, the man with the knife ripped holes in Larry and Tervor's dress shirts and said, "If you know what's good for you, boys, you'll go home and forget this happened. Or, next time, we see your ugly faces, it wouldn't be your pretty shirts I'm slicing up."

Trevor and Larry hobbled to the main street——Clark Street or Belmont, and finally flagged down a cop car after two cars drove by without stopping. Cops rolled down their windows and asked, "What's the problem?" Trevor explained how they had been held up and beaten. The cops laughed and told them, "If you're dumb enough to be walking at this hour of the night down that street, you're asking for trouble."

Trevor mouthed off and told the cops to do their job, at which point the driver pointed at Trevor and warned, "Listen kid, I don't know who you think you are. You're probably some smarty college kid from some fancy school who burns his draft card. You and your kind are a dime a dozen here. So button your mouth, and be thankful you're alive."

Larry intervened, apologizing profusely before pleading with the cops to help them: They were cut up, could they get them to a hospital, his dad was a Democratic congressman from Ohio, they probably wouldn't want Mayor Daley to hear how his son was treated. The cop told them to get in the car and they drove them to an emergency room where they were treated and released. Not wanting to get a Congressman riled up, the police arranged for a taxi to drive Larry and Trevor back to the motel. By then, they had figured out the name of the one we were staying in.

After listening intently, Sugar came over to them and gave each a kiss, then, motioning to Katie, left.

"Gad, you were impressive, Jason, the way you took hold of that blonde," Brian said. "You know how to handle the ladies."

"Yeah, you're more of a stud than I thought," Tom chimed in.

I nodded my head. It was nice to have a reputation as a ladies' man. I wasn't going to deny it. Steve and Eric were nodding their heads.

"When she came over to me," Eric said. "I panicked. I could do nothing. I don't know how you kept it together."

"I just decided to let go and enjoy it," I said.

"But you manhandled her boobs!" Eric said.

"They were big," I said.

"Big. They were gigantic!"

I remembered how they pummeled me and how at the time I must have looked like a fool, but here I was the stud of the night. I liked it.

"Where's Jacob?" someone asked. Nobody had seen them since we came back to the motel.

Tom called out for them and we heard Jacob stir in the bedroom. He staggered back into the main room and got another beer.

"You missed the fun," Tom said.

Jacob shook his head. "I didn't want any part of it. "

"Why not? You some sort of fag or something?" Tom persisted, leaning forward in his chair, his voice strident like an inquisitor.

"You want me to be honest?"

"Yeah, of course!"

"We just recited The True Gentleman as a code of conduct. Remember? I just couldn't get involved with those women. It just didn't seem right."

Tom stood and shook Jacob's hand. "I'm sorry. You're a better man than I am," he said. "You took a stand, stood up for what you believed. We all could learn from you."

Jacob smiled and everyone clapped in appreciation. An odd moment, one I hadn't expected, with one of our brothers daring to be different, to be a true gentleman, and the rest of us affirming him.

II: From wrong to wrong the exasperated spirit...

The Incursion

After our return, we lapsed into a strange ennui, into a quiet satisfaction of being free to do as we pleased. We despised the harassment and the living in limbo for half a year, but the upperclassmen quickly accepted us. A new network of friendships formed and the past slid away as if it someone switched the channel and the old shows were no longer on the air. We could party with anyone. We could come and go without restrictions. And yet, it seemed, some of us turned inward, became strangely reclusive, sitting in our rooms, listening to the Beach Boys or in my case Johnny Mathis. As we adjusted to our new status and established new relationships, we dismissed those in our class who we really never cared for. Some fell out of our lives because we did not have to be with them to survive as pledges.

As a result, new cliques emerged. Some began to drink more with the upperclassmen and joined the party crowd. Some focused their attention on academics and dating. Some created small enclaves and hung around in their rooms, playing poker and gin rummy like retired old men.

I tried to move on, fit in with Tom and Jerry (who, by then, had become as famous as the comic book characters with their notorious parties that lasted well into the night), and tried to hook my wagon to their acclaim. And yet I knew that I needed to study hard to maintain passing grades. Dyslexic without the innate skills I envied in other students, I had to grind out grades one test at a time. I enjoyed the partying and drinking —usually Jack Daniels, black—-but part of me wanted to clear my head and make sense of the degradations of Hell Week. My resentment lingered toward Sean and other upperclassmen, which, even with the initiation, gnawed at me. So I resorted to my standard way of coping and withdrew at times and listened to records and did my assignments.

One evening in April, Paul came into our room and turned on the radio.

"Listen to this," he said. "The President is making a speech about why we are in Vietnam. You will not believe the bullshit. He thinks students at Johns Hopkins University will believe him."

Johnson was speaking: *Our objective is the independence of South Vietnam, and its freedom from attack. We want nothing for ourselves—only that the people of South Vietnam be allowed to guide their own country in their own way.*

We will do everything necessary to reach that objective. And we will do only what is absolutely necessary.

In recent months, attacks on South Vietnam were stepped up. Thus, it became necessary for us to increase our response and to make attacks by air. This is not a change of purpose. It is a change in what we believe that purpose requires.

We do this in order to slow down aggression.

We do this to increase the confidence of the brave people of South Vietnam who have bravely borne this brutal battle for so many years with so many casualties.

And we do this to convince the leaders of North Vietnam—and all who seek to share their conquest—of a very simple fact: We will not be defeated. We will not grow tired. We will not withdraw, either openly or under the cloak of a meaningless agreement.

When the address finally ended with Johnson saying good night to his audience, Paul shouted at the radio and made a feeble attempt to kick it, "That's bullshit! Pure bullshit! We want to take over the damn country."

I looked at him. He paced back and forth. "He keeps sending more troops over there. 20,000. He says it's only an incursion. Then he'll add more. Watch him. Before you know it, you'll be marching onto a plane heading to Vietnam," he said. "You'll be another pawn in his chess game with China."

"But he has some points. Look at what he said about defending South Vietnam," I said.

"Do you read?"

"Yes."

"Well, read about the French and what luck they had. You're going to major in History, right? The country is not made up of a north and south any more than we were during the civil war. There are tribal groups dispersed across the country, some loyal to their local leaders, some to the military governments in the large cities. Look at the country, much of it is mountainous. It doesn't neatly divide into two distinct regions," he said. "It's so fucked up."

I'd heard most of the speech and, based on what Johnson said about our not wanting colonies but only wanting to help the south, I felt

140

sympathetic. Helping out made sense. And yet Paul seemed to know so much more than what was being reported on the news. I wondered where he got all of his information, how he knew so much.

Still I was torn. I wanted to fit in and be seen as a regular guy, more like other guys—patriotic and supportive of the President—and less like Paul, who never seemed to fit in, but never minded being an outsider. I felt at times as if my head were in a mixer, sometimes spinning in one direction, sometimes in another, with my brain in the middle, revolving in convoluted circles. I heard Paul and believed him. I heard the President and believed him. I read about the bombings of the North Vietnam and thought it was wrong for Johnson to sanction them. I read about the new civil rights laws and believed he was right in promoting them. I listened to Jacob talk about how we needed to keep the communists out of the South Vietnam. I knew communism was wrong. I heard Paul about how it was not simple. More than anyone, I wanted to impress Paul with my awareness of current events. But I could not keep up with his pace of reading about current events because I had to keep a narrow focus and study more than he did to get decent grades.

Ever since we heisted the Confederate flag and managed to keep our secret, I felt loyal to him. He was, however, not much fun. His work ethic I admired. His intelligence I envied. But his social life I pitied. He seemed a person relentlessly fixated on attaining a glorious career in public service. I still had no career in mind. I wanted to have fun, so I found myself drifting like an unmoored boat away from him.

At that time, I never imagined that I would ever become a friend of Sean or Randy. But over the last few months of school I did. And that bothered me too. Paul could not believe it.

"What are you doing?" he asked one night in May after dinner when he dropped into our room to pick up some books.

"Hey, people can change attitudes. Look what happen to Randy. For months, he'd have nothing to do with Sean. They never spoke. And now, they're friends again."

"But remember what they did to us. And the flag," he said, holding his arms out querulously.

The Incursion

"They're not that bad," I said, "once you get to know them."

"You're losing it," Paul said, smirking at me.

"You don't understand," I said.

"Oh, you're wrong. I do. I see exactly what's happening to you. And that's the sad part. I want it too, to be in the in-crowd," he remarked. He shook his head. "But I'm not going down that road. It leads to trouble, trust me."

"Hey, you do what you need to do," I said, getting mildly irritated. "I will find out for myself." I turned to walk out of the room. He tapped me on the shoulder. He smiled at me and gave me a brief hug.

"Do what you have to do."

I did.

Girlfriend

By drinking with Tom who had befriended Sean, Randy and several other upperclassmen, I became more accepted by them as one of the party guys and grew to like them. I felt relieved as if I had passed some test that demanded I forget Hell Week ever happened and become just one of the guys. I hung around the parties, since now I could drink anytime I wanted. I found, once I got a little drunk, I blended in and could enjoy myself listening to guys talk about their dates, the hot girls in the Kappa Kappa Gamma house.

I even asked out Suzie Chesterfield. I seemed to be attracted to girls whose names sounded like "Sue," hoping they were like the one girlfriend I had on campus. Suzie was famous at the fraternity. Some guys mocked her last name because, as it suggested, she had big boobs. Tom and I went on a double date to a grungy movie theater, known as "the pit," no wider than a garage that sunk down into a dark cavern at the bottom of which was a screen. We saw *The Greatest Story Ever Told*, a film based on the gospels. With stunning scenes of Christ dragging his cross and his hands nailed to the cross, I noticed Suzie averting her eyes several times. I took her hand in mine and asked, "Is this all right?" She whispered, "I'm fine."

After the film, we went to the Monon Grill and had coffee. Tom liked the film. "Man, that was something," he said. "They made him seem real."

We talked about the film for a few minutes. Suzie mentioned that she'd recently picked up a book that had been banned.

Tom asked, "What is it?"

"Ulysses," she said.

"I read that my junior year," Tom said. "It wasn't banned."

"It's the one by Joyce," she said. "Not by Homer."

"Homer who?" Tom asked. "Is he a homo? Do I know him?"

Suzie laughed, "Funny. Very funny, Tom."

She turned to me, her long angular face which belied a seriousness and intelligence that churned beneath it, and asked, "Did you read the book?"

I admitted I did not. She described the book and the scene at the end with his wife.

"I imagine his wife is supposed to be Penelope," I said.

"Yes, exactly. I loved it," she said. "Especially the—what do you call it? —the final soliloquy is my favorite part, where the wife says, 'Yes I said, yes. Yes I will' is so perfect."

Tom asked, "Do you know of any other girls in the sorority who will say 'Yes, I will'?"

Suzie wrinkled her brow. "What the...? Why do you ask?"

"Our best friend Jerry, he's wanting to date. He's a nice guy and..."

She cut him off. "I'll ask around."

She turned to me, clearly offended by his intrusion, and went on to ask what other books I liked. I told her that I liked Hemingway. She loved *For Whom the Bells Toll,* the final scene when Robert Jordon stays back to protect his love, Marie, so she can escape.

"Can you imagine knowing that you will die, just lying there, waiting for soldiers to come up the pass to kill you?"

"It would not be too bad if you knew, as you laid there, that you had lived, I mean lived fully," I said.

"I suppose," she said. Taking a sip of her coffee, she stared at me. I found that I did not look at her boobs but into her eyes, which were a stunning amber, glistening with a fiery intensity.

On the way back to her sorority, she held my hand and she talked about her family. Her father, a prominent banker in Indianapolis, had pancreatic cancer and was not expect to live. Her mother and younger sister told her, just the week before, that he had a year, at most. That was all.

I squeezed her hand. "I'm sorry."

"Life is not fair sometimes," she said. She brushed a long stand of her hair that had fallen across her cheek back in place behind her ear.

I hugged her at the doorstep. I noticed Tom was kissing his date. Suzie's face, calm and receptive, was only inches from mine. I could feel her breath on my cheek. I tilted my lips and kissed her gently. She responded and pulled me tighter to her.

"Thanks," I said.

"No, thank you," she said. "I hope we can go out again."

"Me too!" I blurted out. She giggled at my response.

"So call," she said, putting her finger to my lips. "Call."

Play by Play

Back at the house, I went to Sean's room. Six guys were strewn like a misbegotten tribe on chairs or the couch or the floor. An open keg sat like one of them on a chair. It was the only one upright. I filled a mug and sat down.

Tom came into the room and pointed at me. "Hey, you would not believe it. Jason made the moves on Chesterfield."

"No way!" Sean exclaimed. "I tried to touch her boobs once and she shoved me away."

"He kissed her and held her. I saw him," Tom said as if doing me a favor.

Sean jumped in. "Hey, Jason. I bet she'd be a good fuck."

I smiled weakly.

"You gonna fuck her, man?" Randy asked. "That would be some fuck. Her boobs in your face. You're one lucky dude."

I sipped my beer and nodded my head. What was I to say? Suzie was a bright, intelligent girl who knew far more than I did about literature and seemed so vulnerable to me as if she'd endured taunts about her body her whole life. She probably was aware that guys ogled her and made jokes about the size of her breasts. I wanted to defend her, but Randy bragged about how he had gotten into Pattie Janson's pants. "She wiggled and squirmed like an octopus. Next time I bet I can get payroll," he said as if by talking about her, he was convincing himself—and those listening—that he was a man.

"Way to go man," Tex, a junior with a Texas drawl as long as his arm, said.

I was stunned how guys recounted play by play what they did on dates, how they felt a girl up, how they got into her pants—every detail as if the girls were like the prostitutes in Chicago merely there as instruments of our pleasure.

As I sat listening to them boast how they had gotten a little, I remembered, back in high school, when I was over at Phil Solerno's house for his birthday. After candles, cake and ice cream, ten of us guys were lounging around in a sun room, sprawled out on chairs and couches and the conversation turned to girls. One guy, a wiry Italian, boasted how he had taken a girlfriend of mine, JoAnne, to the Lazy River Motel and made her a woman. Other guys asked for details and enjoyed the careful exposition of how he disrobed her—blouse, bra, skirt, panties—but the sex part he left vague. Was he making it all up? After his story, others chimed in, telling of exploits or hankerings for one or another broad. Finally, it was my turn. Phil asked what I had done, which, up to that point as a junior in high school, included nothing—not even making-out. Phil told me I was good-looking and I could have any girl I wanted. What was the problem?

I stammered and claimed I just had not found the right girl. Someone asked if I was more interested in boys and everyone laughed. My forehead, as it often does when I'm anxious, quickly poured with sweat. My face, my back and chest became clammy.

"What's wrong?" Phil jibed, walking up to me, standing over me, his hands on his hips. "You a little gay?"

With no ready response, I folded my arms over my chest and looked at my shoelaces—one was untied— and avoided his eyes.

Someone said, "Hey, it's a party. Lay off."

Phil slapped my head, "Hey, Jason, it's just a joke. Laugh already."

I laughed, but, as soon as I could, I made some lame excuse and fled the party, feeling as if I had been exposed and, equally, feeling horrified that guys talk about their so-called dates as if they were meat on racks.

Here I was again, listening to guys brag.

Prior to that night, I had nothing to say because the girls I had dated, nice enough as they were, seemed as uninterested in me as I was in them. We'd smile at one another over coffee or a milkshake and I'd make polite conversation—talk about classes, discuss the weather, inquire about their taste in food or music or movies—but inevitably I'd be gripped with anxiety in the middle of it when I realized I had no idea what to say next. And then large beads of sweat would form on my scalp and like an open faucet cascade over my forehead, cheeks and chin. My date would look over at me and ask, "Are you all right?" I'd look at the table and wipe up a spill. Then my date would suggest it was time to get back to her house. I'd agree and escort her to the door, shake her hand and dash back to my room. Mortified, I could never figure out how a guy managed to get intimate with a girl, to tell her his dearest secrets and to convince her that he was trustworthy and that they should make love. The chasm between "Hello, nice to meet you" and "I love you" seemed as wide as the Grand Canyon. I was clueless how to connect with a girl—with a person I did not know— and yet most guys seemed to have the knack. So, inevitably after my dates, when I returned to the house, I'd go into the debriefing room where the guys would recount their exploits, but I'd I avoided being put in the same position as I was in high school at Phil's house. Before the conversation of dating, I'd excused myself. I'd read and listen to music until late at night, and mostly, sleep on the couch rather than the dorm because the guys, jerking off, caused me to get aroused and kept me awake as they seemed to be priming their pump for a desire, unquenchable in their own hand, that nonetheless lured them to pant and groan and writhe until they were spent.

On this first night, when I did have something to offer, I realized that no one wanted to know how interesting Suzie was, how she knew about Joyce and Hemingway, how she was grieving because of her father's terminal illness. So I left them to their braggadocio and post-date analyses, pleased that rather than subject myself to twenty questions, I could go to my room. Paul was proud of me. Maybe I was learning something about myself.

I enjoyed listening to records, the violet chords of Percy Faith or melancholy of Johnny Mathis singing "It's Not for Me to Say" or the angst of Judy Garland singing "Keep on Smiling" at Carnegie Hall. I loved to sing, "When You're Smiling" and "You Made Me Love You" and, of course, "Over the Rainbow." I don't know what it was about her voice that made me feel as if she were singing to me, to a part of me that yearned to feel something as deeply as she did. I'd sing along with her, putting the volume on high. Since Paul and I shared a room, my singing to myself came on nights that he was out studying or on a date with a girl he'd met and liked. I found the alone time meant more to me than being with others and, at least at the time, felt safer.

The Poet

Suzie's father died sooner than expected. Distraught, she left in mid-semester to be home with her mother who had taken his death badly and suffered a near nervous breakdown. We had one last night out where she told me how her father had wanted her to continue school—and that she planned to come back in the fall—but could not stay since her younger sister needed someone at home. With Suzie gone, I felt empty. I didn't want to date anyone else.

One evening, as I read the newspaper in the house library after dinner, I noticed an oddly colored book, turquoise-green, with a blue oval insignia with silver lettering on its spine. It reminded me of the prestigious Heritage Press books my father had purchased as an investment—objects to admire, not to be touched. I don't know why, but I took the book off the shelf. It was *The Complete Poems of T. S. Eliot*. I blew the dust off the top seam and flipped randomly to a page in the middle. "Time present and time past / are both perhaps present in time future..." That notion struck a chord in me, how past and present were woven into the future. I continued reading:

Footfalls echo in the memory
Down the passage which we did not take
Towards the door we never opened
Into the rose-garden.

I felt as if Eliot had just dissolved my own notion of time like sugar in water and it became something I could no longer wind like a wrist watch, something I could see. Instead of clock time, I was entering my own mother's garden, standing by the yellow and red petals of her roses.

Those footfalls, the ones I heard in the night when I slept in the hotel in New York City, during a senior trip, were of the boy coming into my room, sliding into the bed beside me, his warm body next to mine, breathing as I was, sleeping as I should have been. They were the footfalls of customers going into the door of a small grocery store on 42nd Street,

149

two rows of canned food and chips. They were my footfall through the door I did open, to the bookstore nearby. I stood in front of a shelf and stared at magazine covers with nearly naked guys who were my age on them. I picked up one magazine, than another. On each page a boy, some reference to his background and his likes. Photographs of him, mostly naked. The boys stared back at me, and the heat that rose in my body was not from anxiety as I experienced with the girls, but with excitement at seeing boys like me, advertising their bodies for anyone to take.

Those few lines in the poem were like gasoline sparking my imagination. I held the book in my lap to cover the erection that had poked up at the memory of those boys. I breathed deeply. It was not my book. It belonged to the fraternity library. No one ever read it. I wanted it.

I shoved it under my arm and took it upstairs to my room. I kept the book by my desk and discovered words I'd never encountered before, ones like "appetency." Eliot used it in mysterious ways—"... the world moves / In appetency, on its metalled ways..." I became drunk on the language. "Eructation of the unhealthy souls" might have meant anything to me, but the sound of it mattered more. It was the sound of my pledge brothers vomiting the second night of Hell Week, the sound of sleepless nights waiting for someone to bark out, "Time to get up, pledges."

No one used Eliot's words—not "appetency," not "eructation"—when they spoke. I reserved time to read the poems after Paul had gone to bed. Sometimes I'd fall asleep on the couch with the book in my hand. Eliot was speaking to me with words I'd never heard, about thoughts I'd never had.

The Visit

On one weekend, my mom came to visit me. She arrived on a Friday in her white Thunderbird. I was quite excited. I'd never spent much time with her alone.

We played a round of golf at a local course. My mom was a former physical education teacher and had a powerful swing for a woman. Although slim, she strode with long confident strides and played quickly. When she came up to a ball, she'd pick her club, set the bag down, line up the shot and swing. One shot followed another naturally. I had learned the game from her and had a similar approach to the game. Afterward, we drove into the country and had lunch in a quaint diner.

"How are your classes going?" she asked as she sipped her iced tea.

"Fine. I think I'm getting the hang of it. I have to study more than other guys, but I do well and like my courses—most of them."

"Some you don't like?"

"I have a Speech class and I really get nervous speaking in public. You know, I sweat and feel like crawling in a hole."

"I didn't like to speak in public either. I dreaded it. But, you know, the more you do it, the better you get at it." She fluffed her heir back.

"Are you dating?" she asked.

"Some. Not a lot. I met a real nice girl, Sue, my first day on campus, but we're good friends." I told her about Suzie, how her dad just died.

"I'm so sorry. Pancreatic cancer is dreadful. Most people don't last a year."

"He didn't last even that."

"Sad. Oh, by the way, have you heard from Jeff?" she asked, tilting her head up.

"He called me once. He wants me to come visit him in Urbana."

"That's a long way."

"I know. And I don't know how I would get there and back on a weekend."

"Maybe you'll just have to wait until summer."

"Yeah, I suppose. But this summer, if Jack is better, we're going to Europe, right?"

"Yes, you are. Your father has purchased a car that you will pick up in London. That should be some adventure, a whole two months."

"Not much time for Jeff, then."

"I suppose not."

I liked that she kept asking about Jeff. She knew we were best friends. She understood me sometimes better than I did myself. I missed Jeff. I'd wanted to take off a weekend and hitchhike to see him, but it never worked out. I felt a hollow pit in my stomach when I thought of him.

We chatted about dad and how hard he was working—many weekends at the office. After lunch, I had her drive around the countryside and showed her several of the sinkholes and quarries. She told me how my brother, finally released from the hospital, had been recuperating.

Although I had not been aware of it, I realized that we had a lot in common. She enjoyed literature like me. She'd read *Ulysses* as had Suzie. I changed the topic. "I think that Suzie is an English major. I'm not sure. But I'm thinking of majoring in it too," I told her.

"Oh, honey, that would be wonderful. But give it time. You do not need to choose until next year," she said.

Freed from my father's presence, she seemed more herself, more engaging than when he hovered around her.

"Your brother hopes to transfer to Ashbury," she said. "He has started the paperwork. Your father approves of the move, as do I. Ohio was not right for him. Or your dad. Too many ghosts, his mother dead and all."

"I know," I said. She looked away and sighed.

"It still haunts him," she said. "I suppose it always will."

On Sunday morning, she drove back home. I found that I missed her. She had been my cheerleader throughout high school, coming to every football and basketball game, driving me back from practice, encouraging me to date. My father rarely came to my games. It had been her. She made sure I knew that she cared about what I did.

The Primitive Terror

One evening, Paul came in our room and asked if he could talk with me. I was delighted to see him since we had drifted apart. He asked if I was all right. I asked him why.

He quietly shut the door and stood in front of it, his hand against its frame, as if he were holding something back and looked at me strangely.

"The guys have been saying that you're acting weird," he attested, frowning as he spoke, twisting his jaw right and left.

"So, the guys always talk."

"It's not just weird," he said, not looking at me, his eyes averted, focused at my desk and the book of poems on it.

"Oh, they think I'm weird because I read poetry, is that it?" my voice more irritated than I expected.

"No, no, not that." He pressed his feet together, stood upright like a soldier on duty, came across the room and sat on the couch. He sandwiched his hands between his legs as if tightening a vise.

"Okay, say it. What is it?"

"Well, you know how you have been so excited about your mom's visit," he spoke hurriedly, "and, admit it, how you don't date much, and how you have not much interest in girls, and—all right, I lied—how you're reading poetry, really weird poetry?"

He pointed at the book on my desk. "I mean I looked at the guy, Eliot; he is strange, you have to admit it. I read a lot of books, as you know. And poetry too. But he talks about the wasteland, fire sermons and has cats talk and hollow men and it just does not make sense and you make these odd notes in the margins of a book that isn't even yours."

"Who gave you permission to look in my books?" I blurted out.

"Jason, it's not your book. It belongs to the fraternity library."

I picked up the book and shoved it at him, "Fuck you. Put it back. Nobody was reading it. Nobody could understand him. It wasted away on the shelf. No one ever picked it up. There was dust all over it."

Paul motioned for me to sit down, "I'm sorry. Here, take it back: it might

153

as well be yours—you've made it yours. But it's not the book. Not that at all. I should not have mentioned it." He hesitated again, but this time, his eyes narrowed as if concentrating intensely and he went on, "You listen to music, sing along with it, play Judy Garland who's not exactly hip, stay up late by yourself and sleep on the couch and, the way you talk about your mother, about her visiting you, well..."

He trailed off and pursed his lips. He continued to talk, telling me that he liked me, trusted me, had admired how we pulled off the heist of the flag, and had enjoyed having me as a roommate in the first semester. He had no problem with me, no problems at all. None.

As Paul talked, his face changed. At first he was sanguine, then almost jocular, as if he were letting me know my fly was open, but then his face tightened, his jaw tensed, his words became jumbled, leaping from one thing to another. I interrupted him, "What the fuck are you talking about, Paul?"

He looked directly at me. "I just came from a room with the other guys, Jerry and Ibby, Steve and Luis, and some others, Bill and Sean, and they were saying, all of them, that you act like a... a homosexual." He paused and looked me straight in the eye, "Are you?"

I could tell that he was worried. He had undressed each night, every morning with me. He wanted to be safe. His face pleaded with me to reassure him.

My mind flashed on Steve, overweight and distraught, who, over the semester, I'd spent so many hours listening to, sympathizing with his woes, his inability to get dates. Here he was saying I was gay. I felt a surge of rage quicken in me. I took a breath and pushed it back.

I never imagined someone directly asking me that question, but somehow, as if the lines had been written for me in a play, I knew exactly what to say and do. It was as if I had subconsciously practiced it, rehearsed it, knew how to contain myself, keep my face relaxed, my expression neutral and my voice calm and assured.

"Of course not," I said.

His face wanted more.

So I added, "I can understand their concern; I mean I might worry too. It's just that I like to have alone time. Besides I'm shy. An introvert. It is hard for me to make friends, let alone girlfriends. And I just have not met a girl who turns me on and who is not, as with Suzie, caught up in family difficulties. Many of them seem insipid, full of mindless patter."

He smiled. "That's what I thought. That's what I told them."

"Thanks," I smiled back. "It's scary to think a homosexual might be in our midst."

He laughed and invited me to join the other guys, to get a brew and I did, getting quite drunk, passing out on the floor so someone had to lug me to my room. I woke on my couch. It was two in the morning; a brazen desk light jabbed at my eyes. I went to the desk to turn it off, saw the book opened, paged through it and came to page one hundred and thirty-three as if it had been written for me:

the backward look behind the assurance
Of recorded history, the backward half-look
Over the shoulder, towards the primitive terror.

I pressed my fingers on the words "primitive terror" and held my head in my hand. *Primitive terror.* That was it. Someone finding out that I was attracted to guys is what I feared most, feared most because I could not even accept it myself, and now it had come home to roost, and so, for the time being, I made an effort to attend parties faithfully and date several girls. It was just enough to keep suspicion off me. I finished out the year, looking forward to the next year when I would be an upperclassman and could define how and what I did without having a bunch of guys telling me how to act or what to do.

The Guide

During the summer, my brother Jack and I used our savings to have a grand tour of Europe. We picked up the car that our dad had purchased, then ferried from England across the channel to France and headed off on a two mouth journey that took us through France, Italy, Switzerland, East and West Germany, Denmark, Norway, Scotland and back to London. In Paris, we found a pension on the Left Bank and bought sleeping bags so that we could camp as much as possible to save money. From Paris, we headed south, stopping at small inns, eating bread soup and at one inn trying to figure out if we should eat the whole shrimp, head and all. We feasted on baguettes, local cheeses and wine, and slept on a beach in the Camargue along the azure water of the Mediterranean, the historic sea that Ulysses traveled in his voyages. I thought how Suzie would enjoy being here and wondered how she was doing with her family, her father being lost but unlike Ulysses, lost for good. By the time we wound up and down, in and out of the coastal roads of Provence and Liguria, we were delighted to be in Rome. Even in the scalding heat, we walked everywhere to see the ruins and churches and the sound and light shows which brought history back to life. But we'd gotten tired of being sightseers and, even as we scaled the mountain passes in Switzerland, even after walking deep into the blue icy corridors of a glacier, we wanted to let loose, which we did in Munich at the Hofbrauhaus.

For three nights, we sat at the long tables, ordering pitchers, singing songs we didn't understand and watching the sturdy ladies lug eight large steins at a time. The men, mostly middle-age, drunk like us, slobbered over each other as they sang and drank. By the time we got back to the camp ground, the front gate would be locked, and so we'd climb over the wall and stagger to our tents while trying to avoid the invisible guy lines in a maze of tents.

One afternoon, we decided to go on an excursion to the countryside and visit Dachau, which our guidebook listed as a four star attraction, ten miles out of Munich. At the time, I didn't know anything about Nazi camps.

156

My history books focused mostly on the invasion and the major World War II battles, and, if referenced in the text, the camps were not something our teachers discussed.

At the gate with the sign "Arbeit Macht Frei" on it, which, according to my dad, made sense since a man without work was a man with no future or real freedom. We paid a nominal fee, were given a brochure, and wandered through a large courtyard. We were giddy from wine we'd had earlier with lunch, but as we entered the museum, our mood changed. In glass exhibits, we saw photographs of men and women, starved and bedraggled, staring hollow-eyed at the camera. In other photographs, the corpses like cubist figures were piled fifteen feet high. I found myself getting sick. My brother pulled on my arm, "Let's get out of here." But despite my revulsion, I was captivated and wanted to spend more time looking around. Jack followed me.

Nearby, I saw a man in a uniform talking in broken English to a small crowd of people. He looked as if he was a tour guide, so we went over. The man reached out and shook our hands and explained that at the end of the war he had been a guard at the camp.

"I'd joined the armed forces like many of my friends to support our war effort," he said. "I moved through the ranks and became one of the elite, an SS officer. I thought that it was a good career move. I was ambitious. When I was assigned to the camp, I thought that it was a work camp and a step up, promotion. It was, but it had its price."

He went on to explain how that telling about his experience was his way to remember what he might otherwise want to forget. He came here twice a week. A tall man, dignified with a large square face and silver hair combed straight back on his head, he brought us first to the building where human experiments were performed. More photographs showed tanks where naked men were submerged in freezing water to determine how long they could survive in such extreme cold. Their eyes looked up at the photographer with such desperation. They seemed to be asking, "Why are you doing this to me?" I wanted to reach out and pull them from the water. Our guide said that the men were left in the water until they died. The navy wanted to know how long sailors might last in ocean water if their ship was sunk. In another experiment, prisoners were left in the cold of winter with different types of clothing to determine how long they could survive before freezing to death. He described how some men lost limbs and others lingered from infections wounds that had turned gangrene, while still others were deprived of oxygen—all in the name of "science." On a long wall, and in front of each experiment, the victims stared at me as if I were complicit. The gaunt wide-eye horror in their eyes asked for mercy. Dr. Rascher, the man in charge of the experiments, we learned, believed that he was performing noble experiments on hypothermia to save Luftwaffe pilots and soldiers. He never admitted to doing wrong. He added experiments with heat and fire that became like baking people alive. I was dumbfounded by the extent of the atrocities.

"Come on," my brother pulled on my arm. "We don't need to hear any more of this."

"You may not, but I do," I said and stepped away from him.

"Why?"

"I don't know. I just do."

"You're weird," he said. "I'll meet you outside. But hurry up."

Intrigued by the guide's own complicity, I stayed and followed him to the barracks where, fifty in a room, were crammed together in bunks which looked like coffins hammered next to and on top of each other. I sat on the hard wood edge of one and looked down the rows—an assembly line of horrors.

"I don't want to show you this next stage in the process," he told us, "but this is where the final process began." Down a pathway, we came to an unassuming building that, on three sides, was built into an embankment like a basement floor in a house. The tour guide grew noticeably agitated and was slapping his hand unconsciously against his leg. He told us that these were the so-called showers.

"This is where they were killed," the guard said.

A woman with a large Canon camera that, on occasion she used, snapping a photo of the barracks, asked, "If you don't mind, I just do not understand how anyone could treat other human beings as you did."

The guard stopped, gazed around the complex—his eyes slowly traversing on the wire fence, the gate, the wooden barracks—and took a long breath. "That is something," he said," I've wrestled with— how we

158

became instruments of evil. I suppose you needed to be here in Germany at the time. Our economy had collapsed. People were starving. The new regime took control. Things were improving. They told us that the Jews were to blame for much of what had happened. The newspapers and radio called them swine—pigs—and, well." He sighed. "We believed it. We saw them as animals, no more than swine."

The woman fingered her camera, adjusting the lens unconsciously. "Thank you," she said and muttered something to her companion who shook his head.

A young man, my age, perhaps getting courage from his mother's questions, asked, "Who was sent to Dachau to be killed—criminals?"

"No, not many criminals. Political dissidents mostly," he said. "Jews, of course. Some communists. Some Catholics and even Protestants who opposed the Reich. And homosexuals, of course, a good many of them."

I wanted to ask, "Why homosexuals?" but did not want to call attention to myself.

I peered in the doorway. I thought of the pig in the stream, his large body decaying, left there, and realized that this guard, if he saw a Jew or a homosexual, would have had no more reaction to one of them than I had to the pig. Just another carcass. Dispose of it as the others. The floor, although molded and cracked, looked in places like the cement floors in showers at school, but the room was ten times the size, as if it could hold a couple of football teams. It had no windows. Only cement walls. The guide explained how the prisoners stripped and were herded there under guise of cleaning the lice from the long train trips. The door would slam shut. Cyanide would pour through the vents in the ceiling and, as he told it, with them crammed in so tightly, many died standing up. I imagined the immense dark that came over them as the doors slammed. Naked, pressed tightly against one another, they waited for water, for refreshing water to cleanse them. But none came.

The guide did not linger in that doorway. He wanted us to move along to the next station of death—the brick building with the ovens. His job, he said, was to run the crematorium. He showed how bodies much like pizzas on a metal platter were shoved in the large tubular furnaces, one on top of another, mimicking how he had done his work, motioning how the platter went inside the cavernous hole. Once the ovens were filled, he would gradually increase the temperature, burning them until they were ash. He made sure that there were no remains. Only ash. He showed the instrument panel and the knobs that he turned. He explained that these ovens were carefully constructed with the best materials—heat-proof brick—to increase efficiency and allow him to put the temperature at the maximum level to burn the remains. He seemed proud of the technology and poked at the bricks to show how, decades later, they held up.

He smiled and rubbed his hand over their surface, almost lovingly. But he caught himself and took a deep breath and brought us to what is now a memorial with lovely flowers surrounding it but was the place where the ashes of the dead were dumped.

One of the other people asked if the people in the town of Dachau—the town visible from where we stood—knew what was happening. He shook his head. He did not know if they did. Yet every few days and sometimes twice a day a cloud of smoke, often noxious because some bodies did not burn well, wafted over the town. But he added almost as an afterthought, "These camps are like your prisons in the United States, no? They are set aside, out of town, away from people, and, as with our people, no one asks what happens in them, what sort of things are done to prisoners. 'It's none of our business, right?"

No one disagreed with him.

As I listened to him, I thought how it must have been for a young soldier to find himself in the midst of such evil and not knowing or having a way out. When he described the smell of burning flesh, I remembered in fourth grade, a nursing home near the school burned down, killing, we later learned, ten of the residents. The odor—sharp like vinegar—knifed through the air and the teacher ushered us inside, closing the windows, not telling us what she knew.

I knelt on the ground and touched my hands to the earth, thinking how, under my fingers, lay the remains of thousands of Jews, Catholics, homosexuals, enemies of the Third Reich. I wished that I knew how to pray. But no words came to me. I was silent.

"That is the tour," the former guard said. I stood and brushed off my hands as he passed from person to person, looking us intently in the eye, and shook each hand and thanked us for coming.

"You must not forget what was done. This is why I come here, so others will know and remember, lest we do it again out of some fear or in the name of some deluded ideal."

I thanked him too, but wondered how he lived with himself, knowing what he had done. I gazed at the sculpture of barbed-wire fence and thought of the prisoners, ravenous from hunger, mad with abuse, who leapt on the wire just to be shot, to be done with it.

As if in a trance, I wandered around, revisited several buildings, and looked at the ghastly pictures, the faces of the doctor, so benign, smiling in front of his torture chamber as if it were a shrine. I could not get the images of those men with bones for bodies out of my head. How could anyone do that to another human being?

A City Divided

The awful horror of World War II came back to me when we went to West Berlin and camped outside of the city by an iron fence that divided East Germany from West Berlin, which floated like a democratic island in the midst of a communist sea. At night, I could see the guards marching back and forth with their German Shepherd dogs and rifles so they seemed like Nazis to me and I was in a concentration camp. No matter where we went in Berlin, there was always the barbed wire, always the guards, always the dogs on leashes. I sensed what it might have been like to be the Jew, consigned to a ghetto. It seemed so far in the past, yet the world was still divided into sections. East. West. Political ideology divided them. Eastern Germany surrounded Berlin, its army marching back and forth around it so that those living inside were like animals in a cage. Everyone living in Berlin at that time must have felt the same way.

Hell Week paled when I thought of what happened in Germany, the country of my mother's family. Sean's face flashed before me. Perfect Aryan. Hitler's ideal.

For several nights, I obliterated the haunting images by going with my brother to flashy, packed bars with kids our age. Since the city never shut down, my brother and I clamored to the bars at all hours. Jack urged me to find some chicks, but I rarely did. He'd see girls standing in a clique and introduce himself and I tagged along.

"This is my younger brother," he'd call out.

"Nice to meet you," I'd say.

When he went off to dance with his girl, I would awkwardly ask where the others were from—trying to make small talk. After a few minutes, they would excuse themselves and wander away. Sometime, after the bars, my brother and I would go to Potsdamer Platz at five in the morning to watch the sunrise at the wall. Standing there on the raised platform watching the guards on the other side watching us and at the buildings with their bricked-up windows, made it appear as if the war had never ended but had taken on another shape and form.

Wanting to see East Berlin, we traveled across Checkpoint Charlie, which seem innocuous at first—just a block long with two gates that lifted on either end and between them empty space. But when we left West Berlin and ventured to that middle ground, terror crept into my body. I was leaving the familiar world to enter a territory that was considered enemy land. Crossing that no man's land, I felt as if I was in limbo, neither in one place nor in another. Once the guards inspected our passports and we passed into the East sector, I felt safe. We strolled in a city that seemed, at least compared to West Berlin, to have fallen asleep—or, if not asleep, drugged into a silence. Many lots where buildings once stood remained empty with the bricks strewn about. Few cars. Empty thoroughfares. Museums with few people to gaze at magnificent paintings. Restaurants with empty chairs and tables. Pedestrians in dull gray and brown jackets walking unhurriedly down silent streets. Along one street, when we passed a construction site, some workers asked for a Kennedy coin. We gave several away. We looked at the wall from the Eastern side and I imagined those who dared to cross it, hundreds of citizens, many guards, and died in no man's land. I thought how ugly ideology was, how that guide at Dachau warned me of the evil of it, how it cast people apart and made some think they were better, more righteous, than others. The eyes of the prisoners, particularly of those in freezing water, kept niggling at me. I felt a shiver in my body, a numb ache for escape that I knew none of those prisoners found, unless death is an escape. I never wanted to see those eyes again.

I thought that, after a war, we should have learned about divisions. But here it was, happening again, in what used to be the capital of Germany. Why did people continue to cast one group—or way of life—out? What might have happened to me if I was found out, if someone discovered my attraction to other guys? How would I get beyond those feelings and be like other guys? I knew that's what I had to do. It was not safe to feel as I did. I could be one of the numbered, one left as ashes with countless others.

At that moment, I wanted desperately to drive back to West Germany and from there to get as far away from Germany as I could.

Home Away from Home

And so we headed north toward Denmark but stopped along the way in Hamburg to visit Dean and Karen O'Neill. Karen was the daughter of a close friend of my parents, who'd insisted we stopped by to see them. Newlyweds, they lived on an army base in Hamburg. The housing, much like low- income projects, consisted of rows and rows of one- story attach units with small single-family apartments. Dean, a tall, angular guy, greeted us with a firm handshake. Karen hugged us, clearly glad to have someone she knew.

"I've so looked forward to your visit. You know I love your parents. They are the best. How long can you stay? You can stay as long as you like," she effused. "I'm starved for Americans." A petite woman, she dressed impeccably, wearing the Lord and Taylor blouses and skirts, evidence that her parents, as ours, had trained her well in how to look her best.

We stayed two days, playing Monopoly, a game that always irritated me since it felt as if everyone playing it was trying to cut another player's throat. But once I got into the game, I grabbed as much property as I could, pleased when someone landed on my property so that I could milk them of their cash reserves. We ate steaks and potatoes, "American food," as Karen said, and drank local beer well into the night.

On our second evening, Dean played General MacArthur's famous 1956 address to Congress, the one he made when he was dismissed by President Truman during the Korean War. I listened to it, to his speaking in a deep mellifluous voice, *I address you with neither rancor nor bitterness in the fading twilight of life, with but one purpose in mind: to serve my country. The issues are global, and so interlocked that to consider the problems of one sector, oblivious to those of another, is but to court disaster for the whole. While Asia is commonly referred to as the Gateway to Europe, it is no less true that Europe is the Gateway to Asia, and the broad influence of the one cannot fail to have its impact upon the other...*

His voice full of melodrama plodded on for forty minutes. As I sat there, I wanted to kick the record player. Finally MacArthur spoke of old soldiers never dying but fading away. I would have preferred his dying.

After the speech, Dean said, "You know he should have been President. He was amazing. West Point grad. Very literate. Instead, they put in the bland old Ike. What a horrendous mistake."

My brother agreed. "What a great speech."

"What do you think?" Dean asked me.

"I don't know. It seemed a little over the top," I admitted.

"Over the top?" Dean said, his face flushed. "Over the top?" He stood up, took several steps in my direction, glared at me, while Karen grabbed another beer and gave it to him as if it could quell his ire.

"Yeah." I said, sipping on my beer. "He sounds like some Shakespearean actor in love with his voice."

"Let's order some pizza," Karen said cheerfully.

My brother walked across the room to Dean, standing by him for a moment. "My brother's a little off the wall sometimes," he said.

"What do you want on your pizza?" Karen asked. "Dean?"

"Pepperoni."

"Jason?"

"Anchovies," I said.

"Anchovies?" Dean said, turning around to look at me.

My brother slapped him on the back. "See, I told you. He's fucked up!"

Everyone laughed, including me. I lost at Monopoly that night, went completely bankrupt early in the game and excused myself to wander around the barracks, down one street and another, looking at the identical gray clapboard facades, the single light at the entrances and, coming and going, soldiers, dressed in their green uniforms, and their wives in short skirts. What our army was doing in Germany I was not sure. But we were here, setting up our villages, keeping our soldiers and their wives comfortably ensconced in a gated communities. When I returned, my brother had won big time, having Boardwalk and Park Place. I went to bed and wondered if our army bases in Germany were poised to attack East Germany, to start another war, to wipe out communism. It seemed all like a board game where someone had all the dice, all the moves, and the rest of us waited to throw the dice.

Home at Last

We stayed the night and left the next morning for Denmark, heading ever northward, to Histshals, where we ferried to Norway. While on board, I suggested to Jack that we should have an adventure and go as far north as we could, skirting the Arctic Circle, traveling well into the land of the midnight sun. I'd looked at the map of Norway. There were roads. We could do it. Jack agreed.

The farther north we went, the more I felt free of the dread that had come over me in Germany. We set our goal to reach Tromso, more than two hundred miles above the Arctic Circle. The roads narrowed as we drove into a majestic, verdant wilderness. We'd pitch a tent on a hillside overlooking some vale at ten at night and the sky was as bright as if it were midday. One morning we awoke to the sound of hooves plodding around our tent. We opened the flap and a herd of sheep were grazing around us. We set our sleeping bags out in the tall grass and drank a hot cup of coffee with them. They seemed quite happy to have us among them, coming up and nuzzling at our backs with their snouts. On our way south, skirting the coast, the roads would end abruptly at a fjord. We'd ferried across and pick it up again. The road was like sliced sausage, each link cut by water, and connected again on the other side. We reached Bergen, nestled in a coastal valley, and knew that, by crossing on a ferry to Scotland, we'd be on the last leg of grand tour.

On the boat to Scotland, as I was standing on deck, watching the water swirl and slash against the hull, a man with a beret and long hair came up to me.

"Charming isn't it?"

"Yes, amazing."

"Come this way often?" he asked.

"First time. My brother and I are heading back to London and from there Chicago," I said.

"America?"

"Yes, afraid so."

"Bad time of it this summer with Watts, hadn't it?"

"I'm afraid I don't know what you mean," I said. He pulled out a newspaper and pointed to the headlines, how the black section of Los Angeles had been roiling with riots, blocks burned to ash.

"What's with your blacks?" he asked as if I were in charge of them.

"Fed up with racism, I suspect."

I thought of Dr. King and the confederate flag and how, in a matter of decades, the insults of segregation had moved out of the South and spread north and west. But what could I, as a white person, say?

"You're supposed to be the land of liberty. Is that all illusion?" he said, leaning toward me with a menacing expression. "All like a Hollywood hype?"

"I don't know," I said and moved away from him, wanting to dissociate myself from the riots. I hurried along the guardrail, the dark force of the sea roiling under me, found a deck chair, snuggled into it, pulled my jacket tight around my neck and fell asleep.

Back home, I was delighted to play golf again, swim in the pool, and just relax—and blot out images of Dachau that still haunted me. But at night, I'd browsed through the booklet I bought at Dachau and let the eyes to those liberated survivors look back at me and ask, "Are you one of them?" When I thought of the tour guide, dignified as he was, with his proud military bearing, I wondered if at night, when he wasn't doing his job, when his loved ones were no longer with him, if the faces of the mothers, fathers and children whose corpses he burned came back to him and, if they did, how he could ever forgive himself. Evil finds itself in the hands of the fearful and of those obedient ones who pull the levers and sweep away the evidence. Yet it does not start there. It starts in the mind of someone, someone desperate to get back at someone, to prove himself to be more than he is, and who, by some quirk of fate or by some strange aberration of the will, is empowered to implement the evil. How did that happen? Why did we let it happen? I had no answers to those questions, but they haunted me. Within my own tiny sphere of influence, I wanted to make sure nothing like that happened in the DAE house as long as I had any authority and that no one like Sean would ever control the fate of helpless pledges. I wanted to expunge those faces of the living dead in those horrendous experiments and that room with no windows where the living went in and did not return.

At the end of August, my friend Jeff, wondering where I'd been all summer, called me. We met at his house, went up to his bedroom, and flopped together on his bed. He nestled close to me, turned on his side, his elbow under his head and his head in his hand. He reached over and brushed my hair back.

"You let your hair grow," he said. "It looks good."

"Thanks," I said. "You let yours grow too."

He smiled. "I like it long." He sighed, flipped the hair out of his eyes. "So what you see over there?"

I told him about Dachau, the guide, about those exterminated, about the Jews and homosexuals.

"Homosexuals?" he asked.

"Yeah," I said. "They gassed them, burned them, and left nothing but ashes."

"Shit," he said, "the world is fucked up, you know?"

I nodded and told him about the wall in Berlin. He interrupted me, suggested we take a walk and head down the street toward the drug store where there was an old-fashioned soda fountain with real soda water and flavored syrups, where time had stopped.

"You're getting into some dark things," he said. "You need to lighten up. You can't be thinking about that shit. It'll drive you crazy."

"I can't help it," I said.

"I don't want to think about it. Life is way too short. You can't be bothered with stuff that happened before we were born," he said and slung his arm around my shoulder. "Listen, why don't you come visit me at college? It'll be like old times," he said, kicking at a dead leaf on the sidewalk. "You can forget that shit. I have a place of my own. It's private. We can do anything we want. We can party all the time."

"Maybe."

"Maybe?" he said. "Come on, where's the Jason I used to know?"

"I'll try," I said but sensed that I would not, that whatever it was between us had changed and I did not want to forget, and what we had that was so wonderful was more part of our past than our future.

Leadership

Once at Ashbury, I wasted no time to run for an office in the fraternity. I wanted to have some authority and had some good ideas about changing how pledges and upperclassmen related to one another. Deep inside, after what I'd seen in Germany, I wanted to change the world, rid it of evil. I ran for House Manager and won. It was awkward at first because my brother had enrolled at Ashbury, pledged at DAE, and was one of the pledges under my supervision. We had a talk about it.

"Listen, I feel weird being your boss," I said.

"Hey bro, no big deal. I'm proud of you getting the job. I'll do the work. No favors needed. Can't you see that I'm so happy to be with you?" he said. "I know how to play the game. Just do your thing and I will follow your lead just as other pledges."

Although Jack did comply with my instructions, he also formed relationships with upperclassmen in the house who, because he was older and academically a junior, included him in their parties and other activities. With him fitting in, I ceased to worry about him and I focused on my responsibilities.

The job entailed working with the new pledges and making sure they did their chores, and, each weekend, to stay up late and have an extensive work detail go over the house before Sunday morning. Having checklists of what each duty was and how it would be evaluated soon won plaudits from upperclassmen who claimed the house had never been so clean. I worked along with the pledges, showing them how to use bleach to clean shower stalls, how to make the beds and, even when they were grossed out by the cum stains of certain guys whose sheets were so mottled with blotches that they looked like expressionist paintings, how to get them clean and back on the beds. We scraped the engrained dirt off tiles, kept the kitchen and dining room spick-and-span. I'd developed a strong relationship with the pledges and hoped, with my continued good work, to be considered for the secretary or vice-president job next year. In my pledge class everyone knew if I could get in a position of power, we, as a class, could change how we

170

did Hell Week, making it actually a series of serious challenges, and wipe out the humiliation that we had gone through.

In September, I also started my job as a waiter at the Kappa Alpha Phi sorority. Luis waited there and Sue, a member, had vouched for me. By waiting there, I defrayed some expenses for my dad. I had meals free and put some of the money in the bank. I met some nice girls too. Luis tried to get me to date Carole Henderson, a sophomore and literature major. She wrote poetry. I met her for coffee several times, but she was much more sophisticated than I was. She'd published a book and hung around with other poets. I decided that I needed more time learning about poetry before embarrassing myself with her.

I'd become an unofficial counselor for Steve who'd been in the room when the others had accused me of being a homosexual. Later, he came to apologize for being a part of it.

"I'm sorry man for not standing up for you. I know you're straight. I just felt—well, I don't know—I felt pressure to go along," he said. "Or they might suspect me."

I told him not to worry. I'd taken care of it.

"Everyone is afraid of the gay thing. It's like a stain. You don't want to be near it or it will smudge you too. I get it," I said.

With our relationship repaired in his mind, he'd drop in, bemoaning how he could not get a date since he was so overweight. One evening, he came in looking particularly distressed and sat in a wooden chair I had set beside my desk. As he plopped down, and the front right leg broke, splaying out, and tipped forward onto the floor, he splashed, legs extended, like an enormous hippo splayed out on ice in the middle of the floor. Embarrassed, he scrambled to his feet. Several other brothers—Dennis and Earl—opened the door to see what happened and saw him on his hands and knees in front of me, for I had stood up to help him. They laughed and said, "Look at Steve: he's worshipping Jason," and Steve, enraged, slammed the door in their face.

He went over to the couch and cried. When he gathered himself together, we talked about how snide Jacob had been to him, mocking him because of his weight. He told me that, if he wanted to, he could pay Jacob back for the insults. The previous week, Steve had been ill and went to the dorm to sleep. The school doctor told him that he needed rest. Three days in a row, he heard someone sneak into the dorm and did not notice Steve on a top bunk curled up at the far end in a corner just as I had. At first, Steve made no effort to discover who it was since he felt so rotten. He figured someone was also catching a nap. The second day, at the same hour, the door swung open and the person came in. Steve heard a zipper open. He paid it no mind. But he heard moaning, the bed creak, and peeking through the covers, he saw Jacob masturbating. He did it every day, two and three times a day the whole time he was in the dorm recuperating. He asked what he should do. Having seen Jacob do the same thing, I had no doubt that Steve had a good case to persuade Jacob to stop his harassment, although I knew that some weeks I was just as horny and probably jacked off as much as Jacob did.

I suggested, "If Jacob makes fun of your weight again in public, take him aside later and tell him that you'd been in the dorm for several days recuperating. Tell him that you'd been awakened by someone coming in to jerk off. And then just smile at Jacob and say, 'I thought I might bring that up to some pledge brothers how prolific you are but thought maybe, instead, we could work a deal.' He did exactly as I had told him and Jacob's attitude toward him changed dramatically.

As a counselor to the needy and as a leader, I felt as if I had turned a corner. My grades were getting better. I felt more assured as a student. I enjoyed my history classes and one history of art class.

The Image

Early in the year, I learned that Suzie had dropped out of school. Her mother had a nervous breakdown. She had to take care of her younger sister. But with Tom's help, I met several girls who liked to drink and go out on dates with us. Not romantic types, but just girls who liked a good party. I felt no pressure to connect with them. My reputation as a guy had improved somewhat. Joseph Stein decided that he needed to help me too, with advice on how to date. He seemed to know every girl in the Kappa Kappa Gamma house and dated a girl name Sarah, an attractive blond who hailed from Indianapolis. On several occasions, he came to my room, to talk mostly about girls. His philosophy was to dabble with as many girls as he could, check them out, "give them a test drive," as he called it. Since I played golf, he asked me to give him a few tips on how to play, and we used to chip balls in the side lot. He gave me tips on how best to ask a girl out. He liked casually sitting with them at Jaminotts, introducing himself, asking them where they were from and what they liked to do. These casual interviews often led to dates. He suggested I give it a try. I thanked him, but knew I would never do that. It seemed too blatant, calculated as if dating were some board game with strategies.

On our visits home to Glen Brook, sometimes Joseph's father would pick us up, sometimes my mom, so I'd gotten to know him. Joseph had his life planned—an MBA, start a business, marry, have kids. Although we rarely had much to talk about in common—he had no interest in sports, and I had no interest in the stock market—we managed to discuss girls on our trips back and forth. I admired his tenacity in finding the right girl. He felt as comfortable dating as I did throwing the football.

Although he knew everyone in the house and became a leader of the campus student government, Joseph never developed any close friends in the fraternity. Some upperclassmen resented him being a Jew.

With Tom and me rooming and studying together and going to parties, we became like brothers. After a party, we'd often be the last ones standing and he would pour the last of the Jack Daniels in our glasses and sit, his

173

arm around me, telling about his exploits in Port Washington. Sometimes he'd lean over and kiss me lightly on the top of my head.

"You're the best," he'd say. "The best. I mean it."

"Thanks," I'd say. "You are too."

Tom was taking a photography class and asked if I'd model for him. He'd met another photography student, Tim, who was also a painter and lived in Roberts Hall, and he'd come on walks with us. A tall lanky guy who wore a beret, he liked to pose for photographs and, after he got to know me, suggested that I could make some extra money by modeling in a life drawing class. The professor was always hunting for guys who did not mind posing in the nude. I declined. But I did not mind posing for Tom since we knew each other so well. Not far from campus, a quarry was nestled in the woods. Along its rim, large slabs of rock turned out to be good places for them to have me pose. On hot afternoons, we skinny-dipped, slipping out of our clothes and enjoying the cool water. Feeling awkward at first, I sat on a grassy hillside and watched the two of them splashing each other. Seeing them in the water reminded me of neighborhood boys who used to romp on sweltering summer days in a creek near my house. They seemed so confident and comfortable with their bodies as if they'd never had doubts about who they were and what they felt. I often gazed on them in wonder and yearned to feel as comfortable as they did in their skin.

With his marble-white skin, Tim seemed more like a Greek statue. He and Tom liked to wrestle in the water and eventually, after much prodding, I joined in, seeing how often we could dunk one another. With my arm strength and leg strength, I often won. Afterward, we would sun on the large slabs on the edge of the quarry. Some evenings, Tom and I would sneak out to the quarry and swim, just the two of us, letting the inky water swallow us in its cool embrace.

After becoming comfortable in my own skin, I allowed them to photograph me for their class. When they had to do nude photographs, they'd have me sit on a rock or act as if I were about to dive in or stand in what Tim called Greek statue poses with my arm raised as if throwing a javelin—a whole array of close-ups and distant shots. Their professor thought them very good and wanted to know where he found his model. The professor thought I was quite beautiful, which embarrassed me, and wanted to have me model for him. I told them that I could not do it.

On some weekends Tim hung out in our room, drinking with us. Since he lived in a men's dorm, he'd never hung around in a fraternity house. Handsome with fine facial features—a classic Greek profile—he became a regular until some guys in the annex complained about his being weird, "too artsy" (although they meant effeminate), and Tom, sensitive to criticism, went over to Tim's room in the dorm rather than subject himself to Sean's insults. I'd gone along for several weeks. Tim's dorm room was small— with a couch seconded as a bed and one desk— and forced us to cram together, two of us on the bed, the other in the chair. We talked about art, the latest photographs that they had done as well as some they admired— Walker Evans and his photographs of tenant farmers. I liked the raw, sensual images of people, whose faces belied an uncommon authenticity, a directness of being. They seemed to say, "Here I am as I am," with no airs, no fancy clothes, no fashionable hairdos.

One evening, after drinking way too much, Tom reminisced about his last summer's escapades, how he'd hung around with a wild crowd and had done things I'd never done. One time, his friends—four girls and five guys—snuck into a public swimming pool—quite drunk (he always seemed to be quite drunk) and stripped to go skinny-dipping. Afterward, since he was the odd guy out, he watched in the dressing rooms as his friends began getting it on. One couple invited him to join, which he did in a three-way. He asked if I'd ever done that. Tim mentioned that he'd been in a four way, all guys. It had not been so bad.

"What did you do?" I asked.

"What do you think?" Tim shot back, almost contemptuous of the question.

"I don't know. I mean, what do guys do together?"

He laughed. "You got to be kidding me. They do the same things as you do with a chick."

I did not respond and got another beer to and stood at the window looking out into the branches of a maple tree. I wished I could have leapt onto a branch and jumped limb to limb like a squirrel to get away from the room, from that conversation. All I'd ever done was jack off with individual friends, nothing more. I'd wanted to do more, but hadn't and was glad I hadn't confided anything to Tom or Tim about my limited experience.

We continued to drink, enough to fill a several buckets. Completely inebriated, Tom spread out on the bed and told us that last summer he worked at a gas station, an attendant on a parkway. One evening, at the end of his shift, he'd gone to take a leak and a guy, handsome in his twenties, happened to be in the bathroom too. Tom thought nothing about it and went up to the urinal. The other man eyed him, checked him out, and started a conversation, asking Tom when he was getting off work.

As Tom told the story he elaborated on it, filled in the details, taking delight in our being caught up in it. He tended to exaggerate, adding scenes that may not have happened but certainly made for a better story. I'd learned that because when he told about our double dates, he often described scenes that never happened.

"So I gazed at him—good-looking and, well, you know, good-sized—and told him that my shift had ended. He zipped up his pants. I noticed that he wore top-line clothes. I mean expensive if you know what I mean. Out of nowhere, the guy invited me to a party, and, always up for a party, I went with him, thinking I could hook up with some girls. But this party was different. Mostly guys his age, normal-looking, not fags. We drank mixed drinks. Highballs. Gin and tonics. Grasshoppers. It was interesting. Every once in a while two or three guys would head off to a side room and be gone for a half hour. Someone asked me to join."

He looked at me to see how I reacted—I said nothing, but I averted my eyes. Tom stopped his story. "It was quite an evening," he said, reaching for the bottle to pour himself a drink.

"Tell us more," Tim said. "Come on."

Tom shrugged his shoulders. He looked at me. I didn't know what to say. To make him feel better, I threw out, "That's interesting, really" and he poured us another round of Jack Daniels, then abruptly changed the topic to the next intramural tag football game.

The Princess

In the fall before the weather changed, the fraternities and sororities had a Sadie Hawkins Weekend Festival where gender roles were reversed. What guys normally did, girls did. What girls normally did, guys did. There was a football game among the sororities as well as an auction, a beauty contest, a dance. Men's and women's houses or dorms were paired up so that they could compete as one team. The proceeds went to charity.

Bill Harris and I coached the Kappa Kappa Gamma football team into the finals. The game, much as a game with guys, required the girls either to block to protect their quarterback or to rush and tag the opponent's quarterback and runner. At first the girls hated to get dirty. Some brought towels so they could wash off after plays. They didn't like to shove or grab. Frustrated, Bill and I would role-model for them, showing how to use a shoulder to get around a blocker. We didn't want to hit them or shove them because they might think we were being aggressive. Yet we gently showed them how to push safely, how to hold their arms up and keep in front of rushing linemen. We had them bump into one another lightly at first, harder as the week went on. But it went slowly and often girls would yell at one another in practice if someone shoved too hard. However, late in one practice, one girl bumped into another girl and got a bloody nose. Other girls rushed to rescue her, but she fended them off and started to smear her blood on her face like war paint and the other girls giggled and then another swiped her blood and put it on her face and before long the girls were yelping and smashing into one another. They were ferocious, gobbling up other teams in the festival's tournament, throwing whole body blocks so that their runners could scoot down the field. Their quarterback, left unscathed because of her front line, had all the time to make perfect passes. So we looked as if we would win the championship game for the first time, but we needed to win the beauty competition to take the festival's top prize of a trophy and certificate.

So the girls came over to our house to select a pledge that they could make up for the beauty contest. Out of tradition, it was always a pledge who

177

was sacrificed for the event. Sometimes the victim was the biggest, most burly guy in the class. Other times, as during our freshman year, it would be a guy that might just look beautiful. Luis, thin and lithe, though he came in second, knew how to sway his hips and, with a little padding, he looked like a girl. For this year, the sorority girls chose a pledge, Bryce, who happened to be one of the shyest in the class, a short boy with lovely blond hair and a classic Roman profile. I'd not paid much attention to him, nor had anyone else. He studied hard. He kept to himself. He did his work cleaning. He had a few friends. Overall, he was a nonentity, an insecure, almost frightened guy who did not want to make waves and did everything the right way so as to avoid getting in trouble. He didn't even party. I hardly knew him. Some said that we pledged him because he had money and we needed financial help. From a wealthy and conservative family, Bryce was an unlikely pick. He was handsome and had powdery white, soft looking skin, but I couldn't imagine him as a girl. But, after some persuasion by the girls and several of his pledge brothers, he agreed to go through the hassle. The girls took him off. We decided that several of us in shorts would carry him on stage, carrying an open carriage with him seated in it like Cleopatra.

During the football game, our girls outplayed the Pi Beta Phi team, smashing them to the ground, trampling over them, pounding them, 34 to 14. Our girls came off the field and flicked blood at us to prove they were tough, and they were not only tough, they were winners. With their victory, we only had to win the beauty contest to take home the trophy which usually went to the big houses.

For the final judging of the pageant, the contestants were kept hidden in a large tent until their names were called. The judges sat below a podium and each contestant came on stage, pranced back and forth, showing off their outfits and their makeup. The judges then assigned them a score. A large rowdy crowd cheered as the guys came on stage, often with a special moniker—-Sigma Nu's "Dusty Doo," Phi Delta Theta's "Betty Lou"— along with names of the make-up artists and wardrobe designers, which were displayed on posters. Sigma Nu had a guy with more hair on his back and chest than most guys have on their head. With red lipstick and long eyelashes, he stomped on stage and twirled around, pointing at some of his football buddies, spoofing the whole feminine mystique. Lambda Chi

Alpha sent up a tall, skinny guy who really did look attractive with a wig and a shapely fit one-piece dress, but he walked like a guy, taking long quick steps. The Delta Chi beauty came closest to looking like a girl. He swayed his hips, raised one eyebrow and carried himself as if he knew how it was to be a woman. In addition, the girls made him look lovely with a blond wig and sheer dress that showed off his hips and large bosoms that looked real. By the time it came for Bryce to come on stage, we went to the tent with our carriage and the girls ushered him out. Trevor, Tom, Eric, and I were joking about being a taxi service, our bodies oiled up to make us look buff. We flexed our muscles and waited for Delta Alpha Epsilon's "Miss." When Bryce stepped out of the tent, we stared at him with open mouths. With his blond hair teased out, a careful application of rouge and shiny pink lipstick on his full lips, he looked ravishing. He wore a white gown with frilly lace and carried a gold purse in his white gloves. The girls had taught him how to walk and he sashayed up to the carriage, holding his hand out to be helped to his seat. His natural modesty made him even more alluring. Dumbfounded, we gently picked him up, careful to keep the carriage from tilting. He sat upright and waved as we walked around the stage. Students gasped. Girls craned their necks to see and marveled at him. Sitting just in front of me in his chair, he seemed to exude a latent sexuality, a natural erotic quality as Marilyn Monroe had, the way his body pressed on the silken fabric of the dress and how he bent his head slightly, his eyes modestly averted. "My God she's a beauty!" someone called out. Cheers went up. Students blurted out words to describe him. Unbelievable. Extraordinary. Amazing. When we put him down, he gingerly walked on stage in high heels, stopped at the top, put his hand out for the host to lead him around. For some reason, perhaps awe, perhaps envy, a hush fell over the crowd. We looked on as his singular beauty, a beauty that made him no longer a *him* but had, in a few fleeting hours, transmogrified him into a magnificent *she*. She captivated everyone. She smiled and raised her hand like a princess. She seemed to know what had happened. The once quiet nonentity had become a star. She curtsied. She waved at the crowd which, after the silence, broke into hoots. She threw out kisses just like Marilyn Monroe. She must have been on stage for fifteen minutes. The hooting and cheers rocked the campus. When she walked off, we picked her up and paraded her through the crowds who wanted to touch her, to get their photographs taken with her, who could not get enough of her and who sensed that she was one of those rare, beautiful flowers that bloom once a century and they must see her before she vanished forever.

We knew the contest was over. No one could come close to Bryce. Others came up and strutted around, but everyone could only talk about Marilyn.

But after, back to the house, after the makeup had been removed and Marilyn's clothing exchanged for normal slacks, shirt, and loafers, many of the guys had difficulty with Bryce being a male again. They knew that, for a moment, they'd witnessed some extraordinary transformation and, equally, witnessed something beautiful that had not just to do with makeup but with the inner person that had been hiding inside the shy boy. I know that I looked at him and wondered if all men had hidden in them this feminine beauty or if only a few of us were given that gift. Clearly, he had it. For weeks, he became the brunt of jokes that he took in good humor because we had given him the trophy to keep in his room. He had won it for us. But he settled in, became more relaxed, actually joined in several parties and started dating the very girls who had helped him transform. It was as if someone had switched on a light bulb inside him and he had become himself.

During one school break, Bryce's father came to campus and got wind of what had happened because there were photographs posted on a bulletin board with our certificate for having won the festival and among the photographs of the girl's football team there was one of Bryce. The father pulled it down and tore it up. Before anyone could talk to him, Bryce was withdrawn from school and we never heard from him again.

His roommate told me that Bryce cried the whole time that he was packing up and said he finally found a place he could be himself. But his father would have none of it. I asked the pledge what he was like when Bryce was not dressed up. "Once you got to know him—and it took a while because he was very fearful, shy really— he was a beautiful person."

For weeks, I wondered what happened to him, what his father may have done to him. For all I knew, he'd been enrolled in a military academy. Yet whenever I thought of him stepping out of the tent, my heart skipped a beat. He was the most beautiful woman I'd ever seen, and he knew it, and everyone knew it. For a few hours, he was royalty in everyone's eyes.

The Shrimp Boats

For the weekend of the big house dance, Tom's hometown girlfriend, Linda, flew down to be with him and she brought along with her a girlfriend, Judy, who ended up being my date. She liked to party and Tom thought I could use a good date who didn't put up any fuss. Tom paid for the girls to stay in a motel, one with double beds.

The house decorated for a Hawaiian Luau, with a large pool in front and a five-foot waterfall. Throughout the house, fronds and grass were hanging from the walls. We'd put strobe lights in the main room after storing all the furniture so that there was a huge dance floor. On a stage, Baby Leon, an African American who loved to drink and wail, his songs coming out of him as if they were emerging from the soulful agony of his race, wiggled his hips and spun around like a top, entertaining us with his non-stop rock and roll. We danced until late at night, taking off our dress shirts and shoes, our T-shirts and socks. We'd sway to the rhythms of the music, and, every twenty minutes, went to the annex to imbibe from our supply of Jack Daniels. Judy wore a tight black skirt that rode up on her thighs; when she leaned back on the couch in our room, I could see that she had no panties on.

She smirked as I stared at her exposed body. "Listen, honey," she said. "I'm always ready, willing and able. I hate encumbrances," and dropped her eyes to look me over as if she could undress me with their allure. She wore heavy makeup, dark eyeliner and lipstick the color of chocolate. When we came back to the dance, I noticed that Luis took a fancy to her. He was a good dancer and they hit it off, dancing several numbers, the last one a slow dance.

"Do you mind if I show Judy my room?" he shouted at me over the music. I shrugged and watched them traipse out of the room arm in arm. Tom called out to me to help him pick up Baby Leon who had passed out on the floor. After giving him several cups of coffee, he straightened up like a resurrected god and sang a whole other set with us holding him from either side. When Judy came back, she slid into my lap like a snake. She

182

draped her arm around my neck and gently kissed me. Luis stood for a moment, puzzled, looking at her. She was attractive, no doubt, and Luis liked pretty women. We danced several times. She knew how to move her body and let her chest heave up with the beat of the music. She clung onto me and I could feel every muscle of her body pressed to mine.

By the end the night, after we drove back to the motel, our inhibitions dropped away. We undressed in front of each other, the girls giggling as they watched us strip until we were in our jockey shorts and, after we did, they did the same. We sat on the edge of each bed and had one more round of drinks. With no particular fanfare, we slipped back on our beds and began making out. I could see Tom slip his jockey shorts off and felt Judy push mine down too. We cuddled in our beds. I surprised myself. I felt fine being with this girl. She took my erection and slipped it deftly between her legs. It was moist. Like a suction valve I felt my erection pulled up into her, moist, as if the valve had hold of it, and, once in place, the machinery of love churned into high gear. She knew how to make love and wasted no time in getting me ready for her and I followed her every lead, shifting my weight, moving on top of her, responding to her every move, joining her as she thrust, taking me deeper as she said, "Yes, yes, yes" until I was not sure if it was her or me who was moving, but, most of all, it did not matter since we snuggled close, her arms on my back, my sweat on her body, her nails digging into me and my hips driving back and forth and there seemed no end of it, the body in the body, and then she stuck her tongue deep in my mouth and I cried out and slumped into her arms, drenched in sweat, feeling our lust drain out of us as we kissed softly for a few minutes and then, still holding onto one another, fell off to sleep.

When I awoke in the morning, Tom looked over at me and smiled. I felt good and, although I remembered scantily what had happened, it seemed all right. I performed well my first time with a woman. We lay around for several hours and chatted and, then, after having lunch at the house, which was in disarray, we drove them to the airport and said goodbye. Judy kissed me at the airport and said, "You are a sweet one," and, not sure how to respond, I said, "You are too."

She laughed and ran her hand along my cheek. "Not on your life, honey."

On the way back to the house, Tom asked if I had used any protection, and I admitted I hadn't.

"Neither did I," he said. "We normally do. But I forgot to bring them to the motel and, well, with you going to town with Judy, we just followed suit."

"Is it all right?" I asked, since I'd never done it before.

"Sure," he said. "Judy knows what's up. She'll take care of herself. She's probably on the pill. She's something, isn't she?"

"Yeah, I'll say."

We both laughed.

Aborted

I never gave much thought to the night, except, about a week later, when I was undressing and noticed little brownish bugs, tiny ones that snuck in and out of my pubic hair. Startled, I had no idea what they were or where they came from. They blended easily in my dense underbrush. Later that day, I heard Sean laughing about Luis, who slept in the upper bunk of our bunk bed that was in the dorm, and say that he had the crabs and had gone to the doctor, and had to have his pubic hair shaved and put some ointment on it to kill them. I didn't want to admit that I too had them, lest someone think I had slept with Luis. So, when no one was in the room, using a magnifying glass, I plucked each bug out, one by one, crushing it between my fingers, hour after hour, and shaved myself, just to be safe.

After dinner one night, a few days later, Luis took me aside and, sitting across from me, he said, "You know that girl, Judy, you had as a date?"

I said I remembered her.

"Well, you know, she came to my room, right?"

"Yes."

"I hate to tell you, but we got it on."

I was not surprised and told him.

"Did you get it on?" he asked.

"Pretty much."

He smiled and tapped my leg, "Good. I'm proud of you!"

I smiled.

"But I have bad news," he said.

"What?"

"I think I got crabs from her and, well, I think you should check if you have them," he said.

I joked that my dad had once said there was a song or something that went, "Don't wait for the shrimp boats, I'm coming home with the crabs." He laughed but went on to explain what they looked like and how to get rid of them. I thanked him for telling me, but I never told him that I did have them. It just felt too personal.

Aborted

A month later, Tom had some bad news from Linda: She was pregnant. For long hours, he talked with me about what he should do: go along with it and have a kid or have an abortion. He liked her, but not a lot, not enough to marry her. He called some friends and found out about an illegal clinic in Brooklyn. He stewed about it for weeks. She called him three and four times a week, demanding he do something. He decided that she should get an abortion. I loaned him some money and, on a long weekend, not informing his parents, he flew back to New York where she lived, and she had it done. When he came back, he felt terrible—how he left her off, how she went into an sleazy apartment building, and, after she came out, pale and wasted, clearly in enormous pain, how she would not talk to him, just quietly wept (she was a Roman Catholic) and asked to be left off at a friend's and he spent the night alone in a motel near the airport, getting drunk by himself and took his flight back to school never having talked to her again. Despondent, he drank more and got involved with another girl, Lois, who lived in the dorm. They'd often go to a motel, and he would not show up at the house until late in the morning looking as if he'd been dragged out of a dumpster, his hair disheveled, his face unshaven.

Tom also spent nights at Tim's room whenever they worked on an art project. One evening I tagged along and sat on the bed with Tom while Tim perched in the only chair. We drank and talked as usual about photography, more about Walker Evans, and how he used light, would stay for a whole day to wait for the exact light to fall on a building. I noticed that Tim had a large poster on his wall of Michelangelo's *David*, right by the bed. Timothy talked about Michelangelo being one of his heroes and brought out a whole book with his paintings and statues.

On the way back to our room Tom told me that he'd learned a lot about seeing things from Tim's point of view. "Do you like him?" he asked.

"Yeah, he's a nice guy," I admitted. "Really into the arts."

"I like that about him," he said, putting his arm over my shoulder. "The two of you—and Jerry, of course—are my best friends ever."

For several weeks Tom spent more time with Tim than with me and stayed away overnight.

I stopped dating during that time and withdrew to my poetry and music and studies and enjoyed having the room to myself. Tom seemed to prefer talking to Tim about his private agony and I was not one to intrude.

But a month later, when Tom was coming out of his funk and broke up with Lois and had, he told me he had a blowup with Tim over their art project and suggested that we go on some double dates, which we did. He did not seem particularly interested in any girl. Instead, he seemed to be doing it more to keep his hand in the game. And I was afraid of a resurgence of rumors about my not being interested in girls. We seemed like two actors getting by any way we could.

Before we'd go to pick up the girls, he'd pull out a bottle of Jack Daniels and fill two shot glasses. We'd clink them together, "to love," and down them. Then he'd pour two more, and on some nights, another slug. Our dates never seemed particularly impressed with us, but we didn't care. We took them to the movies or a dance or a bar. They were pretty faces on our arms. No more. After leaving them off, we'd retreat to our room and finish off the fifth. We'd put on Frank Sinatra's album, "A Man and His Music," turn up the volume, take out one of my golf clubs, and pretend to use the grip end as a microphone and sing, "I'll Never Smile Again," "There Are Such Things" and "I'll Be Seeing You" in full vibrato. Tom would put his arm around my neck, and cheek to cheek like Dean Martin and Sinatra live in Vegas, we'd sing into the golf club until we had no more voice and the record player clicked as the needle pulled back and we'd pass out, another empty bottle on the floor along with us.

I enjoyed the freedom of being away from the other brothers in the main house, not having to worry what they thought of me, as there were only twelve of us in the annex, most of them upperclassmen. Tom, who had taken up drinking as a full time occupation, managed to impress them with how well we fit in by proving to them that we could drink as much as they could. He spent more time with them. I spent more time on my studies. To reclaim some of my personal prestige in the fraternity as a quarterback on our intramural football team, I practiced tossing passes for hours, trying to zip a ball though a tire swinging from a branch. Despite painful bursitis in my throwing arm, I believed that if I could prove myself as a winning quarterback and bring some glory to the DAE house, I could cast out any doubts lingering about my masculinity.

Hunger for Glory

Throughout the fall, our tag football team continued to win. With two more blockers to protect me and two more rushers—tall, lanky guys, both former football players—and by adding two wingbacks, a fellow from Alabama whose racist attitudes I had no use for but who could sprint with the best of them, plus my brother who had quick moves and hands like nobody else, we had quite a formable team. When Jack made a cut I knew exactly where he would be. Early on, we dominated other teams, winning by 20, sometimes 30-point margins. By mid-Season, however, I noticed that my right elbow ached after a game so I could barely lift my arm. I iced it, but the pain, at first minor, gradually worsened, throbbing both day and night, the intensity of it undiminished. One morning, nearly in tears, I confessed at breakfast that I doubted I could play.

"No way," Bill said. "I know a doctor at the hospital, an orthopedist. He's a close family friend."

Bill drove me to the local hospital where Dr. Cramer, a balding middle-age man, informed me that I had a very bad case of tendonitis. He recommended rest, ice and aspirin.

"We have a big game coming up, doctor. He's our quarterback. Can't you do anything?"

Bill asked.

The doctor looked at him. "Big game?"

"We have a chance to beat the defending champions. We have never won a championship. This may be the only year we can do it," Bill explained.

The doctor nodded. "I don't normally do this, not at this stage in the tendonitis. But I could give him a cortisone shot. It may quell the inflammation somewhat. But rest, good rest, is still what he needs," the doctor said. He looked at me, holding the arm. He had me lift my arm so that it was at shoulder level. I winced, biting my lip, and gasped for air.

"See?" he said. "My preference is that you give it a rest for the season, for the inflammation to die down. Let someone else take over."

"But there is on one else," Bill said. "Jason has an incredible arm. We really have a chance to take it all, to win the championship."

I added onto to Bill's pleas. "I want to play, but I'll rest the arm until game day and, after this season, I'll let it heal."

Having been a football player, Dr. Cramer relented and gave me a cortisone shot for it, but insisted: No practice. No throwing, No lifting. Ice it. Take aspirin.

My brother had a good arm too, so he played part of the next game that we seemed to be winning easily. I walked the sidelines in a sling, ice on my elbow.

I felt a festering inside me. Without football, without a way to prove myself, I felt as if I would be exposed and be the brunt of accusations about being gay. By being in the limelight, no one dared to question me. Jocks were not gay. That's what I wanted. Bill told me not the play and save my arm. Jack told me that he could handle it. But in the last quarter, when the other team took the lead, I came back in. Jack told me that he'd noticed that their defense spread out when we sent players in a crossing route. If I could do a few downs, he was sure that he could beat their defensive back down the middle. There were only a few minutes left in the game.

My brother faked going to the sideline and then cut deep in a play where he and another guy crossed each other midfield. I threw a strike to him just as he crossed the end zone. A perfect pass, right on his fingertips. He hauled it in, leaping to make the catch. I cried out because I saw where he was headed. As he tucked the ball in his arms, he smacked head first into the goal post. He bounced back, holding fast to the ball and landed with a thud, his legs splayed out.

I raced down the field to him. I felt sick. A large reddish bump had blossomed on the right side of his head. I turned away, afraid of what might have happened. Several players crouched beside him. Jack still held onto the ball, like a teddy bear, but his eyes were closed and his face looked ashen. His mouth was open and he gasped for breath. Someone brought water and dabbed it on his wound. I knelt by him.

"Jack, Jack. You okay?" I called out, pressing on his arm.

He opened his eyes and gazed at me.

"Did I drop it?" he asked.

I laughed, "No, look, it's in your arms."

"Good."

"You all right?" I asked.

"You trying to kill me?" he asked.

"Well, not exactly."

He felt his head, propped himself on his elbow, and looked at the crowd that gathered around us.

"Look I'm a celebrity!"

"Are you all right?" I asked again.

"I'm fine. Sore, but fine," he said, turning on his side.

We helped him up and, woozy, he staggered to the sidelines. Several brothers patted me on the back. "Nice pass, nice pass." I glared at them. How could it be a nice pass when I nearly killed my brother? I helped him to a car and we drove him back to the house. For much of the day, with an ice pack on his head, he lay around, drowsy and incoherent. Bill insisted that we drive him to the hospital.

While waiting for a doctor, Jack held his head.

"I'm all right, really."

"It's just a precaution," Bill said.

In the exam room, after hearing the story, the doctor moved his hand back and forth, asking my brother to follow his finger, and had Jack balance on one foot and then another. He concluded that it was a concussion. Not severe, but serious.

Despite some headaches that week, Jack wanted to practice and would not miss the big game. I realized that he too needed to prove himself. The drive to be the best, to outshine others, was something bred into us both. Why did we have to excel? I wondered if he too had some hidden secret that he had to cover up with outward success. Or was it our dad's injunction "to be the best, no matter what it was"? I suppose the drive, whatever its origin, once it had been started, kept on pushing us because being the best meant that loss was unacceptable.

Sacrifice

Our semifinal game was against the same Delta Chi team we played the previous year. Bent to revenge their loss from the previous year's defeat, they had sailed through their early games. Although I did not tell anyone, my arm still ached, throbbing so much that at night I could barely sleep. But I iced it, and Jack threw most of the practice games. We knew that the same strategy as the previous one would not work. They were ready for us, so we played to our strength. I threw short passes, sure ones. Nothing dangerous and we kept even with them. We ran the ball some with Jeff making some amazing cross cuts, darting away from the defense, for large gains.

But their quarterback ran like Fran Tarkenton, the Minnesota Vikings' star quarterback, who would swirl and dart in any direction. My arm felt heavy and I had trouble getting the ball downfield. One pass was intercepted because I underthrew to Eric. But we intercepted the other quarterback too and the game teeter-tottered back and forth.

It all came down to another final drive. At midfield, we had the ball with less than a minute to go. I had been saving my arm, but now we needed a big play which meant I needed to get the ball downfield. We decided to flood one side of the field with three receivers and to keep Jacob in the backfield, acting as a decoy, making it seem he was a blocker, when, after faking a throw to the right side where we had all the receivers, I would throw across field to him where, we hoped, he would be alone since most of the backs would go toward our receivers. My worry was having enough time and enough strength. With my arm in a sling most of the week and with it being iced day and night, I could toss lightly without pain. But if I drilled a ball, a sharp razorlike pain shot up my arm. Would I be able to make a long toss? I had no idea.

With a snap from center, I faked going to the left and reversed my field, setting up the blockers to cut down the rushers. I trotted to the right looking at my three receivers and pumped several times, and, then, I stopped, turned around and, not having much time to look, heaved the ball toward the left corner of the end zone. The ball had plenty of air under it, and Jacob, sprinting downfield, raced toward it, grabbing it on his fingertips and rolled into the end zone. We ran over to him and carried him off the field. Time had run out. We were in the finals.

After the game my arm felt as if someone had put a knife in it. Back in my room, I applied ice. Pumped up with victory, I was now more determined than ever to prove myself. I would wear my arm out if I had to.

Our final game against Beta Beta Phi, a team we had never defeated, seemed to be impossible. Not only did they have the biggest fraternity but they had several guys who started on the Ashbury basketball team —tall guys, 6'5" and 6'7", who made other players look like Lilliputians. The giants could go anywhere on the field and, as long as the pass was high, they could snatch it, so they moved up and down the field like a well-oiled machine.

Jacob had three ideas about how to defeat them: one, to harass the quarterback who was a straight drop-back type with not much maneuverability; and two, to have Jacob and Eric, who both could jump a foot or more tail their big men and get as high as they could in their face to distract them; and three, to keep Jack in the backfield with me so that I could drop the ball off to him, or he could drop it off to me, and the other team would never know who was going to throw the ball. I could block well because I had been a fullback in high school and he could block for me. Toward the end of the week, Bill drove me to get another shot.

Everyone asked me, "How's your arm?"

"Fine, fine," I'd say, lying. It was not fine.

Some brothers would point me out when I walked to class. "That's Jason, the guy with the arm."

It felt as if my arm had become my identity, a trophy I carried around for people to admire. I looked at it sticking out of my sleeve and thought how it had a life of its own. My body, of course, was attached to it. But my arm became the topic of conversation and concern. A doctor stuck a needle in it. My brothers asked about it as if it were a mortally ill patient.

I talked about it and cuddled it as if it were a child under my care. The closer we came to the big game, the more people asked about it, massaging it, patting it, encouraging it. I was the guy with "the arm." Following doctor's orders, I had rested it the whole week. On the game day, during warm-ups, I threw a few passes and it felt nearly pain free.

The game plan worked pretty well, although none of us anticipated how tall their ends were. They may have stood 6'7" and 6'5", but when they raised their arms, they were over seven feet tall. We rushed their quarterback who made some errant throws, but he still nailed quite a few. With my brother in the backfield, I could spread out the field more, going to my right and, if I did not see someone open, lob it back to him where he could either run or make a pass to someone who, by then, got open. The game seesawed back and forth, our being up, their being up. In the last quarter, they made two big plays and pulled ahead by two touchdowns. But my brother made an amazing play. Caught on our 20-yard line, facing a third down, it looked like the game was out of our hands with little chance of our making a first down. Jack faked a pass and darted toward the line, taking two steps since he had an opened field, but stopped, much to my surprise, for I was jogging toward him, not expecting to get the ball, but he threw it back to me and I saw immediately that Eric had circled behind their players some fifty yards down the field. I knew the play depended on my arm. I set my legs and unleashed the ball, one the best I've ever thrown, a fifty-five yard pass right into Eric's arms and he pranced to the end zone. We managed to fend off the Beta Beta Phi receivers by pressuring the quarterback and knocking down several of his passes. So, once again, we had the ball. Eric suggested he try a cross pattern with my brother and I go to whomever was open. As it turned out, both of them were open and I hit my brother for a long gain. I noticed that the defense was giving both Jacob and Eric room to prevent a long play, so I clicked off four short passes and, on the last one, threw a low one, knee high into Eric who grabbed it and rolled into the end zone. My arm felt sore yet I could still zip the ball fifty yards if needed.

With the score tied and four minutes left, the Betas went to their big ends who came up with catch after catch. But Jacob noticed that the quarterback had a pattern of left, right, and right, left in delivering his passes to the giants. He anticipated the predictable throw to the left, and on one of the passes he leapt as high as I've ever seen anyone leap and snatched it. His momentum left him toppling on the ground with no chance to run, but we had the ball. We had under two minutes to play. We quickly huddled and I threw a few short passes. But they had safeties back to prevent a long bomb. We did not have time to march down the field.

Everything was at stake. I felt as if my life—the gains and losses, the successes and failures—had shrunk into the remaining seconds. For some athletes, their lives were defined by what they did at the critical moment— the dropped pass, the fumbled ball, and the game loss. I knew that, if I kept my cool, my destiny as a DAE might be sealed in these last few plays. In my belly I felt that fire that I liked, the flames of which helped me focus, to pay attention to every move I made. It was as if I was on a stage and I knew, even before any else on stage made a move, exactly what I would do, how I would act, how my arm would release the ball and what would happen.

I called a timeout and went to the sidelines to confirm with my teammates that this was the time to use our trick play.

For the whole season, we had kept one trick play to ourselves. It was designed to use one of our smallest players, a senior named Jonathan, who was probably 5'4" at best. Around campus, he wore only dress clothes— an Oxford shirts and slacks— since he owned no T-Shirt or jeans. He had lace-up high top gym shoes. If someone were to make a prototype of a non-athlete, he would have been it. But he loved football and he had very good hands and when he sped downfield on his little legs, I couldn't help picturing a fox terrier. But he also studied the game and had a good mind for how to deceive his opponents. His notion was that "real athletes" would discount him because of his size, because he looked more like a spectator than a player even though he was on our roster. The safeties would be paying attention to fleet receivers. They were my frequent targets. No one would expect us to throw to him. He would be the rabbit we pulled out of the hat in a sleeper play.

When we lined up, we put most of our receivers on the left, set up what seemed like a regular line, two blockers in the backfield, but set it all up quickly, breaking from the huddle and snapping the ball as soon as the center was over the ball. That would not allow the other team to see that we were one player short. Meanwhile, Jonathan would stand in his civilian clothes *by* the sideline, but *on* the playing field with his back to us as if he were talking to the coach. When I called 'hut hut" he would wait a half second while I darted to the left, looking at my regular receivers and drawing all the safeties toward me, and then, once the coast was cleared, he'd streak down the sidelines undetected. I did as planned, keeping my eyes on my receivers and then turned to look downfield, and, there he was, all by himself waving his arms, and I let the ball go, fifty yards, arching in a high loop to make it easier to grab. A perfect throw. He did grab it and trotted into the end zone, his arms extended, the ball in his right hand.

I grabbed my arm. "Jesus," I thought. "What happened?" I had felt something snap as I tossed the ball. I pulled my elbow next to my body so as not to move it. I jogged down the field and tried to blot out the pain.

We mobbed Jonathan and thought we'd won the game. The Beta Beta Phi captain claimed it was an illegal play—that Jonathan was not on the field, not dressed to play. The referee listened to the complaints. I pointed out that he had gym shoes on and that he was, right there, on our roster, number 34. He had played defense several times, and, yes, he was *on* the field. It was a designed play. The referee conferred with his other referees. When they came back, they went over to me and said, "We can't accept it. He wasn't on the field of play."

"Wait a minute," I said. "Who said that?"

"A referee saw that his right foot was out of bounds."

I slammed the football down. "No fuckin' way. It was legit," I screamed.

"Hey, we know we won," Bill said. "We'll contest the decision. There's nothing we can do now." He grabbed a hold of me and gave me a hug. "Amazing throw!"

I winced and pulled back.

"You okay?"

"Sure," I said, backing up, trying to avoid any embraces.

My brother, having noticed me move away from the mob, asked. "How's your arm?"

"Don't ask," I said.

"Bad?"

"Don't know. Forget it. Let's party!"

We did. We bought three kegs and invited the girls from Kappa Kappa

Gamma to join us. The party lasted most of the night. I felt good, thinking that being an athlete was about the best thing in the world. The girls hung onto me, praising my last throw. Other guys patted me on the back. "What an amazing pass! The referees are a bunch of fools." I could do no wrong. Yet, with each hour, the throbbing in my arm only increased, even after several beers. I kept on drinking, thinking it would blot out the pain. No use. I grabbed ice. No one seemed to notice. All they could talk about was the game, the last play, the glory. They seemed to have forgotten we lost. I hugged the arm next to my body. I sat on a couch, letting others come over to me since moving around, putting any pressure on the arm, nearly drove me to tears. I hardly slept that night. If I lay on my arm, it hurt. If I moved it, it screamed at me. The next morning, Bill drove me to the hospital.

After taking a series of x-rays and examining my range of movement, Dr. Cramer said I needed surgery for a torn muscle and ligament.

"Can he throw again?" Bill asked what I wanted to know.

"Not as he used to. I'm not sure. There's significant damage," he said and turned on his swivel chair to admonish me. "I thought I told you to be careful."

"I did. I skipped one game. And didn't practice much..."

"And?"

"It was the big game. I had to play," I said.

"The big game, huh?"

"Yeah."

"Well, you paid a price. Didn't you? Did you win?"

"No."

"That's too bad since you may sacrifice use of that arm."

The operation did repair the muscle, and with physical therapy, I gradually did gain back the use of my arm. But I could not get back the zip in my passes. My arm seemed to be saying that it went into early retirement and that I'd have to find some other means to prove myself. I still had golf. I had made the team last year and would be on the team in the spring. For most guys, golf was an elite game—for those whose parents belonged to a country club. To be sure, I would have to buckle down to study and I did. I felt confident, assured. Everybody still talked about the last throw and my incredible arm.

A Different Light

After I had lived in the annex for several months, sharing the room at the top of the winding stairs with Tom, my disdain for Sean and Randy, and for the abuses of Hell Week, dissipated with my increased drinking and my becoming part of their inner circle. As sophomores, Tom and I felt honored Sean and Randy had offered us a room across from their rooms. Maybe it was my status as the starting quarterback. Or maybe it was how Tom schmoozed them. But we were the first sophomores to have been welcomed into the annex, a luxury reserved for juniors and seniors and considered the elite rooms in the fraternity.

No longer in the main house, we did not have to keep quiet during study time in the afternoon and early evening. We could party more often—in fact, any time we wanted. Except when I brought pledges over to clean the annex, freshmen were not allowed in the annex. Late at night, after the parties withered to a close, I would be there with them, showing them how to clean the toilets and floors without disturbing the upperclassmen. That was my job as House Manager, a job I was proud of having. When I was most honest with myself, I envisioned it as steppingstone to becoming president, and many of the men in the house thought I would be a good one. I liked being seen as a leader. My brother supported me.

"Hey don't worry about treating me as a pledge," Jack said. "I'll do the work just like the freshmen. You do your job."

I did, yet I kept my party life confined to the annex, since I knew he was of drinking age and might feel I was flaunting my seniority over him.

Tom had no ambitions for leadership: he liked having a good time and bought a calendar with dates of made-up special holidays for every day of the week so we could have a reason to celebrate every day by drinking well into the night if we wanted and, most of the time, we did.

When Sean and Randy were drunk, they became endearing, vulnerable, telling about their fathers who seemed to be quite similar—overbearing men who demanded their sons make them proud. On the long evenings of chasing one mug after another, I learned that Sean, who grew up in southern Alabama, came from a wealthy family that once owned a cotton plantation but in the decades after the Civil War, had fallen on hard times and never really recovered.

As Sean told me, "We damn fell on hard luck. My dad, the worst of a bad lot, never could keep a job. He thought that his name would buy him work. Fat chance. He was like a skunk, thinking his fancy coat and long stripes would open doors. But it closed them." His dad drank fine whiskey, Jack Daniels, sour mash, and liked pretty women. Sean bragged that his dad introduced Sean to women when he was thirteen, escorted him to the local brothel where Alice, a young girl in her mid-teens, took him by the hand to a special room with mirrors on every wall and told him "how big" he was and encouraged him to come back often, which he did. But he admitted that with his dad waiting outside the door, it felt as if he were going to a dental appointment and couldn't enjoy it, although he "got off, of course." By the time he came out of the room, his dad had gone into another room and stayed for an hour. Sean admitted it made him sick to hear his father humping away like some dog with a bitch in heat.

"He treated my mama like crap, scum of the earth, and I will never forgive him for that," Sean said with a sneer on this face. "Oh yeah, I'm not complaining about the sex, nor the booze. But they don't make no difference: there are just some things one cannot forgive."

He described how his pap came out of the side room after getting laid. Staggering down the hallway while tucking his shirt in his pants, he called out, "Hey, Charlotte, come see my boy. He's done already, just like his dad, making quick work with his lady." Charlotte, tying up her silk bathrobe, came down the hall after him, and bent over Sean. She held up his face as an old aunt might do and pronounced, "Why he's cute, Harold, better looking than you by a long shot," at which Harold slapped her, "Don't say that, bitch. I pay good money: you be nice." She withdrew her hand to her face, but smiled at Sean, bending close to him, whispering in a barely audible voice. "Come back anytime, sweet pea."

"What you say, whore?" his pap cried out and she retorted, "I told him to mind his pap."

"Bitch," he flung her the middle finger, "you lie like a rug."

His dad wanted Sean to reclaim the family name and take no less than first place in anything he did. Sean swore he would never to be like his dad. He clenched his fist in the air, "That bastard, I'm not the least bit like him," and his lip curled up in a snarl. He may have wanted to sever any connection, but his temperament made him unpredictable as a child in a toy store. His vitriol boiled over when anyone disagreed with him. He loved goading others. Racist platitudes spilled from his lips whenever he drank. Most of all, he treated any girl as one thing: a potential lay. I didn't know his dad but Sean sounded more like his daddy than he'd like to admit.

I'd seen his cruelty during Hell Week, but, back then, I hadn't known his vulnerable side. His cruelty, lurking inside him now, seemed more pathetic than despicable. He was polished and better educated than his father but clearly his father's ghost haunted and possessed him.

As House Manager, I became a member of the leadership council. Randy was vice president and next in line after John finished his term. Sean was still secretary. I worked with them, having the pledges be particularly fastidious about cleaning their room. Secretly, I had been talking with Eric, who rarely, if ever, drank and, therefore, had nothing to do with Sean and the drinking crowd. He and I shared plans to make the rite of initiation more humane, setting up goals and aligning them more with our "True Gentleman" creed. I kept Eric's ideas in the back of my mind, while trying to impress everyone with my work ethic and my being a regular guy.

I kept up some friendships from the main house. Whenever Steve wanted to talk—and he did—I encouraged him to come to my room and we talked about some new girlfriend that he met and how he feared that she might dump him. Some nights, when Tom was out on a date, I'd still listen to my music and sing along. I read most of T. S. Eliot's collected works and had picked up books by Ezra Pound, Rainer Maria Rilke, and Carl Sandburg. I figured that I could live a double life to get what I wanted. If it meant kissing up to Randy and Sean, I'd do it. Ambition demanded some duplicity.

But what started out as a strategy to put myself in a position to shape the future of the fraternity took a hard turn. Sean invited me to more of his parties. His charm and charisma won me over. A fifth of Jack Daniels dulled my resentment. I could tolerate anyone, even the Pope, if he drank. But I lost contact with Paul who told me that I had compromised my integrity. I told him that it was, as my dad would say, the price of doing business. Paul avoided me. But Sean chummed up to me. After a few drinks, he'd draped his arms over my shoulder, muttering, "You Northern boys are all right, all right." His Southern drawl, the soft lilt of his voice, the way vowels soothed the air—all of those effects blunted those memories of his sitting in the wicker chair smirking at us as we ate raw garlic and onions.

He was even comic, especially with Randy. When Randy was mewling about his date, how she "would not put out," Sean would lie back on the couch, shove his hips up and moan with a deep Southern drawl, "It's all right roomie, y'all can have me; I'll satisfy you." Randy would hop on him, acting as if he were a rutting steer, crying out, "Yippee, ride 'em cowboys!" and they'd fall on the floor, laughing.

A Nazi

One evening, early in November, on a Saturday, my brother Jack had gone to Indianapolis with his new girlfriend, Barbara, to visit her parents. He had told me that she might be "the one" and planned to invite her to meet our parents. I was pleased for him. It made it easy for me. I could let loose without worrying about him, a pledge, seeing me have a good time while he had to toe the line.

Seven of us gathered in Bill's room, all the guys from the Annex—Sean, Randy, Tex and Matt who lived downstairs, Bill, Tom and I. We were listening to Ray Charles and singing along, "I Can't Stop Loving You," at the top of our lungs to and "Born to Lose," wailing about our lost loves, the end of the semester, the long cold nights, and angst of finding dates. In the midst of the ruckus, Sean bemoaned how "Stein has a new cunt every week. How does the Jew do it?"

Tom interjected, "Get real, Sean, your bigotry is showing."

Sean sat up in his chair. "I'm no bigot. It's not that he is a Jew; it's that he *acts* like a Jew," he growled. "He acts as if he owns the campus and every girl on it; he's fuckin' got his way with women. He is so full of himself like some god damn prima donna, like he's got special rights over them. He took my girl from me, you know, Julie, the Kappa—nice-looking broad, too. I dated her for two whole months. He never asked me if he could date her. When he asked her to coffee, she turned me out like a hired hand, left me high and dry. He never apologized or nothing."

"He dates more than any of us combined," Bill chimed in. "He has gone out with every hot chick on campus. I mean, look at him," and then Bill stared at me, "and look at you, Jason, you're a stud, athletic, good-looking and you practically never date. You're always in your room with Steve, talking to all hours of the night. Or listening to that weird music. What's with that?"

The conversation snapped like a whip at me. I quickly assessed what I should say to lash it back toward someone else. Indeed, I did spend hours with Steve who was not liked since he did not drink. Sean called him "one of those straight arrows." I could not defend myself by telling the others about Steve's woes. That was confidential. I pressed the mug in both my hands and noticed how the suds diminished. A tiny thin scrim of them hung over the edge the cup. I looked up. Bill leaned forward in his chair, holding his beer in his hands, rubbing the mug back and forth. He said, "I never thought much about it, Jason, but what is that? I mean you could have any girl on campus, just like Stein, and you wallow away your time in your room reading weird stuff, playing weird music, talking to a weird guy. I don't get it."

Everyone stared at me. I felt as if someone had unleashed a snarling dog, its fangs at my neck. I took a quick swig of my beer, held the mug up, laughed as if it were no big deal, and shrugged and said, "Bill, you should know, I like to drink. Getting smashed is a whole lot more fun than going out with some broad that you don't even know and who doesn't even put out after you've laid out fifteen bucks on a meal and movie that you could have spent buying a fifth of Jack Daniels. You know the sorority broads as well as I do. It's a waste of time. You've told me a hundred times what a pain in the ass those first dates are."

Bill's eyes were still on me. He shook his head, "Hell, if you're a fag, just admit it."

There was a silence. Ray Charles's voice wailed in the background. I could hear everyone breathing. It felt as if Bill's statement tightened like a noose around me and with each second its pressure squeezed against my throat, suffocating me. I looked over at Tom who had retreated to the back of the room by the door. I tried to get his attention, but he stared at something on the rug.

He leaned against the wall. His right leg kicked back and forth. Why didn't he say something?

Bill stared at me, opened his mouth, but then caught himself—perhaps it was the pained expression on my face, the memories of the nights I spent listening to his lamenting his woes dating one girl or another that dropped him like a leper, curtailed his questioning of me—but he stopped, shuffled his shoe on the rug as if rubbing out a spot. He grinned and said, "No big deal," raising his beer to signal an end of the questioning. He muttered softly, "Sorry."

Tom glanced at me and stepped out the door. The record had stopped. The sound of the needle on the end of the record caused Tex to change it. I sipped my beer, licking the foam on the edge of the cup. Sean paced back and forth like a dog on a chain and posted himself in front of me.

He chimed in, "No, wait a damn minute. Hey, I don't know about you other guys, but I don't want no faggot living next door to me."

He raised an eyebrow and asked, "You sure you're not a little fairy?" He waved his hand, loose-wristed at me.

Everyone laughed. I looked around at the faces staring at me, and, acted as if it was just a joke. I laughed too, desperately trying to say the right thing.

"Yeah, a fairy, right!" I bantered. "That's right." I flipped my wrist in a fey manner.

Leaning forward, Sean intoned, "Hey, this is no joking matter. I want to know. How is it you rarely date on your own? Not unless it's a double date? What's that all about?"

My chest constricted. My neck tensed. I glanced toward the bathroom—maybe I could go there as if I had to pee—then I stared at my beer. I had to say something.

"Sean, quit it. You know as well as I do I'm no faggot. We double-dated a number of times before Stein hijacked your Julie. We even came back here and, well, you know what happened."

"Oh, yeah, you took that other broad into your room. What happened? I forgot to ask you," he asked, clearly interested if I got any action.

I decided to be honest since I managed to change the topic, "I had no luck. You know how it is with Kappas. They treat you like dog meat. Don't any of you guys know what I'm saying?"

To my right, I heard someone smack his leg. Tex, a senior from Texas who wore a ten gallon hat and cowboys boots with gold braided insignias, laughed and chimed in, "Yeah, I agree with that. These stuck-up Eastern sorority broads are as stiff as dried-up leather and pointy as a cactus at high noon." Everyone laughed at him.

He enjoyed the attention and I liked how the conversation had shifted away from me.

"Let me tell you about Stein," he said.

He stood up and went over to the keg, poured another mug, and pointed his finger at the doorway. "You all know I don't have much money. I mean I live off a crap scholarship and my daddy, he don't have the means to even send me the clothes on my back and that bastard Stein has insisted that I pay back a measly loan—just two damn bucks—when we were at that townie bar. He hounded me until I paid him, isn't that right Matt?"

He turned to his roommate who was staring into his mug and who, simply responded with a belch. Matt, a quiet drunk, rarely talked, kept mostly to himself but followed Tex everywhere like a trained dog. Tex slapped his leg again, "Well, I'll be. That's the most intelligent things I've heard him say in quite some time."

Unfazed with the distraction, Tex continued, "What does five bucks matter?" He laughed, taking out his wallet and tossing singles in the middle of the room, "What the fuck does money matter? I could give a hoot. But him—it's the wages of righteousness. Screw the damn girls. You can have them. But him? He needs some humility. He made me into a loser and," his voice strident by the end, passionate as a Baptist preacher's, beer slopping over the sides of his mug, he stomped his boot on the floor, "I ain't no loser. I weren't born to lose."

Bill yelled, "No you are not, Tex. But you will be soon enough if you keep slopping that good beer from the keg I bought on my new rug."

Another chorus of laughter brought a smile to Tex's face. He swigged the rest of his beer, turned the mug upside down, "There you are, Bill. No more spills," once Tex sat back in a plump easy chair and propped his feet up like a king, I noticed that Tom had come back and sat on the arm of a couch opposite me. Funny how he glided in and out of a room like a ghost who knew when to appear and disappear. He smiled weakly at me and leaned back, clearly wanting to be a spectator to the harangues.

Sean made a wager, "Someone has got to cut him down a notch, you know what I mean? Someone has got to let him know that he isn't some god damn God. He ain't better than the rest of us." He emphasized "God," drawing out the "o" in his Southern drawl.

By this time, ideas for cutting Joseph Stein down a notch came up. Someone thought to put a swastika on his door, but that seemed too extreme. Another suggested messing his room up since Stein was fastidious, his books in neat piles on his desk, his papers laid out like an accountant's, his clothes always folded, his shirts pressed, a new outfit every day.

"Damn good idea," Sean chimed, slapping his thigh, "We just muss his hair sort of, get his attention, you know what I mean? We'll teach him to loosen up, not be such a...." He hesitated, then blurted out, "Hell, I can say it: a Jew! Show him that he's not the only winner." He started to croon, taking up a refrain from the song on the record player, and continued, "Show him maybe he was born to lose too."

As he picked up on Ray Charles's refrain, we joined him and laughed. After more discussion, which had taken on a solemn tone, someone said, "Let's vote on this, make a pact. We better agree if it's goin' to happen."

Tex shoved his beer up, "I will drink to it." Tom smiled, "I'll drink to anything," standing as he went to get another mug of beer. Bill raised his mug, "Me too," and stood to fill his mug. In a few minutes, everyone had saluted with their mugs.

"Then we all agree," Sean strutted around the room, stomping in a goosestep. "We're all Nazis!"

I stared at him and thought of the Nazi officer who showed us through Dachau. I wondered if he was exposed to the same type of initiation into the SS, the same hate.

Tom smirked at him, mockingly cheering, "Yeah, here's to the numb brained Nazis," and guzzled half a mug.

We sang out in a chorus, "Here's to the Nazis."

Silent as usual, Matt, his tousled blond hair strewn across his face, propped himself with his left hand and tried to stand up but tilted forward instead like a stack of blocks and smacked face down, on the floor. Tom laughed, grabbed him by the arm, lifted him up with a giant heave and aimed him toward the keg, "You need another drink," and by holding his arm in Matt's, walked the five feet to the keg, making sure he didn't tumble again.

"Get something to drink," Tom pointed to me, laughing. "Don't just sit there, buddy: make something of yourself."

Sean was singing a low tune in a Southern drawl, "We're the Nazis." Several others joined it, making mock salutes.

With his hands on his hips, Sean stood in the middle of the room, glowering at everyone, "But you're wimps," he intoned. "Adolf wants to know if anyone will step up and act to protect the manhood of one of its esteemed members." He pointed at Tex who smiled and raised his mug and added," You're wimps, wimps, wimps."

"So are you," Bill countered, pointing at Sean.

"Well, I'll be damned, you got me there," Sean said. "I have to keep some decorum, you know, as an officer and southern gentleman. We Nazis have to keep up a good image. We need courageous new members to represent us in our cause. We don't want no fairies here in our midst." He shot a glance at me.

A quiet crept across the room. Matt had squatted on the floor and was holding onto his mug with two hands, sipping at it like a two-year- old. Tex knelt beside him on one knee to help keep his roommate upright. Tom moved back toward the door. Ray Charles's mournful voice wailed in the background.

This was my chance. I knew it. I realized that I could prove myself to be tougher than any of them, to take a stand, not stir the air with prattle but step forward with action. Although my head felt as if someone had filled it with helium and the front part of my brain had detached and lifted out of my skull, I stood and raised my mug. "I'll do it."

"Here, here! Someone with balls," Sean erupted with a shout and gave me a Nazi salute. I saluted him back.

Everyone laughed and clinked their mugs together.

Sean sidled over to me, put his arm around my neck, and raised his mug, "Jesus, welcome to the real world, kid," and patted me on the back several times. "As an officer"—he was one and I knew it—"I see leadership potential in you, my boy." He ushered me to the door. He told the others to stand and salute me. They did.

"This young man has taken on this sacred duty to honor our pact," Sean announced. "Let's drink to him!"

They drank and saluted me again.

I felt a certain power, a sense that I had upstaged them all, called their bluff, proved I was a man, more of a man than they were. With resolve, I stuck my mug on the end table and strode out the door, bumping into the door way on the way out. Before I had walked six steps down the stairwell, gripping the guardrail so I did not trip, I heard someone whisper my name behind me.

"Jason, Jason, hold up."

At the top of the stairs, Tom was holding onto the railing too, propping himself upright, but he wavered back and forth like a sail in the wind, or a sailor about to fall overboard. He cast his eyes over his shoulder, then whispered, "What the hell are you doing? You out of your mind? This is all a joke. A stupid joke. Don't you see Stein is our pledge brother? You can't go around doing that. Forget it and let's go back to our room and call it a night."

I glanced up at his eyes, both tender and drunk, and then at his shoes, unlaced yet highly polished. I spoke to his shoes because they were the only thing not moving, "Don't mess with me. I am going to do it. You're just a chicken shit, and besides," I whispered back," I'm not going to do anything serious, just move stuff around," and winked at him, then headed off to the main house, not sure exactly what I was going to do, yet not willing to wimp out on my promise. This was my chance. No one would mess with me anymore. I kept muttering to myself, "Asshole, asshole," not sure if I was directing the invective at myself or Stein because, as drunk as I was, I could barely negotiate the walkway. As I pulled open the door to the main house, I nearly fell flat on my ass and teetered backward, yet, almost by willpower alone, I straightened up and headed across the threshold and up the stairwell, my hand on the wall for balance. I kept moving by the bodies coming toward me. They snickered or outright laughed at me as they passed. Bastards. I hated feeling as I did, but I had a mission and hated Joseph for being so damn sure of himself, of being able to date any girl, of always kissing up to me and the other brothers. That didn't make him one of us. It never would. And dating every girl on campus didn't make him a man either. His being Mr. Stud made us all feel emasculated. I would show him. I would do it for Sean and poor jilted Tex and I would do it for everyone.

The Proof

When I got to Joseph's room, I checked the hallway to make sure no one saw me. I knocked and entered. No one there. His room was as it always was: each book neatly stacked, the notepad with a pen on it, the clock on the nightstand, his toilet items in precise rows, a poster of John F. Kennedy on the wall along with a photo of his family—his mother and father and him at his high school graduation. I grabbed his desk chair to keep my balance and took several breaths. My brain throbbed. "Now or never. You've got to prove yourself," rattled through my skull. I swept my arm across his desk, his nightstand and dresser, and shoved everything onto the floor, then took the photograph of his family and—desperate to do something else— sprayed saving cream on it. That was enough.

I swung open the door, checked to see if anyone was looking, closed it, and charged down the hall, bumping into Stew, a freshman, who cried out, "What that hell?" Without excusing myself, I headed to the stairwell. As I pulled back the metal door, I glanced over my shoulder and saw Stew enter Stein's room and turn to look at me. Stein was Stew's pledge father. Our eyes met and I turned away, then hurried to the staircase but stopped on the first landing. What was I doing? I thought how stupid it was, how it made no sense, how I could go back right now, leap up the stairs, go down the hallway, and put everything back in order. I started to go up the stairs when Randy called out my name.

"Jason, hey Jason, you there?"

I stopped and turned around. "Yeah, I'm here."

"Fuck man, come on, get back to the party. We don't want no trouble."

"What brings you here?" I asked.

"Oh, the Fuhrer told me to get you"—he laughed—"Tom and I talked to him. He can be such a fool. He doesn't want trouble. I'm glad I got you."

I held onto the railing and let myself down, careful not to fall. At the bottom, Randy swung his arm around my shoulders. "Glad I caught you. You're a good soldier. You met the call of duty, but it's over." He saluted me with his free arm. I returned the gesture as best as I could. He pulled me closer to him. "Come on," he said. "Let's finish off the keg."

We staggered back to Bill's room. The air, cold with a slight breeze, whiffed across my face. Randy, shorter than I, held me by the arm. I liked the feeling of being a good soldier. I may have done wrong. But it would only take Stein a few minutes to restore order to his room. I was pleased with myself for going on a mission as we climbed the stairs of the annex.

When I reentered the party, Sean handed a mug of beer to me and smiled, "You didn't do nothing, did you?"

I nodded. "I did."

Sean grabbed ahold of my arm. He seemed startled and pleased at the same time. "You did?" he asked.

"I did," I replied, sipping from the mug in my hand.

Several hands patted me on the back. "Well, I'll be damned. You're very efficient. You surprised me." He called out to the others in the room as he gave me a bear hug, "Here's a guy with balls, a guy with real balls!"

Everyone clapped me on the back. My head felt muzzy. I didn't care. I felt powerful, a giant of a man.

The party fizzled out quickly. Looking vaguely disgusted, shaking his head, Bill announced that he had had enough and left, adding as he stepped out the door, "Be careful of my new rug."

Tex held onto Matt and said they were going to their room, but they never moved. Tom left without saying a word. I sat on the sofa and guzzled more beer, then lay back, as my brains crackled and spun.

Sean went to the bathroom, and, afterward, said that he and Randy were going to check out the scene at the Monon Grill where at any hour, day or night, you could get a great cup of coffee and a good meal and maybe pick up a broad. Matt passed out and Jack carried him, cradled in his arms, to their room. Tom came back in and told me that he had to get to bed.

"Don't you want another drink?" I asked.

"No. I've had enough of all of this shit," he said and waved his hand in my face. He went to the bathroom and closed the door.

The Blow

Alone, I could hear noise from the floor below where a new party had apparently started. Though I had tunnel vision, I made my way downstairs

Tex had invited several guys to his room to have a nightcap. I flopped down in a thick, burgundy armchair. No one seemed to be interested in me, so I stared out the window at the lights in a building in the main house, one after another going out except one. I closed my eyes, aware of the voices around me yet not caring anymore what was being said. I could see the barracks in the concentration camp, the long narrow path to the showers and the memorial. I was drifting off to restless sleep.

The door to the room flung open. Shoes stomped in.

"What the fuck is going on here?" someone screamed. I opened my eyes and saw Jerry, my best friend, glowering at me.

I shook my head. "What's your problem?"

"Problem?" he shot back, "Where do you get the right to destroy Stein's room. You, the guy who wants to change things around here? You, the guy with great plans to make things better? What kind of half-ass stunt did you pull? You know what kind of fraternity this is?" He leaned over and grabbed my shirt, jerking me partially out of the chair. I'd never seen him enraged. Although four inches shorter than I was—and half as much in weight—he startled me with his leverage.

"It's one fucked-up fraternity," I slurred.

"It sure is when fuck-ups like you do what you did."

"Get the hell off me," I swiped his hand away, realizing that a group of guys were crowded behind him—Bill, Eric, Tex, Steven, Sam, Luis, Tom, Stephen and seven or eight others, including John, the president of the chapter, and off to the side, Stein—who stared at me and then at the floor.

"It wasn't just me," I pleaded. "Let me explain..."

"It was you. Several freshmen saw you. What kind of example is that, Jason? Big leader. Role model! A new breed of House Manager? Big man, huh?" Jerry jeered at me.

I stood up and stepped back from Jerry, to keep him at arm's length. I caught Bill's eyes. He looked away. Tom had come too. He stood in back of Bill. What was everyone doing here?

"Jason, I need some explanation," Jerry said.

"It wasn't just me," I said.

"You were the only one who entered his room, so don't give me that bull," Jerry retorted.

I turned to Tex and Tom and asked, "Where the hell are Sean and Randy?"

They shook their heads, "Out."

"Out?!" I shouted. "Out where?"

Bill grimaced, "It doesn't matter where they are. They meant it as a joke. Didn't you get it was a joke? A big joke. Didn't you see?"

He was not just talking to me but to the other guys in the room to make his case. They stood around me in a semicircle, some with arms folded, some with hands on hips, or in their back pockets. Jerry's eyes tunneled into me with the intensity of a rabid dog.

"Let me out of here," I said and started for the open door. If I could make a break for it, I felt no one would catch me.

"You will not go anywhere until you explain yourself," Jerry said firmly, his voice pitched higher. I looked to see if anyone—Tex, Bill, or Tom – would help me.

Finally, Tom shook his head and said, "I told you. Didn't you hear me?"

"You told me nothing. Remember Hell Week? You know as well as I do that this house is full of two-faced bastards. And you know what happened tonight," I bit off each word as I spoke. He winced and pushed his way out the door as if he were going to be sick.

"Where the hell is Sean?" I asked again, putting my hand out to fend off Jerry again since he had taken several steps toward me. I flailed my arms in his face, shooing him away and shouted, "Get out of here. All of you. Leave me the fuck alone."

Trying to take control, Bill stepped forward and spoke in a soft voice, "This is not about Sean. You know what kind of guy he is when he's drunk. It's you."

I turned away from him and stepped toward the middle of the room. Everywhere I looked, faces, two and three deep, stared at me. Where did they come from? More were coming in.

Jerry reached for me, his tone calmer as if he realized he had to take control of the situation. He used the tone of some shrink trying to assuage me. "Jason, come on, what is going on? Tell me."

"It's none of your fuckin' business," I pushed him back, "or anyone's. Get them out of here. Where the fuck is Sean?"

Bill called out, this time his voice angrier, "Who the hell cares where he is? You're the one who did it. And you, god damn it, can't deny it. You said you were proud of it."

I stared at him and yelled, "Fuck you, Harris. Fuck you," and turning around, pointing at the onlookers, "Fuck all of you. You're hypocrites. You call this a fraternity where 'honor is sacred and virtue safe'? The fuckin' True Gentleman is a lie. It's all lies and deceit and doubletalk and everyone knows it."

"What is it with you, Follett?" Bill asked.

"I'll tell you what it is, you whimpering ass. You bastards believe in this fraternity crap when you all hate each other. You are nothing but fakes. That's right. Fakes. Don't look so upset. That's the way it is. Everyone is talking behind everyone's back. You are nothing but..."

"Hey, wait, Follett, why don't *you* shut up?"

"No, *you*," I shot back, sneering at him. "You wanted me to talk. Now, go to hell, Bill, just get out of here and leave me the fuck alone."

From across the room, Joseph spoke up, "Jason, I think what you did was unfor ..."

"Oh, bullshit. You're full of it. You think people like you because they call you up at all hours to see if you can get them a date. Actually, Joseph, they hate you, your endless girlfriends, your self-assurance and your damn big mouth. They hate you. Don't you get it?"

Joseph stooped as if I landed a sucker punch. He looked looking around him, tentatively, but no one looked him in the eyes. He shuffled to the back of the room and stood by the door.

"Get out of here. This is not your place," I bellowed. Several guys followed Joseph and retreated to the lobby outside Tex's room and gathered below the stairwell. It was a small space, eight by ten. Tex joined me in trying to get people out of his room and the annex.

"Come on, folks. Let it wait till morning," he said and tried to usher several of the crowd toward the lobby. But no one budged. No one left the lobby. They swung around in a circle again, several in front of the doors, one to the outside, one to the dormitory. Tom stood by the stairs. I wanted no more to do with them, but there was no escape.

"You need to explain what happened," Tom said. He pointed in back of me.

When I turned around, Bill and Jerry were standing in the middle of Tex's room.

"Let's lower the rhetoric, Jason. Let's calm it down. No one is here to hurt you. Come on, just explain why you did it. That's all we want," Jerry said, modulating his tone, his voice more measured, his hand reaching out to me. "I'm your friend for Christ sake. Let me know what happened. That's all I need. I'm trying to figure this out just as much as the other guys here."

They wanted me to explain. How could I do that? How could I explain I did it to be one of the guys? They were phonies. They knew about the pact. They wanted a scapegoat. They wanted to see me hang. I was their Jew. I pointed at the others in the room, "Do me a favor, Jerry, get them out of here!"

Bill stepped in front of Jerry, "Listen, Jason, you need to quit telling us what to do. You need to start..."

By now, there were fifteen guys in the room again, and more coming.

Bill was now speaking for the group. "Listen, Follett, We're tired of this. You have got to quit."

Bill was shorter than I was. I looked down on him and could see that he had a slight balding spot on the top of his head. A square, husky guy, built like a boxer, he tried to glare me down. "Oh, Bill, just lay off, will you? Quit trying to be the big shit."

"That's enough, Follett," he said.

"Goddamn, would you go to hell, just go to hell!"

He stepped back, raised his shoulders like a cat. He opened his mouth and, as he did at night before he went to bed, pulled out his bridge with a false tooth. He held it out for a moment for everyone to see, then handed it to Tom.

"Okay, that's it," Bill said. He stepped toward me, his fists up, moving closer, his face coming closer to mine, not two feet away.

"You don't want to do that," I warned, pushing my hand out at him.

He stepped sideways and, *whap,* slugged me in the jaw; I toppled back where someone held me up and shoved me back in front of Bill. He looked mad, his face rigid, his eyes narrow. He swung again, but I anticipated it, pulled back, which threw him off balance and his punch flailed in the air. I wanted to smack him good and drew back my fist because he was turning around and was not expecting me. I had him just where I wanted him.

Jerry leapt between us, holding his hands up. "STOP it. STOP it," he cried. He gently pushed Bill to the side. He let down his arms. He turned to me, looking at me to see what he could do.

"Jason, listen to reason, just stop and listen," Jerry pleaded, putting his hands up trying to corral me from pacing back and forth and bolting, to stop me from finding a seam in the line, as I used to do in football as a fullback, so I could break through and get the fuck out of there.

Someone called out, "Look at him! He's out of his mind!"

Another cried, "Grab him. He's trying to run!"

Jerry shouted out against the din, "Calm down. *Please* calm down!"

I saw them rush at me, closing in. I had to get out.

"Leave me the hell alone," I yelled, lunging toward the front door. If I could get out, walk it off, figure out how I got caught up in this mess, check with Sean—where the hell was he? He'd know what to say. He'd defend me. He knew what happened. He was the Fuhrer. He made us Nazis. He'd made the pact. It was no joke. We all agreed. We all agreed.

Before I could bolt through the door, Jerry grabbed me by my arm to stop me.

My old instincts, those I'd been trained to use as a fullback to fend off tacklers, came back in a flash. My arms tensed, my body rose up, and I stepped forward to meet him with a blow from my forearm that lifted him——his face blanched as I held him momentarily off the floor—and then flung him across the room. He was amazingly light. His body hung midair—it seemed—for a moment and I could see his eyes, startled, mortified, looking directly into mine, before he smacked against the large window and his head jerked forward and then, more quickly, back, as his arms splayed out, shattering the glass, which then cascaded over him and onto the floor. His head slumped forward and he grasped his wrist, moaning, "Jesus-fuckin-Christ." Blood pulsed between his fingers, seeping onto the floor and he toppled over on his side. His face turned a milky white. His mouth opened like a fish gasping for something, then stayed open and quivered. He stared at me. The blood seeped through his fingers and down his arm.

Bill bent over him, yelling, "Quick, we need to stop the blood." Joseph had returned and tore off his shirt, then ripped it apart and shoved the strips at Bill.

Bill knelt over Jerry and wrapped the strips of shirt around the bloody wrist. He glanced up briefly at me and muttered, "You goddamn fool!"

Stunned by what I had done, I lurched forward to see if I could help, but several guys pulled me back and pinned me against the wall. One shoved his knee in my groin. Another pressed my arms back. I did not resist. They tried to turn me around, but I fell to my knees. I was done and I knew it.

Words sputtered from my mouth, "Oh god, I'm sorry, so sorry, Jerry. I didn't mean it." Several other guys had lifted him by his legs and arms and were hurrying him out the door. I could see that the glass had ripped his shirt in several places. Blood stained the sides of it like splattered paint, and a large dark splotch spread out across the whole back panel.

Before they were out the door, he told them to wait. His face, ashen, riveted me with an intensity I'd never seen before. He was breathing heavily. His jaw twisted slightly to the right, then he whispered, "God damn, what happened to you, Jason? I thought..." and he trailed off and clenched his jaw, his eyes filling with tears. I fell forward on my knees and tried to say something but the two guys whose arms held Jerry upright turned away, alarmed because the blood was pooling beneath him on the floor, "Let's go, let's go, let's go, fast! We need to get him to emergency," and carried him out the doorway.

The two guys holding me tightened their grip, one with his knee in my back, the other forcing my arms back. I fell forward on my side. I stared at the window, the jagged edges of glass like a contorted mouth of a shark. Vomit climbed up my throat but I swallowed it back down. I hung forward, my body shaking, and from out of a pit in my belly, a convulsive sobbing like a squall swept over me as if something had broken loose and, whatever it was, it could not be contained. A knee pressed harder into my back. I saw two shiny shoes a foot in front of me.

Tom's voice blurted out, "Can't you see he's crying? For God's sake, let go of him. He's not going to harm anyone. He's drunk. Leave him to me. I'll take care of him."

My arms released, I tumbled face forward on the floor. Several shoes moved back. A hand came under my chin and held it for a second, then an arm braced my back and pulled me sideways onto my hip. I could see blue trousers. A striped red and white shirt. A collar. A face.

Tom had knelt beside me and said, "Hold onto me," and I gripped my arm around his neck and, with his hand around my waist, he stood me up, balancing me for a moment and, then, partially dragging me, he brought me up the stairs to our room. He put me on the couch and sat in silence beside me. He put his hand on my knee. The sobbing shook my body so much that the tears blinded me from seeing anything. I tried to stop them but it was as if I was grieving my whole life away. He passed me some Kleenex and I grabbed a bunch and patted my face. How much time came and went I have no idea. Tom helped me out of my shoes, shirt and pants and placed a blanket over me. I felt a chill. Before he stood up, he leaned forward and very lightly kissed my cheek and muttered, "It will be all right." He left and I could hear him talk to someone in the hall. He came back into the room and sat in the chair across from the couch. I could hear him breathe. I noticed his shoes were still untied. I tried to look up and see his face but could only see his pant leg, a stain on it, a dark jagged trail that seemed to go higher, but the room was getting darker and was swirling backward and kept falling away from me as if I was drowning in a pool of icy water and was not coming back but being pulled into a vortex, a downward spiral, but I held on by looking at his shoe and the lace and there were more voices and then there was silence and the silence kept coming at me and I tried to push it away, to push away the look in Jerry's eyes which, I remembered, were like the looks in the prisoners' eyes who bobbed in icy water, the eyes of those who knew they were dying, of those who could not stop the savagery. I wanted to scream out, "Stop it, stop it," but the images kept coming at me and everyone one had the same face—Jerry's face—and I swatted at it, trying to push it away. Tom sat by the couch on the floor. He held onto my arms. He rubbed my back, "There. There. It's all right. Go to sleep." The darkness of a room with no windows closed in on me. I began to cry out, "No, no, no." A hand softly caressed my cheek. I wanted to flee from the dark, to find some light, any light. But in the dark, a reassuring voice was trying to soothe me, and I fell into it, into the softness of the voice, let myself float on it and someone laid his hand on my head and said, "Rest," and I did.

The Trial

Sunlight blasted like a siren through the window as someone shook me. "Get up. You need to dress. There's a meeting." I squinted and saw Tom leaning over me. Behind him, John, the president of the fraternity, stood with his arms folded in front of him.

I flopped my arm over my forehead. "Not now. Later. I'm really hungover."

Tom pressed at my shoulder more vigorously," Get up."

I sat upright and peered through the slits in my eyes, but then out of nausea, I slumped back, only to feel Tom's hand on my shoulder, pulling me up again. I put my hand to my face. The skin felt clammy, taut as if I were waking from the dead. Tom and John were talking intensely. I couldn't hear them clearly because my ears were clogged as if I been underwater. A voice was directed at me. I gasped for breath, tried to lean back since the room swirled. The sunlight jabbed at me like a knife.

Then John's voice interposed itself, sternly: "Get dressed Jason. We have some business to attend to—a meeting. You need to be there."

After Tom slapped water on my face and helped me dress, he escorted me down the steps and out into the light.

When I entered the dining room of the main house, the president, vice president and secretary were already seated behind two rectangular dinner tables, which were set up at the far end of the room. They were chatting in muted voices with one another. Other members of the fraternity were seated in chairs, six deep, facing them. Part of the way back, Jerry sat, his hands bandaged. I averted my eyes. I wondered how bad his wounds were. Tom escorted me to a chair adjacent to the front table. The vice president, Randy, recited a phrase that signaled the call to order. The words came from the fraternity pledge and, as I heard them, they had a certain sting—"how good and how pleasant it was for brothers to dwell in unity."

Randy's face appeared sallow, gaunt; his blond hair, wet and combed back. He wore a coat and tie. He never looked at me, but kept his focus on John instead. Sean scratched notes on a paper, his face ashen.

218

The room felt oppressively hot. The old wooden window sashes were warped. Only sharp winter winds could seep through the cracks of the unopenable frames, unless someone opened the door. The air was always still and stifling, as it was that morning.

John folded his hands in front of him. "I think you all know the reason for this morning's meeting. We have a grave problem. The way Jason acted last night. I mean, most of you know—perhaps I should explain with Jason here——the fights and damage to a brother's room and the language he called his own brother." He bit his upper lip and stared at me.

My head throbbed. My hands felt clammy. I glanced at Jerry who was whispering something to Bill. I wanted to crawl under a table and hide.

"I think," John continued, "that Jason has been brought before this meeting because some action needs to be taken." He coughed into his hand and pressed his glasses back up the ridge of his nose. "Personally, I do not think his actions can go without punishment." He hesitated, sensing he had used a wrong word, "I mean without consequence but it is not for me to decide. It is for the membership to determine. Right now I will question him, if that's all right with everyone." He looked around the room and I glanced at the membership, at their expressionless faces, faces staring at the floor, faces of early morning, faces of the hungover, their eyes puffy, their skin pasty. John nodded his head. He knew no one would question him. He had the authority to mandate a meeting, to confront the problem head on— to confront me.

As I gazed at the different members, I thought back on the gala parties when we transformed the house into a Hawaiian Luau, with a fountain and pool in front, and how everyone got drunk, how the campus police crashed the party, cleared out all the coeds, and arrested the drunkest members—— the vice president and secretary among them. I thought of the initiation rituals, the long rhythmic chants of the sacred order contrasted with the general cynicism of most members who thought the ceremonies were phony. I thought of the classes on the fraternity, the graphs of its long history from its founder to the present, from its roots in the Confederacy and racist ideology to its claptrap about brotherhood, from the mysteries embedded in the fraternity ritual to the weekly drunken parties, from making neophytes into members, as if the initiation was supposed to be the emotional apex of our lives, to the backroom put downs of members not in the in-group. I recalled how we stood solemnly with arms folded on our chests, in robes, blindfolded until we entered the candlelit room, everyone serious, somber, how several of us sniggered when we saw Sean and Randy, elegantly clad in purple robes and golden turbans, holding large scrolls in front of them, reading arcane lines that, often, they could not even pronounce. And now, the room as solemn as it had been less than four months before, seemed just as absurd. I clutched my fists. I tried to blot out the vision of Jerry's pale face staring at me, how the blood oozed though his fingers, the knifelike shards scattered on the floor with blood on them, how the faces of Trevor, Brian, and Joseph glowered at me as I was pinned to the floor. I felt as if I could not breathe.

John took a deep breath and continued. "We must address the business at hand." The room was silent. He then rose and walked to the front of the officers' table and sat on the edge of the table. Like a professor, he positioned himself over me and sighed. I recognized the technique from watching Perry Mason do it on TV, how the lawyer casually confronted the witness on the stand, almost speaking like a close friend, before turning the screw and getting the witness to crack.

I wondered if John had chosen this position intentionally. I kept my eyes on my hands which I held in my lap. He was not going to get the best of me. I felt sick; my head was swimming. But I could hold my own. He addressed me directly, said that he had seen Stein's room, had interrogated the freshman who saw me, had witnessed the debacle in the annex, had heard Stein's plea for the need to honor the ideal of brotherhood. Then he looked up and let his gaze settle on Jerry whose wrist, head, and arms were bandaged. He was picking at one of the bandages, adjusting it. He looked awful. I felt like crying. What had I done?

Questions snapped at me, "Did you?" and "Do you deny it?"

I focused on my thumbs, how neatly they crossed. I would not give anyone the satisfaction of making eye contact. It didn't matter anyway. What could I say? I had done what John accused me of doing. His voice, steady and insistent, rattled off one fact after another. I crossed my thumbs over and they fit in the slots either way, my right on top of my left, left on top of right, a pattern.

It was his eyes that startled me. John had crouched down so that his face was right in line with my hands, and he was speaking softly, "Why, Jason, why did you do it?" He stared at me, his eyes glimmering as if he were about to cry. I pulled my eyes away and shook my head. He wasn't supposed to do this.

He put his hand on top of my hands, "Come on, it is not like you. I know you. What is going on?"

I looked up. I was having difficulty breathing. My head was pounding. I could feel the tears brimming inside me but I was like a faucet sealed tight. I was not going to give anyone the satisfaction of breaking down. If they wanted to crucify me, fine. But I was going to wait it out. I had nothing to say. There were others in the room. They knew what happened, what we did. I would not rat on them. If they spoke up, it was their choice.

"Come on," he repeated. "There is something going on here that is not being said. Does anyone have anything to say about what happened?" he asked, scanning over the membership, then back at the officers' table. I took a moment to look at Sean who had been speaking quietly with Randy. He stopped and glanced at me and then shuffled some papers on the table. They both sat up in the chairs and folded their hands in front of them and looked on indifferently, their faces like granite.

"Anyone? Anyone?"

I straightened up in my chair and glanced at the membership, many of them with hangdogged expressions, not looking at me, not looking at John. I stared again at Sean, who clearly was as hungover as I was, and thought how ironic, that he was the secretary, the scribe who would make an account of what had happened for posterity. Would he record patting me on the back, admiring me for acting? He jotted a note on some paper. Next to him, Randy was making notes, too, his jaw grinding back and forth. Then I turned back to the membership and saw Jerry. He stared at me and shook his head. His face drawn, he seemed to be trying to puzzle out what he was seeing. Bandages covered his wrist. There sat the evidence.

I had not said a word. I looked up at the ceiling and out the window. I folded my arms across my chest, hugging myself.

Me against them—that's how it is, I thought.

"Do you have anything to say for yourself?" John asked, this time measuring out every word.

I said, "No."

For a moment, he knelt down lower and peered up at me. Then he took off his glasses and pinched his eyes and wiped his hand on his trouser. "You can go," he told me. "Someone will get you once we make a decision."

The Sentence

I went out of the room by the back door and walked across the street to the field and the woods where Paul and I had buried the flag. I walked to the far end to a playground and sat on a swing and curled my arms around the chains, keeping still. A faint breeze brushed against me.

I remembered the memorial at Dachau. What were the words on it? It said something about uniting to resist evil, and here I was, as culpable as the SS guide. When he spoke about his work at the crematorium—the dials he turned—he could have stopped and said, "No, I will not do this," just as I could have never turned the knob of Stein's door. I could have turned back, but I did not. How easy, I thought, it is to slide into evil, just a matter of seconds and it is done. All it took for me was for the fear, the "primitive terror" to rear its head and I would do anything, even things I found abhorrent, to save face.

The last leaves in the tall hardwoods clicked. The ground was hard like cement. I tried to breathe slowly, let the cool air fill my lungs.

I heard footsteps. It was Tom. He told me that they had made a decision and to come back to the meeting. "What is it?" I asked. He didn't look at me.

"I can't say," he uttered, seemingly more disconsolate than I was. He looked as if he were going to cry.

He stopped, "Why didn't you defend yourself? You didn't start it. You know it and I know it. Why didn't you say what happened?"

I laughed, "Me defend myself? You must be kidding. The question I have is this: why, tell me, did no one speak up? No one said a word about the pact. Not a word."

"I don't know."

"Why, Tom, didn't you say something? I thought you were my friend," I asked.

He clamped his arms across his chest. His cheeks pulled in. "You want to know why?"

"Yeah."

223

"Because I was pissed. I told you not to do it and you did. Why did you do it? It's not like you?"

"Why?"

"Yes, why?"

"Because I'm a fuck-up, that's why."

"No, you're not. You have great ideas. You were doing a terrific job as House Manager. Everyone knew it. So what's up? What happened?"

I stood and shoved my hands in my pockets. For a moment, I wanted to spill out my fears, to let him know that when they called me a homosexual, I lost it. I felt exposed. I shivered.

"It's cold."

"You didn't answer my question!"

"I'm a Nazi," I said.

"That's bullshit. None of us took it seriously. None of us believed a word of that Nazi crap. It was a joke. It was stupid. Sean was drunk. You knew it and I knew it."

"But we made a pact."

"Come on, that was just a joke."

"So that's why you didn't speak up to defend me? It was all a joke?" I asked angrily.

"I'm not where you are. You're the one who trashed Joseph's room. You're the one who tossed Jerry through the window."

"So that's your reason: I'm the *only* one who is guilty?"

Tom took several steps out in the playground and kicked at some stones. "I couldn't speak up, not after what you did to Jerry." Tears glistened in his eyes. "I saw him when he got back from the hospital. He couldn't believe you'd done it. He was sobbing. The doctors said could have died. Did you know that?"

"Is he all right?"

"One bad cut on his head and that one on his wrist, eight stitches, almost got an artery and who knows what might have happened if it were cut. There are lots of little gashes in his back and in both arms. He's shaken up. But he'll be fine."

"That's good."

He stepped in front of me, "Say something. You need to say something.

Defend yourself. That's what's killing you. No one knows why you're acting like such an asshole."

"It doesn't matter," I told him. "I fucked up. What can I say?"

"You could tell what really happened," he blurted out. "I don't care. Tell them about the Nazis, tell them about the pact. Tell everything. Say something for God's sake."

"No one cares," I replied.

"That's not true," he whispered, since he had come back closer to me, not a foot away. "John does. I do. And Jerry—you'd be surprised— does too."

"Well, I don't," I replied, pressing my hand to my forehead because a searing pain flashed across my skull. I nodded toward the house. "It's over and I'm not..."—I hesitated because a flash of rage tore through me, ripping right though my chest as it did the previous night—so I found myself blurting out, "Fuck it, fuck everyone!" and bolted from the swing toward the other side of the street, but, after twenty steps, I turned back. Tom was standing and looked angry. He pointed his finger at me.

"Cut the shit, man. Come back here! There's no time to play hide-and-seek. This is serious shit. Serious. Cool your heels. Pull yourself together. Come on. You're acting crazy. Fuck, man, I don't know what has gotten into you. I don't know you anymore."

He'd taken several more steps onto my side of the street and offered me his hand. I took hold if it and walked back with him. After a few steps, he squeezed my hand, then let go and nodded at the door of the fraternity

Back inside, I sat in the same chair, and John called the meeting to order. He coolly went over the findings, then announced that I had been stripped of my office. "There have to be consequences," he asserted. He spoke about the brotherhood, how we needed to keep the precepts of being a True Gentleman in our hearts and that we must respect and love one another. He was struggling with the right words. He paced back and forth, recounting his own personal agony over what had happened and what he might have done to let it occur. He pleaded with everyone to move beyond this dark night and hoped it would be an awakening for us all. Then, changing his tone, he acknowledged that I had done a good job as House Manager, but that my actions were "egregious" and could not be condoned.

I did not know what "egregious" was but I assumed it was pretty bad.

As he summarized the decisions of the membership, his voice was not as assured as it was at the beginning of his speech; instead it had become distinctly raw, almost hoarse. His consternation manifested it in his face: his cheeks reddened as well as his ears. He took out a white handkerchief and wiped the sweat from his brow. He turned away from me and addressed the assemblage in a tone that was strict and severe. He said that I was still a member, that we all make mistakes, that he expected apologies on all sides, that he knew I would give them and that –this time speaking directly to me, his voice cracking because he was nearly in tears—he considered me a friend, a dear friend, and that our friendship endured, that we were brothers in the bonds. He stood upright as if someone had barked at him to stand at attention. He looked directly at me, his lips drawn tightly together for a moment. Abruptly, he asked for the meeting to be adjourned and someone moved and it was seconded.

It was over.

John shook my hand and patted me on the shoulder. Then he and the other members dispersed, leaving only me, the condemned, behind, as if waiting to be carted off to his prison.

The Long Walk

Once everyone had gone, I left with the intention of taking a long walk to nowhere, but Tom was waiting by the back door and asked if I wanted to get some breakfast.

The thought of being in public jarred me. I could not do it. I thanked him and took off down the street, knowing I had to get as far away from the house as I could.

About half way down the block, I heard someone call my name. It was Paul, standing by a large oak. He motioned for me to come over.

"You all right?" he asked.

"No. How could I be?" I retorted.

"Cool it. I'm not the enemy. I know it must be rough. I just wanted to say, 'Remember what we did last year.' You have a lot of good inside you, man. Remember that." He leaned forward and put his arms around me.

"Thanks."

"I know you need some time. But remember who you are to me is always the guy who made a stand," he said, then shook my hand and left. I did remember how we had made a stand against Sean, but now it seemed so far away that it was no longer me but someone else that had done that.

My skull felt as if my brains had boiled on a burner and were about to explode. I could not see right. I strode dizzily across the playground, into the wooded area behind it and kept walking——past the sorority houses, past the row of homes under the shade of old maples, past the creek on the far side of town, out into naked forest that surrounded the campus. When I walked below the dark expansive limbs, I felt soothed. The trees seemed to contain in their aged forms a strength that came from being rooted deep in the earth, in a place, and in time that I lacked. I felt entirely uprooted. Alone. I found the quarry where Tom had photographed me and where, on several warm days, we'd skinny-dipped, and let the sun caress our naked bodies as we stretch out on the granite slabs and talked about school and our lives and our yearning to know what the future might hold. Here I was and it felt as if the future had slammed me in the face like a collision with an immovable wall.

I sat on the slab and looked into the water, the dark beneath the surface that must go down a hundred feet to the bottom. The light flitted across the surface. I dabbed my hand in the water, swirling it around. I had an urge to leap in, to let the water grab my clothing and for pull me down into forgetfulness where I could look up at the faint light and open my mouth and take it in, the light, the water and close my eyes as my dad's mother must have done as the gas leaked into the kitchen. So I sat there and lazily traced circular patterns in the water's surface that would form and dissipated almost as quickly as my thoughts. The events of the last hours replayed in my head. I was pleased that my brother had gone away for the weekend. If he had been there, he would have spoken up. He'd be outraged. He would have defended me. He would have asked questions. I probably would have responded. But he would have failed and only damaged his reputation in the house. I would tell him later and let him know that it is all right. I deserved it.

I got up, looked around for a path, going anywhere——I did not care——and kept walking for hours, not sure where I was headed, but thinking that if I walked far enough maybe I could erase it all, put it far enough behind me so that I could never find it again.

I wondered if the guard at Dachau took long walks, as I was taking, to erase his past, trying to obliterate the gaunt faces just as I was trying to forget how Jerry looked on the floor. The whole night, and the morning, swept over me like a nightmare that kept rearing its ugly head and kept charging at me. Action meant consequences. I saw that now.

The Nazis ranted about the Jews, and very few raised an eyebrow, but once they became powerful and shaped their hatred into policy, and changed the policy into action, they became more than nattering fools; they became evil.

And I? How had I slipped across the line? I simply wanted to prove I was like everyone else, a man with nothing to hide. I had failed the test if manhood was such a test. It was as if I had become an outcast to my own being. How simple it was to become a Nazi. Join the group. Salute the leader. March off on a mission. No one cared what was said. They only cared when someone acted. Then accountability would open its jaws and snap its iron teeth shut. That was good in a way because what I did was egregious—a stupid and bigoted act—to cover up my fear and divert suspicion of my being less than human, of being a homosexual. Now I was exposed anyway, not as a homosexual, but as a Nazi.

No matter how far I walked—it must have been six miles—I could not get away from myself. I had become the biggest fool of the bunch and I knew it. I knew, too, that I could no longer live in the house: I had to get out. I had to be on my own. Groups were dangerous; I had to avoid them.

Something had broken inside me, changed irreparably that day, yet I had no idea what it was. I did not want to go back to my room, but that was the only place I had to go—at least for the time being. I waited until well past dinner, after people had gone to their rooms and turned off their lights, one at a time, until the windows were dark and, then, I slunk upstairs. Fortunately, Tom was already in bed. I sat at my desk, paging through T. S. Eliot's book of poems that I had found——or, perhaps, it had found me—months ago and read these lines:

In order to arrive at what you are not
You must go through the way in which you are not.
And what you do not know is the only thing you know...
And where you are is where you are not.

It was as if I'd been given an oracle. I knew that I must go on. But where? That was something I had yet to discover.

The Break

After the ugly night and my being stripped of my office, I decided to live off campus. Whatever had happened to me had thrown doubt into my every thought. I wondered why I felt I could change things in the house. Why I had to prove myself. Why I was so ambitious. Why I had violated my principals and let the primitive terror haunt me more and more. I needed time—and space—to think. I spent weeks looking into rooms. I withdrew from most social events at the house, spending more time at the library to read poets I'd discovered—Carl Sandburg, Wallace Stevens, and Sylvia Plath. Tom would invite me to go out on double dates; I was not interested. I had nothing to prove.

I met with Sue several times at Jiminotts and told her of my plight. She commiserated and said that, since she broke off her engagement with her fiancée, she felt at sixes and sevens too.

"Why did you break off the engagement," I asked, startled that she made such a momentous decision.

"It was more him than it was me. When we talked about what he wanted me to do—you know, his expectations of a wife—I realized that he wanted someone who would blend in with the furniture, someone who would keep the house clean, take care of the kids and have a meal ready for him." She laughed. "Funny, those expectations seemed to fit me pretty much to a T two years ago, but it just doesn't cut it anymore."

"Gosh, that's too bad."

Our waitress, a petite girl with a ponytail, asked if we wanted anything else. Sue ran her finger over the menu.

"Can you get me a new life?" she quipped.

The waitress squinted her eyes and looked at her order pad. "I don't think so."

"Then just get me another coffee and one of those chocolate chip cookies. Do you want anything, Jason?"

"New life sounds good," I said. "But the cookie will probably do."

The waitress smiled weakly and walked away.

Sue laughed. "We gave her something to talk about."

"I'm sorry about your breakup. That stinks," I said, putting my hand out to pat hers.

"Oh, no it doesn't suck. It's quite fine. I just need to open some new windows."

"I hope I can do that," I said and, wanting to change the subject, asked, "About you, are you planning to finish school?"

"One more year."

"Great!" I said. "Let's both open some new windows!"

"You got it," she said, sipping the rest of her coffee. "I've got to run along now, but what are your plans?"

I told her my plans to move out of the house into a rooming house. She encouraged me to do what I wanted. I had already decided to move into it in the spring semester. She suggested, with her now being free, that we might go out more often. She promised to keep in touch, but I could tell that she needed time to sort out her decision to break off the engagement. I called her several times to go out, but she was always busy and would always say, as she had in the diner, "I'll be in touch." She never did get back in touch. We drifted apart, yet I knew she was an anchor whenever I felt adrift.

I told my parents and my brother of my needing to get away from the house, but my brother, loyal to the house, urged me to stay.

"Hey, in a few months I'll be a full member and we can party whenever we want! Besides I've only a year left. We could have a good time if we're together," he said.

"It's all right. We still can. I'm only changing where I live."

"You promise you wouldn't just fall off the map?"

"Yep," I said, not sure if I had already fallen off the map.

I told my parents that I wanted to move out of the fraternity to room off campus so that I could focus on my studies. My dad, sensing something wrong, said that he'd like to have a serious talk when I came home for Thanksgiving. I dreaded it. I knew he was wondering why I was taking more English classes when I was supposed to be majoring in History. Over the phone, I explained the increased demand of my academic work. It would be best for me to avoid socializing too much and besides it would actually cost less than he was paying for board at the fraternity, so my father finally agreed with my decision. I made a commitment with the landlord, a former professor, to move in January, the start of the spring semester.

Part II

The Wakening

III: *Ash on an old man's sleeve*
Is all the ash the burnt roses leave.

The Lectures

After dinner one night during Thanksgiving vacation, my father invited me to a game of pool on the tournament-sized table. I liked to play, but had only mastered some spin shots, whereas my father played like a pro.

I decided to break the family rule and discuss politics as we played and asked, "What do you think about the marches Dr. King made for better housing?"

"He's causing more trouble than anything else," he said as if he were merely talking about the weather. I was pleased. Maybe we could have a honest discussion about civil rights.

"But civil disobedience is meant to cause trouble for a higher cause," I said, stepping back as he lined up his shot, a straight one which lined up perfectly with the corner pocket. His ball tipped into the pocket. He dusted the end of his cue and smiled, pleased with his effort, then turned to me.

"Don't tell me about civil rights when I see people rioting in the streets. I've gone to dinners with Mayor Daley. He has no use for King. He's nothing but a troublemaker. A communist. Daley has substantial evidence from reputable sources. The mayor obtained perfectly legal injunctions against the marches. King violated them. That had led to violence. Need I say more?"

"But who caused the violence?" I asked, waiting for him to line up another shot.

"Does that matter? What matters is that he broke the law. King had no right to march in Chicago—he isn't from Chicago. He's enabling upstart radical groups like the Black Panthers to threaten the fabric of our society."

"Dad, Dr. King's march and the Black Panthers are separate organizations altogether. They have no connection whatsoever."

"No matter, they all stem from radical policies both in the South and North and now out West." Our argument spilled over into the antiwar movement. He mentioned that Bill Sayres, one of my classmates at Glen Brook High, had been arrested.

Dad stopped his run, having missed an easy shot, and put his cue stick on the table, handle side down. "Listen to me. I want you to have nothing to do with that antiwar stuff."

"But, Dad..."

"But nothing. Did you see what happens? That David Miller was arrested and sentenced to two years—did you hear me?—two years in prison. Sayres has an arrest record. If you want to go to law school, you cannot have a record. No good can come of it. I assure you that," he said, staring at me. He pointed his finger at me. "I'll not have my son being unpatriotic."

"You cannot control what I do," I said.

He tapped his finger on the pool table and said, "Don't fool yourself. If I pull the plug, you'll be on the streets trying to earn a job like every other decent American. You'll not be involved in such foolishness." He lined up his next shot, a carom off the side that, upon ricocheting into another ball, dropped one in the end pocket. He looked up and grinned. I felt as if whatever gumption I had had plopped in the pocket.

I nodded my head. "Nice shot." During his days working as a salesman in a men's store, he spent many evenings at a pool hall perfecting his game. No matter how many hours of practice, I'd never be better than he was.

After he finished running the table, he asked, "Did you hear what I said?"

"Yeah," and changed the topic to the Chicago Bears and his golf swing. He liked me to check his swing.

My brother asked one night before we turned off the light in our bedroom, "What's going on with you? Dad's concerned."

"Nothing."

"No, that's not true. What is it?"

"I don't know. Dad seems to get on my case about everything. He wants me to be like you and I'm not."

"You're upsetting him. He doesn't like your attitude, I can tell you that. Look, he's done a lot for us—Europe, school, the club—the least you can..."

"Don't give me that crap! He's done what he's done so that he can display us like golf trophies. He doesn't give a damn what we think as long

238

as we conform, as long as we act like good little puppets," I said, turning off the light.

Jack flicked it back on. "Hold on. That's not fair."

"Fair? Fair that I may have to fight in an unjust war that..."

"Who are you to decide if the war is unjust? You some God Almighty?"

"No, I'm not a God Almighty. But I'm a guy that may be drafted."

"I may be, too. But I think we owe it to our country to..."

"Can we not talk about this? I'm tired. We don't agree. We never will. Let's just let each other be, okay?" I turned over to look at him. He shook his head.

"You're one fucked-up guy," he said.

"Yeah, what's new?" I said.

He turned off the light. I stared out the window at the silhouette of an oak tree. Some of its leaves hung on as they usually did, seemingly obstinate despite the persistent frosts. One leaf swung wildly in the wind. It flipped back and forth in a tantrum, and, the next morning it had fallen.

Before going back to school, I brought a plane ticket to New York City on December 26th so I could visit Tom. To avoid another altercation at Christmas break, I figured that, if I went east to visit Tom right after Christmas Day, I would not be around the house and end up in political debates. Since I could pay for the tickets with money earned as a waiter, I was pretty sure Dad would not mind.

Several days later, as I was helping my mother set the table, I told her that I was flying out to New York to spend New Year's with Tom. She gasped and put her hand to her mouth.

"When did you decide that?"

"A few days ago."

"Did you ask your father?"

"No."

"Well, I think you better talk to him," she said sternly.

When he came home from work, after he had his nightly cocktail with my mother, he asked me to talk with him. We went out on the porch. It was an unusually mild evening. He leaned against the railing and sipped on his second martini. I stood across from him, propped up against the sliding glass doors.

"Your mother told me that you are flying out to be with a friend for the holidays," he said.

"Not Christmas Day."

"But for most of the holidays?"

"Yep. Tom invited me and I thought it might be fun to spend New Year's Eve in Times Square,"

"Don't you think it would be proper to inform us of your decision?"

"I figured that if I had the money to do it, you wouldn't mind."

"I most certainly do mind!" he exclaimed. "The Christmas holiday is very important to your mother and she, I must say, is deeply disappointed."

"Sorry."

"Sorry will not do. I think that you need to change your plans," he said. His jaw was set. His ears had turned a bright red. His thick eyebrows formed a little V. He stared at me.

I felt sweat breaking out on my forehead. What would I do? I'd purchased the ticket.

Tom was expecting me.

"But Dad..."

"But nothing," he interrupted. "Call the airline. Change your plans."

I stormed off the porch and walked into the woods behind the house, heading in no particular direction. I heard the porch door swing open behind me.

"Come back here," my father called out.

I hurried away, skirting through the underbrush. *The bastard, the bastard. All he wants to do is make my life miserable.* I found the path that led down to an old cemetery and sat on one of the gravestone—"James Sayer 1867-1929." I thought how I had never and could never stand up to my father. Once he made a decision, it was carved in stone. After a while, I wandered by a stream, partially frozen over and stomped along a jagged path to Butterfield Road, some miles away. The traffic steamed by, cars heading where they wanted to go. Erratic puffs of exhaust trailed behind them as if ghosts had coughed them out and they colliding with the next car. I thought of hitchhiking and heading east, getting away from him, from the house, and from my life as it was.

When I came back to the house, my mother said, "Your father wants to talk to you. He's in the den."

My father was sitting in his leather chair, reading *Forbes*. He looked up.

"Have a seat," he said.

I did.

"Your mother and I talked. She says Tom is a nice boy and comes from a good family."

"I suppose."

"You'd really like to go to visit your friend?" he asked.

"Yes. I would."

"Well, we think that would be nice, a good opportunity for you. And, mind you, we think that it's good that you took the initiative to arrange the trip, buy the ticket on your own."

"Thanks. I didn't want to bother you."

"I know. But, son, we would like to be involved, to know what your plans are. Lately, you have withdrawn and we just do not know what's going on," he said, leaning forward on his elbows. "Do you see what I am saying?"

"I get your point."

"Could you include us in your plans? What if your mother and I were planning some trip or special event? We would not know to exclude you if you failed to tell us."

"That makes sense."

"Can you involve us from now on?"

"I'll try."

"Try?"

"I will," I said and smiled. But I didn't expect there would be any way that I could feel part of the family. A chasm opened like a sinkhole that kept eroding, widening at the edges. They were on one side. I was on the other. But I would play the part, act as I should and get by until I could get away.

He stood up and shook my hand. "That's better. Let's get some dinner."

The first few days of Christmas break, the TV blared from the living room, the commercials for beer and cigarettes and McDonald's specials screamed at us, as we sat around watching the news about Chicago Bears, needing to break out of a pathetic losing streak.

My mom, miffed by my going away, had withdrawn. For several days, she rarely spoke to me and almost looked afraid of me. But in the hubbub of preparing for Christmas, she relaxed and, by Christmas Eve, seemed like her old self. On Christmas Day, we opened presents and Dad fixed his traditional oyster stew. Meanwhile, Mom prepared turkey for dinner and filled it with her special stuffing. Jack mashed the potatoes, and I lined the top of the sweet potatoes with marshmallows. After a long dinner, followed by seconds, we spread out before the TV and watched Jimmy Stewart in *It's a Wonderful Life* with mother, as usual, crying at the end when the bells ring on the Christmas tree, signaling that Clarence, the angel, got his wings.

I'd kept involved with the family like a good son and knew my stint at the house was over. I'd survived. I gathered up my new sweater, slacks, and four pairs of socks, and packed my bag. The next morning, I thanked my parents for a lovely holiday and headed for the airport, ready to go east and visit Tom.

The High Life

When Tom asked me to spend part of the holiday in New York, I felt as if the angel who saved Jimmy Stewart had invited me to heaven. Tom liked the night life and the arts as much as I did. With no constraints, we stayed out late and acted like two sailors on shore leave. On the second day, we had gone through the Metropolitan Museum in search of paintings we had studied in the Introduction to Art class, especially Van Gogh's paintings. We marveled at the reckless energy in the paint, the muscular force of the strokes that still came off the canvas a century later. Then to get off the cold and windy streets, Tom brought me to several bars where I sensed he was a regular because the bartenders greeted him and asked if it was the usual—Jack Daniels on the rocks. We must have stopped in eight or nine bars.

By seven o'clock, when we left the last bar, I had no idea where I was. My feet veered one way and another and seemed as if they belonged to someone else. They'd go in a direction without consulting me and my head would try to follow; I bumped into a man on the street who barked, "Watch it, bub." Tom took control and put his arm around my back.

"That's it: one foot in front of another." Although the sidewalk wavered under the neon signs, although I had an urge to inspect another bar and get another drink, Tom kept us on the sidewalk and told me that, once we got back to his hometown, he would show me a really jazzy night club with cute babes. He aimed us toward Penn Station, where the echo of our shoes hurt my ears. I asked him to let me sit down because then I would not have to listen to my feet but he insisted that the noise would end soon. He glided us through long marble corridors, down one then another flight of stairs, to the commuter train heading to Port Washington. We sat with our arms around each other, not so much for companionship but as to keep from toppling on the floor. He was leaning his forehead against mine and we were talking. With his mouth so close to mine, I could hear what he was saying over the hubbub on the train. He was telling me that it was the train that was moving, not us, and to hold onto the seat because the train made stops. I took my free hand and held onto the armrest. As the train jerked and halted or sped along on sharp turns, I felt as if I were on a Coney Island ride. The train seemed even hotter than any bar. It was moments like this, with perspiration drenching my shirt, I wanted to strip off my clothes.

At the second stop, a tall, stocky man, snappily dressed in a blue pinstriped suit and one of those dress-for-success ties (red with white and blue) and carrying a leather briefcase, sat in the seat across from us. His knees were almost touching ours. He watched us, clearly amused because a grin unlocked his stern, vacant face. "You boys look as if you've had a good time."

Tom nodded his head, "Yes, sir, we have and we plan to have more of it, don't we, Jason?"

He turned to me and patted my cheek. Sheepishly, I smiled at him, realizing that I had little to say because most of my attention was being drawn to sitting upright and not toppling out of the seat.

I looked at the man who had cocked his head to the side. I corroborated Tom's claims with a vague nod of my head, although I had no idea what more to say, but felt I should say something, just to be polite, so I offered, "Yes, sir, my friend Tom here"—I patted Tom on his leg—"knows how to have a good time, a very good time."

The man leaned toward us, "Look guys, do not call me sir. Call me Bob. My name is Bob Johnson. I'm a lawyer with a big firm. Very big. I just got out of a big meeting, a long one, an important and stressful one, and I'll tell you what: You get off at my stop and I will take you to some places that will make sure you and your friend will have one hell of a good time because I need to let off some steam and I know the best place to find some action, if you know what I mean."

Tom took his arm from around me and told me to lean back, which I did, watching the lights in the ceiling flicker as the train reeled and tripped over the tracks. I must have reeled with them, since Tom put his hand against my chest to keep me upright and then, leaning forward, asked Bob questions about this place.

"Where is it?"

Bob explained that it was a private club, one for men only, very hush-hush, but that there were some attractive ladies—and guys, if you were into that sort of thing— that hung out there too and they enjoyed having a good time, a very good time.

"You willing to give it a try?" the lawyer offered.

Tom shook his head, "Not sure my friend here would be into it."

"You willing to give it a try?" he asked me.

"Try what?"

"A private club, very exclusive."

I pulled Tom close to me and whispered in his ear. "It sounds like that guy's trying to pick us up."

Tom whispered back, "Why do you say that?"

"You know, the guy thing."

"Oh."

He leaned forward and said to Bob. "Hey, man, we're not into the guy thing."

Bob laughed. "Oh, I know. I know. That's no big deal. Mostly, guys, it's hot ladies. I know you're ladies' men!"

Tom raised an eyebrow at me. "Want to try?"

"Sure."

Tom signaled the man with a thumbs-up and said, "We're in," then put his arm around my shoulder to keep me steady, whispering in my ear, "We might get laid tonight."

At the man's stop, we followed him out onto the platform. When we were side by side, he slung his arm over my shoulder—he was taller than I was—and whispered in my ear, "We are going to have some fuckin' good times, see some things you've never seen before. If you want to get laid, you will. No problem."

From the station, we walked up a tree-lined street. It crested and bisected another street. We turned left and walked into and out of the puddle of six street lights. We stopped at the top of a driveway that swooped down to a garage and a two-story home, Tudor-style. Its front door light was on along with one light in a second floor room.

Tom gazed around. "These pads run in nine hundred thousand range. Swanky. No place for slouches," he said. I noted the homes, mostly three-story, settled into wooded lots, each built partially into a hillside.

"I'll be just a minute," he told us and instructed us to stand by a tree at the top of his driveway and said, "Hang out here for a few minutes boys. Don't go anywhere. I need to get the car and drop off the briefcase."

"What were your names again?"

"Tom."

"Jason."

"Good. My name is Bradley," he said. "Bradley Jackson." He started to walk down the hill.

Tom grabbed him by the arm. "I thought you were Bob."

"Oh, that's the name I use at the office. But where we are going, let's just say I use another name—it's Bradley, okay?"

Tom nodded.

When he left, I wondered out loud, "How come he changed his name? And how come he didn't invite us in?"

Tom shrugged, "Maybe he thinks we are crooks. Maybe he's with the mafia."

"I think we should get the hell out of here," I said.

"You may be right. Let's watch what he does."

After he went in the door, we heard another voice, and then screaming, at first coming from downstairs, but continuing into the second story. Through the lighted window, we could see him standing, his back to us, pointing at someone. Since the window was opened a bit, we could hear the woman's voice, "No, you are not. You can't do this to me. You promised that it was the last time. You promised to stop. You have a family."

He screamed back at her, "You have no idea what kind of day I have had. No idea. I need to blow off some steam. I can't live like this. I need a break."

We saw the woman charge at him—she wore a pink outfit—and he pushed her away, "Stop it. Let me go. Get out of my way. I'll be back later."

Her screams pursued him out the front door, which he slammed behind him. He opened the garage door and there, inside, sat a swank, black car. He got in and spun the car out and around, facing us.

None of it seemed real, as if we were watching a drive-in movie.

The woman rushed out after the car, her fist in the air, pleaded, "You'll regret this. Come back, Harold. Don't do this again."

246

Tom grabbed my arm, "You hear that?"

I said, "Yeah. She's pissed off. She wants him to stay."

"No, did you hear what she said? She called him 'Harold'."

"So that's his name, isn't it?"

"No it isn't. He said his name was Bob or Bradley."

"Shit," I uttered and felt the need to sober up. I stepped back, trying to hide behind several bushes, but, before I could, Bob—or Bradley or Harold—pulled up beside us.

"Get in boys."

Tom stood stiffly by the car.

"Where's your friend?" Bob-Bradley-Harold said.

"Oh," Tom said, looking toward me. "He had to take a leak."

Stepping out from the bushes, I looked at Tom whose eyes had popped wide-open. He was moving backwards, away from the car, lost his balance, nearly falling. I moved back by him.

"Hey, boys, where you going? Hop in before you get hurt," the man insisted, pushing open the door. "We're in for a good time!"

"I think we better get back home," Tom said. "We're late and, ah, we're gotta take the train home."

"What's your problem?" he asked.

I told him, "You said your name was Bob and then Bradley."

"Yeah, what of it?"

Tom said, "Your wife calls you Harold."

He laughed. "You got me boys. Yep, I'm big in the corporate world, and I wanted to have a cover. My name is Harold Wallace. I'm sorry. But I'll tell you straight. I do have a club, very exclusive, and you wouldn't pay a dime. They do know me as Bradley Jackson. Trust me. It's all on the up and up. Let me treat you."

I looked at Tom and he nodded, signaling that the guy was legit. We hopped in the front seat. It was classy vehicle—a BMW— well-appointed with wooden paneling and a control panel that seemed outfitted with gauges and buttons for a jet.

Private Club

He drove along back roads, past splendid mansions set back from the road, many with stone walls and iron gates. He slowed in front of one that had a guard. Once he pulled up, the guard waved and opened the gate. A long tree-lined driveway, tree lined, led to a large white building with a Grecian overhang where two young valets waited. They greeted him "Mr. Jackson" by name and, after opening our car doors and helping Tom and me out, one of the valets drove his BMW away. Bradley or whatever his name was—took us by the arm, one of us on either side of him, and went to the front door of the club. Once inside, he conferred with a tall man in a tuxedo who looked us over as if we were on sale and smiled, "Sure Mr. Jackson, go right in. Mr. Keer is waiting for you. The show has started. You can have your favorite table."

Bradley pulled us aside as we walked down the hallway. "This place belongs to Keer who has more money than Chase Manhattan Bank, and with it, he likes to have a good time if you know what I mean. He gets the best quality shows for his friends, and, well, I happen to be one." He winked at us. "You will be too soon enough!"

We entered a small room—no more than eleven candlelit tables in it—with a stage at one end, slightly elevated, where two men, young, our age, were seated on a couch. Bradley whispered, "I have a table for us at the front." We moved through the room, excusing ourselves until we found our table. As we sat down, Bradley gestured for us to lean in close to him so we could hear him. "The show just started. Now boys, you may not be into this, but, don't freak. There's something here for everyone. I ordered you Jack Daniels, isn't that what I heard you drink, on the rocks, right?"

Another man, older than Bradley, with long gray hair, dressed in a tuxedo, came up to our table and put his arm around Bradley.

"Who are your friends, Bradley?"

Bradley introduced us.

"Nice to have you boys here," he smiled and shook our hands, then turned to Bradley and said, "Nice taste as always," and added, "Drinks are on the house for those lads.''

Bradley leaned over toward us, "What do you think?"

Tom smiled, "Perfect."

A waiter approached, dressed in a black turtleneck and black pants and delivered our drinks. I sipped mine. Lots of Jack Daniels, not much ice.

Bradley tittered, "Maybe it should be 'get off your rocks'?" and eyed the two boys up front.

Rolling his eyes, Tom smirked, "Right. In your dreams!"

Dressed in coats and ties like two up-and-coming executives, the two young men on the stage sat upright, their hands on their knees, their eyes focused straight ahead as if they were statues. Low, melodious music began and one of the men, a blond, winked at the audience and slid his hand on the other man's knee. The other man reproached the first man, pushing the hand away. Some laughter. The music stopped. When it began again, it pulsated, livelier, stronger. The man who had put his hand out only to be rejected leaned over and kissed the other man who, once the kiss ended, looked pleasantly surprised and placed his finger to his mouth in an impish grin. More laugher. Agonizingly slow flirtation: one touch, another kiss, until one man stood up and, facing the seated man, thrust his groin at the other. More laughter, although awkward because the men on stage seemed not to be funny, but quite serious and engaged, their hands flittering lightly over each other's bodies. The seated man grabbed the buttocks of the standing man.

I adjusted my pants, not wanting anyone to see my erection. My body often spoke to me before I was fully aware of what it wanted. Here it was telling me that it liked what it saw. I wished that I could flick an off-switch, but, the more I looked, the more I grew aroused. I squirmed in my chair.

I felt the first trickle of perspiration drip down my forehead.

Tom leaned over and put his hand on my shoulder. "Are you okay with this?"

Not sure if I should admit that I was or wasn't, I took a sip of my drink. I felt dizzy and squeamish. My stomach was knotting up. I wasn't sure if I was ready for this. But I didn't want to let Tom down. I averted my eyes from the two on stage, yet no matter how hard I tried, my eyes drifted to them. I was captivated by what I saw there—an enactment of my own private fantasy life. Whenever I felt caught between wanting and denying, my body heated up on overdrive. Sweat poured off my face down onto my shirt.

"You all right?" Tom asked.

I felt as if I were in a sauna. "Sure, fine. Just a little hot."

"We can just go, if you want," he said. "We can get a cab."

"It's all right. I'm fine. Don't worry. It's weird, I'll admit. But we get free drinks," I said, forcing a laugh.

Bradley had put his hand on Tom's thigh and was whispering in his ear, rubbing back and forth on his leg. He pointed at the young men, who were my age, no more. Tom looked at me, his face flushed, clearly captivated by the scene. He was not about to leave. That was for sure.

I felt as if some seismic disorder had rippled through my body. Here I was seeing two guys make love. Although I had fantasied about it, I never thought I'd end up seeing guys do it. My stomach churned. I felt as if I were on a rack, being pulled apart. I gazed up at the two on stage kissing tenderly, disrobing.

I took several breaths. It seemed so natural. Yet it frightened me. It was too close.

Tom looked over at me with concern in his face. I smiled at him and clinked my glass against his, trying to act as if I were as comfortable with what I was seeing as I would be watching a football game.

Tom hugged me tightly. "You amaze me sometimes."

Amaze him? I thought. *How about amazing myself?*

By the end of their act, the two men had stripped off not just their suits but their underwear as well. After the applause, they stepped from the stage and moved through the audience. When the blond lad came by our table, given Tom and I were the only ones his age, he leaned close and rubbed his body against Tom who took the young man's ample erection in his hand and gave it several strokes to further applause from the other patrons. Tom pulled the young man by the waist toward me so that the hard shaft was inches from my face. I saw my hand reach out and it did enjoy the feel of it, but I couldn't bear to look him—or Tom— in the face. I let go and buried my eyes in my Jack Daniels, watching the golden liquid swirl around the ice cubes. But when the blond turned toward another table, his muscular buttocks, bathed with the shimmer of the candlelight, drew me out of my chair toward them. I felt like a young child, mesmerized by a stranger in a mall and, oblivious that he's lost, separated from his family, follows him down a crowded corridor into another store. Bradley shouted at us, "Hey, let me have some action, too."

After the boys' performance, several women came out and, more or less, duplicated the show—flirting, making out, undressing, acting out sex scenes, and titillating the audience. The finale included mixed couples who left nothing to the imagination. I'd never watched anyone fuck, so that, as Bradley promised, was a first. After the show, he invited us backstage to meet the performers whom he seemed to know intimately and who were lounging around in a small room, still naked. Bradley gave the blond boy a long kiss and, flipping his hand at Tom and me, called out, "Take anyone you want. It's on me," and, with that, he slipped off into a side room with the boy in tow.

Tom grabbed my arm and pulled me close. "Can you believe it? What luck! I don't care, really, what do you want? Choose."

I stared at the woman who had been fucking, but she was already engaged with several men. Then I looked toward the second and the young man. He was sipping on a drink, while seemingly staring at my shoes.

I looked down; they were scuffed.

"Why is he looking at my shoes?" I asked Tom.

"He is not looking at your shoes," he said.

"What is he looking at?" I asked.

Tom blinked at me oddly.

"You don't know?"

"Not really."

He took his hand and cupped it at his groin. "He's looking there. He likes your 'looks.'"

I blushed. How could I be so stupid?

"You interested in anyone?" Tom asked.

I figured Tom was going to pick up one of the girls. A skinny brunette with long legs and an aquiline face was smiling at him. When he looked at me to identify who was attracting my attention, he noticed that I was looking at the young man who had been in the last act, the mixed couples.

"Shall we talk to him?" Tom asked.

"Not necessarily. I mean those women are attractive."

"Oh, so you want to get it on with them?"

One lady, her blond hair slung across one eye like Marilyn Monroe, blew a kiss in our direction. She looked old enough to be my mother.

"Do you like her?" he asked.

"She's pretty yet..."

"Let's check her out—"

"Really?"

"—then, who else?"

I gazed at the cluster of men talking to the male entertainers.

"You want to talk with them. There's the fellow who came by the table."

"He's nice looking," I said.

"Do you want to talk to him or not?"

"Whatever you want," I said, aware that my stomach was tied up in knots and churning like a washing machine.

"You amaze me," he said. He asked again if I was really interested in talking to the guy. "Whatever you want," I replied.

How could I have known what I wanted? Arousal and ambivalence pinged back and forth like billiard balls inside my head.

"The girls look pretty hot," he said, cocking his head in their direction.

I shrugged. "They do. But they're old, don't you think?"

"There are some nice looking guys, and they're our age, too."

"Yeah," I said, noticing some of them who had performed lounging around, sipping drinks by a bar.

"It might be interesting to find out how you get in this business," he mused, "just in case the job market goes to hell when we graduate."

"Yeah, not a bad idea," I laughed and jumped at his idea. At least with the guys, I could act like I was just wanted to talk.

"This should be fun," Tom said. "What would get a guy to do it?"

"I can't imagine doing this," I said.

"Nor I."

"Okay, let's see what he has to say," Tom declared and went over to one of the young men, who had long brown hair parted in the middle. Tom casually spoke with him and, self-consciously, glanced back, pointing a thumbs-up at me. I walked over and stood by Tom. The young man said us his name was Maurice and that hailed from Philadelphia, the city of brotherly love. He let his fingers drift up and down Tom's thigh. I wondered when Tom might ask how he got into the business, but he didn't seem to be interested in making an inquiry.

Tom rubbed his hand though Maurice's hair. I looked up. When would he ask him? The pale yellow lights in the ceiling pressed in on me. The walls wobbled to and fro as if we'd suddenly hit a squall. I felt my knees buckle and someone cry, "Oh, dear boy" and arms grabbed ahold of me, and a face, a lovely face, close to mine, and the smell of a cologne, a lime scented one, brushed against my nostrils.

The Apartment

When I woke up, I was laid out on a couch. Tom was kneeling beside me. The room was dim. There was one window with a shade pulled down. The long-haired boy, now clad only in his jockey shorts, stood in back of him.

"He's coming around," the boy said.

"You all right?" Tom asked.

"Where are we?" I asked, holding my hands over my eyes, which throbbed as if someone had poked them with a stick.

"At Maurice's apartment," Tom said.

I peeked through my fingers. The apartment was small— one room where I was lying, and, beyond it, another room with a couple of chairs, a long couch, and to one side, a little kitchenette, and another side room. Tom held a cup of coffee in his hand and had me sit up to sip it. Maurice sat beside me, holding me upright. Tom had draped a sheet around him like a Roman senator. I drank the coffee sip by sip, the hot liquid warming my throat. As I came to, I realized that I was also in my jockey shorts.

"Where the fuck are my clothes?" I asked.

Tom laughed, "Oh, you had an accident. They are in the dryer now."

"An accident?"

Draping his arms over me, Maurice hugged me slightly, "Listen, honey cakes, let's just say you lost your cookies and, believe me, honey, a lot of them, enough to fill a good-sized bucket. And besides, you look cute in your skivvies."

"What happened?"

Maurice explained, "You were standing with us and stumbled. I held you up for a second. For some reason, you bolted, started to run out of the room. A big man grabbed you and asked if something was wrong. You put your hand to your mouth and—poor fellow—you puked. I mean puked. Puked over his white shirt, his pants, his shoes. What a mess! He let go of you and you fell to your knees and puked over yourself. I managed to hold you up. Your friend here tried to get you out. Your ride had taken off. I

254

offered to bring you here. You had quite a time of it, dearie."

I blushed and folded my arms over my crotch, trying to cover up, although I didn't need to, since they were dressed as I was.

"Listen, sweetie, you're some hunk and have nothing to be ashamed of," Maurice assured me. "Not at all."

"But I made a mess," I said.

They laughed and Tom said, "You decorated a whole room!"

"I'm sorry."

"No need. You needed your beauty rest. And we were right there to take care of you."

I lay back down.

"Why don't you sleep some more? It's the middle of the night," Tom said, grabbed my foot and squeezed it. The voices faded and lapsed into silence that curled up around me.

When I woke up the second time, light knifed through the sides of the shade. I called out. Tom came rushing in, still in his jockeys. He told me that my clothes were dried. We could leave. I got dressed and Tom went into the side room and found his clothes and dressed too. Maurice seemed to enjoy being in his jockeys. He did look much better in them than in a business suit—and he filled them out, too. Then he dressed too and drove us to Tom's house. It was early morning, the sun barely climbing over the treetops. We tiptoed into the house, carrying our shoes, so as not to wake Tom's parents. We maneuvered down the hallway and headed to bed.

"I need more shut eye. How about you?" Tom asked.

"I could use more. I feel awful."

I brushed my teeth and came back to the room. Tom slipped off his trousers, shirt, and socks. As he was about to hop in the bed, he turned around and came over to me. "You're a good friend," he said and hugged me, then kissed me on the cheek.

"You are too," I said, holding him to me. He smelled of lime cologne. He let go, then stood and moved several feet away. He looked intently at me.

"Goodnight."

"Goodnight," I said and turned over, aware of the lime scent, of Tom and of Maurice, and fell deeply into a sleep that came over me like a long caress.

The next day we stayed at his house watching football games. During lunch, I asked, "I'm sorry for what happened."

"Hey, it is fine."

"Can I ask you something?"

"Sure."

"What did you guys do when I was passed out?"

"Maurice and I?"

"Yeah."

He squinted at me. He took a bite of his turkey salad sandwich.

"Maurice needed to clean up. You know from the show. And I did too." He paused and took another bite of his sandwich. "We showered and sat around talking. He's had a rough life. His parents tossed him out when they found out he was, you know, a homosexual. So he plans to sock money away doing what he is doing and go to college. Pretty sad story."

"He seemed like a nice guy."

"He is."

"Is that all you did?" I asked.

Tom set his sandwich down and frowned. "You thinking we got it on?"

"No, not that. I was just wondering..."

"We just talked. You know I'm straight, right?"

"For sure," I said and decided to change the topic. "What will you do if you are drafted?"

"Look, I have a plan. I could not go to that war. It seems so senseless, doesn't it?"

"Yeah, I guess so."

He scooted next to me at the table, "Here is what you do. You get accepted at graduate school—I plan to go to law school... "

"Me too," I exclaimed.

"Great. They will give you a deferment if you are accepted. By the time the war is over, we will be out and in the work force," he explained. I liked his idea. He suggested I apply to some eastern schools. His dad had contacts. I decided to broach the idea with my father and see if he had any connections. I was worried about the draft. The more I read about the war—our use of napalm, the aerial bombing, the support of a military regime in the south—the less I liked supporting it. I'd heard speakers at antiwar rallies. They spoke about our imposing our will on the country with the only purpose of protecting the south from communist rule. I was not sure why the communist rule was so bad. But I did not think we had the right to dictate what form of government any country should have.

Despite a transit strike that immobilized New York City, at the start of the New Year, we spent the rest of the vacation going to different museums, not drinking much, sitting around Tom's house talking about our goals. We tried to meet up with Tom's old girlfriend, Linda, but she did not want anything to do with him. Though we didn't speak further about it, I mulled over that drunken night, the old men ogling the young men and women, the after-entertainment lounge with naked young studs and girls letting the patrons check them out as horse traders do. I wondered what happened to Bob or Barley or whoever he was, how he must have come home to a wife who probably had grown weary of asking him where he was. The high life was not what it seemed to be, though it excited me. It was filled with desperation and sad stories. I did not want anything to do with that part of it.

One morning, the day before we left for school, Tom and I sat around, reading the newspaper, chatting about the mess our country was in. I enjoyed the *New York Times,* so different than the *Chicago Tribune.* It went into depth in stories and covered a range of issues. They covered events that were never on the nightly news. On page two of the *Times,* we noted that in Tuskegee, Alabama, Samuel Leamon Younge, Jr., a sailor, a nice-looking Negro and a student civil rights activist, was fatally shot by a white gas station owner following an argument over segregated restrooms. It seemed that the pressure to change, however great it was, led to an even greater reaction against change.

A day later, after being dropped at JFK by Tom's parents, we flew back to Indianapolis, to a state so unlike New York that it made my head spin. From the airport, we drove through miles and miles of empty cornfields and isolated farmhouses, of quaint villages and town squares, an orderly world of open space. After being in the congested, hurried life of New York, I felt as if I were marching back in time, retreating from the modern world. I was ready for the start of a new semester, one that I hoped would not force me to change even more how I saw the world, but would let me gradually come back to my old self. I'd gone through enough on the break.

New Roommate

In January, I moved out of the fraternity. My former Spanish professor rented rooms in his Tudor-style home, which was sandwiched between two sorority houses on Elm Street, some five blocks from the DAE house. In my new space on the second floor, I felt exiled and carried regret for what had happened and how the plans I had, the ambitions I was so assured I could reach, had vanished. I mulled over what I could have done differently, but I kept getting stuck as if caught in the groove of a record, just when the music was getting good.

Another worry I had was that now I had to share a room with another student, Jake, whom I knew well from being the House Manager and who was on academic probation at DAE and needed to focus all his attention on getting back on track as a sophomore, not a second semester freshman. If he failed, he would be out and he did not want to fail. In a way, we were both failures and knew it. Yet I felt apprehensive about rooming with someone and sharing the same bedroom. We had a bunk bed. Although I'd shared a room with Paul and Tom, I'd never slept in the same room with them, since everyone slept in dorms.

Jake, however proved to be a frank, open guy. The first night in the room, he admitted his mistakes.

"I fucked up last semester," he confessed, telling me how he would daydream instead of study when he went to the library.

"Don't be too hard on yourself," I said. "Look what a fool I made of myself."

"I know," he said. "Why'd you do it?"

"Shit, man, if I could answer that," I told him, "I'd not be where I am."

"It kinda scared me thinking of rooming with you. You know, the stories. But you seem all right," he said.

"Thanks. I'm not that bad. But I guess you'll have to find out."

I didn't want to tell anyone of my secret fear, least of all to a freshman. But as the weeks went by, especially after we began sharing details about our families, we became closer. His mother had left, just moved out one

259

day unexpectedly. Jake came home to his father sitting on the sofa weeping. I told him about how my father wanted me to be a success and how, sometimes, it felt as if I could never meet his expectations.

We had to negotiate a new friendship in our tight space. Our room had one closet, two desks, one chair and the bunk bed—a very intimate space. The second-floor residents—there were two other rooms, one a single and the other housing three— shared a common bathroom. So we planned when we needed to use the bathroom so as not hold up the other four residents.

A wiry guy, Jake claimed the top bunk and took the desk facing the wall to the right as you entered the room. Most evenings, he kept his resolve and sat at his desk to study. Before undressing, we would chat about his future plans and my own still ill-formed aspirations. He wanted to be a teacher since he loved working with kids. One night we talked about dating.

"Are you seeing anyone?" I asked.

"Not really."

"How come? You're a nice looking guy."

"How come you don't? You're better looking than I am."

I laughed, not sure if I should admit my own insecurities. I decided to take a risk.

"I feel really insecure with girls."

"You do? So do I. Whenever I'm on a date, I don't know how to act, let alone what to say," he admitted.

I looked at his thick black-rimmed glasses partially covered by his long wavy hair. He had a tenderness about him and an honesty that made him endearing. I would never have admitted to anyone what he had just said, but here he was doing it, exposing himself as if he'd nothing to lose, as if his manhood was an open door and anyone could look right in.

"You and I have the same experience," I said. "Sometimes I feel dumb with girls. I think my IQ drops fifty points when I greet them at the door!"

We laughed and talked at length how our inadequacies made us feel like less than a man. By the end of the conversation, we gave each other a hug. Having never lived with another guy except my brother, I found that I was feeling a sweet intimacy that I never expected.

We had a lounge chair in the corner of the room and some evenings when I came back from studying at the library, he'd be curled up in a red and blue silken bathrobe, reading a book. He'd smiled the type of smile that made you feel welcomed as if you were an intimate part of his family. I'd sit at my desk chair and we'd discuss how his schoolwork had been. He had difficulty writing essays and, since that had been my problem my freshman year, I explained how to outline and organize his ideas. I talked to him, too, about poetry and read to him Eliot's 'Lovesong of J. Alfred Prufrock ":

> *And I have known the eyes already, known them all—*
> *The yes that fix you in a formulated phrase,*
> *And when I am formulated, sprawling on a pin,*
> *When I am pinned and wriggling on the way,*
> *Then how should I begin*
> *To spit out all the butt-ends of my days and ways?*

"Isn't that wonderful?" I asked.

"I guess so. But what does it mean?" he responded, shrugging his shoulders.

"He's saying that we all get prescribed ways of acting, ways of being, that are not our choices but rather are imposed by others—our parents, our peers—so we go on acting as we think we should. But it's not our real self. That is hidden away. Yet we continue to do as we are told and finally have to take account of our lives and what then? All we have is butt-ends that might as well be tossed in an ashtray," I explained.

"How'd you figure that out?"

"I just pay attention to the language."

"That's amazing," he said, looking at the words on the page, putting his long finger on them as if trying to nudge them to life.

After I climbed in bed, he'd often stay in the chair in his usual lotus position, with the folds of the bathrobe parted across his knees. Often he would lay down his book, and sit, quite self-possessed, with his eyes closed as if in meditation although, deep in his throat, he moaned, and his legs would flop open and close like an oyster shell. Then I would hear a steady rocking motion and notice his head lean back and his mouth open, until he jerked forward and grab for his white t-shirt or the underpants that he had

261

taken off earlier and he would wipe himself off, while the thick smell of semen pervaded the room. I never complained. He was discrete and I figured that he would not mind if I masturbated after he finished and climbed up in his bunk. In the morning, I'd see his cumstained underwear on the floor by the closet. Although I knew that we had no intention of being intimate—we were both too scared—we had crossed a line and titillated each other, testing how far we could go without actually touching one another. We never discussed our private indulgences. As the semester wore on, we developed a sixth sense about each other's desire, allowing time for our own pleasuring and, if one intruded on the other, to let him finish. When I came in the room one hot afternoon, Jake was already in his bathrobe, his bare chest with the few scraggily hairs showing and his two naked legs exposed. He rested his hands in his lap.

"Thought you were studying for the French history exam," he said, quizzically looking at me.

"I was. The French lost," I said flippantly.

"Lost what?"

"The war."

"Sorry to hear about that," he replied, looking vaguely remorseful.

"Don't worry. It was over a century ago."

"Oh."

"And besides I got tired of the library," I replied, tossing my books on my desk and taking off my coat. I sat at my desk and opened one of my books, keeping my back to him, and added, "Don't let me disturb you."

I tried not to look, but I could hear him take a deep breath. I wanted to concentrate on the text, making notes about Napoleon, but I heard him cry out "Ahh" as if distressed and turned to see if he was all right and, instead, saw him cover himself with a t-shirt, and, as he did, break out in a huge grin.

"Sorry about that," he said. "I was pretty close when you came in."

I replied, "No problem."

Aroused by his blatant exposure, I turned away to let him clean up, go to the shower and head off to dinner. Later, almost as if driven to replay his sexual gambit, after we came back to the room and he'd gone to bed, I picked up and slipped on his robe and came, as he had, in a T-shirt. I remembered the gentlemen's club with Tom, how the guys fondled one another, tenderly as lovers do and thought how, in our awkward complicity, we were doing the same. It didn't feel wrong. It felt safe because we never touched one another, but it was also scary because we both realized how easily we could cross that line. Sensing a danger—the possibility— we became more modest, avoiding masturbation in the room except late at night or on a night when the other was out. But once he surprised me.

One evening when he was supposed to be out of town to visit his father, he came back unexpectedly. He walked in on me sitting in the chair, in my bathrobe, naked except for a T-shirt I had draped across my hard-on and a poetry book by e e cummings that I'd hastily pulled off my desk and held propped in my lap. I pulled the robe closed and pretended to read the book. Jake said a simple hello and went over to my desk chair and sat in it. He casually asked what I had been reading.

"Oh, a new poet."

"What's his name?"

"e e cummings."

"Funny name."

"He changed it, how it's spelled, because he doesn't like conventional spelling."

"I'd like to do that—I mean, change my name."

"What would it be—your new name?"

"John," he said. "I like it. Powerful name, a name of presidents."

We went on talking for an hour. Finally, he said that it was time to hit the hay. He undressed, not turning away as he usually did, but slipping off his shirt and pants and underpants like a man doing a striptease. He reminded me of Maurice, the guy at the gentlemen's club, with his soft silky skin and only a small turf of hair in the middle of his chest and, for a grown man, a sparse crop of pubic hair. I found myself getting aroused. Jake put on boxer shorts and went to brush his teeth, came in, stood by me, not a foot away and chatted at first, occasionally adjusting himself through his shorts. I smiled at him. Neither of us spoke for a minute. He leaned over to hug me.

"Good night," he said, putting his arms around my neck, nor letting go. I leaned in close. I wrapped my arms around his back and held him tight, my lips on his neck. I breathed in his musky odor. I kissed his neck, my lips lightly touching him. His face pressed next to mine, his lips on my cheek, his breath like a moist wind on a windowpane. The door to the bathroom outside in the hall swung open and closed. Abruptly, Jake pulled away and went to bed. I'd grown hard again and felt in turmoil and confusion. I waited for the bathroom door to open and close again and quietly slipped out to the bathroom and finish alone what I was too afraid to do with Jake.

After that evening, he spent less and less time in our room, coming in later, staying at the DAE house. I discovered that I enjoyed the time alone to read and to write some poems. I attended a few antiwar rallies, small ones at the student center. Several pacifists were going from one campus to another to talk about the draft. One fellow, a nondescript guy with large black- framed glasses, told how he had been arrested for burning his draft card. He asked us to pull out our cards. I did. He pulled out a lighter and said, "Do you dare?" One student who I recognized—Tim, Tom's art student friend—came up and put his card over the lighter. Cheers went up. No one else dared to do it. I shoved mine back in my wallet. I remembered what my father had said. I would not cross him. But I knew that soon I would have to make a decision to go or not to go if I were drafted. For now, I focused on my classes.

Over the semester, Jake had managed to keep a B-average in all his classes and, to his surprise and with my help, had an A in his composition class. He also started dating a girl from the dorm, an English major.

"That's all because of you," he grinned.

"Glad I could help," I smiled back.

Without any self-consciousness, as if letting me see him one last time, he slipped off his shirt, his pants, socks, underpants—he liked to sleep nude— and hopped into his bunk. My eyes followed him as a sheet folded around him and he was quiet. We had our ritual, and it never included touch. We were like voyeurs who looked into the mirror catching a reflection of what we dared not to be. We beheld the other as other. We never spoke about it. I suppose it was platonic, yet intimate. Jake was my Snow White— behind the glass, whose breath misted the inner window of my heart.

Mid-semester, after he had improved his grades and was off academic probation, Jake decided to move back in the fraternity. I felt a twinge of loss, sensing that I'd found something with him that I had never experienced before with another guy. But I put the experience behind me. We remained casual friends. Sometimes he'd ask for help in English. The day he moved out, he gave me an English book—-*Modern Writings on Major English Authors*, ranging from essays on Beowulf to T. S. Eliot— with a dedication to me, "To a great friend. This is a book which you expressed some interest in. You have a greater appreciation for this sort of thing than I. Maybe it'll come in handy some time. Hugs, Jake."

Funny how Jake allowed us to have an awkward intimacy that felt almost like that of a kid brother with his older brother and never transgressed into open sexual contact, but skirted much like two scouts, anxious to see where the other side was bivouacked, strayed close as they could to the line without ever crossing it. I became more convinced that my attraction to other guys was something that I could hold at arm's length and dismiss as a momentary fancy.

The Artists

In my Contemporary Poetry class, I sat by the window where I could watch the leaves on the trees uncurl like arthritic fingers. Their pale green, so fragile at first, changed day by day, darkening and filling in the sky so that, after a few weeks, the sun, which had blazed through the window in February, now cast fragmented rays that played back and forth in the wind. Sitting next to me, a guy who wore a beret noticed my infatuation with the leaves.

"Amazing, isn't it how they seemed to agonize before they unfold," he said.

"Never thought of it as agony, but, yes, they seem so tightly wrapped at first, it's hard to believe that they spread out as they do," I said.

"And who are you?" he asked.

"Jason."

"I'm Ruben."

After class one day, he asked if I wanted to go out for a coffee. We went to the Flapping Duck, squeezed into a corner booth and struck up a conversation. He liked the beat poets—

"They let it all out. Sex. Drugs. Spirituality. Nothing is taboo," he said.

"Read me something," I said.

"I just discovered this guy. He rips right into stereotypes. A friend of mine sent me his book. James Broughton. A Beat poet. Listen," he said, leaning forward, speaking quietly so that others could not hear him:

Under the windsong of the redwood trees
we were two Adams together clinging
in the long nakedness of afternoon

Rediscovering close harmony
fingers practiced fresh arpeggios
nipples shone from riper torsos
loins opened into full boom

266

Never had sweat tasted so juicy
or prolonged kiss so penetrant

Who in Eden lives for fashion
for investment   for notoriety?

I must have blushed and looked stupefied because he stopped and put the poem down.

"What do you think?" he asked.

"It's unreal," I said. "I mean it certainly give me a new way to look at Eden without Eve."

"Here, take it. Read it. It will blow your mind."

As we were sitting there, a friend of Ruben's who, he claimed, was another artist——a painter and poet——came in. A handsome guy with a striking physicality that exuded a grace that I'd come to associate with dancers, he seemed to glide, not walk, across the room. He slipped in the booth right next to me and flashed a smile at me as if he'd known me all his life.

"Hello there," he said. "I'm Jackson. You seem familiar. Where have we met?"

I explained that I lived in a boarding house and was a member of the DAE house.

"No, it was somewhere else. Maybe in another life," he said. He put his hand on my shoulder and pulled me toward him so that my face was close to his. He looked intently into my eyes as if he expected to find something there. He let go of me and turned to Ruben.

"I think he is one," he said.

Ruben stared at me. "Maybe."

I felt an unnamed dread seeping up my neck and averted my eyes. A waitress with a blond streak in her black hair was pouring coffee at the table next to ours.

"Yep, I think he's an artist," Jackson said. "It's in his eyes."

Ruben nodded. "I think so too. What is it? How can you tell?"

"He lets you look into him. He lets you be."

"Right."

"What are you talking about?" I asked, embarrassed by the attention.

"Relax," Jackson said. "We have this game—maybe it's not a game—where we search for artists who do not know they are artists. Most of the time we are wrong. But sometimes, we hit the mark."

"You think I might be one?"

"Yeah," Jackson said. He nuzzled up next to me. "Do you?"

I pulled away. "I don't know. I never thought of it."

After class, I would hang out with them, going over to Jackson's room in the dorm. He had decorated the walls with posters of Ginsberg and Kerouac, and his book were shelved with editions from City Lights. He read poems by Lawrence Ferlinghetti. We drank wine and Jackson played jazz on his phonograph. They kept journals and would read their poems. They suggested that I start keeping a journal and I told them that I had one that I started when I went to Europe. I shared some of the poems I had written, mostly imitations, mostly filled with anger, but Jackson liked them.

"You know for a jock——you are one, aren't you? —— you have a lot going on inside that head of yours," he said. He snuggled up to me, perching on his knees in front of me. "Ginsberg used to do this with Kerouac, just look at each other, not touching, just seeing what they could find if they paid close attention to the other. Let's try it."

I stared into his eyes, a hazel color, and at his thick eyebrows. The wrinkles in his brow were like the ripples in the sand after the waves pulled back on a flat beach. His nostrils rose slightly as he breathed. I could smell sweet cologne, lime-scented like the one that Maurice wore at the gentlemen's club that night.

He stared at me. I noticed how his eyes slipped across my body, first up and down my face, then, at my chest and arms and belly and from there, down my crotch and legs, exploring me. I felt frightened, as if he was actually touching me. Perspiration formed first on my forehead and gradually, the more anxious I became, beaded on my cheeks and neck. His eyes narrowed and he reached over, "Are you all right?"

I wiped the sweat off my brow. "Just hot."

"Ruben, open the window," he said. Ruben pushed up the window. Jackson took hold of my hand and pulled it toward him. "Let me massage it," he said. "You seem tense."

"That's all right," I said, pulling it back.

"No," he insisted. "Lie down. I'll massage it. I'm really good."

I lay on the couch and he sat next to me in a chair and pressed and kneaded my hand, bending the fingers and joints. I fell into a swoon, but realized that, although I tried to hide it by bending my knees, I'd gotten aroused. Jackson never said anything, but I could see that he noticed.

After that, we hung out regularly together after class and partied or read our poems. We became friends. Jackson lived in Chicago and told me that, on some break, I should come to town and he'd show me around. I promised that I would call in the summer, which was fast approaching. I knew that, once I got home, I'd be playing golf again and working on the grounds crew—something I looked forward to—since I'd be outdoors, in shorts, rarely a shirt, shoveling sand, raking traps, and fixing broken or damaged bushes, a life of pure physical labor.

The Date

As a member of the grounds crew at the Glen Brook Country Club, where dad was a member, I had to get up each morning at 4 a.m. and be ready by five when Earl, one of the old grounds crew members, picked me up in his beat-up Chevy which had two windows out. I liked riding with him because I'd never known anyone who spent their whole life doing manual labor. I sometimes wondered what it was like and if it was something I could do if I had to. I'd be embarrassed when members of the club would treat Earl and the other staff dismissively.

"They're a nasty bunch of drunks," a friend of my father once said. "How can you stand to work with them?"

I shrugged and said, "They're decent guys. And, hey, you like the course being well kept? They do the work so it is."

For all I knew Earl could have been forty-five or eight-five. He seemed as if he had lived three or four lifetimes. He appeared to be exist in a limbo between age and agelessness. Having worked on the grounds crew since the 1930s, he kept the club's old model-T truck running, dismantling it each winter, the whole engine, cleaning it "whistle clean" and reassembling it in time for the next season. It had a double clutch and hummed at fifteen miles per hour. My coworker—another student, blond haired, thin— and I would sit on the back with our legs dangling as Earl drove us to the back nine where he would leave us off to rake one trap after another, making our way from fifteen back to seven, when we broke for lunch.

Sitting in the shade of a tall, majestic elm, we would listen to Earl tell stories about the members. When he used to be the club's security guard, he'd drive around at night, checking out the gates and the course. He could name who he'd seen out by the thirteen green going at it, some husband with someone else's wife or some waitress who had hopes of marrying into the upper crust. Earl drank vodka most of the time yet never appeared to get drunk. But how could we tell since I never saw him not drinking and never had known him other than he always was. He carried a pint of vodka "cause you can't smell it. That's why those fancy folk drink them martinis all afternoon. No one can tell nothing no how." On the rides to work, he always offered me a nip to start the day right and I'd sipped enough to make me wince. He'd belch a laugh and shove a green object in my face, "Here, take a bite on this," and hand me a cut lime. "It takes the bite off."

He loved telling his stories of the couples he caught over the years going at it and how they paid him plenty to keep quiet. "Nanin't none of my business," he'd say, "I done enough of that in my day, if you know what I mean."

But I had heard a different story about Earl from Hal, a big lug of a guy, one of Earl's longtime friends. He told me what happened on an afternoon when it was too hot to rake anything, least of all a trap. We sat out of sight in a grove of cottonwoods, deep in shade and he told me about Earl's first and only love. After serving in the Pacific front in World War II, he came back to the club to work. He met a lovely girl at his church and finally got the nerve to ask her out. Before his date, he had several shots of vodka to calm his nerves. He took her to a movie. But throughout the movie, he kept taking a nip of vodka to boost his courage. Later, when they strolled together in the park and sat on a bench, he decided to ask her to marry him. But he had gotten so drunk that as he knelt to ask her the big question, he threw up over her dress. He never dated after that. He told them his story one night and it became legendary among the workers. When I heard the story, I laughed. But I felt sympathy for him. Tom and I had gotten drunk too often than I cared to remember before our dates, trying to get the same courage that Earl did. I worried that, no matter how hard I tried, I might end up like Earl with no girl whom I felt comfortable with. It seemed that Hal was telling my story. I wondered if I might end up like Earl, a dismal drunk, frightened of women, doing a dead-end job.

Earl may not have had the education that Tom and I had, nor had our social standing, but we were all equally insecure. But I was still trying, still going on dates, still drinking too much, as was Tom. Earl had learned from experience and had given up. He had a sorry dog, an old terrier, a female, and that was enough.

In my position as a laborer, I felt alienated from the country club set, and Earl seemed as lonely as I was. Somehow, we became good friends. I would go over to his place, a small cottage by a lake, a three-room place that had a couch, two chairs and a table that served as a living and dining room. He fixed a hearty stew with onions, garlic, and vegetables. We drank vodka with a little lime and he told me stories of some fine gentlemen and ladies he had known over the years. When I got home at night—his car weaving up my drive—my parents would ask where I had been. I'd tell them that I was out with the guys.

I knew, however, my relationship with Earl was just an excuse to numb my brain and be with someone who did not care about a world outside his restricted orbit. Somehow, I wanted to know how that felt because, no matter how drunk I got, I could not get rid of the rage and the wanting to make things different. I admired those people who could turn away from the past. The trouble is that I could not forget. It was as if I were intoxicated with the past, mulling it over, drinking in every little moment, trying to figure what it had meant. I'd done that with Tom when we went to the city and to that gentlemen's club. I played those drunken scenes over and over. I wished I could expunge the feelings I had. I wish that I was like Tom. He seemed comfortable with people being as they were. I'd done it with my father, constantly revisiting every conversation, hunting for a way to tell him what I thought without risking his dismissing me, casting me off. I was not sure what made me obsessed with the past but I knew that I had to learn to live with it. How I would learn, well, that was not clear to me, not yet.

Adult Books

In the middle of summer, Jackson and Ruben asked if I wanted to spend some time with them in downtown Chicago, hit some book stores, and talk. Anxious to get away from the house, I told mom that I was going downtown. She asked when I'd be home. I told her not to wait up. I'd be late.

After taking the train into Union Station, I crossed over Canal Street and went toward what I remembered as a bohemian area. Jackson and Ruben told me to meet them at a café on West Adams Street. I found it easily since it had tables out front. My friends were sitting there, drinking iced drinks.

"How you doing?" I asked, greeting both of them and taking a seat.

"Fine," Jackson said and looked miffed. "Don't I get a hug?"

I'd forgotten he liked to hug, as did Ruben. I leaned over and hugged them both.

"That's better," Jackson said. "No macho stuff with us. Drop that football image and just be yourself."

Ruben passed me a copy of Allen Ginsberg's *Howl*. "Have you read it?" he asked.

"No," I said. "But didn't we read some selections of Ginsberg in the anthology last semester?"

"Oh, doll face, that's all expurgated. Listen to this:

"I saw the best minds of my generation destroyed by madness, starving hysterical naked, dragging themselves through the negro streets at dawn looking for an angry fix, angelheaded hipsters burning for the ancient heavenly connection to the starry dynamo in the machinery of night, who poverty and tatters and hollow-eyed and high sat up smoking in the supernatural darkness of cold-water flats floating across the tops of cities contemplating jazz,... who ate fire in paint hotels or drank turpentine in Paradise Alley, death, or purgatoried their torsos night after night with dreams, with drugs, with waking nightmares, alcohol and cock and endless balls..." He stopped and tapped the page.

"Can you believe someone wrote that? 'Waking nightmares, alcohol and cock and endless balls'?"

"Wow!" I exclaimed. I'd not read that poem.

"I imagine we can find even better stuff than this," Jackson said. "I've got a list of poets who publish with City Lights, the publisher who puts out Ginsberg. Let's find them. You need to get your own copies of them."

"You game?" Ruben asked.

"Sure."

"Let's check out the bookstores down the next block," Jackson said. "I know some really good ones not far from here."

We browsed through several stores hunting for Beat Poets who were still considered radical—Ginsberg, Kerouac, and Ferlinghetti. My friends, as aspiring writers, went to readings and spent whole days in the city. They had shopped in avant-garde shops, magic stores, magazine shops, used bookstores, so they knew where they were.

"Look," Jackson said and pointed at "Adult Book Store."

"Let's check it out. We're all adults, aren't we?" he said, appraising us from head to foot.

"Yep, we're adults. Let's see what adults read!"

Once inside, we walked under the checkout counter, which was elevated, with a young man at it. He eyed us suspiciously. Jackson said, "Hi, there!" with a cheery nonchalant voice, and the clerk did not bother us.

Jackson picked up one magazine after another. I stood by him, gazing at the men and women on the covers in various positions, all aroused. It was like the men's club with Tom. I cast my eyes out the window. "Look here," Jackson said. "Amazing!"

He showed me some photographs of women, scantily clad with men fucking them. It seemed gross. Pictures of women seemed like a violation— like watching your mom have sex. I smiled and raised my eyebrows. I knew I was supposed to be impressed.

"Something, huh?" he said.

"Yeah."

He moved to another rack and I followed. "Oh, look here. This is very interesting."

He picked up a magazine called *Hot Nuts* and shoved it at me.

He asked, "What do you think?" pointing at the naked men with enormous hard-ons and other men, young, attractive, spread out like they were Thanksgiving dinner. "Do you think Ginsberg would approve?"

Stunned and unable to utter much except one word, "Sure," I held my breath, trying to fight off my own arousal. He flipped through the magazine and stopped at a page with two handsome young men, kissing one another and between them, sticking up at full mast, their erections. I felt both aroused and numbed by the sight of the men as I peered at what, for years, I tried to deny was my own sexual appetite.

I'd relegated my attraction to men, as some of my fraternity brothers relegated their thoughts about communists: something terrible and opposed to everything they wanted to believe about themselves. I tried to expel it from my imagination, but, here, right in front of me, my body reacted as if the photographs were magnetic and I was filled with iron filings that flung themselves at the images. For years, I had fought with my desires in my own private battle, deep in the loneliness of my room, fantasizing about men, denying men, pretending what I thought was not real but only a phase. Although I did not want to admit it, on some nights, I wanted to kill myself. Or if not kill myself, kill those feelings. When I saw news reports of soldiers aiming their rifles at some Vietcong on a battlefield and firing, I imagined that I too was firing to kill that part of myself that I hated, hated deeply. Of course, I masturbated—everyone did, I suspected—but I never did touch anyone, not intentionally, not since my high school years when I was innocent, just experimenting, not since that guy at the private club. My yearning jostled around inside of me like a canister of fuel, and as I looked at that magazine, the sight of real life satyrs ignited my body. I felt as if I were combustible; in a daze, my eyes fixed on the photograph, and my legs wobbled and, strange as it may seem, I nearly felt faint as I had with Tom that one night at the men's club. What was happening? I put my hand to my face. It felt cold.

Ruben grabbed me, "You all right?"

Dropping the magazine, I looked out the window and saw the light, cracked and jagged, stab the building across the street and headed out of the bookstore. Once outside, I breathed deeply the fresh air as my friend held onto me, repeating, "You sure you are all right? You look awful."

I tried to push him away, "Get off me. I'm fine." I put my hands on my knees, taking in deep breaths. When Jackson came up to me, I lashed out at him, "Damn it, you asshole, why'd you bring me in there?" Rage surged through me, a rage I had never known before, a rage that boiled over, burning inside me as if my body were exploding, as if had ignited a canister of fuel in my chest. I knew it made no sense. I wanted to run, to flee. But I didn't want to make a fool of myself any more than I already had.

He asked me again, "Are you all right?"

I said, "I'm fine, fine."

But, no, I wasn't all right: I wasn't fine. Rather, I felt sick and staggered as if I were drugged. Ruben held onto me. We walked several blocks. I calmed down as we crossed the street into the commercial district. I nodded at him and mumbled something about my being upset, my being under pressure—grades, the draft and all. They took me down the street, and we went into Kroch's and Brentano's, a huge bookstore, where I located the philosophy section and curled up with a book, Viktor Frankl's *Man's Search for Meaning*, who was slated to give a talk on his experience in the concentration camp at school. For a while, no one talked about the incident in the bookstore, but it would not leave my mind.

Later, my friends laughed about how I looked like a ghost, how those images of big cocks, women, and vaginas had put me over the top, how they had to escort me out, having seen how overwhelmed I was. They even poked fun at my rage, commenting lightly about it, as if I was too Puritanical and could not stomach the photographs because of my propriety.

"Well that is that last time Jason will go in there," Jackson resolved. "You will only be allowed in the philosophy and poetry sections from now on!" I appreciated how they attributed my squeamishness to my propriety. It worked for them and worked even better for me.

But it wasn't true. Rather, it was as if I had become a turncoat, had been snuck into a netherworld of aberrant sexual desire and I wanted to see more of it. I wanted to know more about the enemy—those men attracted to men— and wanted to cross the line, to find my way into their camp, see how they lived, to question what made them un-American and to find out if I too belonged there. I remembered how Paul had tried to explain how communists were people with definite beliefs, often very American beliefs about civil rights, about rights of workers and about freedom. But I did not entirely understand him. If they were just regular people, why was our

276

country fighting a war to limit their encroachment in another nation half a globe away? Why were people worried about communists? There had to be something wrong with them just as there had to be something wrong with me, with how I felt.

Confused and perplexed, I told Jackson that I had to catch an early train.

"One more hug," he said. "One more hug for my sickly baby."

I gave him a hug. I felt a sudden urge well up inside me, almost seize me, to cry, to break down sobbing on his chest. Ruben looked at me askance. "You sure you are all right?"

"Fine, fine," I said. "Just pressure. Worried about a lot of things."

"Aren't we all?" Jackson chirped in.

"Yes, aren't we all," I said and hugged Ruben. I raced to Union Station. On the train back to Glen Brook, I decided that I needed to make sense of my fears since they were not going away. I was not sure how to do it. Obsessed with those images I had seen fleetingly, not being able to get them out of my mind, I wanted to go back by myself to see what was there, to explore it alone without anyone else watching me. In New York, with Tom I'd felt inhibited, not wanting to let on, to give him a sense that I was attracted to those boys. Here I was sickened by them. Getting back to the suburbs seemed the best way to avoid dealing with my mixed feelings because I could go back to work at my job, just get outside and build up my body, and to refine my golf game, the one activity that, once I focused on it, allowed me to block out everything else.

War Hero

The next day, after playing a practice round for the club championship, shooting a 75, I met my parents who were having cocktails on the veranda. A young man with short hair, perfectly trimmed, sat at the table across from them and was engaged in a conversation with my dad. I pulled up a chair. He looked familiar, but at first I did not recognize him. It was Dean.

My father turned to me, "How'd you play?"

"Three over—double-bogeyed 16. I can't seem to hit that green for the life of me."

"You need to focus, son. The championship is coming up. You can't do that if you want to have any chance."

"Dad, I know," I said, looking over at Dean. I was afraid that he might still resent my comments about General MacArthur. My dad noted my hesitation.

"This is Dean, you remember? You met him in Hamburg on your European trip—Karen's husband."

I did remember him, all too well. For a moment, I thought that it might be better for me to head off to the locker room. I worried he'd remember exactly what I said had marred our stay there, when we pretended we were not in Germany, played poker, ate pizza, and drank beer. He smiled at me, seemingly glad to see me.

"Good to see you," I said, shaking his hand, surprised by his seeming interest in me.

He nodded at me. "The same. It's been a long time, lot of water over the dam."

My dad stood to help my mother from her chair and then excused himself. "I promised your mother that we would eat inside today. So I need to get into a jacket and tie. But, please, why don't you two eat out here. It's on me. No, no, don't get up."

"That's all right dad," I said. "You don't have to..."

"I want to. He's a war hero. Least I can do for one of our fighting men," he said, clapping Dean on the shoulder.

After he went, I turned to Dean. "Sorry about that."

"Hey, it's no problem. Everyone wants to make me into some war hero. They don't want to know what Nam is like. So they just offer me free drinks, and, now food. Hell, if I play it right, I could be a first-class drunk in no time!"

I laughed. "Here," he said. "Get yourself a drink. We might as well enjoy ourselves."

We watched the golfers trudge up the fairway. Some exuded confidence because they had hit a fine shot on the green. Others looked disgruntled. They slammed their club on the turf and headed into one of the two large yawning sand traps that wrapped like a tourniquet around the green.

Finally, I blurted out, "You know I'm sorry that I offended you..."

"Hey," he put his hand up. "Forget it. MacArthur was a pompous ass, just as you said. And so, as I've found out in Nam this last year, are many generals."

"Really?"

"You bet." He slugged down his drink in one gulp and stared at a man hitting a sand shot from the trap. The ball sailed over the green and hit a tree, dropping into the trap on the other side.

"Not an easy game," Dean said.

"No, not as easy as some think it is. You back from a tour," I asked, "or just on leave?"

"On leave," he said. "Head back next month."

"What brings you back?"

"Haven't you heard? Karen's pregnant."

"Congratulations."

"Yeah, thanks," he said, swirling his drink in the glass. He jiggled it slowly at first, getting the ice to spin in one direction and then, with a quick countermove, spin it in the other direction, trying to keep the ice in the glass, back and forth, each time increasing the speed.

"What are you studying?" he asked.

"Some literature, modern poetry and psychology and, since it is my major, history—French history next semester, the revolution."

"What poets do you like?"

"Eliot. You know him?"

"*Time and the bell have buried the day and the even star has passed away...*Or something like that, right?"

"Yeah, from the 'Four Quartets'."

"I love it. So much wisdom in it. You know at West Point that was my major, literature. You ever read Joyce?"

"I picked up *Portrait of a Young Artist*. It was rough going at first. But I love the scene when the priest admonishes the boys about sin."

"Isn't that fabulous?"

We ordered steaks, medium rare, and two more rounds of drinks, Jack Daniels on the rocks, and talked until my father and mother came out after their dinner.

"Are you boys going to stay here all night?" my father asked.

Dean stood up, as did I, to acknowledge my mother. "Well, sir, it's been good to get to know Jason better. We have similar interests as it turns out."

"Good, good for you," my father said.

"Don't stay too late," my mother said. "Remember, you work tomorrow."

"I know. I know," I said, reaching out to her and taking her hand. She squeezed it and smiled. Her eyes had a faint sadness to them as if she'd seen something that she did not want to see.

They left, greeting friends at different tables. The men, as we had, stood to greet them and my father would say, "No, no, keep seated," but they would stand anyway. My mother knew everyone by name and would chat amiably with the women. They seemed like a couple on a political campaign, greeting their followers.

Dean looked over at them. "They're certainly social creatures."

"Yes, they do that every time we come here and I have to do it, too. It drives me crazy. Why can't they just go to the table and eat?"

Dean laughed. "Well, that's how they make points. This country club set is all about appearances and connections, the more you have, the more points you get."

"Really?"

"No, but doesn't it seem that way?"

I agreed. We ordered another drink and stayed until the bar closed. As we walked out of the club, signaling the attendants for our cars, he put his arm over my shoulder. "You know, we have to get together more often. You are the only guy here who has any intellect and wants to talk about serious stuff."

For the next several weeks, before he had to report back to his unit, we met at the club and chatted about poetry. He introduced me to some war poets—-Wilfred Owen and Rupert Brooke —and told me that he'd write me back at school. Being with him brought the war closer to me, knowing that he, soon enough, would be in the jungles, slogging through swamps and tiger grass while I studied and kept up with assignments.

Club Championship

Jackson and Ruben called me several times asking if I wanted to spend time with them in the city, but I told them I was busy and could not make it back to town. I put my energy into improving my golf game, getting my handicap as low as I could. I'd played golf since I could pick up a club and had a natural swing. The club pro took a liking to me and had worked with me, teaching me the mechanics. After playing the spring on the Ashbury golf team and competing in intercollegiate matches, I decided that I'd gotten good enough to enter the Glen Brook club championship.

I muscled my way through early matches by sinking putts that rightfully I should never have made and found myself getting into the finals, playing against one of the men I admired, a scratch player named Jimmy Lawless, who loved to drink and, even more, to compete. As a caddy, I carried his bag for him many times. He'd start drinking on the front nine and, by the back nine, he'd be plastered. But he could hit shots like no one I ever knew. He'd flub a shot, knocking it twenty yards. His opponent would swell up, thinking that he had him and could easily win the hole. Then Jimmy would pull out a one iron, one of the hardest clubs to hit, and lash a shot 220 yards that landed two feet from the cup, and, much to his opponent's chagrin, would tap it in for a birdie, winning the hole. I admired how compact he was—for a man his age, probably in his mid-sixties—he didn't have a paunch. Even though I was certainly in better shape than he was, he was no slouch. I was sure of that. When I got older, I wanted to be like him—to keep my physique.

In the final match, we had a large following. All age groups had gathered at the first tee to watch us. It was the young David against the older Goliath. He had his entourage of friends who walked with him, his longtime golf buddies and I had many younger, junior members who wanted me to beat the old man. My dad, anxious as I was, followed me too. I could tell in his eyes that he wanted me to do well, to show that I was a fierce competitor, not to embarrass him.

Luckily, I had a caddie, Frank, a guy my age, who liked me, helped me keep focused and offered to do it for free. He'd carried my bag in earlier matches and, afterward, I took him out for drinks. Gaunt, wiry, he enjoyed golf. He aspired to be a pro. Most weeks, we had played on Monday, when caddies could play, and he had a pretty good swing. I passed on tips about how to hit fades and hooks, low and high shots that I had learned from the club pro. Frank knew how to keep me focused on each shot, not to worry about the next one and helped me strategize where to hit shots for the best percent success.

By the third hole I was one down, having missed an easy putt on the second hole. But I birdied two holes in a row and was one up. On the fifth hole, a par five, I knocked a drive right down the middle. Jimmy hit a duck hook that put his ball behind a huge elm. He had to chip it out. My second shot landed fifty yards in front of the green, there in two. Jimmy knocked his third shot by mine. I knew I had him if I hit a good chip, but he had other ideas. He chipped his ball up and in, a four. I skulled mine—jabbing it over the green—and managed a five. Discouraged, I went to the sixth hole, a par three thinking that I had blown the match. Frank pulled me aside, putting his hand on my chest, calming me down, and said, "Stop it. Don't give up. You can do this." I looked into his eyes and he kept patting my chest. I felt as if he was more motivated to win than I was. I did not want to let him down.

My dad was off on the side of the fairway, pacing back and forth, running his hand through his hair, a sure sign of distress. I took a deep breath. I didn't want to disappoint him.

Jimmy whacked an eight iron on the green, twelve feet from the cup. Frank said, "Remember 14," and I did. In the semifinal match, I had to sink several long putts to slam the door on my competition. My favorite putt came on the fourteenth hole. Mr. Johnson, a scratch player, had knocked his second shot ten feet from the cup. When he strode up the fairway, he had a snap in his step that meant he was sure that he'd have me two down with only four holes to go. My ball had landed in the back of the green, on a side hill by the sand trap, and the putt had to go over a mound, slide down a steep slope to the cup.

Kneeling on the green, I looked it over, thinking that if I could knock my ball in, he'd be flummoxed and might miss his, turning the match around in my favor. Frank told me to keep my hands light on the putter, just feel as if I was holding a stick of butter. I followed his advice. I had a sense when I addressed the putt that I'd make it and, as it rolled to the crest of the hill, almost stopping, it crept slowly down, turned quickly and dove into the hole. I shouted and smiled at Frank who slapped my hand as I walked by him to pull the ball out of the hole.

Mr. Johnson looked startled and jabbed his putt past the hole. I won the next two holes easily and went into the finals with Jimmy riding high.

Taking out a seven iron, I chocked down on it, giving myself more control of the shot as the pro had taught me, and hit a bunch shot right at the hole. It hit the flag stick and dropped down, three feet away. Jimmy missed his putt; I tapped in. Frank put his hand on my shoulder as we went to the next tee. "Stay in the match," he said. "Stay with each shot. Play your game."

On the seventeenth tee, the match was tied up. A large gallery, some sixty people, had formed along both sides of the fairway. It looked like galleries that I'd been in when I followed Arnold Palmer and Jack Nicklaus during the Western Open. Seventeen, a long par five, doglegged slightly to the right. Shooting out of a narrow corridor, the drive has to carry a hill about 220 yards from the tee to reach the top of the hill. If the ball carried far enough on the down slope of the hill, a player could almost reach the green. Jimmy teed off first and smashed one over the hill. I followed suit. On our second shot, I pushed mine to the right, fifty yards from the green. He took out a one iron and laced it to the front of the green, several feet from the apron, close enough to putt for an eagle.

Frank took a hold of my arm and pulled me close to him. He whispered, "Keep focused. Don't lose your head. You know how to do this. You've hit a lob a hundred times."

My ball was nestled in the rough. That meant I could not get much spin on it to stop it. The pin was nestled behind a sand trap so I had about ten feet over the trap to negotiate. If I hit it over the pin, I'd probably roll into the sand trap in back of the green. I took out a sand wedge, hoping to hit a flop shot in which the ball lifts up quickly and drops down just as quickly. Frank and I stood behind the ball looking over the shot. As I stepped forward to hit the shot, he patted me gently on the rear. I turned to look at him and he grinned. I felt relaxed and softened my hands so that I could feel the club lazily swing back and through the ball. This was the kind of shot Jimmy loved to execute. The ball lifted up as I wanted it to and hung there and dropped over the trap. I could not see what happened, but Jimmy pointed at me, shaking his finger at me, smiling. The crowd roared. It had gone in! My father leapt in the air. I leapt too. I could not believe it. I hugged Frank who, quickly, gave me a quick kiss on the neck. I pulled back, startled, and looked at him. He flashed an impish smile. "Guess I got excited!" he offered. I patted him on the head. I went to the green and pulled it from the cup, an eagle. My dad came over to me and put his arm around me. "Unbelievable shot, son," he whispered.

Jimmy knelt down, looking at his chip from all sides. Then as calmly as a surgeon, he tapped the ball and it slide right into the cup. No nonsense. The crowd cheered. That's why he'd won the championship five times. I pointed at Jimmy who grinned back at me. The final hole proved to be less dramatic. With the fairway lined with people tee to green, we both hit long tee shots, carrying a trap at the neck of a dogleg. We smacked seven irons to the green, mine above the hole, his below the hole. I putted first, sure I had the line and the ball swung around the cup, leaving it inches from the cup for a tap in.

Jimmy looked over his putt from four directions and talked to his caddy who pointed out the slight slant in the green. He addressed the putt and stepped away. He looked at me and smiled. He loved situations like this when it all came down to one shot. This is what made him a legend at the course. He finally settled over the putt and with a smooth stroke slammed his in and won the match.

The crowd cheered and people poured onto the green to congratulate us, my father included, patting me on the back and turning to others saying, "That's my boy!" and I felt as if, for a moment, I was his boy and knew what it felt like to be the heir to a legacy and find it fulfilling. It was the first time my father ever followed me in a tournament even though I had gotten into the semifinals in several state tournament. I looked down at my hand. It felt good. My father had shook my hand again and again and said that he was proud of me. I was proud of myself, too, proud that I had done my best and pleased that Frank had kept me going. My father embraced my mother who had joined the match on the seventeenth, but kept back in the crowd. She came over to give me a hug.

"Oh, honey," she said, tears in her eyes. "I'm so proud of you."

Other friends of theirs came up to me, saying it was the best match that they had ever seen. They went off with my parents, congratulating them. Dean, who I'd not seen, stood off at a distance and gave me a thumbs up sign. He came over and shook my hand.

"That was some battle," he said.

"I hadn't seen you."

"It was a clandestine operation," he said. "I stalked you the last nine. Impressive."

"Thanks."

"No, thank you. You have guts, and it showed. You need to keep that in mind." He gave me a hug, pulling me close. "Now enjoy yourself. Celebrate."

I felt as if I had this once proven myself, even in defeat. The match was over; I'd lost, but I was pleased. I made a go of it. I felt like a man who had fought another man and had done his best. That is the best kind of feeling. After shaking hands with a number of people and getting a kiss from several of my mother's women friends who said I was wonderful. I noticed Frank waiting patiently on the side of the green. I put my glove and golf balls in the bag and started to pick it up to bring it to my car.

"No," he said. "I can do that for you. You have the green Volvo? Mr. Lawless is waiting for you. You go with him. I'll meet you later."

"You want to wait for me?" I asked him.

"Sure, I thought after all the rounds together, we could go out for a drink," he said, rubbing the irons with a wet towel to clean off the grass stains. I told him that I'd meet him later, but I had to go into the Oak Room for drinks. He said that he had a book to read and he would wait.

"It may be a long time."

He pursed his lips and broke into a half-smile. "Look, enjoy yourself. You earned it. I have all the time in the world. And we will celebrate after you get done."

Nineteenth Hole

By tradition, Jimmy, as the winner, bought drinks. I tried to keep up with him and his friend, Bob, a golf buddy who played with him every week. After several hours, with one beer after another and with Jimmy—he wanted me to call him by his first name now—slurring his words and becoming nearly incoherent, I seemed to have won the drinking round. Jimmy fell out of his chair and his friend and I had to lug him to the shower and undress him. He couldn't manage to find his zipper and we had to tug his shirt over his head. As we undressed him, I discovered that he looked so trim because he wore a corset, pulled tight to give him a thin waist and large chest. Partially made of leather, it had been drawn so tight, he had trouble breathing. When we unloosened it, his body poured out like melted wax. Seeing him, my childhood hero naked, the small bud of his penis under the flab of his belly, made him much too human. His incoherent babble made him seem pathetic. I almost wanted to close my eyes and let the image of him as I'd seen him on the course be the only one I'd have. But he was as he was: old and worn, but still a terrific competitor. We got him showered and dressed and I carried him to Bob's car like a comrade wounded in war, where, just before he swung down to the front seat, he took me by the shoulders and looked me in the eye.

"That, my boy, was the best match I have ever played in all my years here. You're a real champion."

I helped him into the car and leaned over and said, "Hey, in my mind, you will always be the champion." He winked at me and I closed the door. The image of his naked body floated before me and burst like a bubble. I waved as his friend drove him away, the victor, the pathetic victor.

Close Call

As I was walking to my car, I knew the night was over and the summer had come to a close. I'd soon be heading back to school, a junior now, taking some challenging classes. Not far from my car, I saw a figure sitting on the ground. It was Frank. He was still waiting for me by the caddy shack, sitting on his haunches against the building, reading a book.

"Wondered if you still wanted to go for a drink?"

I said, "I don't know. It's awfully late and I'm pretty drunk."

"That's okay. I'm game if you are. Are you?" he asked. His eyes looked pained, almost frightened as if he dreaded what I might say. After he stayed so long to wait for me, I did not want to disappoint him.

"Sure. But I gotta be careful. I'm pretty loaded."

"I'll drive," he said. "I can leave you off here afterward."

"Sure, why not?"

We drove to a local bar, one that was out on Roosevelt Road, and, on weekends, had a jazz band. We sat next to one another in a booth at the back of the bar. After a few drinks, I felt his knee press against mine. He told me that he liked me. I tried to change the topic. We discussed his ambition to be a pro, his swing, and my shot on seventeen. The pressure of his leg was distinct, firm and persistent. I knew that, if I stayed longer, I might get into trouble since his leg against mine was causing me to get aroused. I told him that I had to get home—work started early.

Although clearly disappointed, he said, yes, that he'd drive me back to the club to get my car, but he wanted to buy me one more drink for the road. I drank it more quickly than I should have and felt the top of my head loosen as if someone had taken a can opener to it. On the way, he pulled up to Lake Glen and parked the car beneath the languid umbrage of the trees. He asked if I ever parked there with a girl in high school. I had to admit that I never had.

"I wasn't much for dating," I said.

"Neither was I," he admitted. "Not much for girls."

We sat in silence. He put his hand on my leg and I let him keep it there.

288

I was pretty drunk and my mind had decided to let whatever might happen to happen and not put any brakes on my desires. I put my hand on his leg. After a few minutes, I felt his fingers crawl toward my crotch. It made steady progress. I enjoyed watching it move along like a caterpillar, his fingers inching their way up, so I began rooting for it, hoping it would get where it wanted.

I was pretty drunk, I was sure of that. He latched on my penis and rubbed me, a slow gentle motion. *Oh my god*, I thought. I reciprocated. He was good size, his member right along his jeans, warm and hard. He nuzzled against my neck and kissed me softly. The musk of his body from a long day's work was lovely. I tilted my head against him, pulling him close, our heads cheek to cheek. I was letting myself go as if I wanted to see how close I could come to making love knowing that, if I did cross over the line, I'd have difficulty finding my way back. I noticed, coming up the road, another car. Probably another guy with a date. But behind him, under a streetlamp, clear as day, at the far end of the road, I noticed a police car cruising along the lake. Slow. Stopping occasionally. It's floodlight stabbing into a car. I sat up, Frank moaned and stirred.

"What's wrong?"

I pointed at it and he straightened up.

"This is not safe," I said. "Too many cops."

"I know," he said. "But where else is there?"

I pressed on my hand on his leg. "Nowhere and that's the trouble for us. I can't afford to be front page news, nor can you."

He put his hand under my chin and turned me toward him, kissing me deeply.

Then, as if he too knew the dangers of loving another man, turned on the ignition and drove me back to the club, letting me off and letting me out of his life.

He called after a few days to ask if I wanted to go out for a drink, but I told him I was too busy and had to get ready for school, only a week away.

The Professor

Instead of heading back to the DAE house in late August, as I had previous years, I went to my new room in the boarding house. After Jake moved out in the spring, I had the room to myself and could put my full attention to studies. I still ate breakfast, lunch, and dinner at the DAE house, and, when there were parties, attended them. But I found that I enjoyed my time alone and soon discovered that the old man who rented me a room needed help.

In the first weeks of school, Professor Garcia, who had taken a shine to me the previous semester, invited me to help him with his garden. I often stopped to say hi to him before climbing up to my room and had mentioned to him that I missed gardening as I had as a child. I enjoyed his company and he soon became like a father to me, bringing me coffee at night, checking if I needed any snacks from the store, talking with me when I came back from class. He spoke with difficulty, carefully enunciating each word because, several years before, his son had cracked his skull with a shovel. The two of them were out digging potatoes from their extensive fields. When the professor reached down to snatch up a potato that he had missed, his son was just thrusting his shovel toward the same spot to unearth more new potatoes. The speech lobes of his father's cortex were permanently damaged.

Whenever he came to visit my small bedroom, he knocked and asked, "Are you busy?" I'd always tell him that I could use a break. He would ask how I was doing and, as we talked, I could mouth each word that he was about to speak before he spoke it. The words came out in single file like passengers on an escalator, each pressing forward yet forced to wait for others to emerge. Since his son had gone off to college and he needed help on his farm, he invited me to work for him. I needed the extra money and so I took him up on his offer. He drove us to his farm to harvest potatoes. As he knelt in the soil, I watched his delicate pink hands scooping the firm, moist green-gold flesh that spilled out of the soil. He smiled as we filled bushel after bushel. Each potato fit into the palm of my hand, cool and hard— like bright planets plucked from a dark galaxy. As I lifted the spade above my shoulders to drive it into the mound, he explained, "That's how it happened," pointing to the gash in his head. The scar tissue left a white seam that curved slightly like a scythe, mirrored the curve of the shovel in my hands.

One morning, exhausted after an all-nighter, reading Ezra Pound's ideas about imagism, I heard the professor knock and open my door. He poked his head in and asked, "Studying hard?"

I nodded. "For an English exam."

He sat down on the chair by the bed across from me and said, "Give me your foot. A good foot massage will take the stress out of you and help you relax."

With his long fingers he took my right foot, slipped off the sock, pressed the skin back with a knuckle, and traced firmly up and back on the arch. I leaned back in the desk chair and gave myself over to his ministrations.

Slowly he recounted a story of another boy, before me, of the other boys who had rented my room, about the night the doorbell kept ringing, on and off, with no one apparently at the door until the professor discerned outside, obscure in the alcove, the boy with his girlfriend held propped up and naked against the side door, how each time he thrust into her the bell would ring and so he just listened to it ring on and off until it climaxed like one long, great Hallelujah chorus and the boy let her down and hugged her.

I was not sure why he told me the story except that maybe he had picked up on the periodic rhythmic movement coming from my room when I masturbated, but, whatever it was, the story caused me to get an erection. He eyed my pants, the raised cloth, but he did not let on. He smiled and let my right foot down and motioned to the other. He took hold of it, stripped the sock off and recommended his magic balm easing me out of my own restless skin. He told me a second story, about the another tenant, a tall slim boy who kept to himself, a pre-med student: One afternoon, it started to rain, light at first for half a day, then as the wind picked up, hard, driving against the door and windows, torrential. With the rain battering the house, he had worried about windows left open, dashed up the stairs, bolted into the tenant's room, where the boy sat, naked in a chair, masturbating, as aroused and electrically charged as the storm, masturbating and, so engrossed in himself and his erection and because of the deafening rain pounding on the roof, at first did not notice the professor. The boy kept right on stroking himself. The professor went directly to the window, shut it, and left, but not before glancing over at the young man who, the professor said in his measured speech had an enormous erection. The boy paused but did not flinch with the intruder in the room. He only gazed at the professor and kept his hand on his penis and waited for the professor to leave as if it was as natural a thing to do as brushing one's teeth.

The professor was enchanted by his stories and clearly enjoyed the fact that, based on my own arousal, I liked them too, even while drifting off into a gentle oblivion as he held me firmly in his hands. I thanked him for massaging my feet. He replied, "Oh, thank *you*," and left, gently shutting the door behind him.

The Visitor

In October, well into the first semester of classes, I heard a knock on my door quite late at night—after 11 p.m. Joseph Stein stood in the hallway. I was stunned. I wondered what he might want to say to me; and, even more, wondered why he wanted to talk with me since I had been the vehicle for unearthing the underlying racism in the house.

At first I just stared at him. He was a short, stocky guy, not athletic at all, with closely cropped hair and pronounced five o'clock shadow like Nixon that covered his jaw and cheeks any time of day.

He sensed my discomfort and asked, "May I come in?"

"Sure, sure, have a seat," I offered, trying to compose myself.

As he set himself in the easy chair by the lamp, I looked at him and realized that I had never really gotten to know him. I'd spent time with him, but never intimate time. We'd gone thought Hell Week together, but after that, he kept to his own circle of friends as I did mine.

Reaching in his pocket, he offered me a gift, a small heavy putter blade, gold, that he said could be used as a paperweight since I liked golf so much. I thanked him. We talked about golf for a short time. I was not sure where to go in a conversation with him. Since the incident, I'd apologized and offered him an "I'm sorry" and waited for him to say, "it's all right," and I left it at that. It never occurred to me how naïve I was about his being the brunt of anti-Semitism. Having grown up in Glen Brook, a conservative Republican enclave, not only had I never met a Democrat, I'd never known anyone who was Jewish.

Joseph said he wanted to clear the air. While he talked, I kept thinking back, as if possessed, to the night, and often, found myself totally unaware of what he was saying and had to force myself to pay attention.

"That incident, I know you were dragged into it. You wouldn't do that if you weren't pressured into doing it," he said. "Am I right?"

"You are. It was one of the last things I ever imagined doing, especially after visiting Dachau the summer before."

"Can I ask how they forced you into it?"

"Yes, you can. But, Joseph, to be honest, I'm still sorting out what caused me to do it. I suppose though it would give me... credibility if I knew."

Joseph's brow furrowed.

"Yeah, I know, it seems strange,' I continued. "But I guess I wanted to prove myself to certain guys—you know who—and latched onto a strategy that's totally inimical to me now. For that, I can only say, 'I'm sorry.' "

As he talked, he grew quite animated and kept repeating how he wanted to be my friend too, how he held no grudges.

"I think we can be, too," I offered. I wanted to mend the wound inside me, if not inside him.

"I'm so glad," he gushed. "I mean, the way things happened, the way it got out of hand, I mean, I knew, after driving back and forth that first year, you were not biased and you'd felt good about our relationship— our being friends." He pasted a wide smile on his face. I gave the response that seemed necessary.

"I think we can be good friends."

My own feelings, however, were ambivalent. I never cared for him one way or another, but somehow I caught his enthusiasm, his total concern that we become friends, how we'd be true friends, and what great memories we'd have of each other and what it meant to him, how he respected me. On and on, he kept talking and I kept nodding my head. I don't remember saying more than three or four whole sentences. By the time he'd finished his spiel I'm sure he was convinced we were friends. Not about to dissuade him, lest he spend another hour convincing me how we needed to be friends, I tapped him on the knee and using a phrase I'd heard my father use when talking to another businessman, said, "I'm with you one-hundred percent."

He smiled. A car passed outside the window. I noticed how thick his eyebrows were, almost forming a continuous line across this forehead. He said, "I wanted you to know I forgave you long ago. I heard that Sean put you up to it."

"Thanks, Joe. That helps."

"It's all right," he said, leaning forward. "I want to open up some discussion in another direction. Do you mind if I change the topic?"

"Go right ahead."

What he wanted to discuss is how to be friends with other guys, guys who disliked him and who made snide comments about him.

"What am I to do? I can't change the way I am. I'm Jewish, that's for sure. But I'm also from Crystal Heights and a business major. I mean, I'm more complicated than that. You know that, don't you?"

"Yeah, I do. We're all more complicated than we appear to be," I agreed.

"I want your advice about what to do. How can I get the other guys to like me?"

I shrugged my shoulders and told him, "You know, maybe you should not try so hard. Maybe they're not worth it. Maybe it's better to focus on guys who you know aren't biased and who like you."

He mused for a minute and shook his head, "Never thought of that. I always thought I had to win everyone over."

"What's the point?" I asked.

"I don't know. Maybe I just want to be liked."

"We all do—God knows, I'm sometimes obsessed with it myself, pleasing others, my dad, the professors— but, as I learned last year, sometimes it does not pan out."

He then broached a topic that surprised me. He said that he was interested in changing religions. "I've been going with a girl, Janet and she invited me to come to her church. I like it. The minister is a fine man. I've been thinking that I might become a Protestant," he said. "I don't know. It has been running through my mind. But it doesn't matter. I never go to synagogue any way. So why not become a Protestant?"

I nodded my head, not sure how to respond. "Yeah, I guess so. I don't know much about the Jewish traditions. I'm learning a lot about the question of God and evil in a poetry class— Milton and *Paradise Lost* and Adam, Eve and the serpent. All I know about the Old Testament are the stories about David and the baby being cut in half by Solomon."

"He did not cut the baby in half," Joseph insisted.

"Oh, right, he threatened to," I said and continued. "Clearly, I don't know all that much! You know more about the Old Testament and about how it relates to today's Jews. Modern Jews, I mean, still seem to be outcasts, more a product of Russian pogroms and the holocaust than of Israel and its history, don't you think?"

Joseph winced at my words and laughed, "Never thought of it like that."

"Nor had I," I remarked, "until you brought up the subject."

He asked me more questions about feeling like an outsider and how he could be more of an insider as if I were a guru with magical solutions at my fingertips. I didn't know what to say to him because, well, I had not exactly made many allies in the house after my trashing his room, and had found that trying to be liked was usually a futile enterprise. The more difficult task was being yourself, and I was not very good at that.

I said, "It must be rough feeling like an outsider," and shirked delving into how I had agonized the first months living out of the house and felt as though I had no place where I could feel that I belonged.

He nodded and then said, "You know, now, we have that in common."

"How's that?" I asked, perplexed.

"We are both outsiders: you for doing what you did to me, and me for being Jewish."

I laughed, admitting, "How ironic! You're right."

The conversation lasted an hour, and near the hour's end, it sagged and Joseph offered to go, claiming that he had a date, and then, laughed, "I've always got a date."

"That you do." I smiled. "It seems to be a hobby for you."

He laughed, stood up and reached out his hand, and waited for me to take my hand out of the pocket of my bathrobe. He continued to smile as he walked to the door, seeming to be very pleased with himself. I can't say that I felt the same. It seemed that he had more courage than I had to confront what had happened and to find out what I really felt. I wasn't about to deny his own satisfaction at becoming best of friends—it seemed redemptive— so I told him, "Joseph, This has been a good conversation. I'm really glad you came over."

After that late-night meeting, he made no more attempts to drop by. We had polite conversations at meals, and, during breaks, Joseph and I drove back to the Chicago area, never quite sure of how we stood with one another, yet knowing that he was right about our bond: we were outsiders and that was a basis for some kind of friendship that I never entirely understood. He was a classic extrovert that made an introvert like me feel intimidated by his wanting to become close friends in one swoop. It seemed to me friendship just happened. It could not be contrived. Whether we were indeed friends did not matter as much as I respected that he took the initiative to come to my place, to offer me a gift and to spend time with me. For that, I was grateful and relieved because the harm I had done was at least, for him, behind us. But what wasn't behind me was the primitive terror that drove me to act. What troubled me was, as with the SS officer at Dachau, that being exonerated does not wipe out evil. His coming to my room merely glossed over my guilt and gave it a more appealing veneer. Even if I rubbed it with my own rationalizations, underneath it was as ugly as ever.

Basic Beliefs

Before I enrolled in the Basic Beliefs course to fulfill my degree requirements in religion, the question of God's existence was not something I'd ever given much thought to. God's existence seemed to be like the existence of some guy in China. I didn't know him. I'd probably never meet him. He didn't know me. But I presumed that he existed.

I felt the class might spark my imagination. It might make for interesting conversation with Ruben and Jackson.

The course consisted of lectures, readings, and small discussion groups. In our first classes, we were asked to write a short essay on, "Is there a God? And if so, how do we know it? " I thought those were perplexing questions. I figured if God existed, I was not the person to answer if He did or not. Why question His existence? Why ask me? I had no idea. In my upbringing, we attended church. We celebrated certain holidays, mostly Christmas and Easter. We did not discuss God, nor, for that matter, Christ. My faith in God had swerved one April day, then skidded out of control in high school and never regained traction. In first grade, the Sunday school teacher asked us to draw God. Innocently, I drew my father with a coat and tie and golf club. The teacher, a stocky, broad- shouldered man with a deep voice, picked up my drawing and glared at me, "What do you think you are doing, young man?"

"Drawing God," I answered, lamely.

"This is not God the Father. Look around you. Do you see God wearing a coat and tie and holding a golf stick?"

I stared at the images on the walls, saw a man with a white robe, unshaven, floating among clouds in the top half of the pictures. The teacher grabbed me by the arm, his fingers tightening on me, "Are you trying to be funny, young man?"

I shook my head. "I'm not trying to be funny."

"Well, if you are, I will tell you now: I am the one who makes jokes in here. Your job is to listen and learn."

He jabbed my drawing, "Let me tell you this, young man. If you think, this is God, you are mocking Him." Then, he snatched up the drawing, crumbled it, and dunked it in a trash can.

I held back tears.

"Now draw God," he demanded, pointing at the painting and I drew as best I could the man with a beard whom I had never met. On the way home from church, I stared at my father, wondering whom I could be worshiping if not someone who looked like him. This other man appeared friendly enough, but I wish someone had introduced me to him. I never had seen him in church. Men did not have beards. It seemed perplexing. It did not make sense. I realized that whoever God the Father was, it was not my dad, which meant if my kids went to Sunday school when I became a father, they would not be worshiping me.

From that dismal day in April, the whole idea of Sunday school seemed pointless. If God was anything like the Sunday school teacher, I wanted nothing to do with him.

Having pushed religion to the side of my mind, I gave no thought to God until He bumped right into me in the Basic Belief class. If I were going to pass the course, I had to think about Him. For several weeks, I did minimal work, cramming in some time at the library when I wasn't too hungover from a night out with Tom and Jerry or an evening with Ruben and Jackson. I could wade through the dense theological vocabulary, but I found most of the language so abstract it was initially hard to follow. It was not like poetry. The words were difficult. I had to look them up.

For the first time in my life I was reading real theology and, the more I struggled with it, the more surprised I was because gradually I understood what was being said, and I actually enjoyed reading it. I read theologians like Anselm and Augustine. They asked serious questions about belief and faith, about God. In Sunday school, I never heard a teacher question God's existence: certainty was drilled into us as we were marched toward confirmation. But after that, I put theology out of my mind. I had developed a certain practical approach to the question of God: If God did not exist, it was not my problem. If God did exist, that was fine too, but it was His business. He could mind His business and I would mind mine. As my dad had said, "Seeing is believing," and that was good enough for me. My attention was directed toward things of this world like football games and golf.

God was not half as interesting to me as the Chicago Bears. They could win and lose games. They had to contend with the weather and opponents whom I knew. If they were playing well, I put my faith in them. I had gone to every home game with my mother for years. Getting on the train to Chicago late morning, after church, we trucked along the tracks to the game, and it remained one of my fondest memories of my high school years. God was something that ministers worried about, not me.

The Basic Beliefs course changed that. After a month in the class, I had wrestled with as many questions about God's existence as I had about my own sexuality. For years, I had ruminated about how to cope with desires that seemed to have a mind of their own. But now I was pondering something higher and, it seemed, more profound: the existence of a deity. It didn't happen all at once. Initially I became interested in the class as a spectator, watching students foaming at the mouth about God, amused by the intensity of the discussion, which, for the first couple of weeks, I had managed to avoid by simply looking at my note pad, averting my eyes, and only joining in when I sensed the professor's attention directed at me from across the table.

The class consisted of a formal lecture by Dr. Compton followed in the next period by a group discussion. These were lively, giving fervent believers a chance to speak their minds. Some students were emphatic that we could not question Him in any manner whatsoever, especially regarding His existence. Sarah Reynolds, who carried a Bible with her at all times, would slap her hand down and raise her voice while staring at all twenty of us seated around the long mahogany seminar table. She'd made pronouncements such as "God must exist. Otherwise, there would be no Bible, which is God's word. There would be no standards. How could we know what is bad or good?" She continually confronted the professor as if the arguments she laid down were trump cards that could not be matched. But Dr. Compton would calmly ply her with other questions.

"Well, if He does exist and if He is good, then how can there be evil in the world?"

At that one, Sarah stood and planted both hands on the table. In a shrill, unwavering tone, she asked, "What are you doing? Are you questioning

God? No one has the right to question God. You have no right to question God."

The rest of us at the table recoiled and leaned back in our chairs as if to let the sting of her outrage slide by us. We peered at Dr. Compton and waited for him to rebut her accusations. But instead of replying, he pulled out a match, carefully struck it, and laid it on the lip of his pipe. He puffed several times, never breaking eye contact with Sarah, but clearly enjoying the ritual of inhaling the smoke that soon wafted through the room. He phrased his response precisely: "You say that no one has the right to question God. Are you saying that by not questioning God, we cannot, as a consequence, ask why evil exists or how a benevolent God could permit it?"

Sarah fell back in her chair and paged through the Bible, searching for a passage. She looked at him with her lip quivering. "Can't you see you are intentionally trying to crush my beliefs, the basis for my existence, my faith in God?" she said and slapped the Bible on the conference table.

"If your faith, Sarah," he spoke gently, "is based on unquestioning belief, it has no foundation and will crumble when you face suffering in your life. So I am not crushing your beliefs. Quite the contrary, Sarah, I am trying to help you build a foundation for your beliefs that will withstand the worst of our realities, the harshest experiences, and give you something to stand on that will endure: a foundation that will be flexible enough to stretch to meet the forces that want to tear it apart."

She looked up at him and he smiled at her. The winds in the trees outside the room rustled. I became conscious of my breathing—its modulated rhythm—and of others breathing the same way.

Dr. Compton puffed on his pipe and turned toward me. I took a deep breath and aimed my eyes at my note pad, wondering what to think about what had happened. Fortunately, he focused on a student next to me.

"Mr. Anderson, do you believe evil can exist if there is a benevolent God?"

Relieved to see someone else on the spot, I put my head on my hand and stared at the boy. "I don't know," the student said, "If God does exist—and I do not believe that He does—but if He does, and if villagers in Vietnam are being burned alive by our napalm and Negroes in the South are being clubbed and beaten, how can He stand by and let it happen?" Earlier in the week, I had seen him at an antiwar rally that I had witnessed, one outside the Student Union. He held up posters of napalmed villages. He was one of leaders of the Students for a Democratic Society, a fringe group—communist, I was told by Trevor—protesting our country's fight against insurgent communist regimes.

Then Dr. Compton turned to me. "And Mr. Follett, do you agree or disagree with Mr. Anderson?"

My face flushed. It was the first time he had called on me. I wanted to say something profound.

I rummaged through my brain but found nothing inside my head, only a cabinet with empty shelves. I felt like a fool. I could think about the existence of God when I was by myself, but in a class with others looking at me, my mind went blank. I pushed words out of my mouth: "God must be good or else why would He be God?" I made an odd guffaw, trying to lighten the moment. No one laughed and I continued: "I mean, He is God...but there is evil too, I guess, I mean... I don't know."

Nodding his head, Dr. Compton kept focused on me. "So what are you saying—can God exist or not?" His eyes were intense yet patient. I gazed at my hands, which were folded in front of me, and repeated the question in my head, trying to formulate a response, to compose a statement, some sure answer. Sweat beaded on my forehead. One bead made its way across the rim of my nose. I wiped it away. I was befuddled and could only stammer out another question: "If He allows evil to happen, what kind of God is He?"

Taking it as a question, Dr. Compton called on another student and soon others were weighing in, supporting Sarah or questioning her, each allowed to voice an opinion, adding to the complexity of the question, but no one resolving it.

Determined not to make a fool of myself again and to survive the class, I read the assigned essays and made notes in the margins, trying to anticipate what Dr. Compton might ask me. I attempted responses in class, but the snappy response I was looking for would come to me only on my way back to my room. When asked a question in class, I actually heard as if listening to a voice a long way off. "What does it mean to exist?" "To

302

exist"— I thought and waited for words to come, but I never found words.

I felt like a drowning man swimming desperately against a cascade of questions. I had no idea why God existed. Or why anything—even I— existed. How could I answer that? I had thought that I was really starting to think, to know what I thought when I was with Ruben and Jackson, but in class, instead of becoming more confident, I felt as if I was becoming stupider.

After one particularly grueling class, I went back to my room, where I took a swig from the fifth of Jack Daniels I kept on the desk and called up Tom to see if he wanted to drink. He always did. We swigged a fifth. It was hot in my room, so we staggered outside, past midnight, under the pale green leaves, in love with the warm fall evening, oblivious of the couples skirting around us on their way to the dorms. Eventually, we crawled back up the stairs to my room, had one more round. I tumbled in my bed and Tom staggered back to the fraternity, to his room in the annex that he shared with Jerry. Come morning, the light stabbed at me.

I woke to the realization that the essays on the nature of evil were still on the floor, piled up, waiting for me to pick them up. Nothing had changed. Despite keeping my desk cleared except for two tumblers and a fifth, I knew I had to study harder and so for several hours a day I sequestered myself in a nook on the third floor of the library.

Testing my own thinking was new to me, new to my image of myself. I was becoming smart enough to make sense of poetry and now I was delving into ontological questions, which were different. I discovered I liked reading about questions that meant something, that called into question what I had known or thought I had known.

Getting smashed may have given me an altered state of consciousness and communing with a different way of being, but it was temporary, fleeting. That may have suited me fine in the past, but I was not sure it would do in the future.

The Seamstress

Several weeks later, as was my seasonal tradition, I went to a seamstress, Miss Starett, who took in or let out the waist of all my pants. During the fall and winter, when I played football, I would bulk up, even for intramurals, gaining fifteen pounds and the seams and waist of my pants would tighten. Going to her was cheaper than having two sets of pants. She worked out of a room on the third floor of an apartment building and called her place "the upper room." She kept it spare. There were no books, only a sewing machine with a treadle, a metal table with sewing supplies, several coat stands with dresses, and a rack for pants hung neatly on hangers. It was a tight little room.

A person of rigorous faith, Miss Starett had pictures of Christ with needlework aphorisms framed on the wall—"He is the way and the truth and the light"—and loved to tell me how to avoid straying into heathen waters. On our visit, she checked the seam in my pants, carefully marking it, and inquired about my studies. I informed her of my progress, the classes I had passed. She acted like a kindly grandmother who wanted the best for her grandchildren. I spoke of my hope to go to law school, of how I wanted to be a success like my dad.

She said, "You're very lucky. Your father has provided for you. You are blessed."

"I guess so."

"Be sure of it. He is a good man."

As we chatted, I told her about the Basic Beliefs class. She abruptly pulled away from me and asked, "Who teaches that class?"

"Oh, the Department of Philosophy and Religion," I replied without giving it a thought. I was no longer worried whether I had the smarts to pass it, but I told her that it was challenging some of my beliefs and was difficult. My first paper on the existence of God came back with a C, and a note to "Tease out your ideas more. You have important things to say."

As I talked about the class, I felt Miss Starett grab the inseams of my pants and tug on them like a tourniquet. Her voice changed, becoming quite grave. She spoke in a slow, hushed tones admonishing me, "Did you know, Jason, that there are known communists who teach in that department?"

She held in one hand the white chalk marker, in the other a nettle of pins. At the side of her mouth, she kept three or four pins, point side in, like darts in the mouth of a native.

She raised her voice, "Do you know the danger?"

Instinctively I tried to step back, but she held me fast by the waist band. If she were going to attack, she was in firing range. Instead, she straightened up to her full height, leaned back, and pointed out the window toward campus. "It is a fact. They are in that department. They are there to pollute young minds, convert them to their free-thinking ways. A free mind is a dangerous mind, a mind drunk on its own righteousness and truth." She went to her desk and pulled out a pamphlet, ran her fingers across it. "See here, evidence. You must not lose your way. They will get you to think like communists. They are anti-American." Her soft voice became strident again. "They are un-American, polluted by an evil and Satan himself."

She handed me the pamphlet, which had "John Birch Society" printed in bold letters at the top.

For a moment, I almost laughed. She seemed to act like a salesman for a product that I had not asked to buy. But I wanted to hear her out.

She told me to drop the class immediately. She cautioned how these men could beguile me, cast me under their spell, turning a "nice young man" into one of them.

"Like alcohol, the devil works in subtle ways. You will think that he is not having an effect on you, but before you know it, he will sway you away from the truth." She pronounced "truth" with an assurance that made it sound like a room that had a door you could unlock with a key, and if you entered and arranged the furniture, making it comfortable, you could then live inside of it without fear of being questioned.

Amused even more by her comments, I dismissed it. "It's not so bad. We discuss everything. I enjoy the debate in the seminar. Right now, for instance, we are debating the existence of God... "

"The existence of God?" she squawked.

"Yes."

"That is precisely what I was telling you. He will corrupt your beliefs," she insisted, pulling pins from her mouth as she marked another inseam.

As she warned me of my vulnerability to the satanic force, I realized that I had left the bottle of Jack Daniels on my desk and that I had promised Tom to bring it over to his place and have a shot before we went out to fraternity parties that evening. I changed into another pair of pants. Miss Starett's hands slipped like tiny mice up and down the cloth, tugging harder, pinching, seemingly impatient with me.

"Stand still, please."

She wanted to be done with me, yet she kept firing questions about what I was learning. She asked, "Do you believe in God?"

"Well, I don't know. I've never given it much thought before this class. I'm like my dad; if I can't see something, it's hard for me to believe in it."

"Humm," she muttered. "May I ask how can you question the existence of God?" She jerked the seam of my leg. The crotch of the pants tightened and left me breathless as if she was applying a tourniquet, cutting off all circulation in my leg until I gave the proper and true— at least in her mind— answer to her question. She glowered at me as if I had announced the death of God.

"It's not just me. Many people have questioned it—even theologians centuries ago."

She composed herself with a smile that spread slowly like molasses across her face and stuck her nose close to mine, "Who is teaching this blasphemy?"

Not sure I should implicate any one professor, I said, "Oh, you know, the department." I mentioned several names.

"It is all right," she patted my shoulder gently, "I want to see if I know any of them. You know we all live in the same community."

I told her two of the professors' names. She blanched, "Yes, yes, I have heard their names at our meetings. You may think that I am being overly dramatic. I sense you are even bemused by what I say. But I'll tell you that I'm a member, young man, of the only truly patriotic group. I gave you one of our pamphlets. Read it. Maybe what I have to say has some merit. Isn't that possible? You will find that some people want to protect us. They want to be sure the Christian and democratic values of this country are not undermined. They keep information on these men. Your professors are known communists. Do you hear me, *known* communists. Oh, child, have they tried to change your mind? You must not let them do that. They will twist and turn you. They will beguile you. They will ask you questions and lead you to call into question all that you have been taught, all that your father and mother believe. They will try to win you over with fancy questions and nice words, but they will lead you astray. Unfortunately, they are allowed such freedom in our society to do harm and no one can stop them."

Sticking several pins by the waist of my pants, drawing them in, she asked, "You are a true American, aren't you?"

"Yes," I replied, "I am."

"Well, then, you must be vigilant. You are in the hands of satanic forces. I tell you this because you are a nice young boy and you must protect yourself."

As I took off one pair of pants in her closet and slipped on another, she snipped and chalked and pinned and talked, warning me of the dangers before me. She told me how these forces worked, how they asked lots of questions but never gave answers, how they acted calm and reserved when, deep inside, they burned with evil spirits meant to undermine every true American and Christian. By the time I left I was perplexed by her accusations. I did not think that they were true, but she was so convinced of their truth I wanted to hear what Dr. Compton might say. I had heard him ask the very questions that she mentioned, questions that cast doubts on old truths that I'd never questioned, never in their entirety. I felt more confused about God and evil now than I had ever before. I agreed with her one point about how the class was taught: the incessant badgering of students to articulate their own opinions seemed invasive. No other class called into questions such fundamental beliefs about the existence of God and what we previously thought.

Her questioning the motives of the professors got me to thinking. What if we did not want to tell a professor what we thought about God? We had the right to privacy. We had a right to our own thought. What if we support our government's attempts to stop the spread of the communist influence in Southeast Asia? Our professors had no right to find out what we think. I noticed that they never made commitments to one side or another, just as she said. They were devious in the way they forced us to call into question our old assumptions. They would toss out one question after another. It didn't seem right. I wanted to know what Dr. Compton thought.

After leaving seven pairs of pants with Miss Starett—all but one pair, the one I was wearing—I wandered onto the campus quadrangle. Students came and went, traversing from one side of the campus to the other, following paths cut through the lawn and around the trees. I had promised Tom to meet him for a drink, but I felt my stomach gnarl into a shapeless knot.

Shoving my hands in my pockets, I was determined to get a straight answer from Dr. Compton, to see what he would say when I told him about what Miss Starett said. Then I could go and get drunk. That seemed the right thing to do. Getting smashed would be a kind of celebration, and Tom never got into heady discussions.

Confrontation

I strode to Maynard Hall, hurtled the steps two at a time, came to his office door, which was right off the stairwell, knocked, and waited.

"Come in," came the reply.

I pushed open the door. Dr. Compton, sitting at his desk, smoking his pipe—a thick book open in front of him—turned to me.

"Mr. Follett, what can I do for you?" he asked gesturing to the wooden chair across from his desk.

For a moment, I stood transfixed. I glanced at the room, books as high as the ceiling, different spines on them, some leather and old, some new, piled up like miniature steps, among papers strewn on his desk. Over his desk, a painting by Picasso, the one with the bull and spears sticking out of him, separated two of the bookshelves.

I could not get my mouth open. Like an idiot, I stood dumbfounded. I did not want to sit down for fear I would be drawn into some lengthy discussion. I wanted to keep it short.

"You can sit down," he said, pointing at the upholstered chair. "Are you all right?"

I kept standing, my hands out in front of me, making odd circular motions as if trying to crank up my vocal engine. Once they got a certain velocity, I blurted out, "I gotta ask you something. I was talking to a woman who does my pants, you know, she sews them, and she was telling me that there are some members of this department who are known . . . I don't know how to say it. Well, they are . . . communists!"

I took a deep breath and looked at him, half-expecting that he would snarl at me and take out a sickle and hammer flag and wave it at me.

Calmly, cocking his head to one side, he puffed on his pipe and shook his head very slightly, serious in his demeanor, taking in the accusation, preparing—I thought—for a lengthy explanation. But he did not give a lengthy response. He merely asked, "So?"

In my years as a football player, as a starting fullback charging into the line to gain a few yards, I had been hit by fierce linebackers who flattened me to the ground. But that one word question "So?" knocked me back several steps. I was flummoxed.

I repeated his question, "So?" to take it in.

"Yes," he explained. "So what if they are communists?"

"I don't think that would be right," I said, pleading with him to understand. "They might... be trying to push their political agenda on us and, right now, aren't we fighting communists in Vietnam?"

He smiled wanly, lifted his pipe, pointing to the bookcases, "Indeed, we are fighting against a communist regime in Vietnam. But does a government having a communist regime make it wrong?"

"I don't know."

"So the question might be 'what is a communist'?"

Miss Starett's accusation fell out of my mouth in the form of a question "Aren't they anti-American?"

"Why are they anti-American?"

I told him what she had told me. He nodded his head and poked at the bowl of his pipe, getting the tobacco to ignite.

He shook his head. "Have you read anything about communism?"

"No."

"Do you know what it is?"

"No. Not really. I know our government is trying to prevent the North Vietnamese from making South Vietnam into a communist state."

"Is that bad?"

"I don't know. But I do think the war is wrong. Who are we to tell them what they should or should not do?"

"Exactly."

"But that does not help me understand what communism is," I said, exasperated.

"Do you know who Karl Marx is?"

"No."

"Have you ever met a communist?"

"No. At least I do not think so. I don't even know what they look like."

Dr. Compton sat upright, seeming to mull over his question and my answers, leaned forward, his face sanguine yet circumspect, and said, "Then

310

it seems to me before you listen to the seamstress, who I am sure is earnest in her concerns, and before you worry about what she has told you, you need to read more about it, understand it more, and find out if it is truly anti-American." He gestured to the chair.

I sat down and he pulled several books off the shelf, one enormously thick *Das Kapital* and another, a smaller collection of essays. He held the books in his hand and said, "You know for years I had to take these books off my shelf and hide them—any book on the topic—in my attic, hide them so no one could find them. Do you know why?"

He explained how during the McCarthy era—just one decade before—philosophy professors who taught Marx lost their jobs or were silenced. They were blacklisted and found themselves taking jobs as clerks and shoe salesmen, positions he respected, but ones that someone with a Ph.D. did not expect to be doing. As a young father, he had worried that he would not be able to support his family and decided, much to his chagrin, to hide his books on communism despite the fact that it is a pivotal idea in Western philosophy, his area of expertise. The volumes, Marx's ideas, were like gasoline, too volatile, something he kept out of sight, too great a risk to his livelihood. Of course, he did not abandon teaching about Marx entirely. He presented Marx in classes and carefully brought up his questions about capitalism. But as a professor, he lived in fear. He said how before the 1950s professors could speak their minds, get students to question their thinking, to change their points of view. But because of McCarthy and the general fear of another country—the Soviet Union—open discourse closed its doors for nearly a decade. Many of his colleagues were fired without notice. Out of this threat, the idea of being tenured, protected from political censure, finally allowed professors to speak their mind freely. He asked if I believed in free speech. He asked if it was un-American to silence someone's expression of ideas. He asked what communism was. He listened as I formulated my own thoughts, which still felt more like they were being ground out of a handheld meat grinder. He was patient and listened, often repeating what I had said so I could hear what I said. And then he talked with me as if I had a mind.

I showed him the pamphlet Miss Starett had given me. He perused it, then passed it back to me. "They have very strong opinions. Clearly, they are afraid of people who think differently than they do. They are afraid of communists. They use fear to promote their ideas. They believe they are protecting America."

"Well, are they?" I asked.

"You will need to read more about them and then read what I have given you and then decide for yourself," he said, shrugging his shoulders. "What do you think?"

Here he was asking me questions that I had never thought about. I felt dumbfounded once more, at a loss for words. I began to sweat. He leaned forward, "Well?"

I felt a surge of anger flash up my neck. "She told me you would do this. You would ask me lots of questions and never give answers. You would force me to find answers to questions. You would not tell me how you feel and what you think! She said that is how you play with our minds, how you... how you corrupt minds, how the forces of evil work."

He laughed and swung back in his chair. Miffed by his laugh, which seemed to mock and upbraid me, I stood, convinced that, indeed, Dr. Compton had bamboozled me as Miss Starett had said he would. He was making fun of me, confusing me, playing with my mind, trying to shape how I thought. I bolted for the door. But he stood too, with remarkable agility, holding his hand between me and the doorway.

"Wait, Jason, wait," he said intensely. "I was not laughing at you. I apologize. I was laughing at the language that some people use."

He put his pipe down on a bookshelf. He took a deep breath. "Before you rush out of here, consider this: my job is to get you to question your beliefs—your basic beliefs. That is the title of the class. I'm afraid I got carried away with my role."

I gazed at the floor. His shoes were scuffed, not shined. One lace was torn.

"Listen, Jason," he said quietly, "can we start over? I think some of the questions you are asking me are much more important than some of the ones we ask in class and, therefore, they deserve an answer. Would you stay long enough to listen to what I have to say?" He picked up his pipe and put it down on an ashtray and leaned forward, his eyes intently on me.

I thought that a shot of Jack Daniels would feel wonderful—the quiet numbness rising from my belly and incomprehensible thought drowning in the blissful intoxication. Why hadn't I gone back to my room? Tom was probably wondering where I was. I put my hands on my face—flushed again, sweat pouring off my forehead— and looked up. The professor smiled at me.

We stood quietly for a minute not a foot from one another. He gestured to the chair. I saw how gently his eyes gazed at me. I stepped back and sank into the chair, holding my legs together, noticing the pants I had on were the only ones that Miss Starett had not taken in. Baggy like a clown's, they drooped from my legs.

There was a silence in the room and I could hear a bell ringing in the distance.

When my eyes came back to his face, I saw him shake his head as he spoke. "Yes, what the seamstress said is, to some extent, true."

I was shocked. My mouth must have fallen open. He patted me on the knee.

His voice had an intensity and passion I had not heard before. "Look, you are worried that I am dangerous. I guess I am. I want you to think, and that is dangerous. But as to the accusation that I do not have an opinion, that is wrong. I have very definite opinions. For one, you think I am trying to—what did she say?—"corrupt" your mind? The answer is no: I'm not. Jason, I want you to think for yourself, to formulate your own ideas, not be a mouthpiece for my ideas or for her ideas or for some else's ideology, or some notion promulgated by one group or another. I want you to have your own ideas. I want you to be able to defend them. I cannot do that by telling you what to think or how to believe. If, indeed, I am evil, then isn't it in your best interest to find that out for yourself?"

We talked for an hour. He did not lecture me. He did not tell me what to think. He asked me to think for myself, asked me more questions than I'd been asked in my life. I finally asked him the big question that niggled at my mind: "Are you a communist?"

He mused for a minute, then said, "Jason, I think what you are worried about, and what Miss Starret is worried about, is whether I support our form of government—democracy—and I can unequivocally tell you I do. I believe in democracy. With that said, your other concern is if I am subversive and, in her words, a communist. Is that right?"

I nodded.

"Okay, let me address that question since it is not an easy one. It is never a question of being a "communist" or being "a loyal American," never a question of 'either/or.' No, I am not a communist. But I do believe that Marx has some accurate insights into the dark side of capitalism—its flaws, how it treats the worker as just a vehicle to increase profit—that remain as true today as they were in his time. Remember, he was questioning an economic system, not a form of government. But what he said and the concerns that he had have been expressed by many other loyal Americans. What Marx said helps me evaluate those who promote capitalism as if it were flawless, some perfect economic machine, which it is not. Whatever my doubts are about capitalism, I remain one who steadfastly supports democracy and free speech, the freedom to question governments or an economic system."

He told me about attending a Nazi rally in Berlin in 1937, standing at the edge of the massive throng when Hitler rose to the podium, the floodlights sweeping back and forth, the trumpets blaring, the crowd frenzied, chanting his name. He had seen one face of evil. It came in the guise of an ideology, of a people coming to think that they were right and that others were wrong, and of people who bought the idea and did not question what it meant, how it punished or murdered anyone who disagreed with the idea. He cautioned me that evil has many shapes and guises, ones that came later into his life with McCarthy's despotism. He spoke with passion and with humility. Although I had studied World War II, I had never heard it from one who had been there.

I was at first not sure Dr. Compton had answered my question because I had never thought of democracy as different from free enterprise —but, as I thought about it, I noted that universities have different History and Economics departments. He asked me what I liked about the class and I said, to my surprise, "The discussions, the way you can say what you think and hear what others think."

"Good," he said, "If you want to read more, you can take these." He handed me Marx's books and another that he recommended I read first, by Marcuse. "Do you want to read these now?"

My hand reached out and I held them for a second, then said, "Not now. I have so much I have not read in your class."

"Fine," he chuckled. "Yes, you should be ready for class."

I said, "I guess I should not have said that."

"On the contrary, I appreciate honesty. So many students read Cliff Notes and I have seen your books with notes scrawled all over them; you take reading seriously. Take this one." He handed me a book titled, *One-Dimensional Man*. "I will leave the rest here. Take them anytime." He put them back on his desk.

"I will get them soon," I told him, "and anything else you suggest."

Final Adjustment

Two weeks later, Miss Starett called to let me know my pants were done. As I came down her street toward her white apartment building, I saw the sun glinting though the maple leaves, pirouetting on the sidewalk, shimmering in a way I had never noticed. I realized that I was beginning to see the world differently. I was not sure how, but I sensed something was happening to me. I felt as if someone had lifted a window of a musty room and let fresh air in.

I walked up the gray stairwell to her room at the top. The pants were seamed up and fit perfectly. As I tried each one on, she inquire, "Have you checked, my boy, on the teachers?"

I told her I had. She seemed pleased.

"Well, then," she said in a self-satisfied manner as if she knew what would follow. "Are you going to drop the course?" She held out the next pair of pants.

"No," I told her matter-of-factly. "I like the class and had a long talk about communism with one of the professors."

She looked aghast and held her hand to her mouth. "You did?"

"Yeah," I answered, "He told me how being a good American means supporting free speech and also being open to new ideas—that democracy respects different points of view, including"—I paused to look directly at her— "including communism."

She gnawed on the inside of her cheek and coolly passed me a pair of blue trousers. They fit, just like the others, the old seams pulled out stitch by stitch and the new ones sewn invisibly as if new. Miss Starett avoided my eyes and went about her business, humming to herself.

"Thanks," I said. "You got me to think. And I appreciate that."

"Why, young man, that's *not* all I wanted to do. I wanted you to see the danger in that type of free-thinking and how you stray from the truth. I wanted you to see the inherent danger that the truth faces." She spoke rapidly, racing to sew her doubts into my heart.

I put up my hand. "You got me to think," I said, going into the closet to try on another pair of pants. I spoke louder so she could hear me, "And I appreciate it. But I'm learning the truth comes in different shapes, not in one form. I do appreciate your concern about me." When I stepped out, she looked at my pants and pulled on a seam.

"They fit," she said, brushing lint off one leg.

Her brow furrowed as she passed me the last pair of pants. "My boy, you do not know of what you speak."

I closed the door of the closet, a faint wedge of light seeping past the doorsill, and called out to her. "I may not, indeed, I may not. But I want to find out exactly what I know and do not know. It may or may not agree with you or with Dr. Compton. I just want to keep my mind open."

I heard her smack her lips and when I came out with the last pair, she stared at me and bit at her lower lip. "You're a nice-looking boy."

I paid her and she gave me exact change. I smiled at her and stepped to the door. She folded the dollar bills neatly in her hand, and then placed them delicately in the top drawer of her desk. She said nothing to me as I left but narrowed her eyes as if she were developing a photographic plate to be stored in her memory, one she could pull out and show her friends— "Here is another one of them, another one converted to communism." But her face softened and she said, "I will pray for you," nodding her head with a beatific countenance, kind yet strangely distant. She waved her hand daintily at me as I closed the door, as if she knew I would never come back to her room, never again require the seasonal letting in and letting out.

Back at my room, I opened the book by Herbert Marcuse, *One-Dimensional Man*, and read, "A comfortable, smooth, reasonable, democratic unfreedom prevails in advanced industrial civilization, a token of technical progress..." I read all night and, more exhilarated than exhausted, saw the sun's pale orange light spill through the branches of an old elm and thread its way into my room, unraveling along the carpet, its strands splaying out across the floor with a disarming warmth.

New Tenants

Early the next semester, I discovered that the new tenants in the large room across from mine, and who took the room across from my old room, were involved in the antiwar movement. Previously, I might have been intimidated, worried whether I could keep up a conversation with them. I'd been reading about the war, talking with Paul, but had only recently shaken off my apprehensions about the spread of communism. With the help of Dr. Compton and my better understanding of Marxism and by my spending more time reading journals in the library, I had taken sides about the Vietnam War—I opposed it. But I dared not offend my friends in the fraternity. With them, I enjoyed evenings drinking and going to the movies. I certainly knew that, if I spoke up at home, my dad would not support my opinions.

I fell quite naturally into a double life: with most of my fraternity friends I rarely spoke about my antiwar sentiments, yet I started to help with the burgeoning Eugene McCarthy presidential campaign. Campaign headquarters, set up in a building downtown, several blocks from campus, with a phone bank and boxes filled with campaign flyers, was filled with students night and day. I would eat dinner at the DAE house most nights and during the week work on the campaign, going back and forth like a double agent. I met a girl, an antiwar activist named Jean, who frequently came to visit her boyfriend, a tenant at my boardinghouse. Organized and energetic, she gave marching orders like a general. She said I should break contact with my fraternity friends. "What are you doing with them? Can't you see they're part of the problem? Where are your loyalties?" she asked. I told her that I was opposed to the war, not to them. But I felt the tug of the antiwar movement pulling me further from my old, more conventional friends. My conversations with Dr. Compton had unmoored me, allowing me the freedom to venture into new ways of thinking.

Shortly after my getting involved in McCarthy's campaign, five of my fraternity brothers asked me to go out drinking with them. After a few drinks, we sat around, but the conversation sagged and so we talked about

318

Hell Week, the trip to Chicago, keg parties but even that fizzled and we ended up watching the news. A television at one end of the bar showed an antiwar protest and students, up in New Hampshire, campaigning for Eugene McCarthy. As part of the broadcast, Walter Cronkite reported that Barry Goldwater had just claimed that Nixon, in his fledgling candidacy, was the strongest Republican presidential candidate.

"Nixon," I scoffed. "I suspected he's for the war."

Luis asked, "Jason, what's your take on the war?"

"I oppose it," I said, surprised at how I took a stand and explained my reasons. "We use inhumane tactics on innocent people, napalming them. I don't think we can win it. And most of all, I have no interest in fighting a war I don't understand."

Putting his mug down, Luis told me, "What's gotten into you? You're becoming some sort of nut! How can you believe that garbage? It's left-wing propaganda." I asked if he had read anything in the newly released documents about how the escalation of the war was based on deception and that President Johnson had lied. Trevor, Tom, Jacob, Larry and Jerry turned on me, asking more questions, which I fended off. When they left me off at my room, a cold chill of disdain shadowed me as I walked up the path. When I went to the house to eat, Luis jested, "Here's the resident radical." Others called me, "one of the anti-American underground," as if I were some foreign mercenary. I'd become more of an outsider again. But the accusations, although they hurt, felt less caustic than the ones about being homosexual. As a result, I put more time into studying for my classes, less time at the fraternity.

The new tenants changed the mood at the boarding house. Instead of being a solitary haven to withdraw and study, it became a hubbub of antiwar activity. Every evening, Jean and several women with long braided hair came up the stairs with several guys whose hair was as long. I recognized them as being the campus radicals. One of the women was brilliant. She had been in my Basic Beliefs course and used theological terminology that I had to look up to understand her. They kept the door to their room opened. When I went to the bathroom, I could see them sprawled out on the floor, on the beds, and in chairs as they plotted their next sit-in. They also planned to integrate the female dorms, forcing them to be co-ed. They smoked marijuana, which I had never tried. They laughed and joked. They said "hi" when they met me in the stairwell. One evening, a handsome Negro knocked on my door. Tall, thin, with stunning limpid eyes, he introduced himself, extending his hand, "Hi, I'm Alex."

I shook his hand, soft and warm, his fingers lingering against mine as if to appraise them.

"You're strong," he said.

"Golf," I replied.

"Sure, you need strong hands for it," he said. Pretending to swing a club, he motioned toward the other door.

"You want to come over? We are kicking back and Jean, she says, you might like to join us, since you're antiwar. You were at one of the rallies, right?"

"Yeah, the one in front of the Student Union," I said.

He motioned for me to follow him. "You need a break. Too much studying fries the brain."

I accepted his invitation. Alex pointed to an arm chair where I sat down like a king on a throne. Beneath me, spread out on the carpet, were five others like campers around a fire. They were passing a joint, inhaling it and delicately offering it to the person next to them. They introduced themselves. Two of them were snuggled together—Ben and Sally— and nodded at me. Anne, the one from my Basic Beliefs class, with the terrific vocabulary, waved to me. Beside her was Jean. A guy with long brown hair shuffled across the floor on his knees—his name was Mike—to shake my hand. He knelt beside me, holding out the joint, and instructed me what to do. "Take a hit and hold it."

I put the joint to my lips, inhaled and felt the smoke, cooler and sweeter than tobacco, fill my lungs. I desperately tried to hold onto it, but found myself coughing. They laughed. The joint made its way like a miniature peace pipe around the room. Soon I found myself laughing for no reason, just giggling and enjoying how it felt in my body, laughing at laughter, how it sounded in my chest.

"Your first joint?" Mike asked. He had draped his arm over my knee and stared at me as if inspecting a new species. I admitted it was.

A cheer. "A new initiate!"

A slap of my hand. "Hey, hey."

I stood up as if I had just won a tournament, bowing to them, my arms held up.

"He looks like Richard Nixon. Come on Dick, what's your platform?" Alex called out.

"I plan to run for the president on a... traffic ticket," I said.

"How fast were you going?" Jean asked.

"The speed of light," I said, pointing to the joint. A laugh tickled the room. I kept standing, marveling at how it felt to be on my feet, hovering over everyone else, seemingly floating, my body light as if someone switched off the gravity button.

"Nixon's not running again, is he?" Alex asked. "He's no match for Kennedy and he's a racist as far as I can tell."

Jean who seemed to know everything about politics said, "Yes, he's got a committee and plans to announce any day now. Look, he's been traveling to Europe and South America. He wants to look presidential. The Gallup poll has him ahead of Romney, who at least can build cars. Poor Nixon has never gotten over his loss to Kennedy. What a pathetic loser." She mimicked him, "'You won't have me to kick around anymore.' I can't stand him."

"Where does he stand on the war?" Mike asked.

"Typical, he talks about a strategy to end the war, but he has none," Jean said.

The conversation drifted to the topic of Muhammad Ali and draft resistance .

."He's my man," Alex said. "He says that he ain't got nothing against the Vietcong. That's my feeling, too."

Mike sat up on his haunches, puffing on the joint. "He's got some balls, I must admit. I worry, though. I bet they incarcerate him like the others refusing to go."

"I sure hope not," Alex said as he looked up at me. I was standing in the middle of the room, enamored with the conversation, how it flipped back and forth, like a tennis match.

"Hey, Nixon," Alex said. "You still running?"

I looked down. He seemed far away. He patted the floor beside him.

"Come back to earth. Sit down. Sorry to say, brother, you lost the election."

When I flopped down, I realized that Nixon had been so long out of the public limelight that I'd forgotten about him. I felt unsettled thinking that he'd be getting back into public life. His mannerisms, so much like my father's, left me feeling as if I were watching my dad run for office, as if my dad was weaseling his way back into my life. Mike passed me another joint and put his arms across my legs, leaning against me, watching my face carefully. He must have sensed my distress. He smiled and called to the others, "We need to burrow him."

"Yeah" was the consensus. "Let's do it."

Mike told me to lie on the floor in a fetal position, which I did, and then, close my eyes, which I did, and just enjoy the burrowing. Once on the floor, they surrounded me, and Mike started chanting "burrow" and the others started, too, and then I could feel them nudge me, pressing up against me, their hands burrowing into my stomach, my back, my legs, chest, feet and head, each of them gently bumping into me, their bodies next to mine, male, female, groping me, so that I felt as if I'd fallen into a washing machine, rubbed back and forth, the quiet sensation heightened by being stoned, my skin erotically charged, causing each massage of a finger, each squeeze of a hand to rush over me blissfully, the sensation heightening by the "burrow, burrow, burrow" resonating in my ears.

When they gradually pulled back, they sat on their haunches around me. Mike asked, "How was it?"

"Amazing," was as much as I could say.

We lay on the floor and smoked more weed. Sally and Ben moved up to the bed and, after a few minutes, started to make love, which neither Alex nor Mike seemed to notice, but which kept my attention until Alex, leaning against me, his head on my stomach, whispered, "Don't mind them. They'll be at it for hours. They're like rabbits." I laughed and sighed.

Alex said, "That would be nice, wouldn't it—having it any time you wanted?"

"Sure would," I said, gazing down at him. He smiled and nuzzled against me. We lounged around, lying on each other while smoking and talking about the next sit-in, which was going to be on a Friday at the Roy O. West

Library. Alex suggested that we smoke some weed ahead of time in case the campus cops got hot headed and tried to disrupt it. "It's always a gas to watch them when you're stoned. They look like cops in gangster movies."

For the next few weeks, with different people coming and going at all hours of the day and night, some mistakenly knocking on my door, I became quite friendly with the radicals. Gradually, as I helped fold and send out flyers, as I read more about the costs of the war—the increased number of causalities—as I attended the protests and stood along with my new friends on the sidewalk holding up "Hell No We Won't Go" signs, I spent more time with Alex in my room. He liked to discuss religion—he came from a Southern Baptist tradition—and liked Jack Daniels. He'd give me back rubs when I spent hours at my desk making notes. "Come on," he said. "You need a joint." Although we planned carefully when and where we would protest and how we sent out McCarthy flyers to local residences, I never felt pressured to be anybody other than who I was. Maybe there was the real possibility of being drafted to fight in the war, but whatever it was, I became more of an insider in the antiwar movement and felt more like myself with those involved in the movement.

Manhood

When I visited the DEA house one evening, a former member who had transferred to Ohio State University had come back to visit the fraternity. I'd remembered him as a pledge because he had a wild sense of humor, playing pranks on anyone he could. A consummate salesman, Stan loved to hatch schemes for fund-raising, having us do lotteries on the school bicycle race, or raffle off prizes that he get from local stores—anything to make money. One evening, after seeing the movie *Cool Hand Luke* he got Trevor, ever eager to compete, to see if he could eat thirty hard boiled eggs in an hour exactly as Cool Hand Luke did. I ended up being the bookie, taking down bets. While we boiled the eggs and Trevor pranced around like a boxer before a match, we collected almost a hundred dollars. Practically everyone in the house crowded into the kitchen to see what Trevor could do. For the first half-hour, he socked down one egg after another, getting sixteen down his gullet. But then he slowed down, took breaks, danced and jogged around the room to hoots and shouts, "You can do it, Trevor," and nodding his head, he would sit down again at the table. About twenty-three, he began to look ill. The color leached out of his face. His eyes got puffy. He gagged several times. At fifty minutes, he took his last egg and, standing up quickly, his eyes ablaze, his hand over his mouth, he turned toward the kitchen sink and, before he got there, right through his fingers which were over his mouth, he vomited one of those projectile vomits that splatter against the wall with such force that you'd think the Pentagon might use it as a secret weapon. Everyone cleared the room. No one cared if they lost money. Trevor retched and retched and retched. By the time he finished, nothing was left in his stomach and the kitchen looked as if someone had made an all-out assault on it. It took hours to clean up with buckets and mops. Stan and I did most of the cleaning and, as he said, we cleaned up too, getting forty bucks apiece for our efforts. Trevor did not fare as well and spent most of the next day in bed.

Stan rushed to greet me, "Jason, how are you?"

"Fine, Stan, how are you?" I answered and gave him a hug.

He informed me that he came back for the weekend to make some quick money and asked to know if I wanted to be involved. His scheme was simple: he had several pornographic movies, the real thing, and he'd offer to show them for a small fee—$5.00—and anyone could enjoy the fun. Since I had nothing planned that evening, he said I could be the bookkeeper, as I had been with Trevor, and collect the money. Along with Stan was a friend from Ohio State who was short, cherubic-looking guy and whom Stan called "his little buddy, his side kick." His name was Brom, an odd name. Shy, he immediately tagged along with me, confessing that he didn't know anyone. He was impish, fair-haired with little facial hair. By his looks, he'd never shaved. He ran the projector. Stan spread the word around the house and Brom set up a projector in the upstairs dorm. When anyone came in the door, I collected the money. By the time the film started, the dorm was filled, sometimes two and three on a bunk. Someone yelled out, "Stan, this better be good." It was. A young man enters a kitchen and tells his girlfriend that he wants to stay home. She asks why and he has his hand up her skirt. Well-endowed, he lets down his fly and they go at it, all sorts of positions. Midway through the scene, another stud knocks on the door and there is a threesome, with both men coming. The film got rave reviews. The guys left, not talking much, just going out, seemingly in a trace. Many had their hands in their pockets, divining their own erections, patting them and letting them know that someday, yes, someday they would enjoy such lust.

Living up to his reputation, Stan set up two more showings at two other houses. By the end of the second one, I'd realized that our movies created a mood that was almost sacramental. Guys would burst into the room full of bravado, joking, making crude jokes and, by the end, they left largely silent, in awe of what they had witnessed because the actor seemingly was an expert at making love and was gentle with the woman and she loved touching him, sucking on his cock and, when the other fellow came in, both of them enjoyed him as well. The sex was not the kind that everyone talked about after dates as some conquest, but more so a communion of bodies, each enamored with one another, enveloped in their bodies, taking what was giving and giving what was wanted.

At each showing, my own erection would throb every time the male lead in the film stripped off his pants and displayed a cock and set of balls any male would be proud to have. "Oh, man, look at him", someone would inevitably blurt out, and I did look and was as horny as a rutting stag. Following the last showing, as Stan was counting up the money, he said, "I'm so horny I could fuck a tree."

I joked, "There are plenty outside and most are virgin timber."

"I got an idea," he said. "Why don't we go up to Terre Haute? I know of some really good whorehouses up there. You game, Brom?"

"Gee, I'm not sure,"" he said.

"Come on, it's a chance to prove your manhood!" Stan said. "You game, Jason?"

I said, "Sure, I'm game," and we looked at Brom who smiled and said, "Sure."

Terra Haute

We drove about an hour north and arrived in town at 10. Stan, with the instincts of a salmon heading back to its spawning ground, cut in and out of back streets and parked the car. We followed him to a three-story tenement. In the back of one, a red porch light glowed in the starless night. He went up to it and knocked at the door. A large woman with long gray hair appeared in the doorway. Gruff, she asked what we wanted. Stan handed her a few bills—I could not see the denomination—and she smiled and stepped aside to let us in. "Well, boys, you speak the right language. Go down the hall to the right. There are chairs," she told us—eight set against the wall, but unlike a physician's office waiting room, there were no tables with magazines and the walls were entirely bare. Seated by a doorway were a young boy—he couldn't have been more than fourteen—and an older man with a scruffy beard. Probably ten or fifteen years older than we were, he smiled at us and said, "Nice to meet you boys."

"Nice to meet you," Stan said.

The man proceeded to let us know the boy, Erik, was his son and it was his birthday so, to let him know he was a man, he'd brought him here to have his first woman. The boy never looked up at us, even when his dad introduced him. His hands were folded in his lap as if he were at church. His feet were placed squarely on the floor, but his expression was one I'd seen in high school: of someone waiting outside the principal's office because he'd gotten into trouble. He reminded me of Sean, how his dad had dragged him to a whorehouse and here he was with his dad and no turning back, having to prove his manhood.

"He's a little nervous. But he ain't got no reason to be. This here Sally, she is something special and will treat him like he was her own son," he said, smiling at us. He went on, clearly wanting to talk. "You been here before, boys?"

Stan told him that he'd come several times but that Brom and I were newcomers.

"You're in for a real treat," he said, winking at us.

The door opened and an older gentleman, dressed in bib overalls, came out, not looking at anyone. With his hands in his pockets, he made a beeline down the hall. The woman, young with long blond hair and a thin athletic build, which her paisley pullover dress almost disguised, emerged next. She reached down and took the young boy's hand and he followed her. She seemed gentle and solicitous like a nurse taking a patient to the examining room.

His dad called, "Go and get her, boy!" and slapped his knee, laughing, clearly proud of his son.

After ten minutes the boy came out and the father asked him how it was.

The boy did not look at him but simply nodded his head. "All right," he murmured and sat down with his hands pressed firmly between his knees as if he were about to cry. The father went in next, stayed about fifteen minutes and came out, tucking his shirt in his pants, and told his boy it was time to go, his birthday night was over.

"Mighty fine meeting you," he said, smiling at us. The boy shuffled ahead of his dad and looked as if he'd just had his tonsils removed.

Stan then went in. He didn't take long. Then it was my turn. The woman, Sally, greeted me with a smile, told me to take off my clothes and put them on a chair beside the single bed. One rusty yellow lamp stood on a nightstand. The bed had one pillow. On the floor was a porcelain bowl with soapy water. After I had undressed, she washed off my penis and rubbed it several times until I had an erection. She slipped off her dress and scooted up onto the bed and lay on her back. She opened her legs and with one hand aimed my penis at its target.

"No kissing," she informed me, tilting her head to one side. When I climbed into position, she tilted and stared at the lamp which jiggled erratically as I tried to initiate some semblance of rhythm.

She cried out, "Oh, you are so good," and grabbed ahold of my back and pulled her feet up to my buttocks and I suddenly became aware I was grinding away, a regular piston like a real man. The jiggling yellow lamp was no longer a distraction. She never turned her head to meet my gaze, and so I focused on the wallpaper, a pale pink with funny green ornamental flowers, and soon enough I felt the first inkling of orgasm. She must have sensed it because she cried out, "Do it, do it," not so much because she was at the verge as well (since her words did not ring true) but as a plea for me to hurry up. And so I complied.

Once we were done, she slipped from under me and hopped off the bed and called me over to the basin on the floor and washed me off. "My, my, you are still hard," she noted and let go of me and then cleaned herself and slipped on her paisley dress and sat on the chair. She pointed to a hole in one of my socks and said, "Honey child, you need a good woman to take care of you!"

I thanked her and left and sat next to Stan and Brom who looked up at me as if his wisdom teeth were about to be pulled. Like Eric, Brom had his hands stuffed between his knees.

I said, "Your turn, buddy."

Brom looked down on the floor as if he seen something there. "Really?" he said.

I smiled, "Sure is."

He went in. He took a little longer than I had. After he came out, the three of us walked silently to the car. Stan opened a six-pack and we each drank a beer.

"You still horny?" he asked.

"I am. Let's try another place."

He drove down the street and parked outside another brothel. He leaned back in the seat to gaze at Brom and me. "Was that your first time?" he asked each of us.

I told him that it wasn't because I had done it once before with Judy, although I did not remember much and she did most of the work. Embarrassed, Brom admitted it was his first time.

"Great," he said. "Nothing better than the first time."

While I finished my beer, I thought that, although I had done it once before, the memory of it was so thin that, like Brom, this was the first time I'd ever made love—or whatever they called this—and knew what I was doing as I did it. The mechanics were pretty simple: arouse, insert, pump, and offload. I had it down. I was impressed with myself. I felt like a man. For all the worry I'd had that I couldn't perform, I did. I felt proud, more of a man than I had ever felt before. I couldn't imagine what the poor kid

Erik, only fourteen, thought afterwards. He must have felt like he was doing it with his mom.

As we entered the new house, the Madame treated us like honored guests. She asked our names and what classes we were taking at school. She must have taken a Dale Carnegie course because she knew how to win over customers. Three other men waited in line ahead of us, a very elegantly dressed businessman in a three-piece suit, probably in his 50s; a young farmer, thin, long- legged; and a fat man with the physique of a pumpkin. Unlike the first place, four women were available. When I went upstairs, all four women helped to undress me. Then one took me to her room, apparently because she liked me—"a young one," as she called me. Though she spent a good bit of time sucking on me as if she had a lollipop and enjoyed the flavor, my cock did not want to stay erect. It would fill up, happy with itself, and then topple over. She asked if I done it earlier that evening. I admitted I had. With persistence, she got it working and was clearly pleased. I lasted longer the second time. She gave more instructions, a short tutorial, telling me to breathe, to do some things I had never done before since she sat on top of me and bounced up and down. We tried all sorts of positions. By the time we were finished I was exhausted, sweaty, having had a real workout. When we went downstairs, she grabbed Brom. Up the stairs he went, looking frightfully over his shoulder at me as if being taken in for an interrogation. I gave him a thumbs up sign. He smiled weakly. She coiled her arm around his waist, and they disappeared into the same room I'd been.

After we finished at the brothel, we sat in the car drinking several more beers. Brom and I hopped in back together. Stan drove. Along the way, Brom leaned against me and put his head on my shoulder.

"You all right?" I whispered.

"No," he admitted.

"What's wrong?" I asked.

"I couldn't do it the second time."

"Nothing to be ashamed of," I said. "I had a hard time doing it, too."

"Really?"

"Yeah, really."

He turned toward me, speaking quietly since he didn't want Stan to hear.

"You're nice."

He put his hand on my chest and scooted up close to me, so he could speak right into my ear.

"I'm freaked out. I mean, think of it, Stan goes in, and you go and, well, you both do it and then I go in and do it and that big fat guy he does it, too. Think of it: all of us are inside that woman, even that young kid. It's weird," he said. He pressed his head against me and I could tell he was about to cry. I put my arm around him, and he held onto me.

"It's disgusting," he whimpered. "Really disgusting. Yet, there I was. I did it. God knows why I did it. I feel sick, sick of myself, sick of the whole thing."

I patted him. "It's okay. We're all human. We have needs, animal needs."

"But I'm no animal," he said. "I'm a *Christian*."

Shit, I thought since I had nothing to say. He had violated his religion. Maybe he wanted to prove himself as I did. Whatever the reason, he felt that he'd sinned. I just held onto him, trying to figure out what I might say to comfort him. Although I did not tell him, I felt weird too, having made love—if that's what you call love—to the same woman as dozens of other men. But I felt relief too, relieved that, when called upon, I could do it. I anyone asked, "Had I done it?" I could say, "Yes, three times." I figure that was an accomplishment like a merit badge in manhood.

Brom got me thinking about the whole evening. That first woman h Stan minutes before she had me and, after me, in came Brom, all of coming inside her. And the other men, the businessman and farmer, all them followed us, all of us having the same need, the same yearning to held and told we were good, so good. Once we were finished, we woul go back to our lives, our separate lives, doing whatever we did, comp against other men whom we saw as rivals for grades, for money, for s or for women. But in the ink of night, on one floor of a tenement, we one, united in that procreant urge that Walt Whitman talked abou elemental life force. I wanted to tell Brom that we'd been part of an ; ritual, a bonding with our own sexual nature, but realized that in m I too felt it was disgusting to know, even as the woman cleaned her that Stan, Brom and I had been there, as predictable as machines, de ourselves—our semen— in her, and, after us, all kinds of men, that boy, old as my father, would sidle into her room and do the same thing. She knew how to make all of us feel good and to believe that we were the only ones as she lay back looking at the ceiling or the rusty lamp wobbling beside us. We thought she was ours. But she was probably wondering when the night would end and she could get some sleep.

As soon as Stan pulled up in front of the DEA house, Brom hopped out and, before we knew it, he was throwing up in the bushes. I went up behind him and held him by his belly and helped him get it all out. Stan watched, drinking another beer. "What's with him?" he asked.

"Don't know," I said. "Probably drank too much."

Stan was smiling, his conscience clear and his rocks relieved and, for him, everything was right in the world. We took Brom inside and fixed him some toast and hot tea. Stan wanted to drink some more, so I told him to go over to the annex where there was sure to be a party. Stan dealt out the money, giving us each fifty dollars.

"Nice night's work," he said and went off to the annex.

Sitting in a chair in the kitchen, the lights turned down, I stayed with Brom, listening to him like a confessor, taking in his lamentations that spilled out of him as if someone had released a valve of his woes. We talked some about his disgust, how he violated his church's moral code. He told me that he was a Baptist and how his father, though he was a teacher and lay preacher, did not care what he did, never paid attention to him. His mom, who was special to him, wanted him to be a minister. But Brom liked electronics and was not sure what to do. I told him that God was good about those things and, above all, God was about forgiveness. If Brom could forgive himself—it was just one night and he was a man and temptation could nab any of us anytime—God would forgive him, too. He gave me a hug. As he walked upstairs to the dorm, I wondered how much he'd forgive himself. I already had forgiven myself because I felt proud to have done it. If being a man meant that all you had to do was what I had just done, well, I was on my way and feeling very good about myself. In fact, I actually felt fantastic. Maybe I was just like other guys after all.

Taming the Lion

During spring break, I returned home to find work for the summer. The greenskeeper at the golf course, Mr. Delmore, told me that he could use me as he had the year before, which settled my plans for the summer.

For three days, I went to the Chicago Tribune building to do research for my senior-year history project. I wanted to get a head start on it so I did not have to spend my summer vacation reading old newspapers. My advisor had suggested I choose a topic that was of interest to me, and so I decided to do my senior research project on Robert R. McCormick, the former editor of the *Chicago Tribune*, and his personal war against Franklin Delano Roosevelt and the New Deal. His estate was just up the road off Roosevelt Road. My dad told me that McCormick built a huge fence to block the view of a road named after his nemesis. My father knew the current editor of the *Chicago Tribune*, who gave me access to the archives on the top floor of the Tribune Building. Besides working at the country club, I planned to spend time looking up stories and editorials that represented, as I hoped to prove, not news but propaganda. McCormick had no qualms about publishing excoriating comments about welfare fraud and Roosevelt being anti-capitalist and un-American. His ideas seemed close to Miss Starett's. Maybe she read the *Chicago Tribune*. I realized that bias in the Republican party against the poor and social welfare had deep roots that went all the back to McCormick. Trouble is, I was biased, too. I despised McCormick as much as I did Nixon, who was running again to be the Republican presidential candidate, so it made writing an objective paper nearly impossible.

During the last days of spring break, I decided to visit the Art Institute of Chicago because I wanted to lose myself in something if not mindless, at least beautiful. I knew that, come May of the following year, I would be eligible for military service and for one day I wanted to escape the future that was fast approaching. I did not want to be a warrior and, most of all, did not want to fight in a war that, as I listened to protests at school, made less and less sense to me. Most of my fraternity brothers had made me feel as if I was unpatriotic. When I thought about it, I had my own doubts too.

I thought getting away for a day might help clear my head before heading back to school where I felt like a pariah.

There was an enemy out there to be sure, forces that wanted to destroy America, but it seemed to me that, over the last few years, the enemy changed from being Russia or North Vietnam to it being ourselves. Based on readings I'd done in *Ramparts*, a radical magazine that Dr. Compton suggested I subscribe to, I came to believe the war had no purpose except to feed the voracious appetite of the military industrial complex. If I had to fight, if I really had to, as I did on the football field, I would put up a good fight.

On the nightly news, I could see the soldiers in the swamps of Vietnam, muddy and hot and thought of Dean, out there, trudging in and out of villages where he was a stranger. On the same news, they showed black men and women in the streets marching, demanding their rights. If I had to choose, I would rather go with those demanding their rights here at home. Yet that other war seemed to be getting too close. From a high school friend, I learned that Duffy, a running back on our high school team, had been killed, another senseless casualty. I could see his exuberant face as he spun his tall tales about getting blow jobs while riding down Route 50, and then, his slack face on some tarmac, drained of blood, like a mask. I shuddered. It could easily happen to me in the near future.

The more I wrestled with the notion of a citizen's duty to fight, the more my stomach knotted, tighter and tighter as if some faceless Pentagon bureaucrat was turning a crank to squeeze the life out of me. I had always been a competitor, a football player, a jock— and good at it. I enjoyed winning, knocking someone down, prancing off the field with my fist held high. But killing? I just could not see myself doing it.

I had been despondent for weeks after I saw my brother open an envelope with his 1-A status, confirming he would need to get a medical exam and report next spring to the Selective Service office in Chicago.

"What are you going to do?" I asked him.

"What else?" he said. "Go down and see what happens."

"Aren't you afraid?"

"No. I' pretty sure with my hepatitis, I wouldn't qualify. But if I do, I'll face the music."

I admired his stoicism. I had many more reservations. I talked to my mom about it. She had read many antiwar books and understood the reasons for the protest, although she never spoke openly about it with my father. Sensing my distress, she said, "You love art, go to the Art Museum, take a day off before you back to school."

I took the El that warm and clear day. It went along the Expressway to the Loop, clunking past the office building where my father worked, past the tenements with their back porches crowded with potted flowers, lines of laundry, and wicker chairs. As each scene went by, it seemed as if I was on a reel of film clipping along frame by frame, a bit player in a movie that had no plot and no end. I felt separated from normal reality by this Damocles' sword—the life of a soldier—hanging over me, swinging back and forth in my mind, cutting off the unencumbered life I imagined living— graduating, getting a job, finding someone to love. Everything seemed surreal. Alongside of the expressway, my favorite sign, the Magikist billboard with the huge lips, seventy-five feet wide and forty feet tall advertising the cleaners with the magic kiss blew kisses at me which felt like the kiss of death. Those lips now seemed monstrous, attached to something as yet unseen, that would suck me into its mouth and swallow me whole, obliterate me.

For one day in Chicago, I could look at Van Gogh and those haystacks by Monet and let art distract me. I could forget about school and my history project, about the war and civil rights marches, about the prostitutes in Terre Haute and the naked boys at the men's club in New York.

When I arrived at the enormous steps in front of the Art Institute, two lions guarding the entrance loomed over me on either side of the porticos. I went to the one on the left and clamored on top of it and sprawled out, letting my legs and arms hang either side. From atop the mane, I had a lovely view down Michigan Avenue. For now it was filled with women in svelte dresses and men in suits walking to and fro and pausing as if they were programed to move on the turn of pedestrian lights. I imagined myself as Tarzan. I had leapt on the lion and subdued it, brought its giant haunches under my control. No one seemed to mind me being there, so I leaned over and hugged the beast, luxuriating in the warm sunlight on my face.

From my perch I watched the pedestrians hurrying to their jobs or appointments and felt sorry for them. Everything seem mechanical, too, choreographed, as if they had been scripted to be where they were and the director was hiding in the wings calling out, "Now you go up Michigan. Now you head down Adams." I never wanted to be part of that mechanistic dance.

I'd arrived in the city early, with several hours to kill before the museum would open. After a while I felt I must have looked like an idiot atop those massive beasts, although I secretly hoped someone would photograph me and I would become famous. "Young College Student Tames Lion." I hopped down when I realized I was in the same section of town I had been with Jackson and Ruben. I let my feet lead the way as if they had their own intention, some secret desire that they wanted to fulfill and I was obliged to follow.

As I came to one side street, I looked down and saw a store with a light flickering on and off— "Adult Books." I smiled to think I would be twenty-one soon, officially an adult and do as I wanted to do. While standing on the corner, watching the traffic turn onto Michigan Avenue, I listed all the reasons why it would be fine to go into the store on my own. I was old enough. I could vote too. I could live on my own if I chose to. So naturally I could go into an adult book store. I was an independent adult. I could dismiss all those Puritanical voices telling me what I should or should not do.

I realized that I was like a sinner fighting against the wages of sin when, in fact, I did not believe in sin. So why was I expending so much energy to justify my actions? I laughed at myself. Who was I trying to convince? Fed up with my own machinations, I turned the corner and walked up to the front door of the store, but got cold feet and continued to the end of the block. I turned around and came back, casually checking out the window to see if I could tell what was inside. I walked by the store several more times, trying to assure myself that no one, not this early, was in it who would know me. Giggling to myself, I felt like a spy, casing the embassy of foreign country. I was going to infiltrate into enemy territory and explore—just to see what it was like, and report back, as objective as a CIA agent, still loyal to my country, to masculinity as I knew it, to myself as a regular guy like other guys.

The shop had a metal grid on the outside and from the angle of the door, which was slightly ajar, I could see, as in drugstores, a few magazine racks in the aisles and along the walls.

Nothing special. I made a final pass, went in, and nonchalantly surveyed the racks of magazines, the videos, the booths with numbers on the doors. Where should I go?

A man at the counter, someone in his twenties, thin, handsome, at first frowned at me, as if I had disrupted his tranquility, but, as he looked me over, he smiled, and said, "Good morning." I wasn't sure how to respond. I did not want to give him the impression that I resented him intruding on my private investigation of the premises. I smiled back, but we did not speak. I convinced myself I was merely an observer, there only to see what was in the store that qualified it as being "Adult." That was all. Yet it appeared the man knew what I did not know I wanted, and so he averted his eyes to respect my privacy. I went to one of the shelves of magazines and planted my feet. I took several long breaths.

I opened a magazine at random and saw photographs of naked men, many of them with erections, in various poses. There were women too, but, somehow they seemed offensive to me: it was like imagining women at my mother's age having sex. Not a pretty sight.

But the men were something else and I felt myself getting aroused. I turned away from the counter so the clerk would not see my arousal and headed for a shelf of magazines in the rear, ones I could see with my back to him.

To my surprise, the magazines had men embracing other men, holding each other's erect cocks in their hands and smiling back at me as if saying, "Come on, join us. This is fun." I wanted to say something to them as if they were good friends. I realized then that these magazines were the ones I wanted to see. I remembered that night with Tom in New York, those naked boys on stage. It made me dizzy all over again. At the men's club, I panicked because I was terrorized what Tom would think if he saw I was attracted to guys. But here they were, and here I was with them in my hands, flipping the page, taking in one man after another and no one to answer to and explain what I was doing.

I picked up another magazine and leafed through the pages. My eyes absorbed the men stripping one another, kissing, holding onto each other, or standing as another knelt before him and took the hard cock into his mouth.

Before I knew it, my legs grew weak and the throbbing intensified in my groin, just as it had a year before. I felt close to having an orgasm right there, standing in the store. I could not believe it what was happening to me without touching myself and I tried to assuage the feelings. It was as if the visual images had jumped off the page and possessed me. The urge to ejaculate assaulted me and I felt naked, with no protection to fend it off. Standing there in what, up to then, I had considered enemy territory, I realized I lacked emotional armor. I was defenseless in a summer golf shirt and pants, defeated by my own arousal. I took a breath. I moved from one foot to another. I looked out the window at men with three-piece suits heading to the financial district and other men, looking lost with bedraggled jackets and scruffy beards, wandering the street, inspecting the gutters as if there was a chance they would find lost change. I looked over my shoulder at the clerk with short dishwater blond hair, who smiled at me and nodded as if he knew me. He looked vaguely familiar, but I could not place him.

Maybe I should go, I thought to myself, *before I come right here. This is too much.*

No, I heard another voice inside me say, *You are an adult. You can serve in the military. You could fuckin' die for your country. You can go into battle like other men. You can do this. You can do what you want.*

I took a deep breath and looked at the pictures that seemed to be calling to me, inviting me to strip down and slide into the ink with them. It was as if the whole room exuded sexual energy, vibrating like some primitive, unashamed Eros owned it. The men's phalluses stood up like pride itself, saying, "Here, look at me!" The windows began to throb. The lights radiated lust. I shook several times. The magazines pulled me into their images as though they were sirens and I had no rope to hold me back. Soon I would be swirling down a vortex into the underworld of forbidden ecstasy. With each turned page, my fingers felt as if they were wired electrically and an increasing voltage surged through me.

I was at the brink of orgasm when I heard a voice beside me ask, "Can I help you?"

I turned to see the clerk, not a foot away, looking at me, and, discreetly,

338

down at my pants, which, as I looked down, were delineating what the men on the page sported so openly.

"It seems you have found what you want?" he inquired, his hand by the side of his face, amused.

I panicked, not knowing what to say. "I guess so," I stammered and added, "I'm sorry," thinking I wasn't supposed to be browsing. I put the magazine down and started to head out the store.

He moved back two steps to block my retreat and reached over and touched my shoulder, "Wait, Wait. No, don't worry. You can take as much time as you want. If you need anything else, just let me know. Look at as many as you want."

He looked again directly at my pants and smiled. He removed his hand from my shoulder and put it on his hip. I wanted to flee but felt trapped when another man, not much older than I, entered the store and stood by us. I dared not move, so I just picked up another magazine and looked vacantly at it, hoping my aroused state would subside. The clerk went back to his perch. I put the magazine down and picked up another. The other man who wore shorts and a T-shirt looked at me several times and, getting no response, left. I must have remained for a half-hour. Other men— mostly older, some in suits, very elegantly dressed— came in and out, some coming to the section where I was, which, when they stood nearby, forced me out of embarrassment to go to another section. Finally, I mustered the courage to leave.

As I was heading for the door, the man at the counter, called out, "Hey buddy, can I ask you a question?"

I wanted to keep on going, but my feet stopped and I turned to look at him.

"I suppose," I offered, not sure I wanted to get to know him better.

"What's your name? I think I know you from somewhere."

My whole face flushed. I was startled to think someone knew me and, had recognized me here, in this place. What must he think? But, when I gazed up at him, I saw how earnest he appeared to be: he genuinely wanted to know my name. I thrust one hand in my pocket and pulled my erection to the side, tight against my thigh for safekeeping and out of his view.

"Jason," I said.

"Well, Jason, I didn't mean to embarrass you."

"Oh, it was nothing." I wiped the sweat off my brow.

"No, it was not," he said. "I should have left you alone. I know how it is."

He looked up at the ceiling and shook his head, dropped his eyes and smiled again.

"What do you mean?" I inquired. He leaned over the counter and spoke in a barely audible whisper, so no one else could hear.

"The first time you see it, you know, the images—it's something else, almost overwhelming."

"Yeah," I grinned. I liked that he understood.

He leaned forward on the counter and spoke quietly, gazing at me intently.

"I suppose I shouldn't say this because I'm working, but, hell, you remind me of myself when I first came here, several years ago. I remember how it was. It's like when your fantasy, what you imagined for years, and real images find one another," he explained, "it's like stepping in a cage of lions with a fly swatter."

I laughed and nodded my head. We stood there staring at one another. The store was nearly empty, only a few others in the back. Then he gestured, "You're from the western suburbs?"

I nodded.

"Glen Brook."

"Yes."

"I know you: you played football and won some golf tournament, right?"

"Yes."

"I went to every football game. You were good."

"Thanks."

He motioned to me and explained how he knew me, "Gymnastics—I was on the team, and, well, from the second tier of the gym, we could watch you guys practice." He put his hands to his hips and added, "Come up here. You seem to be a curious fella. Let me show you something that is neat about working here."

I stepped up on the raised platform where the cash register was and, additionally, where, under the counter, four TV monitors showed different shots of the store.

As I gazed at the monitors, he introduced himself and shook my hand firmly. His hand was large and strong, yet very tender and gentle.

"My name is Jim. I don't live in Chicago. I drive in from the suburbs to be down here, you know—it's safer living out there—and, well, now that I work here, I can go out where I want and with whomever I want, but back in Glen Brook, that's where I can afford my own apartment. In the city, the rent would kill you, although the nightlife is sweet."

After I shook his hand, I told him, "I don't live here either. Like you, I live in Glen Brook... with my parents, but most of the time, I'm at school out of state."

"Where?" he asked.

"Ashbury University in Indiana."

"No, not the university, where do you live—your home?"

"Out of town, the western suburbs, in the Armstrong Estates off Park Avenue, at the corner of Butterfield Road."

He was surprised. "I did too, except the opposite side, Willow Brook Farm development. Did you go to Wagner Junior High?"

I laughed, "Yes, I did. In 1955-'59."

He eyed me carefully, "I was earlier, a couple of years, but I remember your class. You went undefeated in every sport, right? You were starting center! Most valuable player. That's why I remember you so well," and slapped my shoulder, "two Wagner boys. What's your name again?"

"Jason, Jason Follett."

"Right, Jason Follett, all conference, most valuable player in two sports!"

As we chatted about Glen Brook, he showed me how the four monitors worked, how he could spy on what was going on in the store from four different angles. We viewed two men in the back of the store talking and exchanging something, and, in another part of the store, one man holding onto a magazine and—it was obvious—playing with himself.

"It gets very interesting," he said, giggling. "You see things here you don't see on Broadway, and *never* on Main Street in Glen Brook!"

I laughed and he told me when his shift was done and asked if I'd wait for him, which I did, because he also wanted to visit the museum. I enjoyed being known as a star athlete. It was an identity I felt proud of, so it made it easier to talk with him, although I suspected we did not have much in common except maybe an interest in the arts.

At the museum, we looked at Impressionist paintings, particularly Van Gogh whose sunflowers practically jumped off the canvas, and then the new exhibits of Egyptian artifacts. Afterwards, we went out to lunch and walked along the lake until we found a place to put up our feet. We sat on a bench under a red maple, looking at the sailboats crisscrossing the lake.

He gave me his number in case I ever wanted to go out.

"You mean a date?" I asked.

Jim laughed, "Don't make it sound so ominous! It doesn't have to be like that. It could just mean we spend time together."

"I'll think about it," I said. I'd certainly called up my other male friends to go out, but that was different: we went out to have fun and meet girls. To ask a boy out just because I wanted to be with him—that seemed weird.

Jim turned to me, gently putting his hand under my chin, and I turned my face toward him. His gesture felt fraternal, something I followed because he had no malice, only a gently turning me like one does a young child to what he wanted me to hear.

"Listen, Jason, you know, the trouble with so many of us guys is that we are trained to think of everything in a heterosexual model: the guy asks out the girl and then they do the 'well, will ya?' dance. It's all about sex, getting some. The guy waits to get rejected. He asks her out again to see if the second time is the charm. The girl plays hard to get. The guy pays for dinner and the movie. The girl acts coy. The guy asks her out again. And so it goes until, in desperation, he marries her. It doesn't have to be that way. It can be just two people having a good time and, well, doing what comes naturally whenever, and if ever, that happens," he said, dropping his hand. I averted my eyes, staring at a woman exiting a store across the street, not wanting to face him, not sure what to say. I didn't want to go out with him, not yet; and yet, I did.

"Think about it," he said.

"I will, I really will," I said, looking at my watch. "But I need to catch a train."

"Fine," he reassured me, patting me on the arm, "fine and give me a call only if you want to...."

I headed off across Lake Shore Drive, dodging in and out of traffic, not looking back for fear if I did, I might go back and cross the line I'd sworn to myself I would not cross and I did not want that, not then, not ever. I would not be tempted. I'd tamed my urges. I'd keep them under control. I tossed his card in a waste bin and rode back to Glen Brook where I walked the streets with parents and their little children in tow. I smiled at the simplicity of it all, how easy life had been when I was a dependent child. Then I winced at the thought of how much more difficult my life was becoming as an adult with so many choices in my hands.

Closing out the Year

A few days later I rode with Joseph—he'd bought a red Mustang—back to Ashbury, somewhat relieved that I could blot out my encounter with Jim and get back to studying, to living a normal life. I talked with Joseph about golf and girls, the usual, and he dropped me off at my room where I spent two uneventful months, studying, hanging out with three different sets of friends—the poets, my fraternity brothers and the antiwar activists.

One evening, a week before the semester ended, Sue who I'd not heard from for more than a year, called.

"Are you busy?" she asked.

"No, just studying for finals."

"Meet me a Jiminotts for old time's sake," she said.

She'd gotten a booth in the corner so we could look out at the DAE house and ordered me a butterscotch milkshake.

"You shouldn't have," I told her.

"Drop the shoulds," she said. "There are too many of those in my life."

"What's up?" I said. "Last time I heard, you'd dropped your old flame."

"Well, it was mutual. Marriage is the last thing on my mind. He ended up heading further and further right. Barry Goldwater seems like a liberal compared to him. And, well, I've gotten more liberal. So whatever flame that we had, had long since gone out," she said. She sipped her coffee. I knew that she was someone whom I could have told about my experience in Chicago, about my anxiety about the war, but, after the long spell without seeing her, I felt awkward and told her that my brother, who, after seeming to find his true love five or six times, had finally settled on a girl he'd met while working at Sears and they might get married.

"That's nice. What's her name?"

"Barbara. She's sharp. I think she'll be good for him," I said. Sue nodded. I realized that she didn't even know my brother and that marriage was a topic I shouldn't have brought up, so I quickly directed the conversation back to her.

"What do you plan to do after graduation?"

"Peace Corps. I want to get out of this country and live someplace else. If I stay here, my mother is going to be asking, 'Are you dating?' and I'll say, 'No' and we'll get into a fight. It's not worth it. If I get away, I can live by my own time clock," she said. She tapped her cup against my milkshake. "And what will you do?"

"I wish they could give me the same choice as you have. I'd love to serve in the Peace Corps. Why is it that we men have to be the ones to go to war and be strung up like puppets to be killed?"

"I suppose it's so that you can come back, brag about your exploits, and run for political office!"

"Yeah, some reward."

"Are you going to serve?"

"I'm not sure. I know that if I get called up, I'll have to make a decision. If I refuse to serve, my dad will kill me," I said.

She laughed. "At least you'll see the bullet coming."

"Thanks, some consolation."

She spun her coffee around in her hand and tapped it against my milkshake. I tapped her cup and, for a minute, we played a game of tag, her cup sliding to one side then another trying to elude my glass. She swung her arm around my glass and pinned it.

"I won," she said, with an impish grin on her face. She brushed back a lock of hair, pursed her lips, and looked me in the eye. "I wanted to say to you how much you've meant to me. I know for a while it got a little strange. I'm sorry the way I behaved—you know, giving you mixed signals."

"Hey, that's over. It's cool."

"No, it isn't. You're a sweet guy and I do love you. You may be confused now about where you are headed, but at least you're giving it some thought. I admire that," she said, putting her hand on mine and squeezing it. "I'll miss you."

"This is getting a little sentimental!"

"So what?"

"Just wanted to point it out," I said. She looked at me intently and withdrew her hand.

"You'll keep in touch?" she asked.

"Sure."

"Here is my address and telephone number. I expect to hear from you, okay?"

"I will."

We chatted for a while, sensing that our time had run out. She'd be graduating, moving on, perhaps to another country. I'd be off to work at the golf course and getting ready for my final year. She paid the bill and we walked out hand in hand. She hugged me and kissed me lightly on the lips. As she turned to walk away, she hesitated and her hand drifted down my shirt to my chest where she patted me.

"You've got a good heart. Trust it," she said. She was tearing up. I smiled. She walked away and I found that I too felt like a yearning to hold onto what had already gone was pulling me toward with every step she took away from me.

The Real World

In a week I contacted Joseph who told me that he could drive me back home in May. He did, leaving me off for what might be my last free summer where I could do what I wanted except for some days spent inside the Tribune building doing research.

Early in the summer, my dad had me set up interviews with several of his friends so that I could begin considering a career after I graduated. I told him that I wanted to go to law school, but he insisted that I also look at the business options.

When I visited the office of Mr. Sayers, the CEO of Commonwealth Edison, he showed me his view of the Chicago. From his picture window on the 30th floor, he commanded a view of Michigan Avenue, which at the time had the commercial buildings on one side and, on the other, old railroad lines and storage buildings. Like an emperor surveying his kingdom, he pointed to that area and told me soon it would be torn up and replaced with an extensive park. He pointed out where a new building would replace an older one. With an assurance of someone who had his pulse on the city, he spoke of the mayor and his plans to improve Chicago. He had me sit in a big leather chair as he sat behind his desk. He wanted to know what I wanted to do. I told him that I was interested in law school, not business.

"Do you have any other interests?" he asked.

"Well, I like what Dr. King is doing, his work with voting rights and with the poor," I said.

"Might you like to work with the poor here in Chicago?" he asked, pointing out the window.

"Never gave it much thought."

He suggested Hull House—he knew the director, a nice man, young, not much older than I was—and told me to give him a call. He wrote a telephone number on a note paper. He discussed other programs in the city. But, as he was talking, I had a strange sensation. The more I focused on him, the smaller he became so that, as he expounded on my options, he

347

shrunk to the size of a pea. If I lifted my hand up, I could have squished him with my thumb and forefinger like a fly. No one would know the better since the only remains would be a smashed fly. Not knowing what was happening to me, I told him that I had another appointment, which I did, and excused myself. Fortunately, when he stood up, he immediately took on human proportions, which made me feel better about him. He shook my hand and escorted me to the elevator.

Instead of going to the other appointments or calling the man at Hull House, I took off my tie and jacket and roamed around the city. Being a corporate man was not in my makeup. What I should do once I graduated festered inside me, but I was determined to enjoy my last summer of total freedom, working on the grounds crew of our club and, after work, practicing shots and playing rounds of golf. For the time being, I wanted to blot out the war and the world, stop thinking about myself and become blissfully invisible.

IV: Love is most nearly itself
When here and now cease to matter...

The Veteran

During the summer, I spent more time with Dean O'Neill, who'd come back from Vietnam earlier to be with his wife Karen. She'd given birth to a boy, Jonathan. Having a son did not make him happy. It cast him into a dark mood. He wasn't prepared to be a dad. He'd become more discouraged about his deployment yet had been doing his best to make it work by shutting out the civilian world, which, with the child, he could no longer do. The small fragile baby frightened him more than the Vietcong. He'd made plans for what he'd do once he completed his obligatory service. He'd decided to go to graduate school in literature. But he was not ready for this homecoming to fatherhood. For the summer, he hung out at the club, trying to adjust somewhat to civilian life. We met quite often to talk at a bar on Roosevelt Road called the Hungry Lion, where we shared ideas about various writers. He told me more about his war experience and about how he his hated civilian life. He felt like a Martian, completely divorced from the vacuous life of suburbanites.

After I had played a round of golf with his father-in-law, Mr. Johnston, Dean met us at the 18th fairway. He was pacing back and forth on the veranda like some caged beast.

Mr. Johnston whispered to me, "It looks like Dean needs someone to talk to. He's having some difficulty. We all see it. Do you mind giving him some time? He so enjoys time with you."

"Sure," I said and told Dean, "My dad is running late. The women are going to lounge around in the Green Room. Do you want to have a drink in the Oak Room while we wait for him?"

"Yes. Yes. I'd like that," he said. He bit on his lower lip. "Let me tell Karen." He went back into the Green Room—I followed him—watching him excuse himself, asking Karen like a little cadet if he could go with me. She smiled and said, "Sure, honey." He gave his infant son a kiss and joined me.

Mr. Johnston called after us, "Have a good time, boys," and sat down next to his wife and Karen.

351

With its dark wood-paneled walls and long mahogany bar, the Oak Room was a haven for men who wanted to play cards and drink. Except for a waitress, women were forbidden to go there. Dean liked this refuge because, since he had come back, his wife kept track of him like an errant boy.

She worried that he might be losing his bearings. At a cocktail party in May, she had confided in me, telling me about his mood swings and his nightmares, asking if I knew what was up with him and why he didn't talk to her. His disposition had changed. His normally sanguine temperament shifted. His temper flared for no good reason. He told her to give him some space, but that only exacerbated her possessiveness. He'd disappeared for several days—she'd called me to see if I knew what had happened to him (I didn't)—and turned up later, telling her that he visited a buddy in southern Illinois, one in his division. They'd gone fishing. But that was a lie. He'd told me that he'd gone to Chicago, rented a room near the lake front and wandered up and down the lake, trying to piece together what he wanted to do with his life. One morning the fog was so thick he could barely make out people ten feet away. As he gazed into the fog, he thought, that it was like his life: if only he had a better eye, he could have seen through the fog, clear across the lake to the Indiana dunes, into another life beyond the one he was living. Although his wife encouraged him to be with his son, he felt it was just another entrapment, not some new lease on life. He'd thought of getting a Ph.D. in literature, studying Joyce, hunkering down into the intellectual life as a way to put psychological distance between him and the war. But nothing seemed promising. It was as if a fog had moved into his mind and no matter how much he pressed against it, he only became more deeply mired in it.

He surveyed the room as if he were appraising how to attack it from different vantage points.

"Never thought of this before, but this reminds me of the Armed Forces Club in D.C.," Dean said, settling back in a leather chair.

"Armed Forces Club?"

"Yes, it's just down from the White House. Very exclusive, just like Glen Brook," Dean replied. He tapped on the table, his fingers clinking down rapidly as if drumming out a Morse code. "Listen, I need to tell you something. Can you keep it between you and me?"

"Sure."

"I've been seeing a gal in your class—your class of '64. She was an old flame of mine, whose name must go unmentioned because she's engaged to someone else."

"That's fine," I said. I did not look at Dean.

"Well," he said, leaning closer to me, "I'm meant I'm currently involved with her."

"Involved?"

"Do I have to explain?"

"You mean an affair?"

"Yeah, and what's worse is that her parents are members here. Her father detests me."

"Damn."

"I'm sure that's what her father said to himself when I showed up at his door wearing my uniform," Dean said.

"Wait a minute," I interjected. "You actually went to her house?"

"I didn't give a shit."

"But you're married!"

"Yeah, that was beside the point. See, I wanted him to notice my Bronze Star with its 'V' for Vietnam. I wanted him to know I laid it on the line for this fuckin' country. Not that he would feel any differently about me. He hated me in high school and that has not changed. The snooty bastard wasn't going to let me see his daughter. Her mother intervened. The old man didn't know his daughter wrote to me in Nam. Every week. She still wanted me. She didn't care if I was married. He was pissed when he heard that she wrote to me. But he put on a smile on his face when I came by, figuring it was, well, friendship. He even asked me into his house, and I went regularly and that's how it started, the old flame hadn't smothered. It came to life by itself. I didn't want it to, but it did."

"You still care for her?"

"Yeah, but that's ancient history now, I reckon. In four weeks I'll be back in Camp Lejeune. No way we could get back together and sustain a relationship, especially with a wife and kid and all. Her father likes the guy she's engaged to, a little Napoleon of an attorney down in the Loop. He's ten years older than she is. Fat and rich."

He slugged down his scotch. "You want another?" he asked, getting up to go to the bar.

"Sure, I'll take another."

He hesitated after a few steps. "I gotta use the head."

I pointed to the swinging double doors.

"Got it," he said and shoved through them like John Wayne, forcing both doors to flap like angry wings.

While Dean was in the john, I'd thought about his girlfriend. Who was she? I'd probably known her in high school. There were not that many of my classmates whose parents were members at the club. I decided to open the conversation up, when he returned, although I was feeling awkward knowing just a hundred yards from us his wife was having a drink with my mother.

The drinks arrived. He came back, scrunched down and propped his head in his hand staring at the golden liquid. "Sweet stuff. Sweet stuff. It clears the mind."

I leaned over the table, and whispered, "I think I know who you are seeing. Is she tall with a great figure and a Scandinavian surname?"

"Yes, she does. You made a huge inductive leap," Dean replied. "She's nice. You like her?"

"Don't know her well. She's quiet. I went to a homecoming dance with her. Her father drinks a lot."

"Probably alcoholic," he said. "She's worried that I might be becoming one too or losing my mind. She and my wife, both. She confided in me that she was uncertain about getting married to her boyfriend. He has a temper. She wondered if I was committed to Karen, if I'd stay with her. I told her I wasn't sure of anything. But at this point it wouldn't be honorable of me to take things further with her."

I burst out laughing. "Further? You must be joking. You're having an affair with her! Dean, I hate to say this because I'm not one to speak, but something's wrong with this picture, don't you think?"

"I know. I know. Contradictions. Just like Nam. We know better, but we just go ahead anyway. The lure is sometimes too much. Last night we were walking around Lake Ellyn Park at midnight. Her house is not far there. Near the boathouse we paused for a kiss. Next thing I knew I was taking her from behind, standing up. She said she had never come that way before."

"Oh, my God!"

"Yeah. Crazy isn't it? Talk about living in the here and now!" He tapped me on the chest. "Keep this between us." His eyes looked as if they were glass. "Between us."

"Sure, sure. But I have to ask, how could you, being married and all?"

He lifted his glass and jiggled the ice. "I used to sit in a bar like this with buddies, thinking, 'This is it, this is my last fuckin' day.' And sometimes it was, for some guys. One nightclub blew up and all they found were body parts, no whole bodies, nothing left of anyone."

"Shit," I said. "How awful. How did you cope?"

"Same as I do now. I keep up appearances. Isn't that how it works here?"

"But you're a dad. That *must* mean something."

He bowed his head, bit his lip, and shook his head. His eyes glistened and he put his head on the table. I looked at him. I could hear him breathing heavily.

The waitress brought us two more drinks.

He sat up and took the glass, raising it to me, "To fatherhood!"

In an effort to change the topic, I asked him what he thought of the war. I added my own take on it: that it was immoral, that we were systematically wiping out villages, committing genocide just as we did with Native Americans and that the President and Westmoreland were deluded fools. I wondered if, indeed, it was true.

From the look on his face, I could tell that he didn't like what I had said, but he sipped his drink and listened, not arguing with me. He just gazed at the grain in the wood, tracing it with the base of his glass. I noticed his forearm, how powerful he was. Overall, he gave the impression that in combat he was not someone you would mess with. A weak half-smile slipped across his face. He sipped the scotch and, then, holding it out, jiggled the ice in the glass, swirling it around rapidly. It never spilled out. He perfected the move. He cocked his head and, speaking slowly, methodically, said, pointing his glass toward me, "You ever think you're invisible?"

"No, but sometimes I wish I were."

"Well, that's how it is when you come back stateside. People look at you. They see what they see. Unless half your face has not been shot off, you look as you did, maybe thinner, maybe less certain, but the same. They do not see the mortars that blasted five of your men and left their intestines splayed out like shredded Christmas wreaths. They don't see the fear behind your eyes, the quicksilver reaction to any snap or crack. They don't see the blood on your hands, nor the nine-year-old kid whose eyes stared up at you after you shot him because he leveled his rifle at you. You want to cry because he was younger than your kid brother, but he was a combatant. No one here sees any of that. They see what they want to see and they don't want you to tell them anything. Not a word. They want you to blend right in, to be homogenized like skim milk, into their card games, their rounds of golf, their cocktail parties, their baby showers, their quiet and orderly life as if nothing has happened. You're invisible."

"Shit."

"Exactly."

"How do you manage?"

"I avoid polite conversations. I've watched them and know what they want me to say. There are rules and everyone follows them. You know them as well as I do. You can talk about your dog, about the weather, about any sport and about food or restaurants or sales at stores. But you can't talk about anything substantive—not religion, not literature, not fear, death, never sex, never how fucked-up our society is and, never, no never, the fucking war... So…"

He tapped his drink on the table. "I find people like you who I can talk to or I'll vanish, just disappear and cease to be—a mannikin propped up for my wife to show off, a war hero."

I thought how I'd felt the same way, how hard I'd tried to act like other men, to pretend that I felt as others did, when I had my own doubts about anyone ever seeing me for who I was—worse, their seeing in me what I did not want them to see.

Dean averted his eyes and looked at the waitress, a young blond girl who

356

wore the club uniform, a short skirt with an apron and a powder-blue blouse. I looked at her too.

She came over to our table. "Can I help you, gentlemen?" she asked.

I looked at Dean who smiled at her, his eyes traversing her from shoe to head. "Yes, you can," he said, then shook his head. "But not right now."

She frowned, then leered at him, and started to walk away when he called out to her, "I'd like to change—not the scotch, but a shot of Jack Daniels on the rocks and a bottle of Bud. My friend here drinks the same."

He leaned back in his chair and stretched. "To answer your question about being seen: that, my friend, is something I suspect I'll be doing the rest of my life. And, yes, I'll be searching for those who are willing and able to hear me out and who don't get all riled up when I tell them how fucked up I am and this fucking world is."

I noticed Dean staring at a large man with a 1950s flattop, a man who had invited him the previous day to join in a game of gin. Dean leaned closer to me and whispered, "Look at him. Remind me. Who is he?"

"Leo Hampton."

"Yeah, look at him. He's one of those invisible men, too. He's keeping up appearances like everyone else here. He talks about golf and the weather. He plays golf with the same three men every fuckin' week, comes here to the Oak Room where the waitress calls him by his name, plays gin rummy, drinks his Miller from the tap in the frosted glass, and takes the cards he is dealt and plays them even though he has—he told me, just as if you'd tell someone you had indigestion—that he has terminal cancer."

"That's quite heroic, don't you think?" I said.

"Heroic? Is that it? Or is it just plain nuts? He calls out 'gin' every fifth hand, maybe, but that's all he does. I'd say it's disgusting. Just disgusting, living the life of a fraud."

He slammed his fist on the table and muttered, "Disgusting."

Several men at a table across from us glared at us, quizzically.

Dean straightened up and continued, "Let me tell you how it was. For me, I knew, when I was in Nam, Mr. Death had me in his sights and..."—he leaned over and grabbed my arm, squeezing it tightly—"you keep this between us, I lived each moment as if it were the last. I'd fuck one chick so many times I was sore. I'd get stoned and drunk and grabbed at life, all I could get of it for that moment because I'd seen brains splattered across my face. My face. I had to wipe them off. Their brains. So when I look at him, Mr. Hampton, and see how he just goes on with the same routine, I couldn't do it. I'd be screaming, 'Can't your bastards see I'm fuckin' dying!'"

Dean sipped his drink and leaned even closer to me, whispering, "He reminds me of someone, though, some football player."

"Mr. Hampton? You may be thinking of him years ago. Don't you remember? He played guard for the Bears."

"A gridiron hero and now a CPA on medical leave from Sears. Some hero!"

"But look at him, Dean, he just does what he has to do. I admire it."

"True enough. He doesn't whine. You want another?" Dean asked, getting up to go to the bar.

"Sure, I'll take another."

He brought us another round. I wasn't counting, but I knew they were adding up because my head felt as if it was slowing filling with helium.

"What will you do when you get off active duty?" I asked him.

"Not sure," Dean replied. "My father wants me to go back to law school at the University of Iowa. I like Iowa, but law school doesn't hold interest for me any longer. I had too many Article 15 investigations and participated in too many summary courts in the Marines."

"Were you ever on the front line?"

"I was, for a while. An officer can serve in many roles, including sitting in on courts martial, and there were many. After I grunted for a while, I was a track platoon leader. Finally they sent me to work with the S-2, that's intelligence. I worked with the various teams. In war, you just play the cards you are dealt."

"What happened in the court martial trials?"

"You do not want to know. That's when a good friend of mine, another West Point graduate told me—and I can see how he felt—that war, any war is immoral and can't be anything else. Responsible for firing mortars, he was given coordinates and checked them and double- checked them but had to fire since some of our guys were surrounded, under heavy fire, so he sent them off and, as it turns out, someone had the coordinates wrong and *blam*, he kills five of our own. Someone had to take the heat. He was court-martialed, sent back stateside. He's never forgiven the Corps. He's joined the vets against the war. He's big in the antiwar scene and I get it, I get it. " He stared again at Mr. Hampton and continued, "Nothing good comes of war; and no doubt our president and Westmoreland are deluded, playing out their roles. They don't give a shit about the South Vietnamese."

"If you feel that Westmoreland is deluded, why do you continue to serve?"

"I come from a long tradition of those who have served their country. I believe in the notion of duty with a capital "D", and doing my part when called upon. There are so many in this fuckin' country club who sit smugly with their drinks and cards, pontificating on the war while my friends are killed in combat," he said, tipping his glass in my direction. "You're one of those who sits on the sideline while others, others you and I knew, die. Like Bruce Capel. Do you remember him?"

"I met him several times when he came back from University of Illinois to visit coach Duchon and played volleyball. He was nice. And he was big and strong, too."

"He was. But he ended up dead like so many others. And the truth in the matter is that we all are complicit in his death and all the others, are we not?"

"Well, yeah, I think we all are, even those of us who oppose the war. I suppose we all have blood on our hands. It's something I feel more than I actually know, although I saw a guy who came back to the States with half of his face shot off. My mom volunteered to play golf with wounded vets last summer. The guy was my age—crew cut, strong, muscular but, the right side of his face, including his eye, looked as if it had melted. I caddied for my mom, but every time he looked at me, I found myself turning away in disgust."

"We're all complicit," he said, clinking his glass against mine.

I didn't know what more to say. There was an uncomfortable silence, and at that point I looked up to see if my dad had arrived. Dean continued to gaze at the grain in the wood. His weak smile was gone, replaced by a thousand-yard stare. He still swirled the ice in his glass. Nothing ever spilled out.

"We should go buy Leo a drink," Dean said finally as he stood up. "Before we have to head out into polite society and make our appearance, I want to go over and say goodbye."

"Why'd you want to do that?"

"I admire him."

"Admire him?! I thought you said he was disgusting."

He put his arm around my shoulder and whispered in my ear, "Don't listen to me, not anymore. Can't you see I'm fucked up?"

"But why *him*?"

He stopped and pulled me to the bar where he ordered another round of drinks. Leaning on the bar, he pointed at Mr. Hampton. "I've kept my eye on him, there in his chair, holding onto his cards, studying them, you know, careful about how he sorted them, placing one suit to the left, another to the right. Have you noticed?"

"No," I admitted. "I paid him no mind."

"Exactly, no mind. Perfect. But *I* did notice. He's careful with his cards, wanting to be sure he gives himself the best chance, leaving a lowly pair there just in case"— he laughed and put a finger to his lips. "Maybe that's why I hooked up with my old flame?" He raised his eyebrows as if inquiring an answer from me. "One last card, you know."

"I suppose," I said.

"Believe me, I'm so fucked up I don't know what I want anymore."

The last drink had socked him in the eyes. He was slurring his words, but he pointed at Mr. Hampton. He wanted to explain what he saw in him.

"So there he is, just doing what he sees as his duty. Duty. Big word in the service. He could be drunk, railing against God, but, no, he's playing his cards to the end." He leaned forward. "You see, that's what I'm doing too, just playing as many cards as I can. Lover. Husband. Father. Soldier. Fuck-up. Shit. I'll play them all and see where they'll lead." He laughed, this time loud enough that everyone turned toward us to see what was so funny. He winced and grabbed his head.

"What is it?" I asked, whispering to quiet him.

"Migraine," he said, rubbing his temple. The skin on his forehead flamed with the burst of a wildfire, spreading rapidly and then, just as quickly, going out and turning an ashen white.

"We should get back to the family," I said.

Dean took the cue, "Sure, you're right," and whispered, looking at Mr. Hampton, "He'll probably die in that chair, his cards laid out, one card short of gin."

We walked over to Leo who knew me from my caddying for him many times. He put his cards face down and greeted us, accepting Dean's offer to buy him a drink and asked, "What's the special occasion, boys?"

Dean looked at him, squinted his eyes, and said, "I'm a dad!"

"Well, damn," said Mr. Hampton, "I should be buying a drink for you!"

We chatted for several minutes and could see, out in the Green Room, Dean's wife waving at us to come over because dinner was being served. My dad had arrived. We said goodbye to Mr. Hampton and headed into the dining room.

Dean pulled himself together, gently took his wife's hand, kissed it, and smiled at her. "You have a nice talk with Jason?" she asked.

"Great talk," he said. "Just what I needed. Thanks, honey. It helps to get away." She kissed him on the cheek, and he smiled at me and reached to take his son, a sleeping bundle, in his arms.

"Are you sure?" Karen asked.

"I'm fine, honey, just fine," he said and picked up the baby, bent over him, putting his lips to his pate and kissed him, whispering, "I love you, my sweet pea." He noticed that I was staring at him and smiled as if to say, "This too is me."

My dad took me by the arm, pulling me toward him, "Well, son, how'd you play?"

"Had a 78. Couldn't putt," I said. "But I hit number 5 in two, though—a drive and a three wood!"

"That's my boy," he exclaimed. "You'll be club champion someday!"

We sat down for dinner and I watched the conversation bounce, almost like a birdie in badminton, among the convenient subjects—golf, weather, pets, television—and Dean smiled his half-smile, winked, and sipped from his wine glass, and I joined in, there being nothing else to do.

By late August, the cool air tipped the leaves and the faint russets and yellows tinged the tops of the maples and ash. I heard that Dean had been called back. I packed my suitcases with the clothes for the next semester. I piled my books in a satchel and left for my final year of college.

361

Upside-Down World

By the fall of 1967, the Vietnam War changed from a simmering topic of discussion on campus to an urgent personal concern. Although many of us had given it some thought the previous spring when a young theology student from Yale came to our college to promote burning our draft cards, we were skeptical because we feared what our parents might do or say. They had bankrolled our education and, well, we were beholden to them as my father had told me. The Yale student had burned his card and, before he was arrested. I met him, and he seemed a regular guy—a bit homely with large black-framed glasses and short hair, not like the radicals with long hair I'd seen on the news. He explained why he believed the war was immoral and had to take a stand against it, which I thought was admirable. I asked him, "What did your parents say?"

He looked at me stunned, "Why does that matter?"

I could not answer him, not there in front of other students, because for me it still did matter, so I left.

Early in my junior year, I thought I would look forward to graduation and be far more interested in fall intramural football season than Vietnam. I was still quarterback of our team. We had a shot of going to the finals again despite my worn-out arm and despite Dwight, a former high school star quarterback, wanting to replace me. And I even imagined that after graduation, I'd be going into law school and working in civil rights with my degree. I had a script and I meant to follow it. Or, at least, that was my plan, a plan that had become frayed over the last year, yet was the only one I had and I clung to it, as a senior, as if it were the only handhold I had as I dangled over the dark cliff that was Vietnam. As yet, I had not pondered how the draft and the deadly carnage might include me. Of course, Dean opened my eyes when he brought up the death of my high school Bruce Capel. I remembered how full of vigor Bruce was, how handsome and engaged he was with us when he joined some of us in a pickup volleyball game. Vitality radiated from him. He slammed the ball over the net and blocked any attempt of ours to get one by him. He seemed invincible. A star college player, he exuded confidence. Our high school football coach used to read his letters to us, since he was among the first ground troops in Vietnam. Capel told the coach how the evasive moves he learned as a lineman helped him evade enemy fire in the fields in Vietnam.

"See," the coach said. "You're learning skills that will help you in life."

A day in April of 1964, Bruce was killed in action. The coach, his face contorted, burst into tears when he told us. It seemed impossible. How could such a vital force be snuffed out? If it could happen to him, it could happen to me. He was the only casualty I had known personally up to September 1967. That was how it was for many of us.

All that changed in September. President Johnson expanded the draft; student deferments would end upon graduation, and no male could avoid being called up. We shared a common fate and felt like a herd being prepared for the slaughterhouse.

In one semester, the campus became a cauldron of protest that transformed many of our lives in ways that made it impossible to live as we had been accustomed to living. We were thrust into making a choice between going to war and resisting it.

With friends on both sides of the debate, I found myself torn between them. Among my DAE brothers, I'd heard them excoriate the longhaired, hippy weirdoes in the antiwar movement. As I'd sit in on the intense discussions and planning sessions of the antiwar group at my boarding house, I would hear them laugh about the weirdo frats with their letter jackets (which I happened to have in my closet), crew cuts, and conventional lifestyles.

But when my fraternity brothers began sporting long hair and beards and chanting "Hell no, we won't go," I realized that change had gone from a slow to a rolling boil. In front of the Student Union, I stood at an antiwar rally and someone shoved at a sign at me. "Here hold it," and I did, pumping the sign "Make Love, Not War." On the steps of the Union, a young professor with a beard and long hair castigate our government's policies. I felt as if there was no turning back. I had to join the fight against the war.

By late October, my friends were also protesting against gender discrimination and doing sit-ins for co-ed dorms. Students were screaming at one another too—conservatives against liberals, prowar against antiwar, civil rights marchers protesting against segregationists. Students and professors were storming off to march in Washington while race riots broke out in cities and hippies were getting stoned while advocating free love, love-ins, long hair, and peace. The lid had blown off the simmering pot that had been our campus.

That fall, each of us got a 1-A status draft card for recruitment into the armed services and we listened more closely as Walter Cronkite reported on the bloody battles in the streets of Saigon on the nightly news. More and more student activists arrived on campus to lead protests; many burned their draft cards and flaunted the selective service and went to prison in what seemed like an assembly line. Among my fraternity brothers, Eric, Trevor and Paul became leaders in the antiwar movement. Some brothers remained in favor of the war—Jacob, who still wanted to be in the Air Force and Ibby who had joined ROTC—became what Richard Nixon, the presumed Republican presidential candidate, would call "the silent majority," but they didn't let on about their support for the war since, among most students, the war had become an anathema.

Nixon had positioned himself as the man who stood above the fray, a man who called for a return to American values. He smiled more in TV interviews than in his past campaigns, although the smile looked as if it, too, had been rehearsed. He acted assured. He was back to his old self— the presidential heir apparent.

Since joining Senator Eugene McCarthy's presidential campaign, I worked with Jean George, a philosophy major and Todd, a religion major, doing door to door canvassing. I liked how McCarthy had broken with Johnson, a man in his own party, and opposed the war. Students across the country flocked to him.

Despite my focus on the primary elections, I decided to challenge myself academically. I took an advanced course in Old Testament Theology from Professor Eigenbrodt, which, more than any other course I'd ever taken, forced me to push my own thinking beyond where I thought it was capable of going. I spent hours reading Gerhard von Rad's *Old Testament Theology*, and Walther Eichrodt's *The Theology of the Old Testament*, trying to make sense of immensely complex arguments about the origins of the Western theological tradition. While I worked at becoming a scholar and became more engaged in the antiwar rallies across campus, for some DAE members, including my friend Tom, nothing changed. They partied every night and bragged about getting laid.

Despite the radicalization of some fraternity brothers, other brothers, especially those who had been recruited under Sean's term in the leadership council, remained avid states' rights advocates. They denigrated Martin Luther King's efforts to broaden the civil rights movement to include worker's rights and opposition to the Vietnam War. Four juniors and three sophomores boasted how they supported the rights of states and of businesses to segregate if they chose to do it. Their argument was that our country believed in freedom of choice and if a person—or restaurant—did not believe in equality, well, that was their belief and no one had the right to tell them otherwise. I'd heard the same arguments years ago about the Confederate flags. At meals they often sat together and made crude statements—"love America or leave it" to insult those of us who were involved in the antiwar and civil rights movements.

The ringleader was Dwight, the new DAE quarterback, who grew up in Birmingham, Alabama, and bragged that he thought Bull Connor, his racist police commissioner of public safety, was a true patriot. Dwight once said, "Bull Conner defended the rights of whites, and he had that right. No one could take it away." He thought that Dr. King's marching to Montgomery had stirred up racial animosity that was not there before he arrived. He should have just left it as it was. Now, his going to Memphis to support the sanitation workers was a big mistake, part of his troublemaking, and most likely, his communist connections. Dwight had seen photographs of King with known communists at the Highlander Folk School and showed me the pictures.

"How do you know?" I replied. "None of them has a sign saying, "I'm a communist," and, besides, if they were, they were probably advocating the rights of laborers and the poor."

"So you're one of those commies too! Watch what happens," he told me. "There's going to be violence in Memphis. He's a troublemaker. Mark my words. He's just another outside agitator, stirring people up and no matter what they say about him, he's just as bad as those antiwar rabble rousers. If they don't like the country the way it is, they should move out. Go to Sweden or back to Africa." Dwight gladly told anyone what he thought. But if I spoke up and questioned him, he'd point in my face and shout, "Don't try to indoctrinate me with your sick ideas."

I stayed away from him. He headed a faction in the fraternity who faithfully watched John Wayne movies every Friday and hung Confederate flags in their rooms. For them, the Civil War was still unresolved; they wanted to do battle as long as they could with any of us Northern liberals.

"You antiwar activists are un-American and undermining our war efforts," he said after dinner one night, trying to rile me up.

Paul took me by the arm and said, "Forget it. You know what good it did with Sean. It'll do no good to try to convince him otherwise."

"Well, look at the scaredy-cats. Afraid to stand up for what they believe because they know they're wrong," he shouted as we headed out the door.

We'd gone to our respective campaign headquarters, me to McCarthy's, and Paul to Bobby Kennedy's, where we each worked to make more phone calls to drum up support for our candidate.

While I was working politically, I discovered that my brother had been doing some intensive work romantically. He called me late one night.

"Hey bro," he said. "Guess what? I'm getting married."

"No way!"

"Yep, in March, during spring break. I want you to be best man. Will ya?"

"Sure."

"I proposed a few weeks ago, to Barbara, the one who works at Sears," he explained. "Mom and Dad are happy. Should be a good time. I've invited other guys from the house."

Funny, I thought, how, for some, the world goes on in its usual pattern—college, job, marriage, as if nothing else was happening in the world.

The Bottom Line

Before spring break, I took a bus home. *Time* magazine had an article saying Nixon was the man to beat. I cringed. As an avid anti-communist, he'd never let us withdraw. With him, the war would probably drag on as it had with Johnson and I would be pulled into it. I felt trapped: To avoid the war, I'd have to leave the country, go to Canada, and disappoint my dad. If I enlisted, I'd be fighting a war I could not imagine fighting. As I watched the raw, untilled fields with their broken cornstalks glide past, I wanted to find a deep hole somewhere out there and hide inside it. The bus left me off in Chicago, where I walked through the cement corridors to Union Station and caught a train to Glen Brook.

My father had called and said that "in no uncertain terms" I had to have a job for the summer and definite plans for the next year if I wasn't going onto graduate school. He suggested that I come home early so I could help with the preparation for my brother's wedding and, while I was there, meet with some of his friends. He'd talked to the President of AT&T and set up another job interview with his corporate friends in Chicago. One offered me a job at a warehouse, a distribution center not far from our house, unloading trucks for the summer until I found out if I had gotten into law school.

The second night home, before dinner, my dad asked what I planned to do after graduation.

"I can tell you one thing," I said, not looking at him, "I do not plan to enlist in the army."

"I didn't ask that," he said.

"You know I oppose the war."

"I'm not interested in what you oppose," he said. "What I asked, son, is what you plan to do?"

"Law school, if I can get into one."

"That sounds good. Do you know which are the best to apply to?"

"No."

"Well, here's some advice, although I know you do not like me to give

367

you any. Apply to Northwestern. Mr. Young, you know, from the club, is on the board. And Vanderbilt where Mr. Warren..."

"The president of Sears and Roebuck?"

"Yes, the same, is Chairman of the Board there."

"Where is Vanderbilt?"

"In the South, Tennessee, I believe, Nashville," he said.

"I'm not interested in the South," I said. "I don't think I could deal with the racism."

He pointed his finger at my chest. "Look, son, if Mr. Warren gives the word, you will be in. No questions asked. Don't be stupid. Give it a shot."

I'd already looked into law schools and their requirements. With average grades during my first two years, I wasn't optimistic about my chances. If Mr. Warren could drop my name, that sounded promising. But going to law school still left me 1-A.

"This war has messed me up." I admitted. "I'm not sure what I want to do anymore. I don't think that law school is a real option. I'll still be 1-A."

He shook his head, stopped, narrowed his brow, and put his hand on my shoulder, "I don't want to hear about the war or your attitudes. I find them offensive. That's not what you should be thinking about. If you're not going to law school, you need to think about what kind of work you want to do. In the real world, noble ideals don't bring home a paycheck. Being for the war or against doesn't matter. You need to earn a living. Let me be clear; I need you to tell me what you want to do."

I stepped back and his arm fell to his side.

I decided to be honest. "I don't know. I don't want to go into business."

"Why not?"

"I'm no good at selling anything, not like Jack," I said. "I'm more interested in ideas and, maybe, helping others, or maybe..."

His ears reddened. He jabbed his finger at me. "Stop it! Listen to me, will you? You need to decide what you are going to do right now. Get it? Right now! No lollygagging around. You hear me? I'll not have my son wallowing around doing nothing or doing things that, quite frankly, smack of being un-American. There's a war. Do your duty and then move on. The bottom line is: Work. Earn a living. Make something of yourself."

"Yes, sir," I said, saluting him.

He raised his hand to swat me, but, once he saw me straighten up and raise my hands, he thought better of it. I watched him. I was proud of myself. For much of my life, when his ears boiled, becoming almost beet red, I'd cower, knowing he'd blast me.

Often when he gotten upset, he said, as an opener, "I probably should not say this," and then spit out vitriol, berating how I didn't put the water softener in the tank properly, or how I had dared to go on the porch in a bathrobe (what would the neighbors say?), how my girlfriends were, well, not the types of girls he wanted around our house and, of late, how my dress and hair were totally inappropriate. He'd sound off, expecting that I would nod my head and, as I often did, comply.

But that night before dinner, I looked him straight in the eye and did not flinch. I let him know not to strike me, not to force my hand. It was not a major battle, only a skirmish, but I'd made a point.

He tightened his lips and turned to walk away from me as if he'd decided to retreat to higher ground.

"And, Dad, don't worry. I hear you. I know I need to make a living and I will. It just has to be on my own terms. I'm not like Jack or you. So give that up. Give me time. It will come together."

He glanced back at me and, with his jaw jutting to one side. He nodded, then smiled weakly. I knew I baffled him. To be sure, I had friends whom he liked, who knew how to act in polite society and were good at golf. But he knew I had some radical friends, too, with long hair and strange clothes, vests with peace signs on them, earrings in their ears. He had no use for them, and they had no use for him. He was afraid I'd gone over to the radical fringe and might embarrass him and my mother and cause the gossip mills, as they had with Jack when got hepatitis, to grind out rumors about me.

Once he snuck into my room to read my journal—I'd noticed it was not where I'd left it—and I made sure never to leave it out again since in it I had questioned the conventional world I'd been brought up in. I quoted Che Guevara, the guerrilla leader who had been killed in Bolivia—"Let me say, at the risk of seeming ridiculous, that the true revolutionary is guided by great feelings of love." Such sentiments would baffle my father and cause him distress because I'd mostly been the good son, the one who starred on the football team, the one who finished second in the Illinois Junior Golf Open, the one that nearly won the club championship, and the one who, despite his long hair, had met some of his expectations.

But I paid the price for being the good son. I felt as if I was a fake like Dean, invisible, putting on a mask, making a good appearance, to keep some fragile connection with my family, when inside I boiled with rage about the war, how napalm melted the skin of peasants, how big business and the military colluded to escalate the war, how Dow Corporation produced a defoliant, Agent Orange, that polluted the land in Vietnam. But here I was, the dutiful son about to eat the supper my mother made who would afterward sit with them and watch The Lawrence Welk Show on TV, drink a Budweiser, and act as if I was my own man, an adult, all the while feeling like a pretender, living a dual life.

How could I keep up the fraud? I didn't know, nor did I entirely understand the anger welling inside of me. Part of it was feeling more and more disenfranchised from my upbringing yet, equally, not being sure what that meant, how it might shape my own future. Part of it was my growing confusion about me, my sexual feelings and my feeling different. I could not name exactly what the "different" feeling was because it had so many faces. I did not fit into the suburban world. I did not fit in with my fraternity. I did not fit in with other guys. It festered at me like an open sore that would not heal.

I fixed him and my mom a martini, dry, only a pinch of vermouth, and sat with them as they talked about the weather, how we could probably play golf by the end of the week, and how the Masters was weeks away and who might stand a chance to win—Jack Nicklaus, Gary Player or Bert Yancey. I spent that evening with them, and those that followed, mending fences, in the little ways they could be mended, hoping that I could keep living the double life without falling totally out of favor.

During the news one night, I told Dad that I had visited a shipping warehouse for Commonwealth Edison and been interviewed by the foreman.

"I'd be lugging supplies off the truck and depositing them in the appropriate places in the storage facility," I said. "But after meeting with him, I drove over to the club and to meet with Ray Delmore to see if any jobs were open on the grounds crew. Since I've worked there previous summers and know the routine, he has one. He hired me."

"Well, good," my dad said. "Now get on those applications."

"I will," I said.

"Good, I'm pleased," he said, smiling. "You ready for your brother's wedding?"

"Yep. Even wrote up the toast."

"Good for you."

The Wedding

The rest of the break, I was swept up in the wedding preparations. I envied my brother. He seemed so sure of what he wanted in life. Having met the girl of his dreams at Sears—she worked in lingerie—he had proposed to her in February and, just as quickly, in late March, he was ready to marry her.

Ecstatic to have one of her sons married, my mother invited hundreds of people to a special pre-wedding at the club. Like a presidential candidate, I shook hands until my hand was sore from welcoming people who passed through the line to greet us. My cheeks grew sore from smiling.

As the big day approached, I drove people back and forth to the rehearsal, picked up prepared food, and went to the liquor store with my dad to lug home cases of wine, gin, vodka, scotch and bourbon for quests who my mother had invited to come over during the week.

The wedding itself, a Catholic affair, lasted an interminable two hours as if each minute had been attached to a medieval rack and stretched out. For thirty minutes, the priest extolled the congregation about the glory of the Church and sanctity of marriage as if he wanted to convert any wayward Protestants to the promise of Catholicism. My brother knelt on the steps before the altar, stone faced, weary, yet elegant in his tuxedo. He bowed his head and I wondered if he'd fallen asleep. His wife, blond, in a white dress with a train that spread out like a fan behind her, snuggled next to him, her head bowed. Everyone had their head bowed but me. Since I'd never been in a Catholic church, I admired the elaborate vestments, having grown up with ministers clad in black. I could not believe the long liturgical pronouncements that praised God, Jesus, Mary and a host of saints. I never witnessed the communion ritual in which the congregation filed to up the altar, one at a time to have the wafer dropped into their mouth by the priest—a process that could have been handled much more efficiently. In my church, bread and grape juice were passed out on trays, and everyone ate and drank at once.

At the reception, I delivered a toast: "To my brother who was always there for me as a kid and who has found one of the most wonderful women to marry. No matter where they go, no matter how far their work and life will take them, he and Barbara, my new sister, will be in my heart." Nothing earthshattering. Barbara danced with me and kept saying how delighted she was to be a member of the family. My dad, near the end of the reception, put his arm around me. "Big day for our family," he said. "That leaves just one more." He glanced at me and poked me in the arm.

I smiled. "Don't get your hopes up, Dad; it may take a while."

"Are you dating any girls at school?"

"Not right now. I'm on sabbatical!"

He laughed. "Yes, I suppose you are."

On the morning my brother and Barbara were to leave for their honeymoon in Florida followed by a week in the Bahamas, Jack called me and asked to meet me for breakfast at the A-1 Diner by our house, an old place with red vinyl seats, some cracked and taped, but a place whose food was plentiful and good.

"So what's up?" I asked after we'd ordered

"Just wanted you to know, Dad is worried about you," he said.

"Why is that?" I said, pouring cream into my coffee.

"You're not like your old self," he said, sipping on his coffee.

"Well, he's right. I'm not."

"You owe him something," Jack said. "Look what he's done for us—school, the club and..."

"Is *this* what you wanted to talk about?" I asked.

"No, not really. I just wanted to let you know how I appreciated your comments yesterday, and Barb, she did too, and how you helped with everything. And that..." He picked at his eggs, shoving one yolk across his plate toward his toast. "I'm scared."

"What?"

"This marriage thing. I'm not sure I'm ready."

"Yes you are. Geez, you've wanted to get married for years, always hunting for the right one. Now you have her," I said.

"You sure?"

"I think she's perfect!" I said, even though I barely knew her.

Jack smiled weakly. "I hope you're right."

The Wedding

The conversation then moved to safer topics: his job at Sears, how he wanted out, and mom—how radiant and happy she was at the wedding.

As we left the diner, he hugged me. "Wish me luck," he said.

"You'll be fine. Don't worry," I said.

When he drove off, the dust roiling up from the car, I wondered what worried him. There was something he did not say. I wished that I had not tossed him palliatives—"You'll be fine"—what good would that do? I almost drove after him but thought better of it. We had not talking about anything meaningful in so long, it seemed futile to try and engage him. We had just drifted in different directions, caught in the different currents of the times.

The next day, I took the bus back to school. Green now dappled the meadows and the cornfields, newly plowed over, exposed the dark, rich earth. I had done my diplomatic job, knowing soon, much too soon, I had to confront the draft and a war that, more and more, made my stomach sick.

Pledge Brother

Although it seemed that spring had come early, a heavy snow fell in early March of 1968. But I was cozy and warm at the boarding house. A large radiator on one wall of my room pumped out heat like no tomorrow. I'd given up worrying about my sexuality—my success at Terra Haute and my drawing the line with Jim left me feeling smug and content—and decided to stay focused on academics and let my doubts fold their wings and be still. I read incessantly and listened classical music; at first standards like Tchaikovsky's Violin Concerto in D, then more unusual pieces by Charles Ives. Since I still ate my meals at the DEA house, I was given the privilege, as a senior, of having a pledge son. Freshmen were paired with upperclassmen who could mentor them as Sam had mentored me my freshman year. The president of the house, Eric, asked if I might help out a shy boy, Stephen, who seemed "thoughtful and deep" —those were Eric's words.

"I think he's a kid whom you'd warm up to. He's very observant, one who likes to sit and watch people. A loner like you," Eric said.

"Thanks for the compliment," I said. I really wasn't interested in encumbering my life any more than it was, but Eric said, "Listen, he's like you were. I think you could help him. At least meet him. Sit with him at lunch."

I did. With long, dark, wavy hair so that it curled in back, Stephen had a serious, reserved demeanor. He blushed when I asked if he was dating.

"No. That's really hard to do, you know," he said.

"Why?"

"I'm shy," he said.

After the first encounter, I told Eric that I didn't think I'd be the best match for Stephen, but Eric insisted. Out of respect for Eric, I met with Stephen regularly at the house to discuss how his freshman year was going. Our session involved more effort than I was willing to make. He practically embodied the word "taciturn." I felt as if I were interrogating a spy sworn to secrecy.

A typical conversation went like this:

"How you doing?"

"Fine."

What you studying?"

"History."

"Doing anything interesting?"

"Nope."

Out of exasperation, at dinner one night, I asked him if he wanted to study in my room. His face beamed, "That would be super. I hate the library."

He agreed to come to my room after supper, the time that pledges were required to be in their room studying or at the library. He was startled when he came in the room since my room was only 10 by 10 feet, with a bed, small dresser, and a desk that was snugly tucked into an alcove by the door.

"Where can I study?"

"You can spread out on the bed, if you want. It's cool. Or when I'm reading and using the bed, you can use my desk." I pointed at it.

"As long as you don't mind." He put his books on the bed, sat on it, bouncing slightly, untied his shoes and slipped them off and picked up the World Literature anthology and leaned back on the headboard of the bed and began to read. He smiled at me.

"Is it going to be all right?" I asked.

"Yeah."

"The bathroom is across the hall."

"Sure. Okay." He started to read and mark the pages with a highlighter. With his long brown hair that fell across his forehead and thick spectacles, he looked studious. He wore jeans and a loosely fit dress Oxford shirt.

I stared at him for a moment, charmed by his appearance and by having him to share my room.

A few friends had come by to talk and drink before we had gone to a party. But no one ever stayed long.

"Is something wrong?" he asked.

Embarrassed by my infatuation, I quickly turned back to reading the book in my hand—*The Fall*, by Albert Camus.

An hour passed and Stephen got up to use the bathroom. I could see across the hall and noticed that he left the door partially open, perhaps, I thought, because the bathroom is so tiny that it is hard to move around. Without thinking, I stared as he unzipped and began to urinate. Despite the indiscretion, I was fascinated with how he stood, with his legs wide, purposeful, his knees bent slightly. At the fraternity or any public bathroom, I never dared to glance at anyone else, but here I gazed as his hands held his cock. It seemed mysterious, as if I had discovered the secret of manhood, and I remembered myself as a little boy at the drive-in movie men's room, standing at the end of the large trough of a urinal, transfixed, looking at the men, lined up in a row, ten penises urinating, until one man laughed and said, "Hey, kid. Did you get a ticket for admission?" and my father, seeing what I was doing, grabbed me and jerked me away.

Stephen turned to look out of the door and noticing me, quickly zipped up and turned to wash his hands. Flustered that he'd seen me spying on him, I got up and went to the window.

When he came back into the room, he stood by the door for a minute quietly. I stuffed my hands in my pockets and spoke, "Not a lot of room in here for privacy. Sorry."

For a second he was quiet, and then said, "I don't mind. It's intimate here. More like home."

His voice, tender, nonjudgmental, soothed me. I felt my shoulders relax. He reminded me of Tim, the clerk at the adult book store. Here I was with another guy whose body felt like a magnet. He walked over to the window and stood beside it as I stared out at silhouettes of sorority girls entering their brick three-storied house.

"You date much?" he asked.

"No. Not really. I mean not this year. I have a lot of reading." He looked earnest and I continued, saying things I had only told Jake, "And besides, I feel awkward with girls. Just find it hard to talk with them."

He nodded his head and pointed to one of my books piled on the desk, "I noticed you read deep stuff—existentialists, French writers—Camus." He pronounced it "cam" and then "us" as in English "us." I corrected him, telling him how to pronounce the last syllable "ooh."

He blushed, "I'm sorry," and reached out to me, putting his hand on my back.

"That's all right. I knew no better until I heard the professor say his name."

I told him the character in the novel was self-absorbed. I quoted a favorite line, "I conceived at least one great love in my life, of which I was always the object."

He laughed and blurted out, "I know several guys in my pledge class who act like that."

We talked for an hour. I asked him the same question that Dr. Compton had asked us about the protagonists in the book, "If someone leapt into the river, would you leap in to save them, or turn, as the main character, and think 'it was too late and none of my business.'"

Without hesitation, Stephen said, "I would leap into the river."

"I mean," he rubbed his forehead, "we all have tough times—want to end it—and later realize that maybe all we wanted was someone to care."

I liked his forthrightness. I wanted to agree with him, but, then too, I equivocated because I had too often doubted myself, wondered if I should act, if I had made the right decision, if someone would make fun of me. Much as the main character in *The Fall*, I compromised more often than I wanted to admit. My own judgmental nature niggled at me.

He seemed surprised that I might hesitate, "How *could* you do that?"

He stared at me, seemingly distraught at seeing someone he admired crumble in front of him. I had to revive his trust and said, "Well, I'm only reflecting sympathy with the character in the story—his own self-doubt. Of course, I would act. I would save the other person just you would. It's the right thing to do." As the words came out of my mouth, I knew that they were lies, something I would tell to keep up the facade of certainty— something I could not really claim, but wanted to claim to keep up his positive impression of me. He put his hand out and poked me in the arm, "Good, good. That's what I thought you'd say."

The streetlights began to flicker on along the street. Stephen leaned back, picked up a book and began to read. He shoved his right hand in his pocket. I gazed down and noticed the outline of his hand cupped on his thigh. He looked at me and smiled.

After an hour, when it was nearly 10 p.m., he spoke and picked up a thread of an earlier conversation, startling me so I turned to face him, "You know, as you were saying, I always feel awkward with girls too. Do you think most guys do?"

I laughed abruptly, took a deep breath and expelled it.

"Good question," I said and thought for a second. "Most guys never admit their vulnerabilities. They act as if they were what everyone wants them to be. I don't know if it is bravado or ignorance." Since grade school, I had wondered why guys act as they do. The tough guy image seemed fake and made me cringe. After I became an athlete, I learned to play the role of a jock, but it always felt like an act. Some guys bragged about how they went all the way and knew how to maneuver a girl as well as they drove a car. That certainly was not me.

As we talked more, Stephen admitted that he had one close friend, Larry, with whom he spent most of his time until he came to Ashbury. The clock on my desk had pushed to nearly 12 o'clock, and I told him that he should be getting back to the house or someone would wonder what had happened to him. He collected his books, shuffled around gathering papers and as he was leaving, slung one arm around my neck and gave me a quick hug, pressing his whole body against mine.

"Thanks," he said. "Thanks a lot."

"Sure," was all I managed to say, but I could have said more. I felt a magnetic energy drawing me to him. I even felt myself getting jittery; my skin tingled. When the door closed, I held onto the wall. I'd become dizzy, and tried to focus on taking long slow breaths. I couldn't figure out what had happened. It was as if someone had knocked the wind out of me. Or maybe it was that I had been holding my breath.

The following night, when Stephen came over, he noticed that I was agitated.

"You all right?" he asked, putting his hand on my shoulder.

I shrugged him off. "Yeah, fine, busy with the McCarthy campaign and lots of schoolwork, several big papers. So, if you don't mind, we can't talk like we did. Let's keep focused tonight, okay?"

His lips tightened and he said, "Sure, whatever you want."

He pulled a book out of the stack that he laid on the bed. I wanted to break the tension, to feel normal again, but it didn't work. I found myself staring at him—how his lips were full and thick, almost Negroid; how the veins in his hands, distinct and blue, seemed like the curved forks of a river; how his hair fell over his forehead covering one of his eyes.

He smiled, "You said you need to work."

I recoiled as if snapped out of a trance.

He stepped back and flopped on to the bed and folded his hands in back of his head. I pulled out the desk chair. I noticed he kept his eyes on me, not at all uncomfortable, more a seeming curiosity about my own inability to work. I put my hand in my pocket, making sure that my state of arousal was not too apparent and went to my chair, pulling it close to the desk so my back faced him. I opened my book and read with fierce concentration, not looking up for what seemed like hours.

A knock on the door startled me. I scooted my chair back, and stood to open it.

"Hi," Alex said. "Am I bothering you?" His sweet smile wafted over me.

"No, come in," I said. As he stepped forward, he reached out as he usually did, to my neck, his fingertips melting into my skin for what was the best massage anyone could imagine.

"You want a backrub. Oh," he said, startled to find Stephen on the bed. "Who's this Adonis?"

"It's my pledge son," I said. "He comes over to study."

"I was thinking of doing the same," Alex said, glancing over his shoulder at Stephen.

"Hi," Stephen said, leaning across the bed, extending his hand.

Alex reached over, "Hi" and shook his hand and turned to me. "I'll catch you later," he said. "Don't want to disturb you." He stepped back into the hallway. I followed him, closing the door.

"Sorry about that," I said. "He's a freshman. He needed to find a good place to study and ..."

"Well, he took my place," Alex cut me off. "That's *my* bed for studying," he said, pointing a finger in mock reprimand at my face.

I smiled. "I know. It won't happen often."

"You sure?"

"Yes," I said, but I wasn't sure. As it turned out, Stephen came over more often as the weeks progressed and Alex, aware of his presence, came less frequently to my room.

My attraction to Stephen was quickly becoming an obsession. It was as if some force had taken possession of me. Not rational, not subject to my discretion, it felt as if it came from my loins and spread throughout my body. I had to pry my eyes away from him and back to the printed page. We would talk late at night, sitting across from one another on the bed. His legs would swing in and out. As the weather grew warmer, he would wear shorts. My eyes would drift to his crotch. I suspected that his did the same. Not since Frank, that night after the championship, had I touched another guy. The old "primitive terror" gnawed at me. I began to drink heavily again, sometimes enough to be passed out on the bed when he came over. Stephen would prop up my head, then sit at my desk, studiously reading and making notes. In my drunken state, I persuaded myself that the attraction was an aberration, just a trick of the psyche, a phase— something that would dissipate in time. I'd had the feelings before, but they were fleeting—the guy at the men's club, the guy in the adult book store, my caddy—and I was able to walk away from them, to draw the line, to know when to stop, just put space between me and desire. But with Stephen, there was no way to avoid what I was feeling. I wanted to flee and disappear. The man in *The Fall* that leapt into the river was me. My body, carried downstream, reached out, gasping, wanting someone to leap in and carry me to shore. The current that pulled at me was my own desire. I could not distinguish if my feelings for Stephen where the same as his feelings for me or if my feelings distorted my perceptions of him. Perhaps, he was just comfortable with intimacy? Perhaps he did not mind my touch? Perhaps none of his glances were meant to be anything other than a friendly acknowledgment of me?

I forced myself to ignore him, to work more on the long paper that I was writing on the nature of evil. I became agitated it he interrupted me.

"Just leave me alone," I scolded him one evening. "I've got to get this finished." He recoiled as if a snake snapped at him. But that did not work to keep him at a distance.

Once he arrived, if I were in the chair, I felt the back of my body radiate with an intensity that seemed unbearable, as if my back were aflame. I never trusted my own desires. Whenever I got an erection as an adolescent, I would question it, finding my distrust of it almost comical. I would think,

"What are you doing? Why are you standing up like that? You should not feel that way." So night after night, I would have a private debate with my own anatomy. My erections did not care about my rationalizations. They moved in, set up housekeeping in my pants and waited to see what I would do. I found myself barely able to think about anything academic. Getting up from the chair, I would walk to the window, my hand in my pocket and pretend I was enamored with the beautiful landscape or the girls walking to their sorority. Stephen would come over and look out too, or chat about a poem that he had read and ask me for my interpretation. Gradually, my erection would settle down and I resumed reading.

The weather that spring fluctuated as much as the presidential campaign. Some days it seemed that winter had her icy fingernails in the air. Other days the heat was unbearable, almost like midsummer. One afternoon, when the temperature had soared into the 90s, I heard a knock on the door. I'd taken off my shirt and shorts, and was sitting in my underpants, while sweat dripped down my neck and off my head. I opened the door. Stephen was standing in the hall, clad in a blue dress shirt and white shorts. He asked if he could study in my room.

"The house on the third floor is a hundred degrees," he explained, "and I just couldn't stand it."

Momentarily taken aback and self-conscious of my being almost half-naked, I reached for my T-shirt and shorts as I gestured for him to come in.

"Don't bother," he said. "It's much too hot. It would be a good day to sit in your underwear, or no clothes at all."

I laughed and said that obviously I had been doing just that.

He put down his books and asked, "Mind if I join you?"

"Go right ahead," I said as calmly as I could and put down my shirt and shorts.

I went to the window to open it wider to take in any hint of a breeze. Putting his books on the bed, Stephen stripped off his shirt, his shorts, folded them neatly, and placed them on the end of the bed and came over and stood by me.

"Hot," I said, keeping my eyes on the leaves outside that barely stirred.

"Yeah, it is," he moaned, holding his hands in front of his briefs, just resting them there.

Despite my conscious intention to be calm, I felt myself getting aroused and stood helplessly as my erection pressed against my jockey shorts. I could see his eyes shifting to me, to look at my body. I became more self-conscious than I had been and made a lame attempt to put my hand over my groin. But it felt stupid to leave my hands on my crotch, so I just let them fall by my sides. My eyes shifted back to the maple tree in the yard, the broad irregular shadow of it across the lawn and then to his body. He raised his arms above his head and I could see the bulge in his underwear, the well-defined cylindrical shape and the tip of it, pointing upward. I knew a lot of guys kept their penis upward so I decided to make nothing of it, just kept my mind on the heat and the potential breeze and not to ponder why he, too, was aroused.

Weeks before, I watched a guy, sitting across from me one evening in the library in very light slacks. He could not see me because he was sitting in a carrel, which, as it was situated, blocked his upper body. He was leaning back in his chair. His penis noticeably snaked across his thigh, and his hand every few minutes patted and rubbed it as casually as if he were comforting a dog at his side. He did that for a few hours and, as he stood, I noticed a stain in his pants as evidence that his caresses came to good use. That was normal. A guy thing.

Stephen's breathing, deep and gradual, jolted me back to the present. I looked back outside and gestured, "Look, no wind at all." The leaves sagged like deflated balloons on the limbs.

"No, none." He raised his hands higher and inhaled deeply. His belly lifted and since the waist band of his briefs were loose, it edged downward to expose the dark mat of his pubic hair and, peeking out ever so slightly, the pink head of his penis.

Neither of us said a word. He continued to hold his arms up, while I stood transfixed before him, enraptured. He gazed at me gazing at him. We stood like two statues of Eros that, because we were marble, could not move. His breath, slow and measured, his taut belly distending and retracting with each breath, my hands by my shorts, his arms in the air. As he let his hands down, he slid them gently down my back and let them rest there.

"Nice," I said.

"Yeah," he said.

I reached around and put my hand on his hip and held him, sweaty and warm, lovely against my fingers. This was it. I had crossed the line. I didn't want to hesitate since I waited so long for this moment. But I let him make the first move. He made no attempt to do anything else, and I felt like an actor on a stage with no script, wondering what I was to do or say next.

He finally turned and moved to the bed, sitting on the edge of the bed. The sweat pouring off his chest and abdomen had turned his briefs transparent, revealing the full outline of what lay beneath. I sat in the chair, my elbows propped on my knees, and we looked at each other. I wondered what he might be thinking, if he were about to speak. If he weren't so taciturn, I would know what to do.

The sweat poured off my face—it felt as if I was leaning into a furnace— and I could feel the wet, almost cool moisture oozing from my erection. My body shivered several times and he asked, "Are you all right?" looking at me with a worried expression.

I said, "Oh fine, just hot."

"I know what you mean," he said, wiping the beads of sweat from his brow. I flipped him a blue towel that hung from the closet doorknob. He wiped his body and legs. I wished that I was that towel, touching his chest with its fine crop of hair between his nipples and the pubic hair trailing up his abdomen and the sleek muscles in his legs.

He let his hand drop to his lap, then and rubbed back and forth with his thumb just below the edge of his waistband. I could see now that, yes, he did have an erection. It began to poke upward beyond the elastic. He smiled and passed the towel to me, then all the while, looking into my eyes, he lay back, again with his hands behind his head to let me see his body stretched out, his erection, proudly protruding. I licked my lips. The animal inside me wanted someone to unhinge the pen. He stared at my crotch where I too was blatantly displaying my own excitement.

There was a ring of the telephone in the hallway. A voice called out, "It's for you, Jason," and I stood, not a foot from Stephen. I was clearly aroused. My erection extended like a bridge between us. Amused, he kept gazing at me to see what I might do. I grabbed my robe and left to answer the phone. It was Tom, asking if I wanted to go to the lake for a swim, I told him, "Sure."

"I'll come right over."

I wanted to tell him to wait, to give me an hour, but he hung up.

I went back to the room. Stephen was stretched out on the bed like a wanton god, one leg up, swinging it back and forth like a metronome. His eyelids drooped and his hand, once more, was resting exactly where I wanted to put my hand. I announced, "Tom called and asked if we wanted to swim. I said 'yes.' You want to go?"

His brow furrowed, "No. I'd prefer to stay here. I'll just read."

"You're sure?"

"Yeah."

"I'll be back," I told him. "Wait for me."

He furrowed his brow, again. "Okay."

I threw on my clothes, grabbed my suit and ran down the stairs. By the time I came back—it must have been midnight—I was slightly drunk and Stephen had gone. He came over a week later to tell me he had met a girl. He was dating. After that, he came back to the room only two or three times; he studied and kept to himself. In a way, I was relieved though still tempted when he entered my room. I could set it aside knowing he was occupied with the opposite sex and could put my energy back into the primary elections and the antiwar movement.

V: I said to my soul, be still, and let the dark come upon you
Which shall be the darkness of God.

The Dream Deferred

A chill grabbed at my throat. Standing outside Ballard Hall— its brick façade looking every inch Ivy League—I shivered in the April air. It had shifted yet again from the brutally hot weather of a week before to bone chilling cold. A few students, hands stuffed in pockets, shuffled across the serpentine walkways that curved around the quadrangle. No one expected the cold. No one was dressed for it.

"Those bastards, those so-called professors, want to abandon everything we stand for," my friend Linda moaned.

"They abandoned McCarthy," I groused along with her, "because the damn polls predict fuckin' Robert Kennedy will win." We had spent months canvassing homes, trudging street by street, meeting people who said that Kennedy was too liberal, one of those East Coast intellectuals; people supported McCarthy because he seemed level-headed, more down to earth.

Earlier that afternoon, we'd spent two hours debating whether Senator McCarthy was worth supporting. He was the first presidential candidate have captured the nation's imagination by questioning Johnson's failed Vietnam policies. But some of McCarthy's vocal supporters were still unsure whether to keep supporting him..

1968 would be a pivotal year for elections. No one could doubt it. Yet no one seemed sure who to support in the primaries. Loyalists who had worked for months for McCarthy equivocated. Many former ex-McCarthy supporters wanted to back Robert Kennedy. He had announced his candidacy late but had the best chance of beating the mainstream candidate Hubert Humphrey. All the recent polls showed Kennedy would trump McCarthy in Indiana. What was one to do?

Although I felt attracted to Kennedy because of his brother, the late president, I distrusted the nasty side of him—his vilification of the Teamsters, his hardball tactics in his brother's presidential campaign. My father told me that he was dangerous. I should watch out: he was a Jekyll and Hyde. He was much too radical. Although I did not want to admit it, I had my misgivings. His growing his hair long seemed a blatant attempt to appeal to us, to the youth.

Another friend who had worked on the McCarthy campaign, Todd, overheard us talking and shrugged, "We might as well support Dr. Martin Luther King. At least he has the garbage union behind him! That's what this election is turning into—garbage."

Linda burst out laughing, "Yeah, garbage! That's what we all end up being, just waste in a commercial society that sells every candidate as if he were a bar of soap."

Todd, who was never shy about telling us what he thought, added, "You know I want to support McCarthy, but I don't know. It looks dismal for him. And Kennedy is strong, at least here in Indiana. Polls show it. And yet politics—something is always rotten in the air."

"Yeah, you think change is charging in on a white stallion and it ends up being a mule who wouldn't budge," Linda scoffed, not disguising the bitterness of her mood.

I laughed, "That pretty much says it all. I thought this election was about change, then we get Kennedy and maybe he's about change, maybe he's the one — he's got a passion that appeals to me and he has a way with blue-collar and minority voters that is eerie, almost spiritual, but he's no King. He's no McCarthy."

Linda chirped in, "It's all a mask, same old, same old. When will it ever end?"

"Don't know," I shrugged.

She came over to me, threw her arms out, "Nice try, you spoke up. You said what you had to say and that's that," and I hugged her back and hugged Todd, gave them a raised fist salute and we parted, each heading our separate ways. Instead of going to my room, I decided to visit the fraternity to watch the news and see what the commentators were saying about the primary.

I took the long walk back — going along the streets instead of bisecting the quadrangle. I needed to clear my mind. I passed through the dappled light on the sidewalk and could hear the brisk April wind fluttering through the frail canopy of leaves.

My history professor, Dr. Herod, had argued for "a practical approach," because even though we had canvassed door to door for months, passing out flyers about McCarthy, the reality was Kennedy had the political clout. He knew how to win. And that's what mattered according to him, but I disagreed and told him that I'd seen McCarthy fend off reporters at an Indianapolis news conference. He was formidable. He might beat Kennedy. "He's savvy," I countered, "savvy enough to take on the president when no one else dared to speak up. He may just have the staying power to beat Kennedy."

Linda, who had started the fledging McCarthy campaign office in her dorm room, had spoken up, citing her own experience talking with mainstream voters who liked McCarthy too. She believed McCarthy would upset everyone and take the Democratic nomination for President. But Professor Herod with stirring arguments for Kennedy convinced seventeen of the twenty McCarthy loyalists to change their allegiance by extolling his brother's unfinished legacy, his charisma, his sizable margin among respondents in polls.

It was 6:30. Defeat left a bitter taste in my mouth. I wandered along the sidewalk, my hands in my pockets, sauntering from one streetlamp to another, counting them, wondering if I too should go with the majority or keep on, stay with Linda who expected me to remain loyal as she was to our candidate.

I had gone with the majority most of my life: wore jeans when they became fashionable, grew my hair long when guys wanted to look more like Elvis than a member of the Mickey Mouse Club. No reason to change now. But maybe that was a good reason to change, to embrace being different. About halfway back to my fraternity, I resolved to hold my ground, although I felt as if the troops had left camp, marched to higher ground, and I was wallowing in the valley, left behind.

Indiana was lock-stepped into Kennedy's camp for reasons I somewhat understood. Kennedy had an uncanny verve and passion — and quoted George Bernard Shaw and spoke of what was possible. A week earlier, Pierre Salinger, President Kennedy's Press Secretary, had come to campus asking us to support "Robert" as he called him. I was impressed with the way Salinger connected with sixty students who attended the reception. I didn't want to leap from one candidate to another for expediency, but I nearly did when I met Salinger. Though still unwilling to give into the Kennedy mystique, I nonetheless pressed through the crowd and managed to get close to Mr. Salinger. He turned to me to ask if I supported Robert. I was honest and said, "Yes, I believe in what Mr. Kennedy stands for, but I stand by the courage of McCarthy to speak up when nobody else would say a word."

I was not prepared to be swept off my feet by the former Press Secretary's wit and charm. Short and pudgy, an unlit cigar in his hand, he looked me in the eye and testily asked, "So you're not with us?" Partially stupefied, I lamely offered, "I might be, but not for now."

He studied me for a moment, shook my hand firmly, "Good lad. Good for you: commit when you are sure. We will need the likes of you. I like someone who stands by his commitments."

As I crossed campus, I could see the lights in the dorms like large insects' eyes and beyond them, the elegant pillars of the sororities, each in a line along the street. They looked, as they had imagined the first time I saw them, like southern plantations shoved together as if they were facades on an enormous movie set for *Gone with the Wind.*

The more I spent time canvassing voters in town and in the rural farm country, I realized that was exactly what our college was: a make believe world amidst the farmers and merchants in this small southern Indiana town, removed from real time and space —the real world my father spoke about, the world his father had encountered in the Great Depression.

My father often admonished me: "Once you are finished with school, then you enter the *real world.* So enjoy your college years. They're a luxury I'm affording you." I never quite understood what he meant by the "real world" because it seemed to me that everything was real, particularly for those of us who were of draft age, waiting for our 1-A status. The Vietnam War hung like a noose over our heads. As the presidential campaign and the civil rights and antiwar protests increased, the college seemed more real to me than the work world because I had time to think, to question, and to find the truth. I did not have to follow a set routine, doing the same thing, at the same job, day in and day out, and earn a living.

By the time I arrived at my fraternity house, I still had not made any decision about Presidential candidates, but I knew I had to study for a French history exam on the 1848 Revolution and an essay that Marx had written about it. I walked up the steps into the front alcove and noticed a number of brothers scampering to the television room, screaming, "Man, oh, man, they got 'im," and thought that some local basketball team had pulled out a last-minute win. I started to step into the television room when a voice interrupted me, "Don't go in there."

Paul, looking pale and withdrawn, stood on the first landing to the upstairs of the house, shaking his head, muttering, "They're a fuckin' bunch of racist pigs." He was glowering at the doorway to the television room as if he'd been sideswiped by someone. He shoved his hand through his hair and grasped the railing to steady himself with the other.

He motioned for me to come up the stairs and join him on the landing. "What is it?" I asked.

Through the shut door, I could hear guys hooting and shouting. It still sounded as if a team snatched a last-minute come-from-behind score in a regional basketball game because the cheers would erupt every couple of seconds. If the local news reported WWIII had broken out during the Indiana basketball tournament, the headlines on the front page of the local paper would still read, "Crawfordville Wins State Title," while somewhere on page five, buried among the news of murders and rapes, would be the headline, "President Declares Global War."

Paul squatted on a stair and put his hands over his face. "It can't be. It can't be."

Paul's face reminded me of my dad's the night he heard his boss had died. The flesh sagged as if it had unhinged from his skull.

I went up the five steps to sit next to him and put my arm on his shoulder. "What happened? Did someone in your family die?"

He turned to me, his eyes filled with tears, "They got King."

"Dr. King?" I whispered in disbelief. "Did you say 'King'?"

"Yeah. In Memphis. In daylight. On the balcony of his motel."

The cheers were louder and Dwight, the tall blond boy from Alabama, strutted out and looked at us, grinning "Did you hear the news, lover boys?"

He stopped and put his hands on his hips, "What's your Northern boys' problem? All mopey because your big nigger man is dead?"

My fist clutched; I straightened up and Paul put his hand on my knee and pressed firmly. I whispered, "No, that's what he wants you to do."

"Oh, look at those boys now; they're like faggots, all lovely-dovey," Dwight sneered and ran out the front door, yelping like a General Pickett charging up Cemetery Ridge directly into Northern lines, thumping his chest in the line of fire.

I stood and took a step after him, but Paul grabbed me forcibly by the arm and jerked me around as he stood. He took my other arm in his hand and pulled me close to his face. His voice was stern and direct: "Listen here, Jason. It was Dr. King that was assassinated. Dr. King. Do you hear me?" He stared at me.

"What the fuck are you talking about?" I shot back.

Dwight had come back in and was grinning at me and raising his hands like Richard Nixon in a victory sign. I tried to jerk away from Paul, but he held me firmly. "It was King that they killed," he said again.

"I know that."

Leaning forward, he spoke slowly in a hushed tone, "Do you remember what we did with the flag, the Confederate flag?"

His eyes radiated an intensity that I remembered in my freshman year: back in March, 1965—the same day Dr. King's march from Selma to Montgomery started. King had crossed the Edmund Pettus Bridge to the onslaught of club-wielding Alabama state troopers. The Confederate flag was flying over our house. We crossed a bridge too, one that required me to stand up for what I believed when I was really not sure what I believed.

Now three years later, as Paul held my arm in the stairwell, the power of our agreement, one we had made three years before, and one we never broke, came back to me. We had done something that became legendary and changed the direction of the fraternity—at least until now.

Even if it split the house, causing enormous in-fighting, the membership had, at least in principle, opened membership to African-Americans. Yet underneath the surface of change, a cauldron of resentment seethed and had finally erupted once again. The cheering from downstairs left no doubt that racists wanted to have their day and this was it.

I turned to Paul who asked me again, "Do you remember 1965?"

I snapped at him, "I remember, of course I do. What's your point?"

"Nonviolence," was all he said. I could see the tears in his eyes and the sad longing in his angular face. I felt my own eyes well up and said, "Let's go. Let's get out of here."

We took the side door to Locust Street with its row of weather worn, residential prewar two-storied homes, and followed the streetlamps that spread their gentle light, circle after circle like little stage lights, into the dark. We wandered, not saying much, swearing indifferently, trying out the sound of certain words to see if, by saying them, they could absolve the torment, *Damn, Shit, Fuck, Bastards*, as if they could obliterate the rage. On one of the side streets that curved to and fro like an entrance to a labyrinth, we saw a girl sitting on a curb; she was moaning as if she had been hit, rocking back and forth, sobbing convulsively.

We ran down the street, thinking she had been mugged. As we got near her, I recognized her as an acquaintance from high school.

I called out to her, "Karen, you all right?" She stood and ran into my arms, pressing herself against me as if we had been long-lost friends. Her body pressed against mine as if she could find, in it, some way to feel alive again.

"I don't know what to do," she blurted out, frantic.

"What is wrong?" I asked, holding her in my arms, "Did someone hurt you? Break up or something?"

"No," she murmured, stepping back a foot and with a circumspect tenderness, touched my cheek, "Well, yes, in a way. Dr. King—have you heard?—he was shot."

We told her that, indeed, we had heard and wanted to get away from the fraternity where they were breaking open the kegs to celebrate.

"It's all madness," I told her. "It's as if someone has unleashed the spitefulness of the nation and no one can stop it."

"Where can we go?" she asked. "I can't stand being around my sisters. They're so smug. They asked me—can you imagine—'Who is he? Why are you so upset? He's just a Negro.' I had another ask, 'What's the problem? He's a known communist.' Can you believe it?"

Paul who had stood quietly listening to Karen, introduced himself and then, taking her by the arm, said, "Come on, I have a place we can go. It will be different there."

We ended up at a bar off campus, mostly for townies, where we sat in a booth and watched the news on a TV set over the bar. Although the town was mostly working-class, I had met people there who were opposed to the war and who like McCarthy believed as much as we did that the war was immoral. I had not discussed civil rights during my soliciting votes for McCarthy, but I now saw that I should have talked about it. That night, most of the men and women at the bar spoke in hushed reverential tones and glanced at the television with mournful expressions and drank as if they were at a wake wishing farewell to some relative. There were no rebels yelping about King being knocked off. A dim numbness settled in my skull as if a light had been switched off and the dark was settling in. Our conversation ebbed and flowed on the edges of incredulity, to what might become of our country, of who might be assassinated next. Hours later, we skulked out, a little tipsy, and arm-in- arm, walked back to Karen's sorority. She said, "I don't want to be alone. Come inside with me. We can sit in the foyer and stay warm and see what else is on the news."

Paul stopped and turned to her, "You must be kidding. Your housemother would never let us cross the threshold! She stands there like the fuckin' Secret Service. I've encountered her more than once. She guards you girls as if guys were on the FBI Most Wanted List."

Karen laughed, "Oh, that's what she does to intimidate the hustlers!"

"I'm no hustler," Paul countered.

"Maybe not, but you're cute and she might have thought you had potential." Karen took Paul's arm, insisting, "She's really nice. And she told me before I left that she would stay up with us because she admired Dr. King and felt awful. And she felt awful that so many girls had no idea how important he was for America and the world and, well, history, world history."

Much to our surprise, the housemother did welcome us.

"Come in boys," she waved us into a side room that she had set up as a safe haven, with the chairs turned inward to face the television. We had never seen the room before, mostly because any callers for girls had to wait outside the threshold, but she had sensed the gravity and importance of the evening and abandoned all her previous intractability. "Sit down, boys, let me get you come coffee," she said and encouraged us to join other students who had assembled before the television.

The housemother cared for us all that night as if someone in our family had died. She brought in muffins and coffee and let us stay well past 1 o'clock. Not much was said, however; but a sense of grace and peace settled over us. None of us could comprehend the enormity of the loss. Not for us. Not for the black community. We'd stumble out a phrase—someone would say, "It's awful" —but it would tumble over itself into silence. Someone would ask, "How could it happen?" and we would shrug. Someone would cry out, "It's a disgrace," and we'd stare at the TV. Our words went nowhere as if they, too, had been snuffed out.

It was at the sorority that we heard Kennedy speak from the makeshift podium on the back of a truck. I leaned forward, wondering what he could say that would have any credibility. I hoped it was not a political stunt, his trying to get votes and upstage McCarthy. Yet he seemed genuine. I could hear his distress, and I kept pressing the fingers of my right hand into my forehead as Karen held my other hand. I was silently weeping; a grief in myself that I never had known existed poured out of me in fits and starts. Although I had never known Karen well—and would never spend time with her again—somehow in those hours we became close. She held my hand and leaned next to me. I put my arm around her.

Kennedy's plaintive voice articulated the shapeless grief I felt, a grief that had been haunting me since the evening Paul and I ventured out after midnight with the flag.

I was struck by how awkward Kennedy appeared to be. He was not a great speaker and had an odd, high-pitched voice with a staccato delivery, yet he spoke with stunning fervor, his face reflecting his own distress as the people surrounding him, largely black, listened to him as if he were, by some kinship with violence and loss, a brother. We leaned into the television as the camera caught his face, dimly lit by some makeshift floodlight. He seemed to be searching for the right words, pleading with himself as much as with others: "What we need in the United States is not division; what we need in the United States is not hatred; what we need in the United States is not violence and lawlessness, but is love, and wisdom, and compassion" —here he jabbed his finger out and then his tone changed as he hesitated and continued— "toward one another, and a feeling of justice toward those who still suffer within our country, whether they be white or whether they be black."

And then he asked us "to tame the savageness of man and make gentle the life of this world." Paul caught my eye as Kennedy spoke those words and mouthed them back to me, "make gentle the life of this world."

When I wanted to slug Dwight in the face after he called us "faggots," Paul had stopped me. I realized now why he had held me back.

When Paul and I strolled back to the fraternity house, an incongruous serenity hung over the campus. Nothing moved. Not even the new leaves. Only a chill in the air. We held our arms close to our chests and scrunched our bodies inward to ward off the cold.

"Did you ever tell anyone, you know, about the flag?" he asked.

I hesitated before I answered. I had been tempted. Tom had pressed me several months before, after he and I polished off a fifth of Jack Daniels. He knew I had some idea who did it because he had seen me and someone else sneak out of the dorm that night. But I told him that I only had to take a pee. He persisted and I only disclosed that I was pleased someone had done it, but that I had no clue. I would never lie to him. I felt good about keeping it a secret.

"No, I have not," I replied.

"Me, neither," he said.

It may have been four years earlier—a long time for us—but as we opened the side door to the house and walked up the stairwell, we remembered how it had been that March evening. Paul took me by the arm and pulled me back outside. "Let's go look," he said.

I knew immediately what he wanted to do. We crossed the street, walked across the small park, past the baseball diamond into the woods. Although it was hard to see, we trotted carefully to the area where we had buried the flag.

The several boulders were still there. Paul stuffed his hands under his arms and gazed down at them. We did not say anything initially; for a long time, we simply stood under the trees and listened to the wind rattling the young leaves above us as we shifted back to that March evening when we put our plan into action.

Paul chuckled, "You know I'm almost tempted to dig it up."

"What for?"

"I don't know. Maybe to shove it in Sean's face, if he still was here, and say, 'It was us. We did it, you bastard!'"

I laughed, "That would be perfect, except, I bet, it must be decomposed by now and he's back in Alabama, probably supporting Wallace for president."

"You're probably right. Best to leave it where it is."

We stood there several more minutes. A gentle wind whispered faintly in the upper branches, and the branches nicked at one another, making a grinding sound.

"There is so much loss in this life," Paul sighed. "It never seems to end. The good get killed and it goes on and on and you can never, no matter how hard you try, you can never get away from that fact. What's left after a loss as enormous as this?"

"I don't know."

"I'll tell you: more loss."

"Yeah, I guess you're right," I agreed.

"And not much you can do about it except go on, make a stand when you can, and hope it will be better someday."

"That's about it," I said.

"Anyway, one flag buried," he chuckled, and then added, exasperatedly, "That's all we could do then, but it's not enough, not now."

He kicked up some of the matted leaves, and I did, too. The leaves tumbled over and splayed in several directions, aimless, and settled down. He took my arm in his for a moment, and said quietly, "Come on, let's get back. We've worn the day out and I want to get back to Kennedy headquarters early. We are making more calls to round up votes tomorrow. Our hope now is in him. What he said tonight convinces me that he's right for the time. And I think he has a good chance of winning. You going to join us?"

"Not now. I want to finish out with McCarthy."

"Good."

"You don't mind?"

"Hell, no. All I care about is that we care about making a change," he said, tugging on me to get back to the house.

I wished him good night at the fraternity door and headed to my room.

I felt sick at heart. The chill in the air seemed to fill my body. But I thought about tomorrow, the work I still had to do. We had a meeting in the campaign office. Our chances did not look good, not based on recent polls, but I'd made a commitment. I would be there.

1-A

With the assassination of Dr. King, with the increasing virulence on campus surrounding the antiwar movement, and with my own internal conflict about being 1-A while being against the war, I had become more frightened about my future. I felt closed in. Doors were one by one slamming shut. The campaign of McCarthy, as predicted, ended in defeat in Indiana. Kennedy's star was rising. When I got back to Glen Brook, I would have no way to work for McCarthy or Kennedy. The campaigns would head out West and I'd be stuck in Glen Brook. I'd told my dad that I'd find work. But work would not keep me out of the armed forces. I hated those words "armed forces." It was as if I would cease to be a person and become an extension of some abstract machine—one of the forces to kill an enemy who was no enemy. My dad would disown me if I told him that I wanted to be a conscientious objector. "What kind of man would do that?" he'd probably ask. "You lost your mind or something?"

So I composed a letter to my parents. I weighed whether to send it or not. Did I have the courage? I had doubts. I did not want to disappoint my parents, yet I didn't believe in the war. It was wrong. The assassination of Dr. King and the increased antiwar rhetoric in the presidential campaign had fueled an enormous battle inside me, one in which my old self—the good son, the responsible young man—had to reconcile himself with a new self that questioned what was happening and what he should or should not be doing. I finally sent the letter and waited with trepidation for a response.

Dear Mom and Dad,

I got two notifications today. One was from Dr. Eigenbrodt, which said that I have received an A in his Advanced Theology class. The other was from the Hook County Draft Board, which said that I had received a 1-A classification as of May 16, 1968.
In other words, I'm grade-A meat for our suicide

program in south eastern Asia.

On the notification, it said that if I wish to petition or appeal this classification, I should do so in 30 days. I shall call you before this letter arrives, but, nevertheless, I'm firmly set against any effort on the part of my government to send me to Vietnam to fight. I must find some way out. I oppose the war.

I may conditionally enter the service, if called. But in that war, I shall not fight. It may seem easy to say, sitting objectively here in this sheltered school. But I know it's difficult to say that I would not fight there, because it may mean going to court, or, if enlisted, a dishonorable discharge.

I hope that I do not end up in such a situation.

My stance not to fight is based on many conditions: that, first, I get drafted; that, second, I'm sent to Vietnam; that, third, I'm coerced to bear arms.

I suspect that I will have to deal with issues related to each of them and that may take a long time to work out.

I wanted you to know that is my stance. Hell, when I see the Vietcong on television, I honestly root for them. I suffer no distress over our soldiers losing a battle. Our war machine can overpower the Vietcong. Our leaders seemed convinced of it. But power cannot make a wrong right. I do respect Dean and others who have served. They do their jobs. They are surely innocent, just pawns in a war contrived by the elders. I do not want to be one of those pawns.

That said, I wouldn't go into the question of guilt and who is responsible for this war at this point. I talked at length last summer with Dean about the war. As a soldier, a veteran, he would not serve again. He told me not to go. He said that it was not only the wrong war at the wrong time, but that it was poorly waged and could never result in a victory.

I would add that I do not feel that I'm forsaking my country. I believe we have the right to protest. I feel amiss that those in the upper middleclass were so late in being called up. Perhaps, if we had been called up earlier, we would not be in this war, or, at least, this war would not have been escalated in such a fashion as it has. That is because the upper middleclass control the country—and, if their sons had been killed off like the poor Negroes and the poor whites and slum-dwellers, then there would have been dissent, more of it, and earlier. As it is, the poor suffered for many years, until their numbers didn't supply the quota for an escalation. Then, Johnson pulled us into it with the draft, and finally, there was dissent by those who could control the news-media and get the attention of the administration.

At any rate, I don't think this war can do much damage to me.

Death is not my foremost fear. But I do fear the despotic nature of our society—not so much because historically it is different than any other society, or, for that matter, because I resent it—but just because I feel that all that so many people cherish and so many have slaved over, quite literally, may blow up in the next few years, right in their faces. That is what I fear, although, even to me, it seems inevitable. It is happening, little by little with one protest march here, with one burnt draft card there, with another protest there, another march on Washington, and right now, all of us divided against one another.

Where I will end up I'm as unsure as any of my friends. I have applied to law school. I do have an interview at Vanderbilt. But going there does not preclude my ultimate decision about this war, since my status would remain 1-A.

Ah, well, I have to prepare for graduation, study for

finals and send applications to the law schools you suggested—to Northwestern and, because of Mr. Warren's connection, to Vanderbilt, although I'm not too keen about the South.

I'm grateful for the chance to go to Ashbury. I have worked and learned in these last four years. I thank you for the opportunity. I intend to keep learning and hope that through knowledge and faith in God, if there is one, and mankind, I may be open to whatever life demands of me. In time, I may grow more hopeful about our future as a nation as hours pass into years and I gray at the temples, and my youth fades into reminisces.

Meanwhile, I face another test, the draft and the bitter smell of an empty shell in a rifle.

I shall let you know what I decide as I determine what is best to do. I look forward to seeing you at graduation.

Love, Jason

Several days later, my father called me and told me that he read the letter and that it was well written. He was, however, very disappointed in me and would talk about it later when he came down for my graduation. "Suffice it to say," he said, "no son of mine is going to renege on his obligation to serve his country in a time of war." After I hung up the phone, I was beside myself. But at the same time I got an unexpected phone call from Doug, my former high school friend, long lost, on whom I'd had a crush He wanted to visit me since he had been called up as 1-A and he was shipping out to Vietnam. He said he needed to talk. He had something to tell me.

Taller and lankier than I remembered him, as well as much more muscular and fit than he had been as a teenager, Doug came to visit me on a Thursday, late in the afternoon. He had to report on Saturday for deployment. Vietnam. I greeted him with a hug. He came up to my room where we had an awkward discussion. He told me that the army claimed that the war was not really to save Vietnam from communism but to contain Red China from expanding its hegemony in the region. I asked him why the government did not say that was the policy. He had no answer. He told me, if I could avoid it, I should not enlist. He feared that he might never come back. But there was no way out for him. He had to go and hope—because he was bright, because he had a college education— he might get a good assignment away from the front.

As we talked, I sensed that not only did he want to warn me not to go to war, but he wanted to tell me something else, something left unsaid when he had visited me at my house at the end of high school.

"It's really good to see you," he said. He patted me on the knee.

I said, "It is. Glad you came."

We stared at one another. I could feel the old electricity between us, some invisible attraction drawing at us. I could just close the door, I thought. We sat together, him on the bed, me in my desk chair, knee to knee.

"How you been?" he asked.

"Good, doing all right."

"After hearing what I've had to say, you going to enlist?"

"Don't know what to do. What do you think, I mean, what else are they telling you about the war?" I asked. "Don't they have some rationale other than the ones we hear on the news?"

"They don't," he said. "That's what I'm saying. It's smoke and mirrors."

"But why are you going?"

"Got caught. Seems it's my fate. I'll make the best of it."

He leaned back, letting his head rest on the pillows, his legs still on the floor. His long body stretched out, his shirt slightly out. I peered at him. He was lovely, just as I remembered him, but a man now.

He asked, "Do you have a john? I gotta pee badly."

I told him, "Yes, in the hallway, right across from my room."

He went out and opened the bathroom door and left it open, while still talking to me, and so I could see him unzip his pants, pull out his penis—just as I remembered it—and hold it in his hand like a gift, one more glance, one more chance to relive nights we spent together as boys.

"We had good times, didn't we?" he called out.

"Yeah, good times."

"I wish we'd kept in touch."

"So do I."

"You meant a lot to me," he said, shaking off his penis and stuffing it back in his pants.

When he returned to the room, we tried to find something to ignite the conversation, some way to connect, but, since he had to get back to base—he'd driven hours to see me—he asked for a hug and I gave him one, a long one, and that was it: he was gone. His visit consumed an hour, yet I felt a yearning for him as if we'd spent days together. If only he'd had more time. If only I had the courage to say what I felt. I missed him in more ways than one.

Several weeks later, I drove to Chicago to report at the Selective Service for eligibility, which, I was told by Tom, meant an aptitude test as well as physical and psychological screening.

At the induction center, we were herded into a large classroom with old-style student desks, the type with the chair and desk as a single unit. I sat in the last row and was fascinated with the patriotic posters on the walls about war, weapons, and America—Uncle Sam pointed his finger at me, his brow furrowed, with the words "I WANT YOU" in bold print. When the officer handed out an exam, explained what was on the test, and how to answer the questions, I was distracted so by the posters, that when he said, "Go" I had no idea what to do on the exam. The questions did not seem to make sense. I filled them in randomly, thinking, if I flunked, they might toss me out as mentally deficient.

Once we completed the exam, we were segregated into groups of ten and marched from one type of inspection to another. The oddest was the proctology exam. We stripped to our undershorts and lined up. A sergeant ordered us to pull down our drawers and bend over. A doctor proceeded to go down the line, one anus at a time, poking his finger up our butts. After that, we were given the standard physical exam: listening to the heart, tapping the liver and kidneys, and holding our testicles while we coughed.

The final hurdle was the psychological exam. We went into a small booth in turn where a psychologist sat in a metal chair with a small desk that had a form on it. He wore wire-rimmed glasses and had a flat top haircut like Jeff used to have. He asked my name, age, birthday and then if

I had ever had psychological problems—depression, thoughts of suicide. I wanted to tell him, "Yes. Every time I think about being drafted," but said, "No."

"Ever had anal intercourse?"

"What?"

"Anal intercourse."

What was he trying to get at? I wondered. I glanced at the form in front of him. He pulled it back.

"Well?"

"No."

"Good." He continued his inquiry. What did I think about my mother? (I liked her.) My father. (He's okay.) Midway through the exam, he asked, "Are you a homosexual?"

The question stopped me. My mouth fell opened. I had not expected it. Was this a question he asked everyone? Did he know something, or sense something like the other guys did at the fraternity? I felt that I hid my feelings pretty well, covered them with my athleticism and toughness, but here someone was probing again, trying to get me to confess. I hesitated. Sweat beaded on my forehead. They lined up, one after another, like sinners at a confessional.

He glanced at me and moved his jaw back and forth. "You alright, kid?"

"Yeah."

"It's a standard question. Just answer it. Are *you* a homosexual?"

I tightened my lips and said dryly, "No."

He peered at me over his glasses and smiled. "Good."

He asked other questions about my family, my stress level, and my health. When we had completed the exams, we were given a card that, in my case, was a passport to the military. It felt like one of those Chance cards in Monopoly: free pass, do not collect 200 dollars, go directly to the nearest army base and war zone. I felt cornered. I wondered if I took enough pills—but what ones?—I could end it and let a dull haze draw over me like a soft blanket. Suicide never seemed an option, but I hated what I was feeling and wondered if that was what dad's mom felt in 1936—cornered, driven to her limit. I detested living in between, caught in feelings I did not want and decisions I dreaded making. I wanted a way out, any way I could find.

I drove back to school since I had an exam in New Testament theology. I tried to blot the thoughts of being in the service from my mind, but I feared I didn't have the courage, despite my letter, to refuse induction. Although I might make an awful soldier, I imagined that I *could* do it, get into it, just as I had with football and golf, and to marshal what was in me to be a fierce warrior. Violence had been bred into me as an athlete. And yet I had come to see that we ourselves were as much the enemy as those Vietnamese whom we called communist and probably, if they were asked, would not even know what the term meant.

A Special Night

During the New Testament exam, Dr. Eigenbrodt, came over to my desk, knelt by it, and whispered that I'd hadn't turned in the final essay on the passage from Matthew.

"I had to go to Chicago for my induction," I said.

"Oh, that's too bad. I'm sorry." he said. "Get it to me soon."

He did not seem distressed that my paper was late. He kept kneeling by my desk and whispered even more quietly, "I'd like you to come over for dinner Friday. Five o'clock. Can you make it?"

"Sure," I said.

"Good," he smiled and pressed his hand on my arm.

A student beside me whistled, nodded his head, and commented, "That's real cool man!" I asked him what he meant. He explained that Eigenbrodt asked only his six best students to his end-of-the-school-year dinner, which was an amazing event, since Eigenbrodt, a gourmet cook, made a three course meal and everyone wanted to be invited: it was a big honor. Six of his best students and I was one. I couldn't believe it.

When I arrived at his small green clapboard house, I thanked him for inviting me and, as my mother had told me to always bring a gift, gave him a bottle of white wine. He told me not to call him Dr. Eigenbrodt this evening, but to use his first name: John. I noticed five other students that I knew—three from my Old Testament class, two from my boarding house who were antiwar activists.

"What would you like to drink?" Dr. Eigenbrodt asked.

"A beer is fine," I said, taking a seat. The other students were discussing the shortcomings of Christianity, how the whole belief system in most churches was not based on the actual doctrine but on conformity, on making people feel good. Anne, one of the student leaders who had spent four days sitting in the girls dorm with a mix of twenty other girls and guys to protest same-sex dorms, was ranting about the system, how fucked up it was and, right in the middle of her harangue, she turned to me and said, "Hey, Jason, you're a member of that DAE fraternity, right?"

I said, "Yeah, afraid so."

"Well, isn't that place full of mommy's boys, wanting to do what mommy and daddy tell them to do?"

"Surprisingly, that's not entirely so," I countered. "Some of them, yes, are jerks. But some of them are as active as you are. Eric, for example, founded our chapter of SDS."

"He's a DAE?" she exclaimed.

"Yep.

"Fuck, I need another drink," she said. "Hell, I need heavy medication! I don't believe it. The fuckin' world is coming apart."

The conversation ranged from the March on Washington to Von Rad's ideas about the Old Testament being a compilation of various religious traditions to Robert Kennedy's ideas about change. We were talking about ideas. We were not just blabbering about the weather, golf, or relatives. We were engaged in serious discussion about significant issues. Although I had serious conversations with students at meetings, in the philosophy seminars, and one on one, I'd never been to a party where serious conversations were the norm. I liked it. We drank for an hour before sitting down to an elegant meal with home-made pasta, three different colors— white, green, and red— with pesto; a salad filled with artichoke, tomatoes, feta cheese, and pecans; green beans with almonds; and more wine and more beer—and conversation, intelligent conversation with people disagreeing and changing their minds when someone made a cogent point. After the meal, John told us to sit around the Steinway piano. Anne whispered, "He is a concert pianist."

He said, "I am going to have you play a game of music charades. I will play a short piece and you will have to guess who it is. It is not some celebrity. It will be one of you."

Everyone laughed, probably because we all felt slightly embarrassed that, in a few seconds, he might be revealing something about us that we did not know. When he played, he did manage to interpret the nuances of each person: how Anne's personality blew hot and cold, full of intense chords and quiet melodies; how Sam, the brain of the group who had memorized Eliot's "The Waste Land," sprawled across the range of notes, becoming more and more convoluted, with themes coming back and overlapping as his mind did when he spoke. When he came to me, he played a soft tender melody, a gentle quiet fugue that built in intensity and then grew quiet again, spilling over into a lovely melody that sounded like a love song (and was, I later discovered, from the ballet *Romeo and Juliet*). By the time he finished, we felt as if someone had caressed us with music.

I went to dinner at his house again a week later. Just me and another student, and, another time, when John had to go away for the weekend with another professor, I stayed at his house—there had been some robberies in his neighborhood— to watch it for him.

When he came back on Sunday night, he dashed through the door arm in arm with Dr. Jamison, who taught French History. Dr. Jamison looked startled when he saw me and let go of John's arm. They had been laughing about something and stopped while John introduced me—telling me to call his friend by his first name, Jackson.

I smiled and shook Jackson's hand. He gazed at John quizzically.

"It's quite all right, Jackson," he said. "Jason is quite reliable. Like you, he likes poetry. And he had a major in history."

John poured us wine, and we talked about Richard Nixon's campaign slogans, how he used fear and racism to rouse voters to his side. Jackson cozied next to John, occasionally kissing him on the cheek. John winked at me and said, "This is probably the only time you'll see history and religion being wholly compatible."

I didn't know why he felt comfortable letting me see their obvious affection for one another, but I felt honored and never told anyone about it. But I liked seeing him with another man and being uninhibited. The sudden realization that a homosexual could be happy startled me. If John and Jackson was a couple, they were, indeed, happy together. They were the first that I had known.

Dead End

In the weeks before I graduation, I felt as if my life had come to a stone wall—either I enlisted or I had to flee to Canada or something worse. I was sitting on the steps in Stevens Hall, moping, feeling I had no real choices. The hall, empty, all students gone to dinner, felt like a sanctuary. I wanted to come to a decision and be done with it. As I sat there, I saw John come rushing up the stairs two at a time, his long jacket flapping behind him. He wore a silk scarf around his neck. He hopped by me and then, when he realized it was me, stopped and turned, catching his breath.

"Is something wrong, Jason?" he asked.

"It's too hard to explain," I groaned, rocking back and forth next to tears.

He slid down next to me, cocked his head, and said, "Try me."

I explained my dilemma. He listened intently. I told him that I had an interview at Vanderbilt Law School, but, even if I got in, I was 1-A and I would be drafted and I could not go to a war I thought was immoral and yet what else could I do? My parents would disown me if I refused to go. I had no money, no idea what type of work I could get. I was trapped. I admitted I even thought of suicide.

He put his hand lightly on my knee and, in a very quiet voice, said, "I have a way out."

"What?"

"First, come to my office. I need to make a phone call." Once inside his office, he offered me a cup of coffee, which I drank, then he sat down and said, "Sit down. Take a breath."

"I can't."

"Give it a try. I'm going to make a call. The Dean of Vanderbilt Divinity School. He's a dear friend and colleague. When you are at Vanderbilt, go see him."

I balked immediately and told him, "No, it wouldn't work."

"Why, may I ask?"

"Well, pure and simple, I have no interest in being a minister. I'm not sure I even believe in God," I explained.

He laughed and informed me that I did not need to become a minister or believe in God. I could study anything I wanted and, later, teach or do something else with the degree.

"But I don't get," I said. "How that will help me?"

"It is simple: 4-D status," he exclaimed. "When you go to divinity school, you get a 4-D status automatically, which means you are no longer 1-A and cannot be drafted,"—he smiled and nudged me in the arm—"which is to say there are some advantages to studying about God, even if you don't believe in Him!"

I laughed and he put his hand on mine, "Willing to give it a shot?"

I nodded. He picked up the receiver and dialed. He spoke to Dean Harrelson. There was some back and forth banter. Then John told him what he wanted.

"I have a student here, an excellent student, who is interested in the Divinity School. He's going for an interview at the law school. Yes, at Vanderbilt. I think that he'd make a fine student. He's been involved in the antiwar movement, has taken my advanced classes and writes poetry."

There was a lull. John nodded. He gave me a thumbs-up. Dr. Harrelson said, yes, he would be delighted to meet with me. Before I left, John scooted close to me.

"Listen, Jason," he said, "I know you feel at loose ends. But you have some cards you can play. You are an excellent student—have a good mind—for studying theology and, besides, you enjoy it. Keep an opened mind. Sometimes the path you end up taking is not the one you expected to take."

He patted me lightly on the shoulder.

"Go on, get something to eat," he said.

I thanked him, headed to the house to see if dinner was still being served and planned my two day trip to Vanderbilt.

My parents wanted me to go to law school, so I made no mention of the Divinity School. In fact, I tried to blot it out of my mind. I knew that my dad might pull the financial plug if I didn't get into law school. His finding out that I might go to Divinity School might be the last straw. Although I wanted to make my own decisions, I did not have the financial resources to pay for graduate school on my own. I hated how I felt beholden to my dad. I resented the pull of pleasing my parents and how it still dominated my own thoughts. Much as I wanted to stand on my own, to be proud of my own opinions, I did not want to disappoint them. They had supported my going to school. But, in the back of my mind like a riptide current, tugging me in a completely different direction was my opposition to war and my disdain for their way of life, a way of life that no longer seemed to lay before me as it had for most of my life yet kept pulling me toward it and away from my antiwar feelings, so that, at any given moment, I was pulled in one direction and then another, casting back and forth in the surf of my indecision.

I had my doubts about going to Divinity School; being with a bunch of ministers just made no sense. I'd never been as closed-minded as my father about religion, who said that he could not believe what he could not see, but I'd never been sold on the idea of God, some fellow out there who can pull the strings and, lo-and-behold, the miracle happens. So I decided to focus on the law school interview, hoping, if that went well, I could then figure out how to avoid the draft after I got into law school.

The Interview

On a Thursday, I drove to Nashville, located Vanderbilt and found a DAE house on campus where I'd been told I could crash during the night. A member of the house, Clark, who had come to Ashbury to finish his last semesters since he had been put on academic probation at Vanderbilt, had driven down with me. He introduced me to his friends and we partied much too late, until one. I went to bed thinking, *I'm not in good shape for the interview, but at least I'm here and I'll give it my best shot.*

I felt apprehensive about the interview, even with Mr. Warren, who was on the board of trustees at the law school and had written a letter of recommendation for me. My dad told me that if he wanted me in—and he did—I was a shoe-in, *if* the interview *went well.* Just those three words "went well" and "if" hung like an albatross around my neck.

The next morning, I sauntered across campus, trying to compose myself by wandering among the luscious magnolia trees with their white, effusive flowers. At 9 a.m. a professor, Dr. Hedgeworth, invited me into his office. Clearly not wanting to waste his time, he riffled through my transcripts and reference letters. He made no eye contact, while he was asking questions about my goals, my interest in law and, then, suddenly he drew his attention to my relation with Jake Warren, the President of Sears and Roebuck, and asked, pointedly, if I knew that he was a member of the trustees at the law school.

I said, "Yes, my father had told me."

He inquired, "Why is it that you chose Vanderbilt over other law schools, say ones, closer to where you lived in the North?"

"I was told it was a good school," I responded.

"By Mr. Warren?"

"Yes."

"Figures," he said.

He paged through my transcript, putting his finger on something.

"You took a lot of religion courses here. You want to be a minister or something?" he asked, pressing his glasses up on his nose.

"No."

"Well, why bother with a course in Old Testament theology, and..." he looked at the course, "New Testament if you're not going to be a clergyman?"

"I enjoy studying theology."

"You do?" he said, paging through my transcript.

"Yes," I said.

"Oh."

Not impressed with my transcript, he tossed it on his desk and leaned back in his desk chair, folding his fingers together tip to tip over his chest and said, "I suspect you may be able to cut it here. But I must caution you that we do not nurse incoming students: they need to be able to do the work or they go. We have very high standards" — he wrinkled his nose as if he'd detected a bad smell and repeated himself—"very high. We don't just pick students from a hat; we pick the best of the very best."

His Southern drawl drew out the 'e' in "very" and "best" so that they sounded as if they had an importance that he wanted me to understand. And I did: I was not among the very best. I merely had a member of the board of trustees who had some pull with admissions.

I nodded my head and, feeling I needed to impress him, told him that I had taken a British Law class and enjoyed it and thought I would do well in law school, since it had always been my life goal, but my response did not matter since, during my speech, he focused his attention on my transcript that sat distantly on his desk. He never once glanced at me. I became anxious and began to sweat. When he did look up, he smiled weakly and asked, "Is it too warm in here for you?"

"No, sir," I managed to say.

"Do you have any questions of me?"

Quite aware that I was taking his valuable time, and also feeling inordinately self-conscious—so much so I was sweating even more profusely so that my shirt was becoming drenched, the stains visible underneath my armpits, I said, "No. I do appreciate your taking the time."

Without standing up, he peered over his glasses and, waving the fingers of his left hand to dismiss me, said, "Well, then, my boy, we're done," and, as an afterthought, added smugly, as I was walking out the door, "Oh, *do* give my best to Mr. Warren, will you?" drawing out every vowel he could so that his Southern pedigree was in full feather.

I looked back at him, and he smiled at me as if he just sealed a lawsuit against me for 100,000 dollars and knew damn well I could not fork over the money.

Feeling utterly defeated, I walked down the hallway out the glass panel doors and into the morning air. I decided to go back to the DAE house and, if I could find Clark, see if he wanted to get drunk again. My fate was sealed; I thought I'd have to enlist and take my chances. I just could not leave the country. I'd have to see, if, once I was enlisted, I could somehow opt out of Vietnam. My dad would be upset that I bungled the interview. Muttering to myself, *damn, shit, god damn*, I wandered up a slope toward the DAE house. I had no doubt Clark would like to drink: he never missed a chance to imbibe. I'd get so drunk this time and see if I could forget what was in store for me.

I stopped by a stone wall and sat on it. The sunlight dappled through the trees above me. Maybe I should go to the Divinity School, I thought. Eigenbrodt might be right: it was an alternative. But I had no idea where it was. It was probably across campus. I'd check into it later. I was still hungover and hungry. All I knew is that I was at the end of the road. I needed to get something to eat. Craig would know of a good place to eat. Breakfast. Eggs. A butterscotch milkshake.

On the way back to the DAE house, I had to go around, or though, a large brick building. As I was coming up to the building, another student— a handsome guy with long brown hair—in front of me opened the door and asked, "Going in?" Seeing now the door was open and how beautiful his eyes were, I walked in. He chatted with me briefly, but then, he hurried up the stairs since he was late to an ethics seminar. He'd left me in a hallway lined with huge paintings of distinguished looking men, white-haired men, with robes and purple and red sashes. Fascinated —they looked erudite and kind—I read the name plates to determine who they were. As I was reading one of the name plates, a voice asked, "Can I help you?"

Caught off guard, I turned to see a tall man with wire-rimmed glasses and a large round face, not unlike the faces of the men in the paintings.

"Oh, no, not really. I just was wondering who these guys were," I said.

The Interview

Taking his time, he told me who each of them were: Deans of the Divinity School, starting with one at the turn of the century.

I was shocked and blurted out, "Is *this* the Divinity School?"

"Yes, it is," he confirmed.

"That's a coincidence. My professor back at Ashbury told me I should come here and meet the Dean, a Mister..."—I floundered because I could not remember his name—"a Mister."

"Harrelson?"

"That's it!"

"And is your professor Dr. Eigenbrodt?"

"Yes."

"Then you must be Jason Follett," he said.

"How do you know?"

"I'm Dean Harrelson," he said, reaching out to shake my hand. "John tells me great things about you. Do you have some time? Shall we talk? You can come down to my office."

"Sure."

He placed his arm across my shoulder as we walked down the hallway, speaking to me with the frankness and openness of an old acquaintance. Once we entered his office, a spacious room with a conference table at one end and his desk at another, he offered me a coffee, which I accepted and which he poured from a pot on a sideboard. We sat in two comfortable leather chairs that were stationed in front of his mahogany desk and talked of the antiwar and civil rights movements and discussed the two theologians whom I'd studied at Ashbury. We discussed the Old Testament and how Eichrodt believed that the covenant relationship was central to understanding the Old Testament and how Von Rad believed that the confluence of the different religious and myths into one story was the strength of the Old Testament. Dr. Harrelson knew both men personally and thought their work was central to any study of the Old Testament. He informed me that he was an Old Testament scholar, and said that I might like to take his class when I came to Vanderbilt. I thought it odd that he spoke about my coming to school there because I had not even applied. When he inquired about my interest in studying theology, I admitted that I really had no interest in being a minister. He raised one eyebrow and said,

418

"Well, Jason, neither did I. The study of history, theology, and archeology really captured my fascination. So don't worry about that."

He went on to explain that the Divinity School accepted students with very different career ambitions. He told me about the program to immerse students in the community, to confront the real social issues—racism and poverty—in Nashville. He admired my commitment to the antiwar effort and agreed with me. I'm not sure how many hours passed before he asked, "Would you like to come to school here?" I instantaneously responded, "Sure, that would be great." He had his secretary get some paperwork, which I filled out, and told me what he needed additionally. He explained that this was not the standard way of applying to the school and of accepting a student., but he had some prerogatives as a Dean, and he would make the exception in my case. After we finished, he put his arm around my shoulder again and said, "You will find that what we are doing here intellectually, morally, and personally is in line with what you want to do. I'm pleased that you will be here."

When I walked across campus, I felt as if someone had put wings on my feet. I raced back to the DAE house, gathered my overnight bag, thanked Clark for putting me up for the night and drove back across Tennessee, to Kentucky, to Indiana, to Ashbury, and to my room, thinking that, at least for several years, I would have a place to go and some time to ponder what I wanted to do with my life. The weight of the war had been lifted off of me. I called my dad, fearing what he'd say.

"Dad, I got accepted at Vanderbilt?"

"I'm delighted," he said.

"But not the law school, the Divinity School," I said.

I could hear his breathing on the other end of the line. I waited to hear what he would say.

"I see," he said.

"Is that all right with you?" I asked and fingered the dial plate of the phone.

"Is that what you want to do?" he replied.

"Yes."

"Then, I'm pleased for you," he said. "But the draft..."

"Dad," I interrupted. "If I go to Divinity School, I have a 4-D."

"What?"

"It's a deferment you get when you attending a theological seminary."

He laughed. "Well, that is, as they say, like killing two birds with one stone!"

"Yes, I suppose it is."

"Congratulations," he said. "I suspect that takes a load off both of our minds."

I said, "It does."

When I hung up the phone, I did a jig around the room, prancing back and forth. When I sat down, I opened my textbook on the New Testament.

Goodbyes

The final weeks of school were crammed with rehearsals for the graduation ceremony, finishing final papers and saying farewells. It was difficult to stay focused on any one thing. The DAE house had an ongoing party any time of day with a keg in the basement. My friends in my boarding house were stoned much of the time. I wandered between the beer and pot, trying to numb my feelings that I'd come to an end, that a part of my life was over. Fortunately, several of my friends wanted to spend time with me and that helped assuage my sense of loss, of doors closing. Tom came over to my room several nights and I pulled out a fifth of Jack Daniels for old time's sake. The first night, we got drunk and hit golf shots out of the window and onto into the sorority's lawn and lay around in my bed, sipping from our glasses, reminiscing and talking about our plans.

"What's with your becoming a minister?" he asked.

I laughed. "Who said I was becoming a minster?"

"You're going to a theological seminary, right?"

"4-D."

"What?"

"If you are in seminary, you get a deferment, a 4-D status."

"Way to go!" Tom gave me a high-five and slapped my hand. "I didn't figure you for a minister."

"I do like theology. I enjoy studying religion. And, you never can tell, I may end up teaching it, who knows," I said, offering him another glass of our standard Jack Daniels.

"Well, pray for me. I'm one fucked-up guy."

"No, you're not," I said, perplexed by his self-deprecating comment.

"More than you know," he said. "Hey, maybe I'll apply for CO. I've not been much for war."

"Not easy to do. But you could claim to be an alcoholic. I'd vouch for you," I said.

"Thanks. Nothing like a loyal friend," he said.

I asked him what he planned to do. He said that he was going to work for Nelson Rockefeller, to be a campaign aide.

But then he said that he had something important to say and hoped it would not upset me. He mentioned that Timothy, the art student, was coming East with him and they were going to get a place together. Timothy was also planning to work on Rockefeller's campaign.

"Why would that upset me?" I asked.

He said, "Well, I should have told you sooner, much sooner."

"Your mending fences with him is no big deal," I said. "I'm glad you will have a friend with you. He seems like a nice guy."

"He is, real nice."

Fidgeting with his drink, running his finger around the lip of his glass, he took a deep breath and looked at me. "I suppose I should tell you, you being my best friend, best friend ever... " he said, hesitating for a second, biting on his lower lip, "I've been seeing him..."

I interrupted him. "Seeing him?"

"Yeah."

"It sounds like you're dating!"

He grinned. The wind from the window caught his hair and it fell over his forehead. He brushed it back.

"Sounds weird, doesn't it?" he said.

"You mean two guys dating?"

"Yeah, you ever know a guy who was dating a guy?"

"No, not that I know of..." I said but hesitated because I met Dr. Eigenbrodt's friend and because I sensed Tom was steering the questions in a direction, so I added, "Unless, that guy is you."

"You got it," he said, looking at me with his eyes squinting and his head cocked to the side, querulous, concerned how I was reacting to the news.

"Oh," I said.

"Are you surprised?" he asked.

"Yeah, I am." I said. "I mean you seemed to be the biggest stud in the house. I always envied you. I..."

"You thought I'd had all those girls, all the ones I'd take to motels on weekends."

"Yeah."

"Well, I did!" He laughed. "I did."

"And..."

"There is something about Tim, something I can't name, but, after Linda, I just never felt right with any girl although I damn well tried and, I must admit, had a good time trying. But with Tim, it felt right. I suppose it's something you'll never understand."

"Fuck!" I said, gulping down my whiskey.

"You all right?" he asked, noticing my fidgeting with my glass, twisting it in my hand.

"I'm not sure."

"What *are* your thinking?"

"I'm not sure I'm thinking anything," I said. I wanted another drink—that was for sure. I poured another glass full. He smiled and poured himself a glass.

"What are you feeling?" he asked.

"Confusion," I said.

"Here's to confusion." He tapped my glass and laughed.

"Confusion," I echoed, laughing too. My face felt flushed. I felt sweat creeping across my forehead. *Damn*, I thought. *This is too much. Too close.*

He leaned over and gave me a hug. "I knew you'd understand. You're the only one I dare tell this to."

"I'm glad you did," I said, thinking to myself how anyone could do what he was doing. I could not imagine it. What would people say? What would his parents say? How would he get a job? Questions raced through my head, but I blotted them out and listened to his story.

He talked about how he came to understand how he felt attracted to Tim, and how he planned not to tell his parents, to say they were just rooming together and let what happened happen. He admitted that he had no plans for the distant future. He'd work on the Rockefeller campaign and find some way to avoid the war.

We drank more than we usually did and took a long walk out of town, back to the quarry where, late at night with only the moon as light, we stripped and swam together, paddling out into the middle of the pond, letting the milky moonlight drape an invisible cloak over our bodies. I felt an enormous sadness and I suppose he did, too. The water seemed to quell it, allowing it to dissipate in the recurrent circles of water that eddied out of our hands. We swam side by side, doing the breaststroke out into the middle of the quarry, letting the moonlight settle in around us like an embrace. After treading water for a while, we swam to shore and sat on the slab at the edge of the water where he had taken photographs of me—which I'd never seen. Both naked, we held onto each other, just rocking back and forth. His body, warm and muscular, clung to mine. I felt his chest breathing in and out. The ache inside me seemed to swell. I'd never told him how I felt for him, and now, after he told me about Tim, I supposed I never would. I knew that he was a friend when I desperately needed one. We dressed silently and walked back to campus. Somehow I knew that I would never see him again.

He whispered, "I'm sorry."

I asked, "For what?"

"For deceiving you."

"Oh, that doesn't matter. I mean, what matters is that we were..." I caught myself, "we *are* best friends," As I told him that, I realized that I was already putting our life together in the past. He asked that I keep what he told me, his disclosure, between us and I did. But it was not just between us, because it fell on me like an enormous weight of something bigger than either of us. It seemed as if he'd done a cannonball in the water and its wake had enveloped me so that I was still reeling, trying to keep above water that was spilling me out of the pool in a direction I never expected to be taking.

Questions came over me: If he was going to live with a guy, what did that mean about me? Did he feel the same about me? If he did, why had he never told me? Why had I never put the pieces together—they were certainly there: the private club, the lime cologne, the nights at Tim's room, the affection after our drunken nights. I shirked them off, thinking that I would worry about finding answers another day. I was glad that he told me his secret. It made me feel better to know. I wasn't the only one who felt as I did. That was good to know. But his confession came at the wrong time. With school ending and the goodbyes, I had so much to figure out in these last days. I had to make plans for the next year, get a place to live and decide how I could support McCarthy's or Kennedy's campaign, depending on how the last primaries went.

"You sure you are all right?" he asked, putting his arm around me.

"I think so," I said, letting myself sink into him for a moment.

"We better get back," he said.

"Yes, lots to do. Not much time," I said.

Slowly, dragging out each moment with each step, we sauntered back toward campus. But Tom seemed to have drifted off in his own reverie, not saying a word. He paused when we approached Delta Tau Delta fraternity. In the floodlights, we watched two guys coming out, carrying suitcases to cars. Their fathers and mothers, like ants in a row, were lugging armfuls of shirts and boxes. I remembered that I had not yet boxed all my books and started to pick up my pace toward the DAE house.

"Wait," he said, grabbing me by the arm.

"What?" I asked.

"I've been thinking that I need to make another apology."

"It's okay, I told you. I'm..."

"I know you're fine. But I'm amazed that you are. You may not know it, but I heard the rumors your freshman year about you being a homosexual. I was in the room when guys brought it up. I was there that night when Sean and Bill accused you. And I said nothing," he said, not looking at me, his eyes cast to the trees above us where the floodlights caused the leaves to shimmer and dance in the light.

"What could you say?" I asked.

"I could have said that they had the wrong guy. But I was scared. I wanted to say something, but finked out," he said. "I knew you were different. I knew you better than they did. You're a loner. But you're straight. I didn't say a thing."

I kicked at a broken branch on the ground. His bringing up that night caused a knot to tighten in my stomach, a knot that bound me to it and contained my own inner secret encased in my own dread and fear. I'd managed to forget it, to wipe it from my mind—my primitive terror. The wind rustled the leaves above us. Several limbs nudged against one another. A squeak. A moan. Silence.

"Jason, did you hear me?"

"I did. It's just hard to go back there. It seemed my life stopped back then."

"Well, I know you're not..."

"Thanks. I appreciate it." I said abruptly. "There's not much we can do about it. That's over."

"Yeah, it is and I'm sorry." He walked over to me and gave me another hug. I could feel that he was crying, a contained gasp with intermittent sobs, and I held onto him. I was not sure if he was crying for me, what had happened to me, or for him, what had become of him, but I pressed him next to me. The wind flirted with the leaves. Car lights licked across us. Several cars went by, the faint sound of their radios and of tires on the pavement and the sight of the tail lights, red, blinking in the dark. Several girls passed by on the other side of the street, arm in arm. When he let go, he shrugged.

"Sorry. I'm a mess."

"It's fine," I said. "It's fine."

As we approached the house, I reassured him that his secret would be safe with me and, after leaving him off, headed back to my room across campus to put my books in boxes and pack up my clothes, my own heart feeling as if all the blood had been squeezed out of it and it was empty, beating on in its emptiness.

The day before graduation, Paul asked me if I wanted to go for a walk and I told him that I did but worried that he too might have a confession to make. He didn't. We went to the burial ground for the confederate flag, and he took out an envelope and told me to read what he'd written. It was some words from Dr. King's speech in Memphis—"I have seen the Promised Land. And I may not get there with you, but I want you to know, tonight, that we as a people will get to the Promised Land."

Paul said, "Those were his last words and I thought this would be as good a place as any to bury them." I handed him back the paper and he sealed it in an envelope. He pulled out a serving spoon and dug a hole a few inches deep and laid the envelope in it. Not a religious person, at least not a churchgoer, he knelt down and put his head in his hand. Instinctively, I knelt down, too.

"Damn," he said in a voice choked with pain. "Damn."

I glanced over at him and his face was filled with tears, steaming down. He tried to wipe them away but they kept coming and I found that I was crying, too. For what, I was not sure, but I knew that so much had been lost in these last months and, if there was any hope, any lone voice carrying on the message of hope, it was Senator Kennedy, but I also knew that his campaign, good as it was, was likely to run smack into the Democratic establishment, and his victory would not come easy. Deep down, I realized, too, I was weeping for Tom, and for me, for all we had not said, for all he knew and I knew that would never be said.

"I wanted to come here," Paul said, catching his breath, "because what we did back then, how you joined me... I think you really didn't understand what we were doing with the flag—did you?"

I shook my head, for I knew he was right; I'd made a stand but had no real idea what it meant. I trusted him and went along. Later I was glad I'd done it because somehow it absolved what I did to Joseph that horrid night. Doing right did not obviate that wrong, but it did give me hope that there were better angels in my heart and I could follow them.

"Well," he continued. "I appreciated that you trusted me and went along because in my life it was the most important thing that I have ever done. You know what I mean?"

I reached over and squeezed his hand.

"Yeah, it is for me, too." What we'd done would endure as a touchstone, something I could look back on with pride. At least, I hoped it would be. Moreover, Paul had stood by me when I had messed up and had stood up for what he believed in the face of brutality and violence, and I was proud to know him, to count him as a friend.

"We just have to keep taking stands," he said, "or else they will kill us off one at a time and nothing of the dream will be left but caskets and tombstones and life will go on as it did, unchanged."

He pushed the dirt over King's words. We stood up and patted the earth down with our shoes.

He told me that he wanted to go to the bar where we had gone the night King was assassinated. We walked the mile, sat and drank. Paul didn't say much beyond that he wanted to stay in touch. I knew that I wanted to keep in touch with Tom, but was not sure since he seemed to have crossed over a line and would be going in a direction that I could not go. But with Paul, we had come through fire and the fire was still within us.

Early on the morning of graduation day, my parents arrived from Glen

Brook and helped me pack the car with my books and clothing. After I gave my landlord a hug, I went over the philosophy office to wish Dr. Compton and Dr. Eigenbrodt for a last goodbye. When I got to Dr. Compton's office, he had me sit and gave me his home address and telephone number.

"Now I expect to hear from you," he said. "You're no longer a student. Consider yourself a friend." Not a man given to touch, he stood and gave me a quick hug.

"You are on a journey, a voyage, and, now that you are on it, you cannot turn back. Learn to trust where it will lead you," he advised me. I started to get teary-eyed and he admonished, "Now, none of that. This is not a goodbye, it is just a farewell and we will meet again, I hope quite often. I want to read your poetry. Someone said you are writing some."

I blushed and admitted that I was trying to, but felt quite inadequate.

"That's where we all start anything worthwhile: feeling inadequate. Competence takes a long time and only after much effort," he said, patting me on the shoulder.

I shook his hand and went down the hallway to Dr. Eigenbrodt's office. The door was open, and he welcomed me in with a handshake. He told me to come by anytime and that he had a room I could use. "You know where I live."

"Yes, of course," I said, thanking him.

"And another thing—since you like poetry," he said and handed me *The Collected Poems of Hart Crane*. "You'll like these," he said. "They're among my favorites. A bit hard to get into, but no harder than Von Rad."

"Thanks."

"Be sure to take a course from Dr. Harrelson," he said.

"I will."

It was as if each of us was waiting for the other to say something, but neither of us knew what it was. He led me to the door. "Stay in touch," he said and held my hand, looking at me intently for a moment and then he said, "Oh hell," and clasped me to him in a full embrace. I held him, too, feeling his body next to mine. He let me go. I could see that there were tears in his eyes. I broke away, not wanting to turn back, and hurried down the hall. My heart ached as if someone had cut it in half.

I went to the DAE house for lunch and said goodbye to some of my pledge brothers, hugging them and telling them I would stay in touch, although I sensed that I would not. Stephen came over and handed me a present.

"What is it?" I asked.

"Open it," he said.

I ripped off the wrapping. It was a recording of T. S. Eliot reading his poems.

"Where'd you get it?"

"Never mind," he said, slinging one arm around my neck and pulling my shoulder to his. "Thanks. You helped me a lot."

I stared at him. He was looking toward the sidewalk. His girlfriend stood not ten feet from us, looking at us. He shrugged, "Got a date," then turned and went off with her.

Left alone in the dining room, I riffled through Crane's poems and found one I liked, but could not entirely understand, and yet it echoed what Dr. Compton had told me in a way.

Infinite consanguinity it bears—
This tendered theme of you that light
Retrieves from sea plains where the sky
Resigns a breast that every wave enthrones;
While ribboned water lanes I wind
Are laved and scattered with no stroke
Wide from your side, whereto this hour
The sea lifts, also, reliquary hands.

And so, admitted through back swollen gates
That must attest all distance otherwise—
Past whirling pillars and lithe pediments,
Light wrestling there incessantly with light,
Star kissing star through wave on wave unto
Your body rocking!
  and where death, if shed,
Presumes no carnage, but this single change,—

Goodbyes

Upon the steep floor flung from dawn to dawn
The silken transmemberment of song;

Permit me voyage, love, into your hands...

I read it several times and felt that, yes, I was wrestling with light and, yes, I wanted to find my own voice, to have a transmemberment of song, and, too, to keep on the voyage, whatever it was, and if only I could find someone whom I could hold as dear, I would gladly glide into their hands with love.

The graduation ceremony itself, set in the common with the blazing heat on us, was anti-climactic. My mother clung to me, her arm in my arm. She was crying and kept saying, "Oh, don't mind me. You're my baby, that's all." My dad took photographs, careful to make each shot count. He took many photographs of me with Tom and Paul, with Eric and Trevor who wanted to be in everyone's photographs, of me with Dr. Compton—Dr. Eigenbrodt had skipped out early to catch, as he did every year, a cross-country train to California.

As my parents and I walked to the parking lot, my father pulled me aside and said, "I'm glad it worked out, son."

"Me, too," I said.

He hugged me and said, "Vanderbilt is a fine school. I'm proud of you."

I lingered in his arms a moment. I knew that we had struggled and that the struggle would not end there, or anytime soon, but sensed that, for now, we'd come to a reconciliation that would hold up and allow us to carry on.

I looked at him as he walked to the car, his blue sports jacket, the white collar of the shirt, the pressed slacks and shoes polished and fine and thought he'd done his best and always looked his best and what more could I ask.

Just as it had four years ago, my parents' car pulled away down Locust Street and out of town, past the lone statue of the WWI soldier in the square, past the cornfields and the gently rolling country, to Glen Brook and to my summer job raking traps on the golf course and to what I thought would be the end of the struggle.

Assassination

Although not working for McCarthy anymore, I kept attuned to the California primary that, if McCarthy won, might give him a good shot at his being the nominee. But my loyalties had shifted to Kennedy whose speeches seemed to come from his heart and inspired me to believe that he could unite the country. I planned to listen to the results on the night of the primary but, with the time difference on the West Coast, and with my having to get up at 5, I went to bed early.

The next morning at 5:30 a.m., I drove to work as the ruddy pinkish rays of the sun peaked above the trees along Roosevelt Road and turned on the radio as usual. Wally Phillips on WGN was saying that Kennedy had been shot. I thought, for a moment, he was speaking of John Kennedy, but then he said Robert, Robert Kennedy. I pulled off the road. Stunned, I sat in the car hearing the replay of Bobby's final words and then sounds of gunshots. Other cars sped by me, men in suits heading to work.

How could they go to work? I thought but I followed them. I went to work, but kept coming in off the course from raking traps to check the news. Eight o'clock no news. Nine, the operation was over. It was successful. He was recovering. His wife was with him. The next twelve to thirty-six hours were crucial. I kept breaking into tears, right there, on the golf course as I shoved and raked back and forth. I felt an ache that seemed to come out of the earth and rise up in me, right into my belly and pour up and out of me as it had when Tom told me about himself. At lunchtime, when I was eating a sandwich, no improvement. Still critical.

I told my boss I had to go home and left work early.

When I came in the front door, my mother asked, "Is something wrong?"

I couldn't believe it. Something wrong? How could she ask that?

I said, "Kennedy has been shot."

"I know that. Is there something wrong with you?"

"Yes. I'm upset."

"It's certainly unfortunate."

"Yes, it is," I said, heading past her. She took my by the arm.

"Aren't you going back to work?"

"No." I said, pulling away from her.

"Do you think it's a good idea?"

"Do you think it's a good idea to assassinate Bobby Kennedy?"

"Honey, that's not fair," she said and walked off to the kitchen. I went to the TV as if it could assuage my fears. But it only confirmed them. Experts pointed to where the bullet lodged, to right by his ear, to the lobe of the brain. Graphic images of the brain, the functions found there, and what senses he would lose if he survived were discussed.

Would he be able to campaign? Would he have his faculties? If he survived? To me that was not an option. He had to survive. The network replayed the chaotic scene in the hotel kitchen.

His face, those last moments, as he looked up at the cameras pointed down at him, seemed to be asking, "Can this be?"

After Sirhan Sirhan pulled the trigger on his .22 caliber handgun at point blank range into the back of Robert Kennedy's head and the busboy Juan Romero crouched beside the injured Senator, holding up his head, I recognized the look in Kennedy's face—it was the face of Che Guevara being propped up by one of the military junta, the mask of death, of the eyes looking into the dark void.

Bobby lingered in a coma for most of the day. I held onto whatever shred of hope I heard. He was breathing. His family was with him. I went back to work. The golfers hit their shots. They drove their carts. The flags on the greens fluttered. The next morning, I heard on the ride to work that he'd died in the night. I raked traps in the circular pattern, row on row of grooves. My back baked and sweat glistened on my body as I tried to keep thoughts from entering my head. Since school ended, I had not bothered to get a haircut and I had let my hair grow. My mother scolded me, but her petitions for me to look as she thought I should—to shave, to get my hair cut— did not matter. Something had snapped inside of me long before that day. The replay of bodies pressed into the kitchen, Kennedy reaching out to shake the hands of staff, a tussle and then the camera jostled, someone yelling, "He's been shot," another screaming, "Get the gun, get the gun" and then my mind went blank. If there was to be a future, it died for me in those words.

For two years, I had gone to meetings, listened to speakers, read in magazines how we as a country were the major arms dealer internationally. We designed, built, sold, and used the most heinous weapons that spared no one—not solider, nor citizen, nor any living creature. At Ashbury University, I had paged through magazines at the library and had read how we were napalming villages in Vietnam, incinerating homes and those inside them in rivers of fire. The Kennedys were culpable. President Kennedy had condoned assassinations in South America and Asia and Cuba. Robert Kennedy had ruthlessly squelched those who opposed his brother's policies. Yet I heard something in his voice, some abiding sense of compassion for those whose voices had been silenced, whose lives had been shattered, whose sons had been slaughtered and whose hopes had been denied. Through his brother's death, from his friendships with the civil rights leaders—and from their taking him to see the impoverished people of this land—and with his listening to antiwar protesters, he came to realize that compassion must prevail over disputation and blame. He may have been a man ruled by ambition, as my father claimed, but I came to trust him and find in him a strong voice for humanity. Looking back, I find his last words still haunt me—" What I think is quite clear is that we can work together in the last analysis and that what has been going on in the United States over a period of the last three years, the division, the violence, the disenchantment with our society, the divisions whether it's between black and white, between the poor and the more affluent, or between age groups or over the war in Vietnam, is that we can start to work together. We are a great country, an unselfish country, and a compassionate country. And I intend to make that my basis for running... I would hope now that the primary is over, that we can now concentrate on having a dialogue... on what direction we want to go in the United States: what we're going to do in the rural areas of this country, what we're going to do for those who still suffer in the United States from hunger, what we're going to do around the rest of the globe, and whether we're going to continue the policies which have been so unsuccessful in Vietnam... I think we should move in a different direction." He articulated in that shining moment a vision that he and many of us held—and he seemingly possessed both the will to make it happen and the heart to persuade others to follow him. I had come to believe in him and I paid a price for it: my belief broke in two.

After work that day, I walked down the road by our house, crossed over into the cemetery and the woods beyond where there was a pond so perfectly circular it seemed someone had circumscribed it with a compass. I sat and watched the sun drip the last paint of sundown on it and the moon slid into its surface like a medallion. I contemplated how I had been mesmerized by the hour by hour news, by detailed analysis of where the bullet entered the brain, by what functions might be left, and by questions about if he should live. Charts and diagrams. Experts and prognostications. Candlelight vigils at the hospital. Hourly updates. Replays. Time tipped back on itself and could not move forward. Then he died. News updates dropped off the air. Scheduled TV programs came back into their time slots, and I was here at a pond. Clouds danced across its surface. I wanted to swim out into it, dive deep inside and hold my breath. But I sat there and let time pass.

Over breakfast the next day, my father said, "It's just as well. He was not electable." My mother said, "It was a pity. He had such a nice family." I turned to my journals and wrote. Nothing I could say could change what had happened, but I had to try to make sense of it.

June, 1968.

After the California primary, Senator Robert Kennedy, the second heir to the Kennedy legacy, was shot in a hotel kitchen. Early this morning, he died and the news played his famous speech in South Africa: "Each time a man stands up for an ideal, or acts to improve the lots of others, or strikes out against injustice, he sends forth a tiny ripple of hope, and crossing each other from a million different centers of energy and daring, those ripples build a current which can sweep down the mightiest walls of oppression and resistance." He's dead. His words and deeds, in the hearts of the despairing, in the minds of the hopeful, across all ages, young and old, will be remembered as I remember them. As a nation, we'll bury

434

him as we did his brother, as we did King, with much pomp and with long lines of those who loved and admired him waving handkerchiefs, waving goodbye.

But what next?

What next?

I have no answers. There are no answers.

Something ended. Another door closed—whatever hope that Kennedy may have inspired died with him. His death cauterized a wound that I had inside me, a wound that would always be there, sealed over but ever raw underneath. It was like Bruce Capel, one day slamming balls over the volleyball net, looking like he exuded all the vitality in the world and a year later, dead. How does one make sense of it?

After dinner that evening, I again wandered down the driveway and across the street to the cemetery. As I passed the headstones and read the dates, I thought how there is probably a headstone somewhere with its dates already inscribed waiting for each of us. I could not fathom how a man at the height of his life, having won his arduous campaign, having spoken of his beliefs about mending the brokenness of our nation, could be plucked out and transported across some mysterious boundary to be among the dead who were to my right and left in the cemetery. So many doors seemed to be opening in these last years, so many questions being asked, so many possibilities opening before us and, with the quickness of a bullet, slammed shut. I knelt by one grave and ran my hand across its marble surface—so cold, smooth— and slammed my fist into it, once, then again, until the pain registered and the blood came and then I sucked the blood, its bitter taste, and cried because there was nothing else to do.

One night, I called Paul, who was equally distressed. He cried, his voice small and weak, but said he was going to carry on. He had worked on the Kennedy campaign and had been there in California with him and now planned to go to the convention in Chicago along with Eric and Trevor to protest the war. He said, "Life is so fucking fleeting. I don't think I'll make it to thirty."

"I feel that way too."

The Line Drawn

At dinner one night at the start of the Democratic convention, I told my dad that I planned to go into Chicago, to join my friends.

"Oh, no you're not!" he said.

"Why not?"

"I'll tell you why not. I will not have my son involved in any protests, that's why!"

My mother said, "Howard, please not at..."

"Yes, at dinner. If you dare go down there, I'll tell you right now, if you go there, consider any financial support for Vanderbilt to be finished," he said, slapping his napkin on the table. "Now, if you'll excuse me." He got up.

"Howard!" my mother yelled. "Please."

He looked at her. "Our family is falling apart. And I'll not have it."

I shoved the roast beef with my fork. My mashed potatoes were cold. My mother put her napkin to her face. I sipped my beer. The front door opened and closed with a bang.

"It's okay, mom. Don't worry."

"I hope so."

I finished the meal and helped her clean the plates.

"What will become of us?" my mother asked.

"We'll go on," I said and hugged her.

After she went outside to find my father, I drove off, not sure where I was going. I ended up by the Illinois River. As a young teen, I spent days on the river with my friend, Doug, who had a Chris-Craft and would take us to an island, where we built a fort and used to pretend we were Indians and skinny dipped. It was Neverland and we were remnants of the lost boys who would never grow up.

But now I was.

When Paul called again to invite me to the protest, I told him that I couldn't because of what my dad had said. Surprisingly, he understood.

"Hey, we all have to figure out what price we will pay," he said. "Your future, it's important."

I felt guilty as I saw the ugly spectacle in Chicago unfold on TV, the police clubbing students, the tear gas, the sirens, the paddy wagons. Several times I drove to the Eisenhower Expressway and headed toward Chicago, but I always turned back. Instead, I spent long hours at the club hitting shots, one after another, until I could land every shot within ten feet of the pin. Instead of coming home for dinner, I ate at the club. I'd play golf until dark and go home to my room. After Humphrey accepted his nomination, Paul called me to let me know that he was heading back East. He asked if I could meet him at the airport.

I was shocked when I saw he had a large gash over his right eye and several bandages on his arms and learned he'd been beaten by the cops— one of the protesters who went through the window at the Hilton. He was discouraged. He thought if Kennedy had been there, he would have reached out to the antiwar protesters and told Mayor Daley to pull back his police force. But now, Paul said, the Democratic Party with its warring factions was ripped in half and the Republicans and Richard Nixon were left with a seemingly righteous message about bringing law and order back to this country. Grief had turned to rage and rage had collapsed in its own incandescent fury, and, exhausted, the fires of hope for change flickered out as did the lives of King and Kennedy. Paul seemed defeated as he boarded his plane for New York, where he planned to teach in the inner city. I didn't hear from him for the rest of the summer, except for a postcard with a cryptic note, "The gyre has turned, the world unloosed. Never turn back."

In those last days of summer, as I played golf and went out with friends to a bar, hunting for girls, I still followed the campaigns. Nixon wrapped up the Republican nomination, the balloons cascading over him as he stretched out his arms, his fingers in a V, knowing that he'd reclaimed his dream of being President. Humphrey darted across the country, the happy warrior, trying to distance himself from the Democratic convention and from Johnson. It seemed like a charade, two men speaking to a country numbed by grief and I turned my back on the campaign and raked the traps, line by line in the sand, and tried to forget what had happened.

The Salesman

Before I headed off to Divinity School, my brother and his wife invited me to a cookout they were having for their friends, young couples that I had heard my parents speak of glowingly, telling me how proud they were of my brother, how his friends were ambitious, buying homes, moving up the corporate ladder, planning families. Their praise was a way of contrasting my brother's friends with the likes of mine who were protesting in the streets, being beat up by police, smoking pot, and giving the finger to the establishment. Jack had been working as a salesman at Sears for several years and had recently gotten a promotion. We didn't agree on much. In fact, we stopped talking about politics long ago when he tried to broach the topic with me one evening of his junior year. He supported our country. He did not oppose the war. He always had, and claimed he always would, vote Republican. He liked Nixon. He believed in prosperity and he wanted it for himself.

The invitation was probably the result of pressure by my parents for him to make an effort to include me more in his life. It was the first time I had been to his new apartment since Barbara and he married in early April, before I graduated from college. I had seen Jack a few times on weekends during the summer, playing golf at the club, but we never socialized much since he was busy in his new career. As a young salesman for Sears, he put in long hours and was saving to buy a house, to settle down, to do what I couldn't imagine doing.

When I arrived at their door, Jack gave me a quick hug, then muttered, "Can't you get a haircut? You trying to look like a reincarnated Kennedy?" and brushed my hair back from my forehead.

I smiled, "You're worse than Mom," but as he kept picking at my hair, I snapped, "Leave my hair alone. I'm no Kennedy. I'm just me. Just leave it be, and, please, no jibes about Kennedy, you know how I felt about him."

"Okay, okay, calm down bro," he stuffed one hand in his pocket as if he were searching for something but took it out with nothing in it. He pointed to the apartment.

"Nice digs, huh?"

"Yeah, you have a nice place."

He smiled at me, but looked agitated, his jaw tight until he whispered, "I need to talk with you later—it's important."

"Sure, whatever," I retorted, still put off by his comments about Kennedy.

Before he could respond, we were cut off by the stentorian noise of the gathered quests in the living room, seemingly all talking at once as they grazed around a bar and nibbled on hors d'oeuvres. I took a deep breath, thinking, "Oh shit, another cocktail party." Having grown up in a household where my parents regularly had cocktail parties and where, as the dutiful sons, we had to mingle with the guests, while offering to refresh their drinks or passing around crackers with sliced cheese or shrimp strangled with bacon, I hated cocktail parties. My initial reaction was to head to some quiet spot and observe the quests as they engaged in the art of small talk and smiled as they listen to other people's prattle. I checked out who was there: at least twenty people spilled from the living room out onto a porch and into an adjacent TV room. This was no small party. This was not going to be easy.

The political divide between my brother and me, however it started, had made our relationship tenuous at best. But he put on an exuberant manner and he took me around his apartment, introducing me to couples who enthusiastically greeted me, nodding because, as I watched him work the crowd, he was selling me as he did merchandise on shelves. "This is my little brother, the one who's going to Vanderbilt." He joked with them, flattered them, make me seem like someone they would naturally want to know, to have as a best friend. I'd never noticed close up his acumen at sales. He could sell anything and now I was the latest product.

Surprisingly, I felt special. I liked being sold. It was something I could never do for myself. But here I was being touted as a guy everyone should know. Despite the fact that I did not want to know any of his friends—they seemed smug and conventional—I began to believe as he did: that I was someone who could be their best friend. I patted people on the arm, asked how they were, noticed what they wore, commented on the snacks, the beer, the pre-season football game on TV. I could make polite conversation as well as anyone, at least for a moment. I could turn on the engine of charm, but it would never last long and, as if by habit, I would stare at people, notice the gloss of a woman's lipstick, the nervous tic of a man who picked at his ear, or the banter about the latest sitcom.

My brother did not quite know how to explain when someone asked, "What does he do?" He told them that I was going to seminary and trailed off, so I rescued him with a lame joke, "Oh, you know, I am one of those radical intellectual types who smashed through the windows of the Hilton." No one laughed. Blank eyes stared first at me, then at my brother, and so, in a desperate gesture, I offered to help cook. Jack pointed to the porch, "That's probably a good idea." I sauntered over to the grill.

Barbara was poking gingerly at some chicken parts as if she was afraid of upsetting them. She greeted me with a kiss. I hadn't seen her since the wedding and she had gained some weight.

"Marriage has done you good," I said, "You look really good."

"You think so?" she asked, tentatively.

"Oh, yes," I said. She looked radiant, her hair combed into a halo of tinted blond hair. We chatted for several minutes and she excused herself to get more hors d'oeuvres while I was left to douse the chicken with barbecue sauce and flip them regularly, until my brother came over to man the grill and told me to go inside, have a good time and enjoy myself. I went back to the living room, but I felt out of place and worried my comments about being radical had put people off.

My mind kept spiraling back to the conversation I had with Paul when he called from the Lincoln Park precinct police station in Chicago after he'd been arrested. "This is the revolution, Jason, and nothing will be the same. You cannot go back to the world that you are used to."

But my commitment to the antiwar effort seemed more a charade now that King and Kennedy were dead. I felt as if I had died with them and desperately wanted to feel as if I were alive again. And so I downed several beers and soon felt woozy and mellow. I munched on scallops wrapped in bacon, five of them, and crackers with anchovies and cucumber, ten of them. The alcohol provided my emotions with an instant vacation, and I felt more like socializing if only just to show my brother that I could do it as well as he could.

I noticed a petite woman with a tight pink blouse eyeing me. She had an intense expression and I liked how she was appraising me as if she was considering what I might offer her. I wondered if she might be propositioning me. She was sitting on the edge of a sofa and leaning forward, exposing her ample breasts. She knew what she was doing. She did it well. I was impressed: a woman who knew how to flaunt her body and enjoyed it.

I wandered over and asked if I might sit next to her. I swung my leg over the arm of sofa and perched on it. She wiggled backward and looked up at me. As we chatted, I discovered that she was a publisher for a sales magazine and her name was Tammy. She grew up in Indiana, not far from where I went to school. We talked about the farmland in southern Indiana, the expansive cornfields broken by gentle streams and occasional sinkholes, the rolling hillsides. She knew about the local folklore, the intense basketball rivalry of two towns I did not know and, as a young girl, had picnicked by a creek not far from the university. Her father had several close friends who were faculty members, but she could not remember their names.

Surprised that I was enjoying the conversation, I asked her, since she seemed articulate and nuanced, and since I wondered if she might be an anomaly at the party—an actual liberal, "Are you against this stupid fucking war?"

"What did you say?" she smirked as if she had misunderstood me.

"Are you against this stupid fucking war?"

"How dare you ask me that!" she retorted, edging away from me. "And, please watch your language."

"Sorry about that. I do random surveys like this—" I offered, trying to smooth over what was clearly a gaffe—"you know, checking what the silent majority thinks."

"I am *not* the silent majority." she upbraided me, "but I *do* support our nation and our President and am not, since you asked, against war and never have been, nor will I be. I have my own opinions," she stated emphatically, "and I keep them to myself and don't impose them on others." Then she turned to face a man who had heard her raise her voice and had seated himself next to her.

"Honey," she said. "This man has insulted me." She whispered something in his ear, then, told me that she believed Barbara might need help and left. Her husband stared at me, at my hair, and in a deliberate manner, jabbed at my chest with his finger, then sneered, "My advice to you, bud, is get a haircut and get a life."

"Oh," I said, "that's original."

He stood, gave me a look of contempt, and left to get another beer. I flashed him the finger.

I was alone on the sofa. I gazed at the TV which had a football game on, the Chicago Bears and Dallas Cowboys. The Bears were at mid-field on a drive. The score was tied seven to seven. Without my effort I could have pulled an invisible cloak over myself, but in my half-drunken state I convinced myself that I should make an effort to engage with other guests, even if my first attempt did not pan out too well. I went over to the tub and fetched another beer.

My brother, conferring with the woman with big breasts, glared at me, and then leaned in close to her to finish hearing what she was saying. He spoke seriously to her and whispered something in her ear. She gave him a hug, then smooched him on the cheek and went to the porch to find her husband and put as much distance as she could between herself and me.

My brother strode over to me. A frown dented his forehead.

"*Why* can't you stop your political garbage?"

"I just asked her if she was against the war."

"Do you have to get everyone to think like you do?" His face was red from too much beer. He came closer and whispered in a strident tone, half, it seemed in apology, half in rage, "Listen, I love you, bro. I put up with your long hair, your dressing like some radical SDS freak, but you are in *my* house and so have a little respect. You're way out of line. Okay?"

The back of my neck heated up. I leaned into him, "Lay off your righteousness. And as for respect? Some respect you show. I'm fed up with all your conventional crap, the complacent bullshit, the pretense of this cocktail-party world that goes on indifferently while we napalm one village after another, wiping out a people, in the name of freedom, and no one raises a god-damn finger, no one does a damn thing except to assassinate anyone who asks a god-damn question."

"Don't use the Lord's name in vain," he shot back.

"The Lord's name! You have got to be kidding? You have no use for religion. All you ever worshipped was the almighty dollar."

My brother cupped his hand across my mouth, hushing me, "Shut up, will you?" He flicked his head to the side and I could see that everyone had stopped talking and was staring at us.

"Get out of here," he murmured, pointing to the front door. "Did you hear me? Now. You're creating a spectacle."

I stood up, bowed to his guests, "So nice to meet all you nice people. I must be going. I have a revolution that I am late for. Thank you all for the scintillating conversation and thank you, my brother, for a lovely evening," I took a swing of my beer and strode out.

My brother, at first confounded, stood with his mouth open, but then came after me. Before I got to my car, he pulled me by my shoulder and jerked me around to face him. His fist was drawn back.

"What the hell has gotten into you?" he barked.

I slapped his arm off of my shoulder and looked at him, not sure if I wanted to hit him or shove him away and dismiss him from my life.

"Hey, did you forget? I believe in nonviolence, so drop the fist," I retorted.

He stared at me. "What has happened to you?"

"Happened to me?"

"Yes, happened to you?"

"I happen to be fed up with this life. God, do you not see what has happened to us, to our world? The fuckin' country is torn apart. King and Kennedy assassinated. Are you paying any attention? We're fucked, Jack. We're totally fucked up. Everybody who cares about anyone is killed. No one gives a damn. Not your hoity-toity friends. No one. Our leaders are bankrupt motherfuckers who only care about getting elected and keeping the good-old-boys in power. Do you not get it?"

"You're out of your mind. You've become so caught up in your own thought that you can't think. Listen here, brother: you say I don't know what is happening. That's not it at all. What's happening is that you do not see what is going on in your own family."

His voice rose yet he kept it modulated, never shouting, although it felt as if it verged on being a shout, but a contained shout, so I turned to get away from him. I had no use for him, nor for his so-called friends, nor for his excuses.

"Look at me," he said, moving to get by and stand in front of me, "Stop walking away and look at me. I'll tell you what is happening: Barbara is pregnant and we're going to have a baby and I have to make a decent wage. That's what is happening. So get off your high horse."

"Pregnant?" I gasped.

"Yeah," he said, half-suppressing a smile.

I hugged him spontaneously.

"Why didn't you tell me?"

"Brother, we don't talk about anything. All you talk about and think about is the war and civil rights. Don't you see how far you are so immersed in some other world that you don't know who we are anymore? Mom and Dad don't know who you are anymore."

I took a breath and placed my arm on his shoulder, patting him, pulling him closer to me, drawn into the realization that he was going to become a father, a role I could not imagine. That was big: he had a legacy. His life would carry on beyond him.

He repeated what he had said, "You've alienated everyone around you. Mom and Dad ask me what is wrong with you, why you've become so angry and withdrawn. They don't know who you are. "

"Neither do I," I confessed, "but I do know that I cannot live as I have lived. I cannot go where I have been raised to go. I cannot be who I was raised to be. I must go another way. Can you understand that?"

He stared at me, tears in his eyes, and shook his head.

"No. I don't understand that," he said.

"Well, if you cannot understand it, can you at least accept it?"

"Yes, I suppose I have no choice."

"I don't believe any of us have choices anymore."

He put his hand on the back of my neck, hugging me, and then took a deep breath.

"You're going to go where you go. I just can't go with you. I have a life and I like it. I do."

"Sure you do," I said. "Do you know if it is a boy or girl?"

"A boy," he whispered sadly as if he was telling a secret.

"What is it? What's wrong?" I asked.

"I need your advice. You're the only one I can talk to about this." He took my arm and we walked toward a nearby grove of willows, talking as we went. "She is seven months pregnant."

"Great!" I intruded, "Two to go."

"Not great," he said. "Remember: we were married six months ago. She was pregnant when we got married. What do you think Mom and Dad will think?"

I stopped and turned to face him, "Think? My God, Jack, you are their son, their first son. They'll be happy. Oh, so very happy."

"You think so?"

"Of course. Of course."

"I didn't know who else to talk to. My friends, you know, they are good people. I like them, but many are Barbara's friends, and they're Catholic. You know how that is."

I chimed in, "Well, you could always claim it was an immaculate conception."

He slugged me in the arm tenderly and laughed.

"I love you, bro," he said.

"I love you, too," I said, smiling at him.

We strolled shoulder to shoulder under the willows. He offered to get me another beer, went back in and came out. We sat in the grass and talked about our childhood, his job, his honeymoon. I asked him what he told his guests and he laughed and said that he told them I had some emotional problems.

"Yeah, it's called Vietnam and segregation," I said.

He stared at the willows and said, regretfully, "You know I do see it, bro. I do see it. It's bad and I know there are many things that are wrong. But I can't go there. I just can't. That's how we are different. You can. I do, well, I do what I do. I sell people what they want and sometimes what they don't want but buy nonetheless after I make them see it's what they really need."

I had never heard him be as forthright about what he did. I told him I understood and knew that he was a salesman from an early age. He exuded confidence. He could get any girl to go out with him—even the ones that every guy drooled to date. His smile could crack the stone face of the sphinx into a smile.

He wanted to know if I wanted to go back into the party.

"No thanks. I think I've had enough," I said.

"Good," he said, "I didn't want you to go back!"

We laughed again. It was good to be able to joke about the worlds dividing us. He walked me to my car and as I slid into the seat and pulled out, I felt as if I had gone into the enemy camp, done battle with one of its most fierce warriors, been wounded, and then patted on the back for doing a great job. I stared at him, drink in hand, heading back to his apartment, to the other couples, comfortably talking about pets, children, weather, golf, or the next football season— talking about topics that everyone approved of and would never lead to differences in opinion. I could not help feeling that Jack, Barbara, and their friends were a separate species, worry-free, and content, so alien to the world I inhabited. They knew how to be in style, I thought, how to appear as they should appear: exemplars of happiness and the right life, a life I did not want to live. But I had no idea what life I did want to live. What I would become was still a mystery to me. There remained parts of myself that seemed shrouded in a veil that I as yet had not been able or willing to uncover.

The Lake

I drove off and went to a nearby lake where I could walk by myself and watch the moon lounge on the surface of the water—its enormous weight shining, pressing, moving without disturbing the water, not a ripple, like a good clear, uncluttered mind floating upon the surface of emptiness. Still drunk from the party, I walked toward the shoreline. The lake mirrored the moon, nearly full, that peeked in and out of a few wisps of clouds. The air had cooled. I lay back on the embankment and thought how inviting the water was. I stood up, took off my jacket, undid my belt, tugged off my shoes and stripped, walked down to the water's edge, careful not to slip on the rocks, and stepped out into the lake.

I remembered how Tom and I had done that those last days at Ashbury, how we'd held onto one another. Being with him in the water felt like something sacred and primitive, something that bonded us even as, week by week, we drifted off into our separate lives. It felt like a baptism: immersion in the water, sliding in the darkness that was inside it, slipping into its liquidity, feeling it gradually encase my body.

As I edged my way into the water, I noticed how, the reflected images of the moon and stars began to tremble and shimmer around me. The lake cradled the sky and the sky moved as I moved. I swam out beneath the shadows of the trees with the moon looming over them. As I swam, the reflections moved with me and the shadows seemed to extend outward from me to the middle of the lake. From the shore, a park lamp glimmered on the water and it too would move as I moved. I dove under the surface and looking up could see the luminous fragments of the moon bob along the wake of my dive. It seemed that by being immersed in the lake, I could slide from image to image without hindrance. How elastic it was—the moving, the turning to find the moon trailing along after me as I swam, finally to shore—how seamlessly everything outside me, along with my thinking about it, came together.

But, after I came out of the water, my body cold as I sat shivering on a patch of grass to dry off, I thought how I'd not find it so easy to enter the next part of my life. I would have to find another life. But, as yet, I did not know what it was, nor where I would find it. I could not reenter the life I'd been raised to be in as my brother had. I had to cross over some boundary, as those men I'd most admired crossed over from their brilliant lives to challenge fate, and, even, to face death, and to discover what was on the other side. I knew only that I had enrolled in Vanderbilt Divinity School and had a 4-D status that exempted me from a war. Perhaps while I was there, studying religion, I would discover the life that would be entirely mine.

As Dr. Compton said, I was on a voyage and could not turn back. I may have no compass and no clear and final destination, but that was all right. I dressed and walked to my car and drove home, a home I had for a few more days, before I went off into the life that was waiting for me like the moon out there—waiting in the cool water, deep in the middle of the lake.

About the Author

Bruce Spang, former Poet Laureate of Portland, recently published *Boy at the Screen Door* (Moon Pie Press, 2014). He lives in Falmouth, Maine with his partner Myles and their two labs. He is currently working on his next novel about Jason's years at Divinity School and his work in Appalachia. He's completing a book, *Putting the Arts Back in Language Arts*, based on his experience as an English teacher.

CPSIA information can be obtained at www.ICGtesting.com
Printed in the USA
BVOW03s1232080914

365591BV00002B/28/P

9 781939 739421